AWAKENING

CU RUA PUBLISHING, LLC

Book Cover Art by Jeff Brown of Jeff Brown Graphics
Interior Maps and Illustrations by Arwen McCain

ISBN 979-8-9994664-0-2 (hardcover)
ISBN 979-8-9994664-1-9 (paperback)
ISBN 979-8-9994664-2-6 (ebook)

First Edition 2026

Published by Cu Rua Publishing, LLC
P.O. Box 5 Willow Spring, NC 27592-9998
curuapublishing.com

To the God who gifted me with an over-active imagination,
The family members who encouraged me not to give up,
The friends who graciously listened to my wild tales,
And the fur creatures who snuggled by my side.

Contents

Map of
TERSAITH
Sea of
Earnorr
GRENDOLEN
EASTLAND
OCEAN
Dorthrin
River
Deltapoint
Fertine
River
The
Flats
Lornadian
Range
Chain of
Plenty
MIDTIER
Lowood
Border
Branch
Moorland
Ruins
Outer
Branch
Ismoad
Peak
Cassia
Mountains
MATUI
Cassia
Falls
The
Drylands
RIVI
OCEAN
Midsor
Mountains
Parton's
Pass
Plesties
Range
Occori
Jungle
SPANS
Lyntolian
Sea
0
500
1000

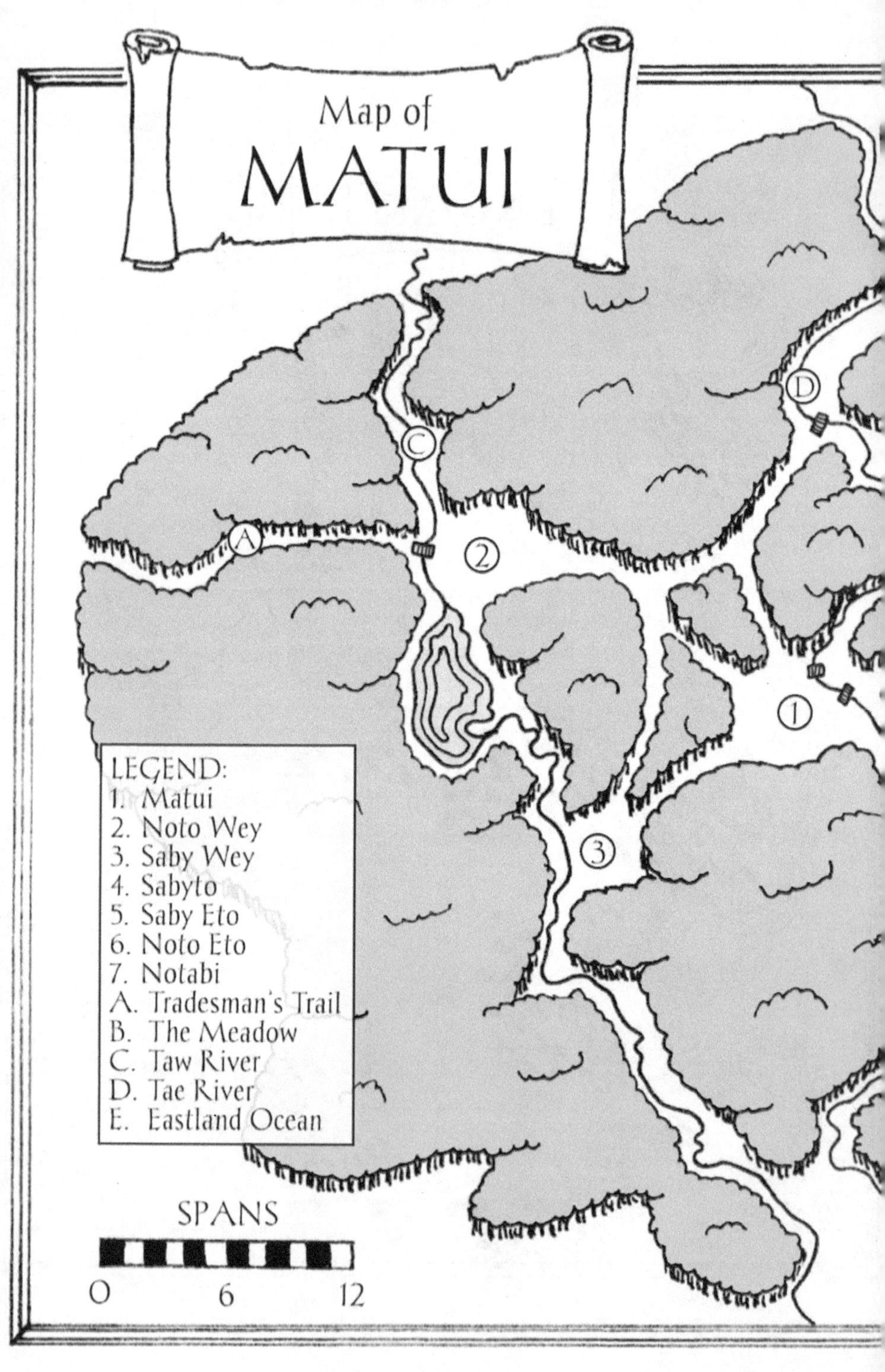
Map of
MATUI
A
C
D
1
2
3
LEGEND:
1. Matui
2. Noto Wey
3. Saby Wey
4. Sabyto
5. Saby Eto
6. Noto Eto
7. Notabi
A. Tradesman's Trail
B. The Meadow
C. Taw River
D. Tae River
E. Eastland Ocean
SPANS
0
6
12

7
E
B
6
5
4

PROLOGUE

The Prisoner

The prisoner stiffened as the sound of footsteps broke through the constant noise of muffled cries and beatings echoing down the dungeon's stone corridor leading to his cell. His ears listened intently, counting the tread of feet. Three, maybe four men? One pair walked with more certainty and determination than the others. It didn't matter that he could no longer see through his swollen eyes; he knew who it was and what this last visit meant.

He let out a slow, staggered breath. Any faster and his cracked ribs would have protested. He could have endured more beatings; after all, he'd been prepared to die in order to take his secret to the grave. But *this*? This, he had no defense against. The screeching metal hinges of the cell's wooden door ground against one another as the accompanying soldiers led Faction Colonel Varcor Orna into the dank room. The prisoner did not give him the satisfaction of attempting to lift his head in recognition of the man's station. He hoped Varcor saw it as a sign of defiance, but the truth was, it hurt too rotting much to move.

"It will be painless," Varcor said, not bothering with introductions or formalities. He knew the prisoner was acutely aware of who he was and what he'd come for—a chilling realization. Yet, it was the lack of human emotion in Varcor's voice that made the prisoner's stomach knot up. The faction colonel had earned quite the reputation among the Grendolen army for his... less-than-savory methods in acquiring what he wanted. "Compared to what you have already suffered," Varcor continued, "this will be a swim downstream." The prisoner listened as the man's boots clicked softly to his right as he slowly paced the floor. "The less you fight it, the easier it will be, and the faster this will all be over."

Behind him, the soldiers who accompanied the faction colonel into the cell were preparing something. A few moments later, a pungent smell hit the prisoner's nose, causing him to gasp, which in turn sent shivers of pain throughout his bruised rib cage.

"*Elements...*" the prisoner wheezed through his tight lungs.

Rot. So, his guess had been correct. There was a reason most kingdoms of the world of Tersaith banned the use of Elements. Sure, they could cure anything from a receding hairline to adding some spice to your nightly activities, and because of that, if you knew where to look, you could acquire a pouch or vile on the quiet. But those kinds of Elements were more or less harmless if you didn't count the odd side effect or two. The Elements Orna practiced with, however, were on a different level. It was said they could eat a man from the inside out and keep him alive to experience the agony during the process. It was said they could carry plagues that selectively affected its victims. It was said they could make you do things you didn't want to do.

Bracing himself against what was to come, the prisoner spoke boldly, hoping his words wouldn't betray the defeat he actually felt.

"You don't honestly think I'd make this easy for you," he challenged. Varcor's boots scuffed to a halt.

"I thought you more educated in the Elemental arts than that," the faction colonel chastised, sounding almost amused at the notion. "You will eventually give up the information I need, no matter how hard you fight against it." The prisoner knew he was right, but it wasn't in his nature to give in so easily. Perhaps he'd be the first to overcome their effects. He *had* to believe it. What other option was there?

"What? Give up what you want to know now and deny my own enjoyment of making you *work* for it? I think not." The prisoner paused to take in another painful breath. "You know what will happen if you take this information to him." His voice had grown quiet and more solemn. It was a last-ditch effort, but it was all he had.

"I am fully aware of what Lord Agnarr intends to do with the information. Did you think to dissuade me because of it? Without our lord's leadership, the Grendolen tribes would have continued bickering in their squabbles for another thousand cycles instead of coming together as the dominating empire we are today. Kingdoms rise and fall, that is a simple fact of time. The nations he conquered to create this empire will eventually come to realize they are better off for it."

"You actually believe that, don't you?" the prisoner said in disgust.

"I cannot fathom how you see it otherwise. Lord Agnarr took their mediocre lives and trivial governments and brought them under his control. He gave them *stability*. He created order from chaos."

"You and I have *very* different definitions of those terms."

Varcor let out a snort in response, a rare show of emotion for the man.

"Our opinions on the matter are moot, and my time grows short. My lord requires the information you have and therefore you will relinquish it to me. You *cannot* fight the Elements."

The prisoner gritted his teeth. His time was up.

"You are but a puppet, Varcor," he warned. "When Lord Agnarr has squeezed all he can from you, he will light you aflame just like the many tribes and kingdoms you've burned to ashes in his name."

Varcor bent down until his breath could be felt on the prisoner's ear.

"You *will* tell me what he wants to know," the faction colonel whispered. "The irony being, you won't die from the process, but by the end, you'll *wish* you had." Not waiting for a reply, Varcor turned to his silent partners and grabbed something from them. More footsteps were heard as they came around to flank the prisoner's sides and hold his arms back. Without warning, one of

Varcor's gloved hands grabbed his throat. The grip was like a vise, *dangerously* strong, with more power than any mortal man should be able to wield. It seemed the whispers regarding the faction colonel's private use of the Elements were to be believed.

With the prisoner clutched easily in one hand, Varcor shoved a glass vial in between his captive's lips and poured a sour liquid into his mouth while one of the others present plugged the man's nose.

No amount of coughing or spewing would keep the concoction from being ingested. As the Elements made their way down into the prisoner's body, they left a burning trail in their wake until he felt them pool in his empty stomach. The sensation was like that of touching ice so cold, you couldn't tell if your skin was burning or frozen, only that it caused immense pain. His body began to shake and convulse, its natural instincts kicking in, wanting to rid itself of the toxin within. But nothing came out of the prisoner's mouth until Varcor spoke.

"Did the heir of Moorland survive the fires?" he asked calmly as he slightly loosened his grip on the captive's throat. Tears streamed down the prisoner's face as his mind tried to fight against its own body. No! It was too soon! Surely, he could hold out for longer than *this*. His insides, however, worked against him, pushing air out involuntarily until he vomited the answer in one forced breath.

"*Yes*," the prisoner admitted against his will. He could almost hear the pleased smile as it spread across Varcor's face.

"Where has she been hiding?" he demanded coolly. This time the prisoner's body did not revolt and give up an answer on its own. But that was because he had no answer to give. He had no idea what happened to her after that night. Moments passed. His interrogator let out a slow sigh, then paused suddenly.

"Where did you last *see* her?" he pushed, changing his tactic. The prisoner could *feel* he knew the answer by the way his body reacted before his mind remembered it did. If the heir had managed to survive all this time, knowing where he'd last seen her would give the Grendolens a viable lead on where to begin searching for her. In vain, the prisoner struggled against the effects of the Elements coursing through his blood.

"An old... ttt-tunnel," the prisoner struggled, "used by ssss... servants."

"And where did this tunnel lead?" Varcor coaxed.

"D...ddown through the castle."

"Where did it *end*?"

"The bottom of the... cliffs."

"North, south, east, west? Give me a *direction!*" The prisoner gathered every bit of remaining strength he had into holding himself back, but it was of no use.

"*South*," he heaved, "toward the coast."

As soon as the answer escaped his lips, a bitter shame washed over him. He'd not only acknowledged to the Grendolens that the only heir to the Moorland throne had survived the massacre but had also directed the enemy on where to start looking for her.

The prisoner hung his head and wept long after Varcor and his soldiers had left until the Elements played their final part and pulled him into a restless unconsciousness.

CHAPTER ONE

Meera

A low fog clung around Meera's booted feet as she silently weaved through the dense wood stalking her prey. It was only mid-Lyfmoad and yet even in the early twilight she could tell the day promised to be a warm and humid one. Meera had been on the hunt for several days with nothing to show for it and had nearly given up when she spotted the tracks of a buck making its way east. Normally, she wouldn't go after such big game at the beginning of Lyntensol, as they were in rut, but Meera was an excellent tracker and she could see the animal was favoring his back leg. After following it for several spans eastward, it was clear to her it was an injury it may not recover from, and as they say, waste leads to want. Such a prize would make an excellent trade back in Notabi, her home village, and there were always ever-present items on her list of needs the trade would lessen. That, and she could finally afford that throwing knife set she'd been eyeing at the market. Sure, she had two sets already, both of which were on her person at that moment. But could one really ever own enough?

The forest Meera ran through was vast, and every tree, from young Sasson saplings to the towering Bora, was considered part of Matuian territory. It stretched over eighty spans across the plains below the Cassia Mountains all the way to the coast of the Eastland Ocean. Within the forest flowed two swift rivers, providing fresh water and food to the Matuians, the occupants who lived within. Over three thousand cycles ago their people split off from their nomadic kinsfolk and settled in the area. Throughout that time, the Matuian population had spread through the forest, creating a network of seven villages all linked like an interconnected web to form a rough hexagon shape, a sacred symbol among the tribe. Within its center sprawled Matui Village, the original settlement and now the tribe's largest village. The Matuians themselves were a seclusive people and had kept their population low for the very purpose of not drawing attention to themselves. So strict were they on this, that whenever their population grew too big to accommodate the seven villages, a large contingent would be sent south to rejoin their nomadic kinsfolk. No one from the outside was allowed to cross over into Matui's borders, save those of their own tradesmen, Meera Rammel Lavonna Tarmanon being the *one* exception.

Had Meera been a Matuian native, with fully black eyes that could see in the dark, navigating her way under the thick tree canopy through the maze of vegetation would have been a breeze. Sixteen cycles living among them, however, had given her plenty of time to adapt to her surroundings. She still couldn't see in the dark like a Matuian, but the bluish hue of the luminescent moss that hung from the Sasson trees provided just enough light to guide Meera's way as she closed in on her prey. This was great news to Meera, as it turned out that carrying the number of weapons she had tended to get heavy over long distances.

The injured buck finally came to a stop in a meadow located about eight spans south of Notabi. It was a familiar setting. Meera had spent countless nights over the cycles laying in its grass, watching the moons Orynis and Oryna dance across the sky. It had long become her place to rest whenever she needed a sanctuary from life's troubles. That, or when she knew it would be better to go there than punch the face of whoever was annoying her. Nature had a way of calming her down when nothing else seemed to work. Trees, especially, were great listeners. Never once had they ever tried to argue or talk back.

Kneeling next to a large Bora tree positioned at the meadow's edge, Meera pushed back strains of the long wavy red hair that had been clinging to her neck. In a moment that had become somewhat of a ritual of good fortune, Meera pulled out the large hawk pendant that hung around her neck under her shirt and gave it a kiss. It had been her mother's and the green crystal the hawk's wings held reminded Meera of her mother's green eyes. Once the pendant had been safely tucked away again, she wiped away the beads of sweat that had gathered on her forehead and readied her trusty bow. It was old, one she made many cycles ago, but it had never let her down on a hunt. Meera studied the animal before her as she waited for the right shot. It was clearly in pain and if she waited too long the meat could grow too tough to trade, but Meera refused to loose an arrow unless a clean kill could be made. The animal had suffered enough as it was. At long last, the buck took a few steps to her right, lining up its heart perfectly with her vantage point. Slowly releasing a calm breath, Meera closed her eyes and said a silent prayer.

May the soul of this creature rise to find you, Yveth, and may it live anew forever in the Afterealm.

Belief in the Creator had always been a staple in Meera's life, as it was for most of the people on Tersaith; however, living among the Matuians had deepened her faith, as every aspect of their culture was grounded in their devotion to obey Yveth's will and that of his god-kin, the Ancients. Confident her prayer had been heard, Meera pulled her bow taunt and prepared to loosen her arrow. Just as her fingers were beginning to relax their hold, something directly behind the deer caught Meera's eye, giving her pause. Whatever it was also caught the attention of the injured buck and spooked him. Eyes white with fear and pain, the animal bolted as fast as his limp would allow into the cover of the trees on the other side of the meadow.

Rotting Nihility! She cursed in her mind.

Annoyed, Meera swung her arrow point in the direction of the thing that had startled her prey, ready to take it down in its place. The growing morning light revealed a tall woman with long, dark-green hair as she took a few steps out into the clearing.

Rot.

There was no guessing who it was. Meera could spot Chief Usoti's daughter a thousand spans off. If the elaborately beaded hides the woman wore hadn't given it away, the white circular tattoos above her brow and under her eyes stood out against her tan face as a sign to all regarding her station.

"You ruined my shot, Katula," Meera complained, her own pale complexion growing red with anger as she walked out from the tree cover toward the woman.

"I have been here since before the sun rose, Meera. You were the one who barged in and ruined *my* shot," the other woman challenged, her Matuian black eyes narrowing. They had never gotten along.

"Three days, Katula. I've been out here *three days*," Meera emphasized, "and I had been tracking that buck *all* night. It's not my fault he chose to come here."

"It's just one buck, Meera. Besides, it's not like you were expecting to find one anyway. It's Lyntensol. They're in rut," Katula remarked, as they met up in the middle of the meadow. The way she said it implied Meera knew nothing about hunting, which angered her even more.

"Just one buck?" Meera stammered, her anger rising. Katula had a way of bringing out the worst in her, and apparently this encounter would be no different. "Katula, that may not seem like a lot to you, but in Notabi, one buck would be a feast for the whole village!"

"Don't be crass, Meera. I didn't mean it like that." Meera cocked an eyebrow in doubt, but the truth was she was just too rotting tired to argue by that point.

"Fine." Meera's stomach chose that moment to alert her and all living occupants within the meadow of its hunger.

"I snared some hares," Katula noted. It was an offer to share, a way of trying to smooth things over.

"I'll check my own traps," Meera retorted. She then quickly added, "But thanks."

"Are you headed back to Notabi then?"

"Not yet," Meera said, shaking her head. "I'll have to swing west and check the traps before heading home."

"I've got to head back to Matui. I'll walk with you to Donotabi bridge, if you like," Katula suggested. Meera looked at the woman who was her sister in every way save blood. Katula could drive her mad sometimes, but every once in a while, the Matuian's stony exterior would break and a normal person would emerge.

"Alright," Meera agreed, hoping she wouldn't regret the decision. It was at least an eight-span walk, and Katula wasn't usually the talkative type. The two women grabbed their belongings and began making their way west toward Donotabi, roughly translated into the common tongue to mean *trail that leads to Notabi*.

As Meera predicted, the day grew hotter as the sun rose above the trees. Below their cover, humidity hung in the air and clung to everything it touched. It was normal for Matui. Even in the coldest moads of Wyntersol the temperature would rarely go below freezing. They hadn't even caught sight of a snowflake in several cycles. Meera missed the snow, especially in the Sumorsol moads when the heat and humidity cloaked every orifice and made it feel like she was breathing in steam from a kettle.

As uncomfortable as the weather was for Meera, the lack of conversation was even more so. Especially when Meera knew there was something on Katula's mind she refused to say. When they had walked over six spans without one word being said, Meera decided she needed to intervene as the loving, caring almost-sister she was.

"That's it," Meera announced abruptly, turning to Katula. "Out with it! What's going on?"

"What do you mean?" Katula asked, taken aback by Meera's abruptness.

Stubborn and rotting hardheaded! That stony face of hers didn't even budge.

"You've got something on your mind, so out with it already," Meera repeated. Katula let out a slow sigh but didn't immediately respond. They walked on for a little more before the Matuian finally answered.

"I'm thinking of swearing the oaths and becoming sagen." Meera stopped in her tracks, genuinely shocked, causing Katula to look back and turn around. "What? Do you not approve?"

"No. It's just that..." Meera paused. "Katula, it's a *lifelong* commitment."

"I know," the other woman said, lifting her chin and regaining her composure as she continued walking. Still taken aback by the news, Meera quickly caught up and matched Katula's long-legged pace.

"Don't you have to serve as an apprentice to the sage for several cycles before you can become sagen?"

"Two cycles," Katula corrected. "And I have." That was news to Meera, but then, ever since she'd left Matui Village and made Notabi her home, she hadn't seen much of Katula.

"I'm sure your father and grandmother are very proud of your decision," she finally replied.

"Implying I would swear oaths to Yveth in order to satisfy their pride, Meera Tarmanon, is a shameful thing to suggest!"

"Maggots, Katula! Watch what you say!" Meera chided, shooting a look around the woods in case anyone was in earshot. Only Katula's family knew her true name. To the rest in Matui, she was simply Meera, one of the fortunate few to have survived the Moorland Massacre.

"Sorry," Katula apologized, looking unusually chastised. "The point still stands, though. I would never say the oaths for any selfish desire." Her almost-sister was a lot of things, but a liar wasn't one of them. If anything, Katula was *too* serious.

"I know you wouldn't, Katula. But they must be proud. *Two* women from the same family to become sage! It's quite unusual."

"Natta *is* over the moons about it," Katula admitted, referring to her grandmother's given name rather than her title as sage. Meera detected a slight smile in the corners of Katula's face, revealing to Meera just how excited she was about it.

"And Chief Usoti?" Meera pushed.

"Father is, too, but you know him. He doesn't wear his emotions for all to see like Natta does." Meera nodded in understanding and smiled fondly. That sounded just like him.

"How are they doing? It's been a while since I've been able to travel that way," Meera asked. It wasn't exactly the truth. She'd traveled down to Matui Village on several occasions, but each time she considered stopping in to visit the Min family, something kept her from doing so. The move to Notabi hadn't exactly been under cheerful circumstances. It was hard enough perusing Matui's market without getting pummeled with snide comments. Meera didn't fancy finding out what the locals would say if they saw her spending time with Chief Usoti's family again.

"They miss you," Katula noted, referring to her father and grandmother. "You missed Natta's last experiment. It blew the whole top of her workhut clear off." In normal Katula fashion, the Matuian kept a straight face as she spoke, but Meera couldn't help but grin as she imagined the chaos the event must have caused. The sage was *always* pulling stunts like that. It was one of the reasons Meera respected the old woman so much. "And Father," Katula continued, "has been preoccupied with the latest numbers coming out of the other villages. He is preparing to send another group south by the end of Lyntensol." That was news, too, though not unusual.

"When do you plan on swearing your oaths?" Meera asked, coming back to the main topic.

"Solmoad 16th," Katula announced firmly.

"Full moons," Meera remarked with an approving nod. It was clear Katula had everything planned, as always. She'd probably already written out step-by-step instructions for the ceremony three moads ahead of time. Meera almost felt bad for whoever had been assigned to help Katula.

"Meera," Katula said, stopping and turning to the redhead. "Would you bear witness?"

The request took Meera by surprise.

"You really want me there?"

"Yes."

"Won't the elders be upset?" Meera questioned reservedly. Katula's tan face darkened.

"You should have never let the elders push you out of Matui, Meera. It was my father's *wish* for you to become kinblood and for us to be true sisters."

"Katula, you and I both know the elders would have never let a Moorlander become kinblood, *especially* one to the chief's family. The fact that Chief Usoti was able to convince them to allow a Moorlander into Matui's borders was nothing short of a miracle from Yveth." Katula continued walking but didn't respond right away. It wasn't until a clearing could be seen through the thick foliage, signaling their approach to Donotabi bridge, that Katula broke her silence.

"Kinblood or not, I would like you to be there and bear witness," she said, keeping her black eyes forward. Meera knew, in Katula's own way, the request meant she thought of Meera as a true sister. The unspoken words meant more to Meera than she wanted to admit.

"I'll be there," the Moorlander eventually promised with a firm nod. A few moments later both women broke through the trees and into the sunlight. They were not alone. The first person to pass them traveling south was a female Runner. There was nothing unusual about that, as Runners were a constant in Matui. They delivered messages between the villages multiple times a day. But not far behind her followed two more Runners along with a large group of villagers Meera recognized from Notabi.

"They're leaving for the southern tribes already?" Meera asked.

"Father wasn't going to send anyone until another moad or two," Katula remarked out loud, her face growing concerned.

"Why the hurry, then?"

"You, there!" Katula called to one of the Runners. A man almost as tall as Katula immediately broke away from the others and ran toward them.

"Katula Min," he acknowledged with a bow.

"Has my father issued the order for them to join our nomadic kin?" Katula demanded, nodding her head in the direction of the crowd nearing them. The Runner looked up at Katula in surprise but faltered when he caught sight of Meera. For a moment, the Runner just stared. It wasn't just the oddity of Meera's red hair or pale skin compared to the Matuian's dark-green hair and tan skin that always seemed to grab their attention. It was the red eyes. From far off, they appeared brown, but upon closer inspection, they were a deep blood red. It always seemed to unnerve the Matuians. "Runner!" Katula yelled again, prying the man's eyes away from Meera. "What is going on? I demand an answer!"

"My apologies, Katula Min." The Runner bowed again. "I thought word would have reached you by now. The Grendolens have been spotted off the coast. They sail on *hundreds* of ships! A whole armada! Word reached Notabi last night." Alarm shot through Meera as memories of the fires that burned her kingdom to the terra resurfaced, flames that nearly ended her own life.

The Grendolens... here?

"When were they spotted?" Katula asked, keeping her composure.

"Two days ago. By now they'll have reached the shore. Runners were sent on ahead to Matui last night," the anxious man assured her.

"Then news of this will reach my father soon, if it hasn't already," Katula surmised. "And the other villages? What of Noto Eto? It will be the first village the Grendolens reach."

"They have been alerted." The Runner nodded curtly. "I myself beg your forgiveness, Katula Min, as I must leave for Noto Wey right away if I am to bring them news by nightfall."

"You've done well, thank you," Katula said, dismissing the man. Without delay, the Runner took off southward, anxious to carry word to the other villages.

"After all this time," Meera breathed out loud, trying to wrap her head around what they'd just heard.

"It was *always* a possibility someone would come for the Tercara Scroll," Katula remarked matter-of-factly, her black eyes looking over at Meera.

"Yes, but... Katula, the *Grendolens*," she stressed.

"We've had three thousand cycles to plan for such a time as this. Already the evacuations are underway. My people know what to do. Come!" the Matuian called confidently, waving for the Moorlander to follow. "There's no need for you to return to Notabi anymore. We'll need to hurry if we're to reach my father before the evacuees crowd Matui's streets."

With that, Katula launched into a sprint toward the bridge, not bothering to look back to see if Meera followed. Begrudgingly, she did. After all, what else could she do? This was *the* evacuation, the one Katula's ancestors had put in place all those millennia ago, when they swore oaths to Yveth's god-kin to safeguard the Tercara Scroll. In its very text, the scroll warned of such an event, that one day someone may come to use its knowledge for ill. That prophecy was the sole reason the Matuians chose to break off from their nomadic kinsfolk and live such seclusive lives. It was why every generation, after coming to settle in Matui Forest, was prepared to evacuate at a moment's notice. But, as Meera ran to keep up with her taller Matuian sister, she couldn't help but wonder if the Grendolens had a different reason for sending an armada to the most seclusive place on Tersaith.

Two questions plagued her mind. If they found out she had survived, would the Grendolens really go to such lengths to hunt down the remaining heir to the Tarmanon line, even if she had no kingdom left to rule? And if so, how many of them could she send to the depths of Nihility before they took her down?

The sun had set by the time they reached Matui Village, and while the women were able to outpace the evacuees flooding south from Notabi, villagers from Noto Eto on foot or cart had already begun pouring in and clogging the streets. Noto Eto was closer to Matui than Notabi; however, it was also closest to the shore—where, by now, if the Runner's details held true, the enemy forces had already made camp. The location of Noto Eto, however, wasn't placed haphazardly, nor were the other six villages. Each sat directly along the banks of either the Tae or Taw Rivers or one of their tributaries. All flowed southward, providing a hasty retreat for those fortunate enough to have a piwakey, a traditional Matuian-made boat, available to them. Their narrow frames were perfect for paddling the waterways, but not all Matuian families had access to one. The rest of the evacuees would have to make their way south on foot or, if there was a tradesman in the family, by pony and cart.

It was one of those carts that narrowly avoided running over Meera as she did her best to follow behind Katula as they zigzagged through the chaotic streets. The cart's cavity was overflowing with belongings, younglings, and a staggering number of chickens. The looks on the occupants' faces, however, were what really caught Meera's attention. It wasn't a look of fear but of determination. They had been ready for this and were anxious to see the plan through.

At long last, the two women reached the Green, a grassy clearing used for ceremonies and celebrations. At its far end stood a long-domed hut where Tineus, the Matuian word for meetings, took place and from where Chief Usoti governed his people. As soon as Katula caught sight of one of the guards stationed outside of the hut, she grabbed Meera's hand and pulled her into a faster run.

"Bitun!" Katula hailed, waving to him as they came near. The man's age showed through the lines around his eyes and the fading green hair around his temples, but his exposed arms were covered in white tattoos, attesting to his skill as a warrior. Meera recognized him as one of the chief's personal guards.

"Katula Min," the guard answered, bowing and touching the back of his thumb to his lips before extending his hand palm upward. It was a sign of deep respect.

"Is he in there?" Katula asked, referring to her father. Bitun gave a curt nod in confirmation.

"Word about the Grendolens reached us around midday," he replied grimly. "Your father called an immediate Tineu, and the elders agreed to an official evacuation. You are to go directly in and speak with both your father and the sage." He then looked directly at Meera, showing no hint of discomfort in doing so. It was a rare thing for Meera to experience, and it instantly propelled him into her internal category of people she respected. It was a small list. "It is fortunate you arrived together," he explained, "as they have requested your presence as well." Not wanting to waste any more time than they already had, the wizened guard pulled back his spear and quickly motioned for the women to enter.

The inside of the long hut was windowless and dark, save for a small hole in the roof set directly above a large fire pit. The scent of smoke, wood, sweat, and clay instantly transported Meera back to the first time she had been brought there, back when, against many of the elders, the chief insisted she stay and live among the Matuians. The fire within the ringed stone pit provided the only light, as Matuians had no need of a light source to see in the dark. The flame served more of a symbolic purpose. It was never allowed to be extinguished, until the passing of the chief who had initially lit it upon swearing their inaugural oaths. Chief Usoti's own fire had been burning for many decades. The evacuation triggered by the Grendolens' arrival, however, meant his would be the first fire to die out before his passing, bringing a sudden end to a Matuian tradition that had begun countless generations ago.

As Meera's Moorlander eyes adjusted to the darker interior, Katula easily led Meera down the rows of wooden benches circling the central fire pit and brought her before her father. Sixteen cycles had passed since Chief Usoti adopted Meera into their tribe, and yet she still felt humbled whenever she was brought into his presence. He was everything Meera believed a leader should be: strong, proud, and honorable. While his hair had long since turned a light green and wrinkles now etched the shadows of his face, Usoti Min stood tall, and his black eyes still held a keen alertness in them. White tattoos fully covered his arms and chest, many of them depicting beasts of myths, various motifs, and also marked his number of kills in defense of his people. Around his brow and eyes dotted similar tattoos to those his daughter Katula bore, only his were larger and more numerous, marking him as the Matuian's leader. Elaborate necklaces and bracelets decorated with shells, beads, bones, and bright-colored feathers hung around his neck and wrists, and upon his head sat a crown carved from the bough of an ancient Bora tree. Unlike the ornate throne Meera remembered her father had in Moorland castle, Chief Usoti sat on one of the many simple benches, with the seven elders and the sage spread out among the others positioned closest to the fire.

Despite the differences between Katula and herself, Meera had always held the chief in high regard. In truth, he had become the closest thing to a father she had since her own parents were killed by the Grendolens. Runners found Meera on Matui's northern border near death at the age of seven, and it was Chief Usoti who had insisted his own physicians tend to her wounds. They said it was a miracle from Yveth that she survived. Katula's mother had passed from an illness the sage could not heal several cycles before. Seeing the girls were so close in age, the chief brought Meera into his home, hoping the two would be a comfort to one another. But several cycles later, when he asked her to swear the oaths and become kinblood, Meera declined. By then, her presence in Matui Village was upsetting more than just the elders. Arguments had begun breaking out among those unwilling to break with tradition. Meera wasn't just any stranger, she was a *Moorlander*. The rift eventually pushed her to pick Notabi, the most remote and smallest village of the seven, as her home.

"...Remember, the evacuation *must* draw the Grendolens' attention southward in order to give the scroll bearer enough time to make it out of Matui," the chief finished saying to one of the elders.

"But what of the Tercara Scroll?" one of the female elders asked. "You have not yet spoken of its destination."

"That is sage business, Elder Sari," Katula's grandmother broke in forcefully. Meera knew from experience that she wasn't someone you wanted to cross. "Would you have it so that vital information would be readily available should the Grendolens capture one of you?"

"No! Of course not, Sage!" the women exclaimed, aghast at the notion. "My deepest apologies! The scroll's safety was my only thought." It was then Meera and Katula's presence was noted and the conversation cut short.

"You have your orders," Chief Usoti announced to the elders. "See they are carried out."

"By the will of Yveth," all seven said in unison as they bowed and gave the sign of respect.

"By the will of Yveth," the chief echoed, signaling their dismissal.

"Father, Natta," Katula called to her family, once the elders had taken their leave.

"Took you long enough," the sage chided her granddaughter. Neither Katula nor Meera took any heed. It was the sage's way. "Where on Tersaith did you get off to, anyway?" The old woman's faded graying eyes looked past Katula to Meera. "Ah, so you too have come. Good! We have reason to speak with you both."

"Bitun said as much," Katula acknowledged. "I ran into Meera while out hunting north of Tae River and we happened upon a Runner bearing the news." At this, Katula paused and took her father's hands. "Is it true then? The Grendolens have come for the scroll?"

"Scouts have confirmed their landfall, I'm afraid," he nodded. "They will reach Noto Eto by tomorrow, Matui in a day or two, depending on whether or not they brought horses." Katula's eyes widened. There were no horses in Matui, only ponies. The dense forest was thought too thick for them to traverse and the narrow trails between the villages were managed easier on foot or by trader's cart. On horseback, the Grendolens would be forced to travel at the most two abreast through Matui, but it would still mean a swifter advance.

"What of Matui's warriors?" Meera interjected, sending all eyes to her. "You must be sending a large force to hold off the enemy while the evacuees use the time to escape. I want to volunteer as one of them." There wasn't much that shocked Katula's stony composure, but Meera's proclamation obviously stunned the woman.

"Don't be so brash, Meera! Have you forgotten what they did to you? Your parents? Your *people*?" Meera's face flushed red with anger.

"Of course I haven't forgotten, Katula! The pain of it *haunts* me. There's not a day that goes by where I don't feel their loss."

"Then you must know they wouldn't hesitate to send your soul to Yveth if they found out you survived," Katula reasoned, crossing her arms.

"How do you know that's not the real reason they're here?" Meera challenged, her voice growing soft as the gravity of her own words hit her. The idea apparently seemed as preposterous to Katula as the idea of Meera staying to fight the Grendolens.

"Enough you two!" the sage interjected, waving her arms in the air. "It's been like this since you both were younglings. Never could get along. Ha!" she suddenly laughed, smacking a wrinkled hand on her knee with a clap. "It makes sense now why Yveth brought you both here together." The smile on the old woman's face warned Meera she was up to something.

"Revenge can be a powerful motive," Chief Usoti said, turning to Meera. "You, among us all, have more reason to feel its pull. I caution you, though, Red Daughter, do not let it rule your better judgment." Normally, Meera would have punched whoever dared point out her oddities square in the face, but with the chief it was different. It was a term of endearment from a man who not only saved her life but took her in as one of his own. Feeling conflicted between wanting to heed his advice versus seeking revenge on her enemies, Meera respectfully challenged his words.

"If you were in my place, would you deny me this one chance to avenge my parents' deaths? Even if they realize who I am and send my soul to Yveth, is not laying down my life for the memory of my people a valiant death? What other purpose could Yveth possibly have for me if I traveled with you south?"

"You will not be traveling south with us, my dear," the sage announced matter-of-factly.

"Natta?" Katula called, confused.

"I thought that is what you wished of me, to go with the evacuees," Meera replied.

"We have need of you elsewhere, youngling! One that would allow you to exact revenge on the Grendolens and possibly keep you alive in the process." Meera looked from the sage to Chief Usoti skeptically.

"What *kind* of revenge?"

"While the enemy forces are pulled southward after the evacuees, the Tercara Scroll must be taken far away from Matui," the chief explained. It was Katula's turn to interject.

"You want a *Moorlander* to carry the scroll?" Even to Meera, it was unthinkable.

"Katula Min, do not behave like a dolt! Our laws are clear; only women in service to the sage can even look at the Tercara Scroll, let alone carry it," the old woman barked, before growing more serious. "You have been studying its text for two cycles. In fact, I would go so far as to say you can translate it faster than my old eyes can at this rate."

"What are you saying?" Katula pushed.

"I have chosen you as the sagen who will take the Tercara Scroll to Pawtoton, and your father and I would like Meera to accompany you on the journey."

"*Me*?" Katula gasped, showing more emotion than she probably intended. "I'm not even sagen yet!"

"Which is why your father and I will be performing the ceremony tomorrow tonight."

"What? Natta, I'm not ready! I have so much more to learn!"

"Did you say *Pawtoton*?" Meera interjected, still stunned by the unexpected proposition. The sage nodded firmly.

"It's the only place more secluded than Matui, and there are rumors it holds *vast* libraries of histories. It should be quite safe there until we can return home." For once in Meera's life, both she and Katula were thinking the same thing. Pawtoton was a land of *myth*, a place of youngling's tales. It was filled with snow beasts, giants, and flying creatures that could breathe fire.

"Natta," Katula staggered, unsure how to respond. She looked to her father, but the chief was of the same mind as his mother.

"The Tercara Scroll will be safe in Pawtoton," he assured her. "The Grendolens do not know of its existence."

"*Does* it exist?" Meera challenged, still in disbelief.

"Of course it exists!" the sage countered, waving her hands in the air at the suggestion. "Do you think because it is woven into our stories it isn't real? I would say it's the very opposite. That, because it is a part of our oldest stories, it very much *is* real. Katula is ready for this," the sage encouraged, looking at her granddaughter. "I wouldn't have chosen you to become sagen if I didn't think you were ready."

"Will you go with Katula?" the chief asked, turning the attention back on Meera. She didn't answer right away but sat quietly while a battle raged in her head. Long ago Meera had promised herself that if ever Yveth gave her the chance, she would exact revenge upon the Grendolens for what they had done. Would denying the enemy of what they were after *be* accomplishing that promise? The chief seemed to think so. If she stayed and fought side by side with the Matuian warriors, how far would she get before she died in battle, or worse, get caught, tortured, and eventually killed?

"I'll go with Katula," Meera finally confirmed, "if that is what will hurt the Grendolens the most."

"Ah, you see?" the sage beamed with a ready smile. "It is as I thought! Yveth guides our way," she said, turning to the girls. "You two will travel to Pawtoton together!"

CHAPTER TWO

Darmond

It had been a bad week for Darmond. Actually, the entirety of Wyntersol had become a collection of blunders that had conjoined into a reeking cesspool of his own making, threatening to pull him under. A bit dramatic, but that's how he felt. Up to this point, he'd been the *best* at what he did. No one was as good of a spy as *Darmond the Cunning*. It was a working title. Then suddenly everything changed. It had gone to rot ever since he failed his last mission. Others failed, sure, but not *him*. At least, not until now. Yet, here he was, now in Flowanmoad, an entire sol later, and still paying dearly for his mistakes by doing the job no one in the Resistance would have ever volunteered for—a form of penance, in his mind.

Plenty of other fleaborns had grown up on the rough streets of Midtier, yet none of them had turned out to be as skilled in Darmond's particular talents as he. Blending in to gain the trust of others and learn their valuable secrets had always come naturally to him, even when he was a youngling—secrets others tended to pay quite a bit of coin for. He *used* to be the best. After recent events, however, he wasn't so sure that was true anymore.

Taking a step back from the small, dirty mirror he was peering into, Darmond surveyed the armored image reflected at him. There were plenty of things Darmond *didn't* like about the Grendolens, but their armor was not one of them. They had expertly crafted gear. The chainmail, made from a rare metal they mined up north, was lightweight and resistant to rust. It was no wonder the enemy was as successful as they had been in conquering the lands south of Grendolen; with their greater numbers and superior armor and weapons, the Resistance had little chance of pushing back their advances.

Yet, despite all the aliases and jobs he'd pulled off over the cycles, never would he have ever imagined his life decisions would lead him here, infiltrating the Grendolen military by posing as one of their own soldiers. It had certainly proved to be his toughest assignment yet, and it didn't help that his own mistakes had landed him there. He was only in his late twenties and had ages to go before he grew old and began to lose his edge. He'd been working with the Resistance since he was young enough to pickpocket, and his skills had only improved from then on. Every mission had been a success, every challenge had been easily overcome. His peers said he had good fortune; others believed Yveth favored him. So, what happened? When had all that changed? Now it seemed like everything he touched turned to rot. Not knowing the answer to that question had haunted Darmond ever since he'd taken up his position with the enemy's encampment nearly four moads ago.

Without his unique talents and skills, who was he? His familiar, well-chiseled face and stark blue eyes stared back at him from the mirror challengingly, as if daring him to answer the question.

Maggots, man! Pull yourself together! There's a reason Yveth blessed you with your good looks and skills. Best not waste *it. Everyone hits a dry patch now and then, and you're no exception.*

"Bae! You've been staring at your rotting reflection for near-on the *entire* morning! Stop fawning over yourself and move over so the rest of us can have a go." Darmond looked up, acting surprised he'd spent longer than he meant to in front of the tent's solitary mirror. The young Grendolen soldier who had addressed Darmond by his alias, Bae, was accompanied by a gathering of several other soldiers, a mix of men and women who also occupied the tent. All were casting annoyed looks in his direction. Little did they know the self-indulgence Bae showed was just a part of the act Darmond had put on for his current role. Well, maybe not *all* an act.

Giving his dirty-blond chin scruff a rub and winking at the mirror, he stepped out of their way.

"My apologies, gentlefolks," he said, lifting his hands in defeat. "You know how the S.O. likes everything to be all sheen and shine for inspections."

"That we do, don't we folks?" one of the beefier soldiers mused, stepping closer to Darmond. "'We must always present ourselves as if Lord Agnarr himself were addressing us.' Isn't that what Commandant General Doth says?" the soldier quoted. Darmond caught a hint of mischief in the man's tone, so he held back the quip he was about to let slip. "Unfortunately, even after all that preening, you're still in no state for Soldier Officer Emidd's inspection." The man gave Darmond a look over and clicked his tongue disapprovingly. "Soldiers, we're going to have to help the lad out, don't you think?" Without delay, several in the group grabbed hold of his arms.

Note to self, Darmond thought wryly, as he saw the bucket of mud being brought over. *Never underestimate just how jealous others can be of your rugged good looks.*

A little while later, Darmond stood in the inspection lineup along with the others in his pod, a term the Grendolen military used to signify a grouping of twenty soldiers. Each pod had an S.O., soldier's officer, to oversee them; however, the one standing in front of Darmond looked less than pleased at his appearance... and *smell.* Turned out it wasn't mud in the bucket after all.

"What is the meaning of this, soldier?" S.O. Emidd barked, his face reddening with anger and breath fogging the air. Even with Lyntensol nearing, the northern weather was still crisp with the last dregs of Wyntersol. Darmond knew better than to cross the man, so he kept his salute and stance as rigid as possible until the S.O. signaled for his reply.

"My apologies, sir," Darmond began in Bae's Grendolen accent. "I was performing a routine perimeter check of the camp when I came across a rogue grizzling. Nasty bugger, sir, just as the locals described—tusks as sharp as a tit and eyes as beady as balls on a cold day, let me tell you. But not to worry, sir! I sent him screaming to the deepest bowels of Nihility. Only the rotting thing held me up longer than could be helped and left me looking like a muck stall in the process." The S.O. cocked his thick, graying eyebrow as he weighed the story he was just weaved. Darmond was well aware that the military had only moved into this particular region recently and were not yet familiar with the wildlife that inhabited it. Had they done their research, they would have known that grizzlings, wild and dangerous though they were, did not bother traversing the Flats and instead kept to the northern foothills of the Cassias.

"See it doesn't happen again, soldier," S.O. Emidd growled. "I'll lash you myself if you report to my lineup one more time in this state, *grizzling or not!*"

"Yes, sir!" Darmond responded, holding his salute. He breathed easy knowing the others in his pod wouldn't rat him out, as the S. O. tolerated very little and would have disciplined them all for their poor conduct. Emidd backed away from Darmond and turned to address his whole pod.

"You can rest assured there will be no further *grizzling* encounters, soldiers." At this, he shot Darmond a knowing glance, saying very clearly without the use of words that he'd not bought into his lie.

Maggots and rot, that man's more informed than I'd given him credit for. He really *was* losing his touch.

"Our brief stay in the Flats has come to an end," the S.O. continued. "Commandant General Doth has given orders to vacate the area and head north." At this, muffles could be heard from the others who were taken aback by the news. Tactically, the sudden move didn't make sense. The Grendolens had finally managed to push the Resistance's opposing forces back across the Dorthrin River, claiming the area to its east known as the Flats. It was the largest region they had conquered since the Kingdom of Moorland fell to them sixteen cycles ago. So why pull up stakes and vacate what had taken them so long to win? It was the question every soldier in S.O. Emidd's lineup was thinking. Everyone except Darmond. He wasn't at all taken aback by the news. As a matter of fact, this was precisely why he'd infiltrated their ranks and what he had waited moads to hear.

About rotting time.

"We are to meet up with the naval fleet at Deltapoint," their leader announced, "and from there, board ships heading south." The S.O. paused for a moment, letting what he said sink in. "Time to pack up, soldiers! We're bound for Wildwood."

Darmond couldn't turn to see the reaction of the others, but he sure could hear the gasps escape their lips. *Wildwood.* No one *ever* went to Wildwood, or Matui, as the natives called it. Not the Midtierians and certainly not the Grendolens. Once Emidd was satisfied his soldiers had accepted the startling news, he barked out the remainder of their orders before sending the pod marching in neat and orderly lines back to their tent to carry them out. Darmond marched along with the others in silence as his mind reeled over the news they'd been given. At long last his moads posing as a Grendolen soldier had paid off.

By the time the army had broken camp, Darmond was more than ready to see an end to his time among them and embark on the next stage in his plan. Perhaps his good fortune had finally returned to him. It was time he parted ways with dashing Bae in favor of one of his more *approachable* aliases.

Marty sloppily emptied his tankard and placed it down with a thud in front of him. Letting out a belch that could blow the scabs off a fleaborn, he pushed it forward and hailed the barkeep.

"Another," he demanded in a slurred voice. The barkeep ignored his rude behavior and went about refilling it. Darmond had been wrong before about the Grendolens' armor being the one thing they did right. They also made *delectable* ales. Which was saying a lot, as the ales back in Midtier were something of a boasting point for the locals.

Having so many delicious personalities gathered in one place worked to Darmond's advantage. He was always looking for new personas to adopt, and what better place to do it than in the military's designated ale-tent stationed in Deltapoint. It was chock full of soldiers and sailors alike celebrating their upcoming sea voyage. The area itself had been under Grendolen rule for several cycles as it sat on the banks of the Fertine Delta, an expansive wetland where the Fertine River emptied into the Eastland Ocean. Whoever controlled Deltapoint controlled access to the river and any kingdoms or settlements found along its waterways. Needless to say, the Resistance's loss of Deltapoint had struck a huge blow, not just for the Midtierians on the battlefield but for all the people along the river who now found themselves under Grendolen rule. The town itself was quickly changing from a small coastal settlement into a bustling trading port, as it offered easy access for their numerous ships to dock offshore and was only several days' sail north to their most southern occupied city. Even the ale-tent Darmond sat in had a more permanent wooden building already being constructed next door.

For a while Darmond sat in silence, soaking in the mannerisms and accents flowing around him. Even some of the same soldiers from Bae's pod were within the makeshift establishment, although none of them had recognized him. No one ever did. Marty had always been a foolproof alias and had served him well many a time.

Darmond took the refilled tankard from the barkeep and raised it in thanks to the man, making sure to spill some with the gesture. Marty, the drunkard with a rural tradesman's accent hailing from the Flats, brought out his weighted coin purse and placed one too many tin chips and copper tenners on the bar as payment before sinking his greedy lips into the liquid. It took only three additional tankards to lure his prey over.

"Evening, friend! What are you having?" a smiling sailor asked, taking a seat on the stool to his left. Darmond sized him up without taking his eyes off his tankard. Too short.

"I's enjoyin' the ben-o-fits of a fine Grendolen red ale, Sir," he mumbled through sips. A second sailor sat down to his right, and this time, Darmond turned to look at him through Marty's bloodshot eyes, a simple trick he'd learned back in his youngling days involving certain herbal mixtures. The second man was much more promising. Not too short, not too tall, and of a lower naval rank. Perfect.

"A Grendolen red is the finest there is, and that's the truth of it," the newest sailor said matter-of-factly. "Shame we don't have anything to celebrate, otherwise I'd toast to that." Darmond cringed inwardly at the man's feeble attempt to goad him into paying for drinks.

Amateurs.

"Barkeep! A round for may new friends here!" Marty called in a Flats accent. Then, putting on a solemn face, he said to the two men, "You find may mournin' the loss of may uncle, lads, his soul rest in Yveth's sweet embrace." The two bowed their heads in reverence as they echoed the last phrase. It didn't matter who you were or where you hailed from, everyone always showed respect for the Great Creator.

"Now all that's left of the fine man hay was is the inher-o-tance left to may. Only seems fittin' to raise a tankard in remembrance." The sailors were handed their ales and together with Marty, they toasted. It didn't take but two drinks down their gullets before talk began flowing about the navy's imminent departure. It all sounded like the usual chatter one would hear from sailors before setting out to sea until Darmond heard mention of a name, one many of the others within the ale-tent had been muttering all evening.

"Jerrna Wess?" Marty repeated with a slight slur. "He one-o' your officers?" The taller sailor nearly spit out his ale bellowing a laugh.

"No, man! He's the rotting *commandant admiral* of the fleet!" The other sailor joined in the laughter and slapped Marty on the back. Unperturbed, Darmond pushed on.

"With him bein' in charge o' the Navy an' all, why all the fuss about him comin' along?"

"That's just it, Marty, my friend. Why send the C.A. to transport the military? It's not like they're expecting to encounter a sea battle where we're going," the shorter one said. The man had a point. "There're plenty of shipmen captains under Commandant Admiral Wess that could easily see the job done, and yet Lord Agnarr, the emperor himself, personally requested he lead the fleet."

"And not just him," the shorter one added. "Did you see what's sitting pretty at the docks?"

"That I did," the other replied, "the *Seventh Sister* herself, pride of the Grendolen Navy! And she doesn't make an appearance for any ol' reason." Darmond made a mental note to remember the name as he ordered another round of drinks. Best keep the ale flowing if you want the conversation to follow suit. Darmond knew the reason behind the military's sudden upheaval and new orders, but what he hadn't yet figured out was why such a large portion of it was being sent. Finding out how much of the Grendolens' naval force would be needed to transport the military was disconcerting. He didn't know much about the Matuians who lived in Wildwood, but he knew enough to know the force being sent there was excessively more than what was needed to subdue them, especially when considering the Grendolens' superior weaponry.

As the two sailors chatted on, Darmond continued to mull over the situation until a dark thought settled on his mind. The more he considered it, the more it made sense. The Grendolens had *no* intention of subduing the Matuians. The only reason a force of such a size would be sent was to wipe out Wildwood's inhabitants altogether. The final pieces of the puzzle clicked into place. It was clear now what Lord Agnarr intended. The Matuians would be made an example of, a strong statement to anyone else who dared go against his will. It was a sobering realization, one that made it difficult for Darmond to keep up Marty's happily drunk guise as the evening stretched late into the night.

An unknown number of tankards later, the two sailors finally ended their drinking spree and used Marty's money to pay the barkeep, promising to see him off home along their way. Darmond kept up his drunken alias as they led Marty through the packed streets filled with tents and wooden constructions before eventually winding their way into Deltapoint's older settlements. It was only a matter of time before they ducked into a dark and narrow alleyway perfectly out of sight from any nosey passerby.

Just before the two sailors turned to attack him, Darmond sprang into action, using the back of his own head to hit the shorter man in the nose, breaking it upon impact. Before his tall companion could respond, Darmond threw a punch in the man's gut, knocking the air out of him and causing him to fall to his knees. The short sailor with the broken nose, however, began making more noise than Darmond was comfortable with, so he knocked him out first with a kick to the head before turning his attention back to his main target. Coming up behind the larger of the two sailors, he pinned his arms around the man's neck with one arm and covered his nose and mouth with the other. If he was going to use his uniform, he'd need to keep it blood-free. After a few moments, the sailor's struggling faded and Darmond let him drop incapacitated onto the street.

Dawn's early light would find Darmond reporting for duty as Linklo, an awkwardly shy sailor aboard the *Seventh Sister*, while Marty's two would-be robbers were just waking up to find themselves gagged and bound in the cargo hold of a trading boat headed up the Fertine River. Dawnday, the start of a New Cycle on Tersaith, was only two days away, and Darmond couldn't help but feel like his fortune had finally changed for the better.

Bring on, 3131 T.C., Darmond confidently challenged fate. It felt good to be back in action.

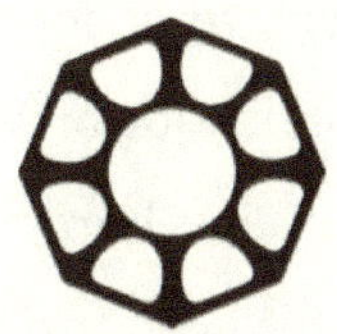

CHAPTER THREE

Katula

"Put·this one in the green satchel," Katula's grandmother demanded, handing her a vial filled with a deep orange liquid. "That'll cure a bad case of icebite should the mountain weather turn ill." Natta didn't even bother turning around. Her eyes were too busy focusing on the task at hand, providing Katula with as many Elements as she could for her journey to find Pawtoton—if indeed it existed. Natta, of course, seemed confident it was not only real but that the giants who supposedly lived there could be found somewhere to the west, within the expansive Cassia Mountain range. The giants from the stories Katula heard as a youngling were said to have kept vast libraries full of long-lost histories and tales. Those same giants could eat the meat right off your bones. Katula glanced over at a dark leather tube propped up against the work hut's wall. In it, safely rolled up, was the Tercara Scroll ready for its journey.

Let's hope the giants of Pawtoton are willing to forgo a taste of Matuian in exchange for a glimpse of my people's most precious relic, Katula mused.

“Do you really think it will be that cold by the time we reach the Cassias?” Katula questioned, while she obediently bagged the vial. She had never stepped foot outside of Matui, and yet now she was expected to not only cross over its borders but traverse lands wholly foreign to her. The idea of it both thrilled and overwhelmed her. Not that Katula would let those feelings overcome her ability to carry out her duty. Her people were counting on her to keep the Tercara Scroll safe. She would not let them down, no matter what.

Natta paused and turned her faded green head to look Katula in the eye.

“My dear, in some areas the snow never melts,” she explained, graying eyes wide. Natta then turned her attention back to the well-used wooden shelves lining her workhut that, since Katula could remember, had always been packed with dusty scrolls and Elements, glass vials filled with an array of colorful liquids, and wooden boxes stuffed with various dried plants. Now they stood mostly empty, save for the dust rings where the items once sat. “Ah, here it is!” Natta exclaimed, grabbing a small wooden box. On its lid was an image of a Bora tree, carved in the traditional flowing knotwork of her people. The sage’s wrinkled fingers pried it open, gave it a sniff, and held it out for Katula to smell. She did so and instantly wrinkled her nose.

“Natta, that’s awful. What is that? It smells like rotten fish.” The old woman nodded with an excited smile.

“Ha! It’s terrible but one of the most important Elements I can provide you with,” she laughed before growing serious. “It’s pollen from a Bora tree. Mix a small pinch of this with two drops of Jynyn blood, the blue liquid in the leather satchel, and you'll get a heat source that burns without putting off any smoke. Now, two drops are important, because if you go over that amount, the vapor has a tendency to render one unconscious." Directions like that had been going on the entire day, as Katula's grandmother and father were set to head south down the Tae as soon as Katula spoke her vows and the Sagen Ceremony was over. Not knowing when they would see each other again, Natta threw herself into imparting as much knowledge and wisdom as she could in the small time they had left together.

While her grandmother continued to hand her vials, jars, boxes, and pouches of Elements to stow away, Natta gave a thorough, verbal list of what each one did, how to use it, and what might happen if Katula didn't follow her directions to the letter. Katula frantically hung on every word and tried not to allow the magnitude of what was happening to distract her from concentrating. She was to become sagen of her people that night, and yet there was so much more for her to learn. All sagens that had come before her would have been familiar with the information Natta was providing long before swearing their oaths. But Katula thought she would have had more time, and instead focused most of her studies on the script and language within the Tercara Scroll. It's not that she didn't know *anything* about the Elements. She knew some. If you had bad breath or a case of bunions, Katula knew the proper mixes to concoct remedies for them. The things her grandmother had her packing, however, were on an entirely different level. Mix one Element with another and you created a new blended Element that could fill the stomach if you were without food. Yet, if you mixed the same two ingredients without knowing the correct amounts, they could very well explode, taking you along with it. The Elements weren't something you could just throw together and see what happened. You had to know the exact amount to mix in for each concoction, which was why, when the Ancients offered the Matuians the knowledge of Elementism in payment for safeguarding the Tercara Scroll, the exchange was so readily accepted. To study the Elements, one must follow strict laws, which was something Katula understood and one of the reasons she had chosen to become Matui's next sagen. The idea of spending one's life dedicated to Elementism in service to her people gave her a sense of fulfillment nothing else did. Katula's grandmother had married and raised a family, all while carrying out her duties as sage. There was no law saying you couldn't marry if you chose the profession. However, Katula had never harbored feelings for anyone, nor had any inclinations toward marriage or mothering younglings. Her strength was found through intense study, which could only be accomplished without the added distractions a family would bring. Besides, her people *were* her family. For Katula, joining the lineage of Matuian women who had served their people as sage was the highest honor. The first step toward that goal was acting as apprentice to the sage. That night, before she left her home, she would take the next step and become sagen, and sagen she would remain until Natta's death, where the title of sage would pass on to Katula until her own death.

It was well into late afternoon when a knock came at the sage's workhut. Annoyed at the interruption, Katula roughly threw open the old door.

"What do you want?" she barked. Bitun stood there, panting as if he'd been running. Immediately Katula changed course. "What's wrong?" The old warrior bowed.

"Forgive me, Katula Min, but your father sent me to fetch the sage." At that, Natta turned and shuffled her old legs to the door to listen. "A Grendolen scout has been captured and Chief Usoti requires Elements for the interrogation," he explained. Tingles ran through Katula's spine.

A Shadeblight in Matui! Katula had never seen a Grendolen. There was no way she was going to stay and pack. She *had* to look the enemy in the eye for herself to see what kind of person would willingly inflict so much pain on others.

"Tell my son I am on my way," Natta confirmed, before cocking an eye at Katula. "And tell him our soon-to-be sagen will be attending as well. She'll need the experience." Bitun bowed and took his leave.

"How did you know?" Katula asked, surprised by her grandmother's actions.

"That you wanted to see the Grendolen?" Natta guessed. "My dear, I've known you your whole life. You may think you hide your emotions from the rest of us, but to me it's as plain as rain on your face." The old woman smiled affectionately, then motioned for Katula to come in for a hug. Katula was not a hugger, but with Natta, she always gave an exception. "My dear sweet girl, you are more than capable of doing what your people require of you," she soothed, somehow reading Katula's thoughts. Natta always seemed to know what Katula was thinking. "But if this is the last time I am to give you advice..."

"Natta, don't say such a thing," Katula protested, pulling back and looking into her eyes. She couldn't bear thinking of never seeing her grandmother again.

"Now, now," Natta said, pulling her granddaughter in closer. "Not all paths are laid out before the journey," she quoted. It was a line Katula was familiar with, from the Tercara Scroll. "As I said, you are more than capable, but remember this, two voices can create harmony, whereas only one voice carries the weight of the entire song."

"You are referring to Meera," Katula guessed, reading through the subtext. Natta pulled away and nodded.

"You are a strong woman, Katula Min! You *both* are. Don't let that come between you. You're sisters! Use your strengths together." With that, Natta turned and fished out a jar from one of the satchels. "Come! Let's go get our first glimpse of a Shadeblight and see what he can tell us," she smiled, shaking the jar. Katula quickly picked up the packed bags and carefully looped them around her shoulders before following her grandmother out onto the suspended wooden walkway that connected the workhut to the Min family's other dwellings high within the trees. Silently she sent a prayer to Yveth.

If it be in your will for me to return to Matui, please let there be a home for me to return to.

Down below, on the terra, Katula found her surroundings eerily void of its normal sounds. Her home village had always been bustling with traders coming back from outside their borders or with families on the go. Now the tree huts and dirt roads sat silent and empty. Not a dog barked or a pony neighed. When they reached the Tineu hut, a handful of guards stood by Katula's father with the rest pointing their spears at the Grendolen, who had been bound and sat on one of the benches. As soon as her father saw the women arrive, the chief waved them in. A flash of jealousy stung Katula when she saw Meera was already in attendance. The Moorlander was *supposed* to be gathering vital supplies for their journey. Meera, however, paid no mind to Katula. She sat directly across from the bound captive staring with her red eyes narrowed with one hand on the hilt of a dagger and the other on a small throwing ax.

Yveth save us! She's going to kill *the man before we manage to get anything out of him,* she inwardly complained. Bloodkin or not, Katula's patience for her hot-headed sister was always in short supply. The Grendolen himself had a rather relaxed pose despite his restraints and current situation. Being the first Grendolen she'd ever laid eyes on, Katula couldn't decide whether the calm demeanor meant they should be worried because additional enemy forces were already on their way, or if the man really didn't know how dangerous Matuian warriors could be. Two of their guards took off the enemy's black helm, finally revealing a face underneath. It was not at all what she was expecting.

"He doesn't look like a Grendolen," Katula remarked to her father in the common tongue, so the captive could understand.

"No, he does not," her grandmother agreed, adopting the same language. She placed her weathered hands on the man's face and gave him a good look over before pinching his nose and stepping back with a satisfied look. "Not tall enough for a Shadeblight," she remarked. The captive gave a sniff and turned his blue eyes on the pair.

"I'll have you know I was the tallest in my pod," he said indignantly. He then added, "What's a Shadeblight?" One of the guards smacked him across the face.

"Quiet, captive! Show respect to Chief Usoti's family!"

"Ouch!" the captive complained, yawning his jaw in pain. He was about to get another warning when Katula's father held up his hand, signaling to stop.

"You were found alone on our eastern borders," he said to the captive. "How many more of your kind have already come ashore?"

"By now, *plenty*," the captive acknowledged readily. "And they aren't *my* kind. From the looks of it around here, you've already started evacuating. That was a good move on your part. They won't be expecting that, and it may hold them off for a little while, but not for long. The Grendolens have sailed here with an entire host of well-trained soldiers, and I should know, I pretended to be one of them. A *host*," the man emphasized, blue eyes narrowed. "That's an army *ten thousand* strong come to wipe your people off the map." It was Katula's turn to narrow her eyes.

"We are a strong people," she warned, her voice almost a growl, "and you are *very* close to finding out *how* strong."

"I'm sure you are," he replied, unfazed. "But not against a host. And I know you know this, because you've evacuated. So, let's get to the point, Prickly. Why would the Grendolens suddenly decide to send such a force *here*, in the middle of nowhere?" Katula snarled at his comment but held herself back from saying more.

"It is obvious you know and want to tell us," the sage intervened, with a knowing look in her eye.

"Alright," he admitted, flashing her a smile. "It could have to do with resources. This is quite the little woodland oasis you've got going here, and the Grendolen Empire is in the business of growing its naval fleet. But why sacrifice the labor force that could harvest the lumber for you? No, they're not after your timber. They're here to make an *example* of you. It makes one wonder what you did to warrant Lord Agnarr's wrath. Only, it isn't just *revenge* the emperor is after, is it?" He paused and eyed the chief. "He's sent his commandant general here, which means you've got something Lord Agnarr wants."

"And what would that be?" the sage pushed.

"Her," he replied, nodding toward Meera. Stunned that the Shadeblight thought any of this was about Meera and not the Tercara Scroll, Katula turned to her sister. In a blink of an eye, the Moorlander had unsheathed her dagger, pulled out her ax, and was halfway around the fire, headed straight for the captive. Katula quickly stepped between the two and tried to hold her sister off.

"Get out of my way!" Meera hissed, looking past Katula toward the enemy.

"He has information we *need*," Katula warned, still taken aback by the enemy's admission.

"*Sit down*, Meera," the sage ordered sternly, before taking a seat herself next to the captive. "Guards, leave us." The guards looked to Chief Usoti in surprise, who weighed his mother's words before nodding and requesting they wait outside.

"Do not think that by their leaving you are safe, captive," the chief warned once they'd gone. "One false move and I'll personally send your soul to Nihility." Then, turning, he addressed the sage. "Mother, I think you owe us an explanation as to why you so readily trust this stranger, one who wears the armor of our enemy."

"Oh, there's no danger with this one," the sage confirmed with an air of certainty. Meera stopped trying to push past Katula but kept her weapons at hand.

"Thank you," the captive replied coolly, nodding his head in respect to the old woman.

"Natta, he is a *Grendolen*," Katula stressed to her grandmother.

"I think all in this room are very aware that not all things are what they seem." At that, the sage glanced Meera's way. "This man is telling the truth. He is no Grendolen soldier. Look at how the uniform is slightly small in the sleeves! See how his shoes are too wide? This isn't his uniform. Besides, I made sure to dose him with a good amount of Tannison when I examined his face."

"Impressive," the captive said with an air of admiration before stopping short. "Wait, *what* did you dose me with?" Katula's grandmother ignored the captive and just smiled. Tannison was a vapor made from Elements that, once inhaled, would entice a person to tell the truth.

"If he is no Shadeblight, then who is he and what is he doing in that armor?" Katula demanded. The sage looked expectantly at the captive.

"My name is Darmond," the man replied. "I work with the Midtier Resistance as a spy. I infiltrated the Grendolen army and found out they were actively hunting the surviving heir to the Kingdom of Moorland. My plan was simple: acting as one of their sailors, I would let *them* lead me straight to her. And as Yveth would have it, I was able to break from their ranks once they landed on your shores and reach you before they did. I mean to take the heir back with me to Midtier, where the Resistance can help keep her safe. Maggots, I am talking *a lot*! What did you *do* to me?" he charged, looking concerned.

"What makes you think I'm the heir?" Meera demanded, her cheeks still flushed with anger.

"The fact that you aren't Matuian is pretty much all the proof I need," he countered. "Unless you're harboring more foreigners in these woods..." When she didn't respond, he added, "You're the right age and fit the heir's description, although those red eyes were *not* mentioned in the report." Meera let out a hiss.

"How did the Resistance know she was alive," Chief Usoti asked, his brow furrowed.

"My superiors are still trying to find the answer to that, but the point is, the Grendolen emperor found out. Whatever gains Lord Agnarr's interest, gains the interest of the Resistance."

"What is this Resistance you keep referring to?" Katula demanded.

"We are the ones that have been keeping the rest of Tersaith free from the Grendolen Empire. The Resistance has been fighting them back for a long time now, even before Moorland fell. Your people have enjoyed peace, while mine have paid dearly for it." Katula's father chose to ignore the comment, but the man realized the broken branch he'd walked out on. "Rot, that was more than I wanted to say. That stuff you dosed me with really works."

"You said the Resistance would keep my Red Daughter safe, but what is their interest in her? Why go to the length of risking a spy such as yourself hiding among the enemy and bringing her back with you?" This, at last, finally stopped the overly talkative Darmond, who seemed to be weighing how to best answer the question. The Tannison couldn't force words out of him, but it did lower one's normal discrepancy. It allowed truthful conversation to flow. Katula could tell the man knew as much and was trying to figure a way around it.

"Father, this man cannot be trusted, even with the Tannison," she pleaded in Matuian, so the captive wouldn't understand. "Sending an army here for a Moorlander? We all know what they are really here for, the Tercara Scroll. It was prophesied why."

"A tree's foundation is made strong by many unseen roots," the chief cautioned. "We are not privy to how the prophecy will come to pass, only that it will. This man's appearance at such a time as this cannot be ignored. Your grandmother is wise. If she trusts him, we need to hear him out." Katula let out a frustrated sigh but nodded in compliance.

After a few moments of hesitation, the Midtierian took in a resolved breath and turned to Meera.

"Have you wondered why the Grendolens were coming for you?" he asked.

"No," she shot back quickly. Then more quietly, she added, "Maybe... But *why*? I have no kingdom to rule! What threat am I to the Grendolens? Am I just a means to an end?"

"An understandable conclusion, but no," Darmond disagreed. "No offense, Red, but you're not worth sailing an entire host after." Meera's grip on her dagger tightened.

"It's *Meera*, to you," she seethed, "and you were the one who implied as much! If not simply a means to an end, then *what*?"

"They sent a host because Lord Agnarr, leader of the Grendolen Empire, believes you have something he wants. The Stone Key."

"A what?" Meera laughed, a mixture of confusion and disbelief. "I don't have any keys!"

"It's one key, the Stone Key, and it's no laughing matter, I can assure you. Lord Agnarr believes the Stone Key unlocks an ancient weapon, one he would very much like to get his hands on, and he thinks *you've* got it. That's why he sent ten thousand soldiers here. He doesn't care a *rot* about you or your little ruin of a castle. He wants the *key* because he wants the *weapon*." *This* grabbed Katula's attention. Perhaps the man was a root of the tree after all.

"This, then, is the *true* reason the Resistance sent you," the chief broke in. "They want Meera to bring them this Stone Key you speak of so they can use the weapon against the Grendolens themselves."

"It would finally give us the edge we need to beat back the enemy once and for all," Darmond admitted.

"I'm not going *anywhere* with you," Meera snarled, "no matter which side you're on."

"This key," Katula remarked, suddenly very focused on the man. "What does it look like?"

"No clue. But the good news is, I don't think the Grendolens do either."

"Natta," Katula called, turning to her grandmother and switching to their language. "Isn't there a reference to a key in the scroll? Something about a 'key of stone'?" The Midtierian spy grew annoyed.

"Hey! What are you talking about? You just dosed me with Yveth knows what and made me reveal *highly* classified information. You owe me the truth." Natta nodded to Katula indicated she should speak in the common tongue again.

"Natta!" Katula protested, still speaking in Matuian. "I am not about to go talking about the very thing I've been tasked with protecting in front of a complete stranger. One who was sneaky enough to hide among the Grendolens."

"*Roots*, dear," Natta tsked. "My soul tells me this man needs to hear what you have to say." Begrudgingly, Katula obeyed and repeated herself in the common tongue.

"I believe there is a reference to a key of stone in one of our ancient scrolls."

"Scroll? What scroll?" Darmond asked, his interest clearly kindled.

"Indeed, you are correct," the sage recalled, growing excited. "There *is* a passage! It reads, 'Yet if we cannot find it in ourselves to extend the graces bestowed on us to those in need of it, how then can we face Yveth in the end? Therefore, life, the greatest gift of the Creator, must be held sacred. For does not a key of stone hold only death?'"

"Death," Darmond mused, narrowing his blue eyes. "Sounds sinister enough that it might actually be a promising lead. What scroll is this?"

"The Tercara Scroll," the sage informed him. "Written by the Ancients themselves." Katula's tan face went ghostly pale. How was she expected to keep the scroll safe if her grandmother refused to keep it a secret? For a moment, Darmond's chatter stopped as he weighed the new information.

"Wait a moment. Are you saying this scroll you have is over *three thousand* cycles old?"

"Yes," the old woman replied matter-of-factly. Darmond's eyes went wide.

"Just to clarify things here, you have in your possession a scroll written by Yveth's god-kin that *mentions* a key of stone during the time the weapon is rumored to have existed?"

"Correct. I suspect now that is why we were requested to safeguard it all this time." The realization of what Natta had just pieced together hit Katula like a gale off the coast. Taking a seat on one of the benches, she struggled to keep her composure.

He really is *a root! The time of the prophecy is here, and this man is part of it*, she marveled to herself.

"A weapon from the Ancients' time doesn't hold well with me," Darmond finally responded to those in the hut. "If even half the stories I've heard about from back then are true, using this weapon could be devastating. I'm talking about the end-of-life-on-Tersaith-as-we-know-it devastating. I *need* to find the Stone Key before the Grendolens do." At that, he turned back to Meera. "You may not have the Stone Key now, but maybe somewhere in your memory your family made mentioned of it?" Meera shook her head.

"I was a youngling when I... when all that happened. I don't remember much."

"That won't matter to Lord Agnarr. He has *ways* to make people remember. He openly practices Elementism. He can use the Elements to pull memories out of your mind, even ones you forgot you had." Katula looked at her grandmother in surprise. She had not heard of any other people on Tersaith practicing Elementism, nor to such a degree.

"Can the emperor really *do* that?" she asked Natta.

"Unfortunately," the sage confirmed gravely. "There are Elements that can force one's mind to open. I wasn't aware, however, that the Grendolens practiced Elementism."

"Wait, *you* use the Elements?" Darmond asked incredulously, suddenly uncomfortable with the old woman sitting next to him.

"All of our sages do," Katula noted. "As I am about to swear my oaths as sagen, I myself am learning to use them. The Tannison you were dosed with was made using Elements." Darmond's skin took on a sickly green hue.

"The Resistance in Midtier," the chief cut in, pointing the question to the man. "Do you have a way to communicate with them?"

"Not here. I'd have to reach the Cassias. My hope was to take Red here," he said, nodding to Meera, "and send a carrier pigeon once we reached Vardia. It's a trading town just past Ismoad Peak." That information caught the attention of Katula's father.

"That area is familiar to you, then? You have traveled there before?" Chief Usoti asked.

"Sure, loads of times." Darmond shrugged casually, still under the influence of the Tannison.

"It looks like the roots have been laid out before us," the chief announced, turning to his mother. The sage nodded, catching on. Seeing the look pass between the two caused Darmond's smile to fade.

"Why do I get the feeling I just talked myself into doing something I'm not going to like?" he asked, looking worried.

A short while later, Chief Usoti struck an accord with Darmond. Knowing the Midtierian spy wanted to dig into Meera's past and the Tercara Scroll for information about the Stone Key, the chief gave Darmond permission to accompany the women westward as their guide through the Cassia Mountains in return for brokering an alliance between their two people. If the Midtierians and Matuians joined numbers, they would both have a chance of turning the tide and reclaiming their lands and freedom. Darmond was all too eager to comply, and with the sun already setting, he was released and sent with Meera and several guards to finish gathering supplies for their journey.

That night, on Lyfmoad 18th, both Tersaith's moons were in between their full and withering gibbous phases, allowing their light to shine brightly on the Green's clearing. The Watchers were what many called the moons. Orynis, the larger of the two, dominated the sky with his blue haze. Oryna, however, with her gray-white hue, sat at his right side, like two lovers who danced through time together, unwilling to part. Only eighteen days ago, all of Matui had gathered together on that same Green to celebrate Dawnday, the first day of the New Cycle. As they had done for generations, Katula's people had lit lanterns, walked out among the forest, and sang songs to wake the trees from their Wyntersol slumber. Now that the evacuees had fled and all their warriors had gone to hold off the Grendolens, a pensive silence hung around the Green like a funeral shroud—silence that Katula could find in the forest readily. In the villages, however, especially Matui, the most populated of the seven villages, noise was constant. The sudden lack of it, where once it thrived, came as a shock to Katula. To find her home emptied of not only its people but also the *sounds* that usually accompany the normal hum of life unnerved her. Even more so, as she wondered if those beautiful souls and voices would ever be able to return home.

A Sagen Ceremony would have usually warranted a large turnout of spectators, but the only witnesses to Katula's initiation were her family, their personal guards, Meera Tarmanon, and one Midtierian spy. None of it was how Katula had expected things to go. She had spent the past two cycles planning her advancement to sagen. She had even commissioned a new beaded dress for the ceremony, one that would never be made at this point. Her mother had passed away from a sickness when she was a youngling, and she had no other siblings, unless you counted Meera. It was just her father and grandmother now, and both seemed set on Katula taking the Tercara Scroll to Pawtoton. It didn't seem to matter to them that she had no map or inkling of *how* to get there. And now she was to be accompanied by not only Meera, but a spy who very much wanted a look at the scroll she was about to swear to protect.

Katula slowly took in a deep breath, trying to calm her nerves as she approached the small gathering before her on the Green. Coming to a stop, she turned to her grandmother and gave a sign of respect, bowing and touching the back of her thumb to her lips, then extended her hand palm up to the sage. Her grandmother wasted no time.

"Katula Min, daughter of Usoti Min, Chief of the Matuian tribe blessed by Yveth's god-kin to guard the Tercara Scroll," the wizened woman addressed. "You stand before your people and the Watchers, who bear witness to the oaths you are about to swear.

Oaths that are lifelong and binding! Before those gathered, declare now if you intend to make them."

Circumstances may have changed the way Katula planned things to go, but there was no doubt in her mind about committing to becoming the next Matuian sage. It was all she had ever wanted.

"I will swear the oaths on my life and adhere to them until my dying breath," she replied confidently, black eyes stern.

"Then kneel and prepare yourself," the sage commanded. Katula kneeled, pushed back her long green braids, and looked up into her grandmother's eyes. Never had she seen them so full of pride. The chief handed his daughter an ornate bronzium bowl and the sage poured the contents of a pouch into it. Striking flint, a spark lit the powdered Elements and burst into a bright blue light.

"See my offering, Orynis, as it burns to mirror your light," Katula recited, looking up at the larger of the two moons. "May it continue to watch over me and never burn out." As soon as the Elements dimmed, the sage emptied the contents of the second pouch into the bowl. This time, the flame burned a bright white. "See my offering, Oryna, as it burns to mirror your light. May it continue to watch over me and never burn out." As the last of the Elements burned, Katula's grandmother lifted her head and began singing a chant, first to purify the air and hearts of those in attendance before the oaths were sworn, and secondly to call to the trees of the forest, for they, too, would bear witness. Satisfied all was ready, the sage turned to Katula and addressed her.

"Do you swear to serve as sagen to your people until the time comes for you to ascend to become their sage, or until Yveth calls your soul to his side?"

"I swear to this oath before Yveth, the Watchers, and my people," Katula replied solemnly. Giving a curt nod, the sage dipped her thumb into the ashes of the burned Elements and pressed it to Katula's forehead.

"What do you ask of Yveth?"

"I ask for blessings of wisdom," Katula replied, "and in return, I promise to use it in both deed and heart." Putting her thumb into the ash again, the sage then pressed it onto her granddaughter's lips.

"What do you ask of the Watchers?"

"I ask for blessings of bounty, and in return, I promise to never exceed that which they have given.

"What do you ask of your people?" the sage finished, dipping her thumb into the ash and pressing it to Katula's chest.

"I ask for blessings of fellowship, and in return, I promise to never turn away those in need." A wide smile spread across the old woman's face.

"Your oaths have been witnessed and accepted. Rise now and know these oaths have forever changed you. Katula Min is no more. You are now Katula, Sagen of Matui, bearer of the Tercara Scroll."

There was no great feast to celebrate the newly appointed sagen that mild Lyntensol night. No singing and dancing on the Green until the wee light of dawn. Instead, there was a final burst of energy to finalize preparations. While the others were busy with their tasks, Katula's grandmother pulled her off to the side.

"I fear this weapon the spy speaks of," she admitted, whispering in Matuian. "There were many such weapons when the Ancients walked Tersaith, and none of them good. If the Grendolens should get a hold of one..." Katula watched her grandmother's face cloud over in concern. In truth, she had never seen her look so worried before.

"If it does exist, Yveth has known of its existence since it was made. He will not abandon us now," Katula encouraged, trying to comfort her. "Besides, Meera doesn't remember anything." At that, the sage looked directly into Katula's eyes.

"That is what worries me most. The Midtierian is right. The enemy could use the Elements to *make* her remember." The old woman stood there, a heavy conflict in her mind clearly reflected on her face. At last, she came to a decision. "Katula, my dear, I think we may need to break one of our most sacred laws, and I'm afraid you're going to have to be the one to carry it out." Katula's eyes widened. She liked laws. They gave her comfort. They kept the world in order.

"Natta, what are you talking about?"

"The only way to make sure Meera doesn't know anything is for us to administer Elements of our own."

"That doesn't break any of our laws."

"No, dear. But not telling her we're doing it *is*."

"What?" Katula gasped, barely able to keep her voice down. Giving a Matuian Elements without their permission went against not just one rule, but *all* the rules. Despite their different backgrounds, Meera was close enough to her family to fall under that rule.

"I know, I know!" Natta said, lifting her hands in surrender. "But there's no other way. If we were to tell her, it could alter her memory of what really happened in her past. Meera needs to remember without being influenced in any way. Otherwise, it could skew the results." Katula hated that what her grandmother said made so much sense.

"How much are we talking about?"

"Eight doses."

"*Eight*?" Sagen for less than half a night, and she would be agreeing to break the rules not once but eight times.

"We'll need to mix it up fast. They're almost finished packing the piwakeys, so I don't have much time." Katula followed her grandmother over to a bench near the Tineu's fire where her own belongings were being stowed. Katula stood watch as her grandmother rummaged through the bags and expertly mixed the Elements together. As soon as she was done, the sage turned to her granddaughter and packed the vial with the memory elixir back into the leather satchel.

"Remember," she warned, "there are eight doses. Give one dose of two drops every four days. Once you start administering it, you can't stop. If you wait too long in between doses, the effect could wear off before the full memory of her past is restored. If you give it too often, you run the risk of compacting her memories and distorting their truths."

"One dose of two drops every four days eight times," Katula repeated to confirm.

"I pray Meera doesn't remember anything," the sage admitted, clasping her granddaughter's hands. "Because if she does and there is a weapon this Stone Key unlocks, it would mean the spy was right, and it would need to be found and destroyed before the enemy gets their hands on it."

All too soon, the piwakeys were packed and ready to transport her family southward during the night, and her last goodbyes were said. As Katula stood on the banks of the Tae River and watched the most important people in her life paddle downstream, she couldn't help but feel a piece of her soul had broken through its bodily cage and left with them.

CHAPTER FOUR

Finnik

Finnik stood at the starboard bow aboard the *Seventh Sister*, warily eyeing the dark, ominous cliffs towering above the tall ship as it sailed past them in the night. Behind him, on the quarterdeck, Commandant Admiral Jerrna Wess barked out orders as he expertly maneuvered them out of harm's way. A shout arose above from the crow's nest, alerting those on board that a more approachable shoreline was spotted. Sure enough, the dense, *glowing* forest of Wildwood peeked into view a few moments later. Positioned directly above the dark trees blanketing the strange land, hung the Watchers, providing ample light as they slowly made their way across the sky.

The ship lurched suddenly with the waves, causing Finnik to stumble forward and grab hold of the taffrail. He growled at the waters in defiance and quickly regained his composure. He had never been fond of sailing, and this voyage was no exception. It had been a direct command, however, straight from Lord Agnarr himself, and Finnik took his duty to the empire seriously, even if he saw little point in dragging the Grendolen army halfway across the sea to track down a kingdomless heir.

Necessity dictates, he chanted to himself, giving his velvet black forehead a rub.

"Commandant General Doth?" a young voice squeaked from behind him. The boy saluted by placing his right hand flat against his chest and bowing his head. Finnik looked over the sailor with a cynical eye. Was it just him, or did all the newest recruits seem to be much younger these days?

"I've not got all night, seaman. *Spit it out*," he demanded impatiently, his brown eyes narrowing.

"C.A. Wess has asked that you join him on the quarterdeck to discuss preparations for disembarking," the sailor rushed, referring to his superior's abbreviated title. Finnik noticed the boy's eyes did not make contact with him directly, which wasn't surprising. Most people acted that way when coming face-to-face with a Doth, one of the most prominent and wealthiest families of Grendolen. Still, if one signed up to join the mightiest military on Tersaith, they should know how to look their commanding officer in the eye, Doth or not. Annoyed at the boy's lack of training, Finnik left him without so much as a nod and made his way across the ship; his heavy, determined strides were an outward display of the confidence his sea legs kept threatening to undermine, while also warning the busy crewmen running around to keep a clear path.

The *Seventh Sister* was indeed a robust ship. They'd painted her a glossy black with red and yellow trim to match the Grendolen sigil colors. Despite her large cargo hold, she was still the fastest two-masted brig in all the fleet. The ship's name derived from a prominent constellation found in the Tersaithian night sky that comprised of seven bright stars, known as the Seven Sisters. It was a well-known belief sailors held that, if you could spot the brightest of the stars in the constellation, Varwonen, the Seventh Sister herself, she would always guide your way home. Many sailors kept a small carving of a female figurine depicting Varwonen with them during their voyage as they believed it brought them good fortune. Some even went to the extreme of tattooing images of the constellation on their arm to further add to their fortune. The very ship Finnik sailed on even boasted a gold-painted figurehead carved in the fictional woman's likeness. Finnik, however, was not fond of such superstitions. He played life by the rules. Growing up under a long line of generals in the family has that effect on you. Honor, duty, and loyalty were the codes he lived by.

Had his mission not been so urgent, their journey would have been made over land. Dependable, *solid*, land. Yet, that hadn't been the case, and it had placed Finnik and his own soldiers at the mercy of this superstitious sailing lot. Age and experience had hardened him enough to know that the only thing worth putting your trust in was the empire itself. It had existed long before the rise and expansion Lord Agnarr had brought on, and it would continue to stand strong long after Finnik's time on the world came to an end.

Necessity dictates, he reminded himself again, taking in a slow, steady breath.

The commandant admiral stood with his shoulders back and hands clasped behind him, his eyes coolly scanning the ship and swaying night horizon as he oversaw his sailors performing their orders. Dusty gray hair, a touch darker than Finnik's own short white hair and beard, poked out the sides of his wide bicorn hat, which held a red ribbon pinned in the center, indicating his naval rank. In the few moads that Finnik had sailed with the man, he had come to learn C.A. Wess was not a person you wanted to cross. Something Finnik could appreciate and respect, as he, too, kept a tight rein on his own men. When the general had received his orders from Lord Agnarr and realized he and his men would be sailing a little over one moad, he had grown concerned. Soldiers did not do well penned up in small places for an extended period of time with nothing available to blow off steam. But a meeting with the admiral had eased his worry. Wess had seen to it that Finnik's soldiers were kept occupied and in shape during the voyage. All in all, the journey had been a smooth one, much to Finnik's satisfaction.

"Ah, Commandant General," Jerrna Wess acknowledged as Finnik climbed up the stairs.

"Commandant Admiral," he replied with a curt nod.

"It seems we have made it past the cliffs with not a ship lost," the admiral said, a clear tone of pride in his voice. "Many a crew have gone missing rounding them, and that was in broad daylight. The Seventh Sister surely guided our path this night." Jerrna's eyes stopped scanning his ship and turned to the general.

"Indeed," Finnik managed, not wishing to get into a debate on superstitions. The admiral hadn't been happy over the prospect of navigating the cliffs in the middle of the night; however, he'd eventually given in after Finnik reminded him of how important this mission was to Lord Agnarr. The element of surprise could very well determine the outcome of the upcoming confrontation with the Matuians, and that could only be acquired with their swift and unexpected arrival on their coastal borders.

"We are nearing the shores and will be ready for your men to disembark by morning," Jerrna continued.

"I will have my men at the ready, Commandant Admiral."

"I have no doubt on the matter," Jerrna nodded before casting his eyes down toward the ship's lantern-lit deck. "As agreed upon, I'll send a portion of my sailors to assist on land."

"Good. As soon as we make camp and the scouts have reported back, I'll be giving orders to push west. If we are to catch the locals off guard, we'll need to strike fast."

"All is in order, then..." Jerrna paused as his eyes narrowed and focused on one of the sailors below. "Torin! What is that rotting fleaborn doing with my ship's foresail?" he demanded, directing the question to his closest commanding officer.

"He's a new one, sir," Torin said, his face cringing as he observed the seaman's behavior. Without waiting for a command from his superior, Torin barked at the officer overseeing the men on deck. "Jay, look to your men, ya maggot! You've got a sailor out of line!" The man named Jay turned quickly and saw his new charge loosening one of the foresail lines.

"What in *Nibility*? Get your *rotting* hands off that line, Linklo!" Jay bellowed, as he ran over to the man and shoved him aside. The man in question threw up his hands in frustration, shouting back at Jay something about misguided directions.

"Torin," Wess hissed through his teeth. "See to it that man is properly disciplined."

"Yes, sir!" Torin responded with a firm salute. Once everything had returned to the regular rhythms on the main deck, the admiral turned his attention back to Finnik to finish their conversation.

"When can we expect your return?" he asked.

"No more than four days, a week's time," Finnik replied. "These are a reclusive people, Commandant Admiral, with primitive weapons. Indeed, we may even be back by Lyfmoad 21st," Finnik concluded confidently. As always, he had researched his enemy extensively before drawing up his plans of attack. The Matuians were not advanced; his men would be up against small clusters of warriors armed with bows and clad with leather. It was true, though, that Matuian-crafted bows and arrows were known throughout Tersaith for their accuracy and durability, which was why they were the tribe's largest export. But what was an arrow when up against Grendolen armor, made from virtually indestructible noiramite metal? A metal whose discovery had brought about the empire's recent rapid expansion. Revealing its compounds to Grendolen is what propelled Lord Agnarr into power at the young age of nineteen. And he hadn't been content to rule only the far lands of the north. With his use of noiramite, Lord Agnarr painted a broader vision for the empire, one where the borders stretched ever southward, where the might of Grendolens' military forces could become the largest on Tersaith, and where the wealth from those they conquered would be redistributed throughout the land. The people of Grendolen believed those promises, the Doth family among them, and many of Lord Agnarr's promises had already come true. Some had not. Finnik may not agree with how the leader of the empire went about fulfilling those promises, but it was not his place to disagree. No matter how many kings rose and fell within his life, Finnik would remain faithful to the empire and serve his people.

Lord Agnarr had made it clear Finnik was to deliver a swift end to the Matuians, as payment for their betrayal in hiding the Tarmanon fugitive. The sooner they captured the Moorland heir, the faster she could be brought back to Grendolen for interrogation. She held valuable information the emperor needed. That was the sole reason behind bringing such a large force, and why, in turn, they were forced to sail rather than march. With an estimated five thousand able fighters among the Matuian's population, Finnik brought with him one host of his army, a total of ten thousand trained soldiers. Still, the battlefield was to take place among the dense forest of Wildwood. If rumors were to be believed, the place was wholly unlike any other forest found on Tersaith, filled with a myriad of toxic plants and creatures that could kill you. Thus, Finnik had taken great pains to prepare his soldiers, knowing the unfamiliar terrain was the one advantage his enemy had over him.

Finnik didn't want to risk encountering anything... *unusual* when it was still dark in Wildwood. Best wait until light to strike into the unknown. They decided to make landfall on Lyfmoad 18th and make camp up against the small sandy cliffs just below the tree line but not within the actual forest. Once his tent was erected, Finnik wasted no time setting out his plans and plotting his final steps before his scheduled meeting with the selected commanders he'd chosen for the mission. They consisted of a host commander, two faction colonels, and two assembly captains. All but one had served under Finnik previously. Host Commander Baska Sarell was the only one of the five who had fought alongside him during the attack on Moorland. While the others had proven themselves in other battles, the colonel had played a major part in the success of the kingdom's overthrow.

"C.G. Doth, sir?" a voice said from outside Finnik's tent flap. He looked up from his wooden desk, surprised at how fast the time had passed.

Is it already evening? Finnik wondered to himself, realizing his lamps had long been lit by one of his attendants.

"You may enter," he called, covering up his work. A scrawny boy, no more than fourteen cycles of age, entered and cautiously approached Finnik.

They really are *getting younger. Either that, or I'm getting* older.

"Sir, if I may," the boy said, thankfully with more confidence than the sailor on the ship, "it is nearing time for you to meet with your officers. If you follow me, sir, I can lead you there, through camp."

Nodding, Finnik motioned for one of his personal guards to follow. As he walked along the rows of small tents erected just below the unnatural woods, Finnik studied the faces of his men. Many cast weary glances at the forest, as if expecting something horrifying to pop out at any moment. It was the unease of the woods that kept conversations between his men unusually subdued, and it didn't help that Finnik had ordered them not to light any campfires in case it alerted the enemy to their presence. The war horses they had brought with them on the voyage were restless as well and were unsettled in their makeshift pens. Thankfully, the hounds had wisely been kept aboard the ships and would stay there until he gave the order to advance into Wildwood.

As Finnik approached the large command tent, several guards stood to attention and saluted. Inside, multiple lanterns glowed with a warm, natural light, and he could see its effect reflected on the five faces of those within.

"Commandant General," Host Commander Baska Sarell called, noting his arrival. She was his second in command within the Grendolen army. Her feminine features were an even match to her strength and cunning, making her one of the most dangerous women Finnik had ever known, and one he highly respected. Underneath the red cloth wrapped around her head, he could see the tail end of several black braids poking out. It was how she always chose to wear her hair for battle.

"H.C. Sarell," Finnik greeted her with a nod as he made his way over to the central table. A rough map of Wildwood's terrain was spread across the large table, littered with figures representing their army and those of the Matuian tribe. The map itself had been acquired through a native tradesman they had captured before embarking on their sea voyage. Elementism was not openly practiced in Grendolen, and Lord Agnarr's use of it was still something Finnik was growing used to; however, in the tradesman's case, he had allowed it. The map they tortured out of the man *had* to be accurate if Finnik was to know how best to strategize their advance.

The soft mumbling of the others within the room died down as he approached.

"You may proceed with the current report," Finnik commanded, never one to waste time with idle chit-chat.

"Yes, sir," Baska saluted, turning to the maps. "We expect to hear back from our scouts soon with updated information about the exact location of the two most eastern villages. In the meantime, I believe the maps provided sufficient detail to follow the scouts' routes.

"As you can see from this map, we know that the layout of Wildwood's seven villages are roughly based on a hexagonal shape. However, trails leading in or out of this rotting Nihility are far and few between. If the information we gained is to be believed, the only trail that exits the forest is to the far west. We estimate it to be at least more than eighty spans from our current position." As she pointed, one of the other attendees, Faction Colonel Varcor Orna, quietly moved figures to designated areas on the map. "Meanwhile, we assume they will send the majority of their warriors to block our advance along the coastal trail inward, somewhere around their northeastern village," Baska added, her green eyes giving Finnik a quick glance. "If our initial numbers are accurate," she continued, "their fighting force should hold no more than a faction, around five thousand warriors, once the weak, old, and young have fled."

"Even if our numbers are wrong and the other villages hold similar populations as their largest village, I am confident our strength in numbers will have them surrendering before the day is out, Commandant General," Faction Colonel Varcor Orna, to Finnik's left, surmised. Out of them all, Orna was the only one Finnik hadn't fought alongside. A stout man with an unusually pale complexion and short black hair, Orna's lack of emotion was sometimes found off-putting to the soldiers around him. Having recently moved through the ranks at an unusually fast pace, Finnik hadn't had time to get to know the man as well as he would have liked beforehand. The plans Finnik had drawn up for this attack had been meticulously combed over, as with any move he made on the battlefield. Part of that planning had included those within that very command tent—all save for the F.C. Yet, Orna was there at the express order of the emperor, Lord Agnarr, which meant his presence was something Finnik would *have* to accept. However, it didn't mean he had to make it easy for the man. If Orna wanted to advance under Finnik's command, he would have to prove himself.

"I wouldn't be so quick to underestimate the Matuians," Baska warned Orna, bringing Finnik's thoughts back to the present. "This forest is *their* terrain. They know every tree, rock, and hollow, not to mention what will kill you and what won't. To push that information from the forefront of our minds would be foolish."

"I agree with Host Commander Sarell," said Faction Colonel Han Wesdo through his thick graying beard. "We aren't just here to put an end to these plaguemen. Our advance will send them scattering to every possible exit. If we are to capture the prey we are after, every exit, no matter how small, will need to be covered. Especially these two rivers." Though usually reserved, Han's strength was in predicting the enemy's strategy, which was why Finnik had brought him along. "If the information we've received is to be believed, both rivers running through their territory run southward. My recommendation is to send a large contingent to cut them off."

Wesdo was right. When the command to invade Wildwood had been issued to Finnik, the first concern he had was how difficult it would be to march an army into an unknown forest. Having the map drastically improved his odds of success, but finding the Tarmanon heir in all that mess was going to be akin to locating a quiet spot to nap in the middle of a battlefield.

"Yes, that was my assessment as well," Finnik nodded curtly. "We must first cut off their exits, locate our prey, and then burn every single rotting tree in this Yveth-forsaken land. Don't let their familiarity with the land fool you. The Matuians have *never* seen a force the size of which we'll be throwing at them, and that is *our* advantage. Let them scatter like roaches into our traps! Remember, for the last sixteen cycles, these plaguemen have defied our emperor. No mercy shall be shown, no quarter given!"

Those around Finnik saluted and cried out in agreement.

"F.C. Orna, I want you to take command of the cavalry. You are to lead a troop north above the forest and make your way westward. Place men here and here," he noted, pointing to the two northern river entrances. "However, your main task will be to cut off their exit to the plains." Finnik paused and narrowed his brown eyes at the man. "Your advance must be swift! If you leave tonight, I estimate at least a three-day ride, putting you there by Lyfmoad 22nd."

"It shall be done, Commandant General," Varcor Orna saluted.

"F.C. Wesdo," Finnik called. "Tomorrow morning you will take a full faction and sail south. With the rivers being the natives' fastest escape, I want those southern river exits *covered.*"

"By your will," Wesdo acknowledged with a salute.

"As for dealing with those warriors," Finnik noted, looking at H.C. Sarell. "Do what you do best. Take three assemblies. I want them cleared by the time my personal unit moves through. The rest will stay here on the coast. I'll send for more troops once I'm stationed in the central village."

A smile spread across the woman's face as she saluted. "With pleasure, Commandant Doth."

"I remind you all, only those within this tent know Lord Agnarr's true orders. Our first priority is to find our prey. *Anyone* caught escaping must be thoroughly interrogated if we are to locate what we are looking for," he emphasized. "Our prey has spent the last sixteen cycles hiding. She'll have grown complacent, like a hare that strays too close to the fox den. She may bolt, but we must have all exits covered."

“By your will, Commandant General,” they all agreed simultaneously.

“One last thing,” Finnik cautioned, his face growing serious. “On Lord Agnarr’s orders, when our prey is found, she is to *immediately* be brought to me. She is not to be harmed, interrogated, or searched. Failure to adhere to that command would mean the Stand, not just for you, but your entire family. Do I make myself clear?” The harsh warning didn’t dissuade their eagerness, however. Finnik could see they took it seriously.

“Sir, pardon my interruption.” One of his soldiers stood at the tent’s entrance and gave a hasty salute before continuing. “Some of the scouts we sent out just arrived back.”

“And?” he growled impatiently.

“It seems the Matuians knew of our landing, sir. They’ve already started evacuating!” An icy wave washed over Finnik as all his meticulously thought-out plans crumbled like sand upon a shore. The whole reason he had pushed Commandant Admiral Wess to risk rounding the cliffs at night was so their ships weren’t spotted. If he was going to recover the time lost, he needed to act fast.

“Have the evacuees reached their southern borders?” he demanded.

“Our scouts didn’t make it that far, sir. But they did report that the eastern villages were nearly emptied, and a large portion of their warriors were gathering.”

“Orna, Wesdo,” Finnik barked, turning back to those around the table. “Ready your men. You leave tonight. H.C. Sarell, send for the hounds. Your force advances by dawnlight.”

"There's something else, sir," the solider added.

Finnik read the tone of his voice. What else could possibly go wrong?

"There's been talk among the sailors. Apparently, one from the *Seventh Sister* is missing. Scuttlebutt has him pegged as a Resistance spy." Finnik's face remained calm, but internally his mind was racing. A *spy* within the Grendolen military? And not only within the military, but aboard the ship *he'd* sailed on? The very one he'd held meetings containing highly sensitive information about Meera Tarmanon on? If there was a spy, just *how much* did they now know?

"This doesn't change our plans," Finnik finally announced to those in the tent. "Keep to your orders, as planned. I will have my command tent stationed in the central village. Once your advance inward is complete, report back to me. In the meantime," he said, turning to the guard, "I need to have a talk with C.A. Wess about these spy rumors. I want a boat ready to take me out to the *Seventh Sister* by dawnlight tomorrow."

The commandant admiral confirmed Finnik's fears the next morning. There had indeed been a spy about the ship, none other than the one named Linklo that Finnik himself had witnessed being called out while on deck. The spy's supposed link to the Resistance wasn't confirmed, just a guess. A likely connection, though. The Resistance was the only order within Midtier that had managed to muster up a sizable force to fight the Grendolen army. And while Finnik knew the Resistance had spies within its service, their organization's infancy left their troops untrained and often disorganized. The fact that one of their spies had actually managed to infiltrate the Grendolen military came as a surprise. Especially since Finnik had placed spies of his own within the Resistance. Not one of them had alerted him to a spy being sent aboard the *Seventh Sister*. Had their messages of warning gone astray or had the Resistance managed to conjure up a decent spy?

Another more worrying thought crossed his mind. If the spy was good enough to pass even Finnik's scrutinous eye, were they equally capable of finding the Tarmanon heir before him?

He had grossly underestimated the Resistance, it seemed, and he would have to pay the price if he didn't figure out how to gain back control of the situation. It wasn't just Finnik's life on the line. Every Doth in Grendolen would be sent to the Stand to burn along with him.

Not ready to let that happen, Finnik immediately penned a message and sent it to his most trusted spy within the Resistance, demanding an explanation. It would take some time for the carrier pigeon to deliver it and for a reply to be received, but that worked in his favor. It gave him time to sort out the mess in Wildwood. Before any word of his failure reached Lord Agnarr's ears, Finnik Doth was determined to have things back in order.

It wasn't until midday on Lyfmoad 19, 3131, that Finnik was back on shore after meeting with the commandant admiral. Waiting for him was his own unit of highly trained soldiers and a contingent of servants and supplies that would follow in his wake as he pushed west toward Wildwood's central village. On horseback, they made good time and by late afternoon, reached what was left of the natives' northeastern village, where they made camp for the night. Baska Sarrel hadn't wasted any time clearing out the area. Bodies of Matuian warriors littered the forest floor, sometimes even requiring Finnik's men to clear a trail before they could pass through. While it was clearly a Grendolen victory, there were some surprising finds they came across. Pits filled with some type of ape-like creature dotted the landscape that many of Finnik's soldiers had the misfortune of falling into. Of those who did, none survived the encounter. They were found dismembered and half-eaten. But on the whole, Finnik considered the eastern invasion a success despite the lack of villagers to interrogate.

Let them run into our traps, he thought to himself. *They won't get far.*

Seven days later, Finnik sat in his command tent, listening to an update from F.C. Wesdo. It was not good news. By the time he had reached the rivers, an unknown portion of the evacuees were able to escape south before their defenses were in place. However, according to his report, the waters there were treacherous and some of the natives had succumbed to the rapids. The only good news Finnik could gain out of it was that Meera Tarmanon had not been found among the bodies. Even if the worst were to happen and the heir managed to slip past their defenses, Finnik could easily hunt her down. If she died, however, it meant the loss of the information Lord Agnarr required. Finnik didn't want to even consider whatever consequence would befall him should that happen. All he could do now was wait. Wait for F.C. Wesdo to interrogate the remaining evacuees and wait for F.C. Orna to report back from the west.

And wait he did.

By Lyfmoad 27th, F.C. Orna had failed to report in. Growing impatient, Finnik sent a pod west to retrieve the man. At last, two days later, they returned. By that point, his anger over F.C. Orna's lack of communication had grown enough that, emperor's pet or not, Finnik was ready to make an example out of him. Yet when the leader of the pod reported to Finnik, Varcor Orna wasn't with him.

"Why the *rot* is Faction Colonel Orna not with you?" he bellowed.

The man dropped to a knee in submission before answering. "Forgive me, C.G. Doth," he pleaded. "We reached the western border a day ago, but F.C. Orna wasn't there."

"*What*?" Finnik growled in disbelief.

"There were no signs of fighting, sir," the man quickly explained. "No tracks indicating any evacuees went west on foot."

"Are you saying the faction colonel never made it there?"

"No, sir. There *were* signs F.C. Orna and his troop were in the area, however... Commandant General, sir," the man paused, daring to look into Finnik's eyes. "Their tracks headed *northwest*, toward the mountains." The gravity of what the man was saying slowly crept into Finnik's mind. There was only one reason F.C.

Orna would defy his commandant general's orders and head away from Matui territory. The man had successfully captured Meera Tarmanon and intended to claim the victory as his own. Varcor Orna was positioning himself to take over Finnik's command.

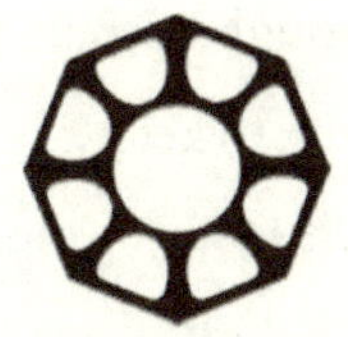

CHAPTER FIVE

Meera

Meera hadn't slept for three straight nights and it was starting to get to her. Twice now, she could have sworn she saw a white bird of prey watching her from the cover of the trees. The only thing was, the sightings were spans apart and to her knowledge, no such bird existed in Matui.

Careful, Meera, she warned herself. *You're losing your grip on reality.*

They had departed Matui Village before dawnlight on Lyfmoad 20th, having worked through the night gathering provisions, and begun making their way toward Noto Wey. Taking the lead in their single-file line, of course, was Katula. Meera had been too tired to argue otherwise, so she took up the middle position. Behind her walked Darmond, leading the chestnut horse he had stolen from the Grendolens' encampment to ride to Matui. The warhorse had now become a packhorse. Meera couldn't help but think it was happier with its new lot in life. Even with the horse's help, however, all three travelers were still burdened with belongings. Darmond had been insistent upon bringing such a large amount of supplies, citing various scenarios he was sure they'd encounter along the way. The sage may have had enough faith in Yveth to trust the Midtierian spy, but Meera made sure to keep an eye on the man. Every once in a while, she'd look back his way, prepared at a moment's notice to put a blade through his skull if need be. But by the time they reached Noto Wey, and Katula finally allowed them to stop and make camp, Darmond hadn't done anything to warrant Meera's wrath.

"What in *Nihility* is in these satchels?" the Midtierian complained, glad to put the heavy bags he was carrying down for a bit.

"Those?" Katula asked, glancing over. "Those are full of Elements."

The man's face went white and his body froze. "Elements," he whispered, wide eyes looking at the bag.

"Yes. I'd put that one down gently if I were you. It holds the more volatile ones," Katula remarked, her face as solid as stone.

"*Volatile*?" he wheezed.

Meera gave Katula an impressed nod, knowing full well she would have never given such dangerous Elements to the Midtierian spy to carry. She hadn't realized Katula could actually summon a sense of humor within her stony exterior.

"We sleep there tonight," Katula announced, ignoring Darmond's concern and pointing to one of the tree huts within the village. All were vacant now. "I'll take first watch."

Dinner was quick, some dried meat, a slice of bread, and a handful of berries for each of them. With food in her belly, sleep wasn't far behind. As much as Meera didn't want to let her guard down around Darmond, her exhaustion eventually won out. She hardly remembered laying on her bedroll before realizing someone was attempting to rouse her from her sleep. When she saw it was the spy, Meera nearly stabbed the man in the arm.

"Whoa, there, Red!" he whispered, backing away from the blade Meera produced upon waking. "You nearly took my arm off."

"Call me Red again and I will," Meera grumbled quietly.

Darmond nodded but didn't move.

"What?" she asked, eyeing him suspiciously.

"I don't know how you did it, living here in Wildwood for so long. This place gives me the chills."

Meera sat up and smiled. It wasn't a friendly one. "Didn't think you'd admit to being scared," she taunted.

"Scared?" he shot back a little too loudly before checking himself. "I'm not scared, I'm just not used to seeing plants that give off their own light," he whispered.

"You mean the moss on the Sasson trees?"

"No, the flowers," he emphasized, pointing to the tree hut's door. "Out there."

Still groggy from sleep, Meera got up to go see what the rot the man was talking about, keeping her knife close in case it was a trap.

It wasn't. Down below, on Noto Wey's Green, stood a small cluster of flowers swaying in the breeze. They gave off a reddish-orange light, making them appear as tiny flames.

"Huh..." Meera said, raking her fingers through her mess of red hair. "We don't have any of those in Notabi." For a moment, both of them stood quietly taking the sight in.

"How'd you manage it, all these cycles?" Darmond asked, breaking the silence.

"Manage what?"

"Being here on your own. Leaving your homeland."

"It wasn't like I had any homeland left to go back to," Meera countered, turning to look at Darmond. Even in the dark, Meera couldn't miss the similarities compared to her own. It had been a long while since she had seen any other people besides the Matuians. How odd to suddenly notice the blue irises and the whites of his eyes, or the lighter color of his skin. The likeness conjured up images in Meera's head of faces she'd lost long ago. Uncomfortable with the unexpected memories, Meera shifted and turned back to face the Green.

"I'm not going to harm you," Darmond noted, misreading her body language.

"I know," she lied.

"I can see your knuckles turning white around that dagger you're holding."

"I know you won't harm me because I'll shove this dagger into your heart the moment you try anything," Meera replied coolly.

The man actually *smiled* in response. "I can tell we're going to become great friends, Red," he remarked. Before she could protest, Darmond gave her shoulder a pat that nearly knocked the wind out of her and took his leave.

Other than the unique flowers, the rest of the night was uneventful, and at the first signs of dawnlight, Meera woke the others so they could resume their journey. Tradesman's Trail led directly to the western boundary of Matui Forest, where the plains stretched until they reached the foothills of the Cassia Mountains. With the lack of cover they would encounter on the plains, Darmond insisted they make camp that night just within the forest border and rest as much as possible. As soon as they left the cover of the trees, they would have to move quickly and cover as much terra as they could in hopes there were no enemy spies within the area. Having never lived outside the forest, the idea of being exposed didn't sit well with Katula, so she agreed to the plan. Out that far west, there were no tree huts for them to take advantage of this time, so the trio chose a secluded spot by a small stream near the border, not too far off from Tradesman's Trail.

When Meera's turn to keep watch came, the last one of the three, a thick fog rolled in along the forest floor. With dawnlight still a ways off and the Watchers already ducking below the horizon, the dim glow of the tree moss reflected against the low cloud, creating a rather haunting landscape. Spotting a few of those glowing flowers peeking out of the mist like small flickering embers didn't help.

Perhaps the spy has a point about this place, Meera thought to herself, unable to shake the feeling that something was out there, watching her. The tree cover was too thick to track the stars, so Meera relied on the sounds of nature to measure the passage of time. The nighttime insects of Matui had a soothing cadence and they nearly lulled her back to sleep, until suddenly, without warning, they all stopped in unison. The unexpected silence shocked Meera out of her dozing, making her bolt upright and ready her bow. Holding her breath, she strained her ears, hoping to pick up on whatever startled the nightlife. It wasn't the first time Meera wished she had Matuian eyes to see through the fog. When no culprit presented itself, and the nightlife continued its warning silence, Meera decided it was time to wake the others. With an arrow nocked just in case, she crept over to her companions and carefully shook them out of their slumber and motioned for them not to make a sound. They immediately sprang for their weapons—Katula for her bow, and Darmond his longsword.

"We need your eyes," Meera whispered to Katula. "There's something out there, and I can't see *rot* in this fog."

The Matuian gave a firm nod and scanned the area but came up short. "There is nothing as far as I can see, but the trees are thick. My sight doesn't go far," she replied.

Just when Meera was beginning to think she'd overreacted, the sound of voices and horses carried through the forest. All three travelers turned their heads.

"Grendolens," Darmond confirmed grimly, "and from the sound of it, heavy cavalry. Every one of their mounts will be a warhorse, like Pignut, here."

"Pignut?" Meera repeated, looking in the direction of the chestnut gelding left tied to a tree.

"He needed a name, and I happen to like hickories." Darmond shrugged.

The horse itself had also caught wind of his previous companions and began nervously stomping the terra. Worrying he may give away their location to the enemy, Meera quickly went over to the horse and began trying to calm him down. After some soft words and rubs, the gelding settled.

"They've cut us off," Katula realized, bringing their attention back to the present. "I estimate there's at least a good fifteen to twenty of them out there blocking our only exit. How did they even know about Tradesman's Trail?" The women cast suspicious glares at Darmond.

"Don't go looking at me. They must have a map, one *I* didn't know about. As far as timing... I told you, if Lord Agnarr wants something, his army will stop at nothing to get it. They'll push their horses to the brink of death if they have to."

"What do we do now?" Meera asked, taking in Pignut's size. "There's no way we can outrun twenty warhorses, let alone one!"

For a moment, all three fell silent as they contemplated their predicament.

"Who said we have to outrun them?" Katula challenged at last, an idea popping into her head. Meera and Darmond followed the Matuian's gaze over to her satchels full of Elements.

There were indeed twenty Grendolens stationed on the edge of Matui's border and the plains. A pod, Darmond called them. He had also been telling the truth about how far the Grendolens would go to please their emperor. While the soldiers showed signs of fatigue from their long journey, their horses were in much worse shape. Three had succumbed to the strain upon arrival. Not wanting to start a fire and alert others to their presence in the area, the Grendolens had left their carcasses piled together in a heap against the tree line. It seemed, though, the enemy had enough good sense to see to the welfare of the remaining horses, as they had been left to rest by the stream in a roped-off area.

"They left two guards," Darmond noted with a smile to the women, being sure to keep his voice low. "This will be a swim downstream. It should only take me a few moments to incapacitate them," he noted confidently. "Once they're out cold, I'll signal for you to move in and... do whatever it is you do." At this, he gave Katula and the box of dried Elements she held a wary eye.

"There is no way I'm staying here," Meera announced, stowing her bow and doing a quick check of her knives, daggers, and throwing ax. The excitement on Darmond's face fell flat.

"Maggots, Red, have you lost all sense? *You're* the one they want. Your capture could negatively impact millions of Tersaithians. Do you really want that on your conscience?"

"Don't try to guilt me out of this," Meera protested. "Whether you chose to believe it or not, I know nothing about the Stone Key Lord Agnarr is after, and you and I both know you'd never be able to take down both of those guards without one of them alerting the others." With that, Meera kissed her hawk pendant, got up from her hidden position, and made for the guards. Behind her, Darmond let out a string of faint curses as he tried to catch up.

The guards were positioned on both sides of the roped-off area, so as Meera and Darmond closed in, they eventually had to split up. Meera was about to cut left and go after the larger of the two guards when Darmond beat her to it. Infuriated, she doubled her speed, determined to prove herself in the task Darmond seemed so sure she'd fail. In the cover of fog, Meera snuck right up behind the woman. But just as she was about to spring forward, the guard on the left suddenly disappeared. The movement caught Meera's guard's notice, forcing her to jump on the woman's back and cover her mouth before the soldier alerted the others. It was an awkward struggle, but eventually, Meera was able to brandish her blade and run it across the guard's neck. Meera didn't let go until well after the woman's body slumped to the terra. For a moment, she stood dazed. Never before had she taken another person's life. Sure, she had hunted plenty of times, but that was only ever for food, for survival.

This was *for survival*, she realized to herself, looking down at the woman's body. The last time she had seen Grendolen soldiers, they had been burning her people alive. Darmond's well-built frame broke through the fog.

"Are you all right?" he asked gruffly, his face a mix of concern and anger.

"Fine," Meera lied.

"Well, hurry up, then. Katula's already in with the horses." Meera chose to ignore his attitude and followed him under the ropes and into the makeshift pen. Katula had gathered two warhorses by their reins and was feeding them something from her hand.

"It will take a moment or two for the Elements to kick in," the Matuian warned them, upon their return. "I'll walk these two back with me to camp. In the meantime, you two will need to see to the others." Meera took a good look at the horses surrounding them. They all looked on the brink of exhaustion, but that was going to play in their favor. Moving quickly, both Darmond and Meera untied one of the ropes from its tether and threw it to the terra.

"Come on," Meera called softly, pulling one of the horses by its reins. The poor thing didn't budge. Despite the situation, she couldn't help but feel sorry for the animals. Reaching into a small pouch on her belt, Meera pulled out a piece of dried fruit she'd been saving and gave it to the large beast. The gelding puffed excitedly and ate it without reserve.

"There you go." She smiled, giving its nose a rub. The scent of fruit managed to gather the other horses' attention and soon the remaining fifteen followed Meera out of the confines of their pen and further down Tradesman's Trail, away from the Grendolens and back towards Matui. Meera was just beginning to allow herself to believe they were going to make it out alive when the alarm was sounded. In a flash, Darmond sprang to action. Using the blunt of his longsword, he smacked the horse he had been leading on its rump.

"Ride on! Ride on! Ride on!" he yelled. As tired as those horses were, at the sound of the command, they took off, bolting into the dim blue fog toward Noto Wey. Before Meera could respond, Darmond grabbed her by the arm, spun her around, and began racing toward their camp. Halfway there, three soldiers brandishing longswords burst through the trees. Knowing they couldn't outrun them, Darmond pushed Meera down onto the terra behind a tree and ran to meet the enemy. Anger boiled through her veins.

If we get through this, I'm going to give that rotting fleaborn a black eye! But as she pushed herself up, her hand felt something hard lying next to her. Feeling around she recognized what it was and gasped. It was her quiver and bow, left there while they took care of the two guards. Realizing Darmond had shoved her there for that very reason, Meera's anger was quickly doused. Throwing on her quiver and nocking an arrow, she went to join the fight.

By the time Meera rounded the tree, Darmond had engaged two of the soldiers in combat, their swords loudly clashing in quick successive bouts. While the Midtierian expertly kept on the defensive, Meera spotted a third guard moving in from behind. With a *twang*, her arrow flew from her bow, and with a *whack*, it hit the man's black helm, only to ricochet off into a nearby trunk.

"Neck or face!" Darmond advised with a yell between strikes. The soldier she had missed turned his attention to her with a shout of warning to the others. It was cut off, however, when Meera's second arrow pierced his right eye, flinging his body backward to the terra. Meera nocked another arrow and tried targeting one of the soldiers Darmond was fighting, but she couldn't get a good shot without risking hitting him.

Two more Grendolens broke through the fog, distracting Meera's attention. In one breath, she loosed an arrow. It hit true, penetrating the soldier's throat. Seeing his companion go down, the second soldier ducked behind one of the trees.

"Rot!" Meera cursed. To her left, Darmond deflected a blow from one of his assailants and used the momentum to swing his blade around and up into the man's chin with a strong thrust. The second assailant wasted no time and ramped up his attack on Darmond. But again, she couldn't come to his aid. The Grendolen pursuing Meera peeked out from the tree trunk and threw a dagger. Ducking into a roll, the blade just missed her, and as she rose Meera released an arrow at the man. It hit just below his eye socket in the left cheek. No sooner was he down, however, than four more Grendolens arrived and ran straight for Meera. Realizing she was outnumbered and seeing Darmond was in no position to help, she turned around and ran, hoping to lure them away. It worked.

Jumping over limbs and avoiding trees, Meera outpaced them enough to give herself an advantage. As she ran, she nocked an arrow and, as soon as she saw an opportunity, pivoted and shot the soldier closest to her. He went down without a fight. The next one to close in on her position, however, easily avoided the same fate. Meera guessed she was of higher rank than the others based on the markings her armor bore. Reaching down to nock another arrow, Meera came up short.

Rot, rot, rot! She was out. How had she not realized? Unhooking her quiver as she ran, Meera threw it and her bow aside and pulled out two matching daggers. She hated to admit it, but at that moment, Meera would have loved to have Darmond's skill with a longsword. Going up against a highly trained swordswoman with two daggers wasn't going to be pretty. All too soon, the woman had caught up and Meera was forced to turn about and attack. The suddenness of Meera's advance threw off the woman momentarily. Using that, Meera lounged into a grapple. The closer she was, the less damage the woman's longsword could do. The Grendolen, however, recovered quickly and kicked Meera full in the stomach, sending the air out of her lungs and her body sprawling onto the forest floor.

"You're no Matuian," the woman spoke in the common tongue, looking surprised. Meera's eyes widened as she realized the black hood on her cloak had come off in the exchange, revealing her red hair. Peeking around the woman, Meera could see her companions were not far behind. If she was to survive this, she'd need to take this woman out before the rest reached her. To make matters worse, she'd dropped one of her daggers in the fall and couldn't reach it. But there was no time to deliberate what to do. As Meera jumped to her feet, she pulled a throwing knife out of her sleeve and threw it at the woman. The blade hit its mark and cut across the woman's cheek. It was just enough of a distraction for Meera to attack again. Leaping forward, she punched the woman in the face and lifted her left hand up to sink her remaining dagger into the woman's exposed jugular.

The woman, however, used her dominant sword hand to punch Meera in the skull using the pommel. The hit knocked Meera back into longsword range and, immediately, the woman took advantage of the opening by swinging from above. Had Meera not ducked to the left and used the woman's own momentum to grab her forearms and headbutt her, it would have been a killing blow. The headbutt, however, backfired as Meera forgot just how strong Grendolen armor was. She cried out in pain at the impact and staggered backward. The woman lost no time and raised her sword to strike.

At that moment, Meera heard a loud cry from the trees above. The Grendolen must have heard it, too, because she paused and looked up. Out of the fog, a white bird of prey streaked through the air and dove straight at the woman's face, its sharp black talons finding their mark and digging in. The woman let out an agonizing scream and dropped her sword as she tried to swat the bird away. Without hesitating, Meera picked up the sword.

"Look out!" she warned the bird. As if it understood, the creature fled to the cover of the trees as Meera swung the sword. It hit perfectly between the helm and armor, digging into the woman's neck. It wasn't a clean cut, but it did the trick. Pulling out the sword, the woman's body thumped lifelessly to the terra. Meera's victory, however, was short-lived, as the other soldiers from the group had finally caught up. Using one hand, she threw another knife at the closest enemy, this time catching the man's eye. He went down writhing in pain but alive. Lifting the sword, Meera turned to face the two remaining. They reverted to their training and began circling her on both sides.

"My, my! What do we have here? You don't look like one of the natives," one of them taunted, seeing her hair and pale skin.

The other smiled. "Looks like we're going to get that bonus after all, Gerdiun. They said anything unusual goes to the F.C. and this one looks *mighty* unusual," said the other soldier. There was no way she could fight them both, especially not with a weapon she wasn't trained with. Not knowing what else to do, she lifted the hilt above her head, dropped the tip, and swung it around her in a circular motion. The plan worked for a few swings by blocking their blows and protecting her body, but soon their cuts came at a faster pace, one she couldn't keep up with. The defeating blow came from behind, delivered by the one named Gerdiun. Her swing blocked the brunt of the cut, but Gerdiun's follow-through sliced straight through Meera's leather armor and cut into her side. In pain, she cried out as she let go of the sword and fell to her knees.

"Now, now. Don't go spoilin' the goods," the other soldier warned Gerdiun, lowering his sword. "She's no good to the F.C. if she's dead, and I want that rotting bonus they promised." Meera grasped her injured side, trying to apply pressure and slow down the blood loss as the two men circled together to face her.

Gerdiun's face fell in disappointment but in the next moment held a look of shock as a dagger ran across his throat, quickly dispatching him to Nihility. His limp body dropped to the terra, revealing Darmond who'd snuck up behind the soldiers. His nameless companion quickly recovered from his own shock and came at Darmond with his longsword. The two clashed together with skilled, precise moves as they trampled down the vegetation around them. Their exchanges were so fast, it was hard to keep up with the fight.

As the Grendolen cut downward from his right shoulder, Darmond moved to his left and tried to pull off the same killing thrust that had worked before. This soldier, however, was much quicker and knocked Darmond's sword right out of his hands. The Midtierian's recovery was just as quick, though, and with a lunge and twist, Darmond wrestled the Grendolen's own sword away. Realizing he was suddenly outwitted, the soldier bolted away. Darmond looked like he was about to pursue the man but then looked back at Meera and let out an aggravated yell.

"What's the damage?" he demanded, forcibly moving her hand from her side to take a look. Meera pushed him away and immediately regretted the sudden movement. She sucked in a sharp breath in pain before she could respond.

"I'm fine," she lied.

His blue eyes narrowed on hers. "I *told* you this would happen."

"You said I'd be captured. I *wasn't*."

"And what would have happened if I hadn't been here?"

"Would you two knock it off?" Katula's voice cut in sharply. Meera and Darmond looked back to find Katula standing there, holding the reins of three horses.

"How did you find us?" Meera asked. Katula's face hardened when she saw Meera was hurt.

"How bad is it? Can you ride?"

"I'll be fine," Meera lied again.

"There are more Grendolens on the way, and I saw some heading off to try and find their mounts. If we don't leave now, we'll be cut off for sure."

"That last soldier saw her," Darmond told Katula, his face shadowed with anger. "If he makes it back to the others, they'll know we aren't just a small group of evacuees trying to flee."

"We don't have *time* to go after him," Katula warned. "This is our only chance to make it to the plains. You can either come with us or take your chances with fate. It's up to you." Katula then eyed Meera with that stone-cold stare of hers. "Grab your things and let's go."

With great effort, Meera stood, reclaimed her bow, and recovered enough arrows to refill her quiver before taking the reins of the large black horse Katula offered her. With an even greater effort, she mounted.

With a resigned sigh, Darmond mounted Pignut and waited for Katula to mount her light tan gelding.

"What's the holdup?" he asked, frustration still heavy in his voice.

"I've never ridden a horse," Katula admitted as she awkwardly pulled herself up into the saddle.

"What?" Darmond shot flatly.

"I've been around ponies and have driven carts," Katula explained coolly. "I'm sure riding a horse follows the same principles."

Darmond lowered his head and gave his face a rub. "You're telling me the person who came up with the plan to dose the horses with Elements, steal them, and *ride* them across the plains all the way to the mountains, has *never* ridden one?" he asked incredulously. "It's barely dawnlight and this day just keeps getting better and better..."

"Well then, since you are the expert, lead the way," Katula suggested.

All too eagerly, Darmond and Pignut shot off, leaving an injured Meera and inexperienced Katula to try and keep up.

Thankfully, Katula's plan to scatter the enemy's mounts had worked to clear most of the soldiers from the border. The few soldiers left raised their swords and rallied as soon as they saw the three travelers riding their way, but they were no match for fully armored warhorses, and they jumped out of the way as the three came bearing down on them. Looking behind, Meera could see the shock on the soldiers' faces as they faded from view. Finally escaping the tree cover, they were relieved to see dawnlight beginning to stretch over the plains. Morning had come. With the sun on the rise and no more tree cover, Darmond had been right to calculate how hard they would have to push the horses. Whatever Elements Katula had given them, though, seemed to work, as their mounts rode as if freshly rested. It wasn't until midday, when they hit a small stream meandering along the prairie's grasses, that Darmond allowed them to stop for a brief rest.

"Your horses are falling behind," he noted. "Dismount and unburden your horse from its armor. We'll need every bit of energy they can give us." Looking to Katula, he asked, "When can you give them more of those herbs?"

"It's too soon. Any more Elements now and we risk their hearts giving out," she advised. Meera attempted to dismount, but her wound sent a sharp pain through her body making her gasp, miss the stirrup, and fall to the terra. Cursing, Katula ran as fast as her wobbly riding legs would allow to her sister's side.

"I think it's time I look at that wound," she said, helping Meera up.

"We're short on time," Darmond warned, scanning the plains. "Be quick about it."

"Be that as it may, Meera's not going to make it any further without treatment."

"Treatment?" Darmond questioned. "Gracious, Prickly, how often do you use those rotting Elements?"

"I'm the sagen, remember? It's what I have been trained for."

Darmond eyed the satchels filled with Elements with a wary glare before taking another look at Meera's condition.

"Make it quick," he said begrudgingly.

"You do know I can hear you both," Meera wheezed through gritted teeth.

"*You* don't get to weigh in," Darmond shot with an edge to his voice. Gone was the cocky Midtierian that had smiled his way through Chief Usoti's interrogation back in Matui. He was genuinely angry at Meera. Annoyingly, she knew he had good reason to be, which only caused her to stew in her own anger even more.

"You two can fight it out later," the Matuian cut in before the conversation grew more heated. Out of her green satchel, Katula produced a small, lidded bowl that held a thick light-green salve inside.

"Here," she said, handing it over to Meera. "Put some of this on. It should help keep the wound from getting infected."

Meera pulled her tunic up and sucked in a breath at the sting of the Elements as she applied them. "Thank you," she managed, breathing a sigh of relief as the Elements began relieving some of her pain.

Katula gave a nod but turned back to Darmond. "If we're going to make it to the mountains, we're going to need to exercise a bit more patience with one another." At that, Katula turned to Meera, making sure she knew what she said was meant for her as much as it was Darmond.

"Fair enough," the Midtierian replied.

"How's it feeling now?" Katula asked Meera.

"Better, actually."

"Enough to get us through to nightfall?"

"Yes, I think so." Katula nodded and handed her the bowl.

"Apply it as often as you need it until it stops bleeding and a good scab forms."

With that, she packed up her supplies and readied her things. Meera dug out a spare garment, tore a strip of cloth off, and wrapped her torso as tight as she could manage before standing and gathering the strength to get back on her horse. Her head hurt something awful after the blows she'd received, but she wasn't about to bring that up after being the one who'd gone and got herself injured.

Darmond pushed them hard for the rest of the day and late into the night. By the time they stopped, the Watchers, now approaching their withering quarters phase, had already begun lowering in the sky. Katula had refused to allow a fire to be lit, but they were all so exhausted it didn't matter. Even still, Katula insisted on checking Meera's wound before they slept. Both women were shocked to find the cut nearly healed. Meera praised Katula's knowledge as a sagen, but Katula seemed to think the salve, though potent, wouldn't have closed the wound that quickly. Both concluded the wound hadn't been as deep as they originally thought.

Meera's headache, on the other hand, had only been made worse by the jostling of riding a horse. She barely remembered laying down before Darmond was shaking her awake again. That morning was the hardest. Katula's Elements may have helped close her open wound, but it still felt like someone had stuck her like a pig and left her on the spit to rot.

For many days thereafter, much was the same. They rode hard, rested only when they had to, and never lit a fire. Every nightfall, the horses would be given their dose of Elements, providing them with enough energy the next day. With nerves running hot, conversation was in short supply, and when it did happen, tense.

Eight days from the morning they bolted out of Matui's border, they finally reached the foothills of the Cassia Mountains. While the trees in the foothills were not as tall or thick as the ones that grew in Matui, the hills they encompassed provided ample amounts of coverage with their nooks and hollows. At last, they could take a proper rest. Even still, Katula refused to allow them to light a fire.

"I still say there's enough distance between us now that lighting a fire won't be an issue," Meera pressed. It was the first real conversation any of them had had since Meera's injury and so far, it wasn't going well.

"We just spent weeks outrunning the Grendolens, and I'm not about to jeopardize all that by lighting a fire and giving away our position," Katula coolly countered, busying herself by unpacking things. Despite her reserved appearance, she, too, sounded exhausted. Rot, they were *all* exhausted. Meera was starving, too, and if she didn't get a good meal in, she wasn't sure she'd have the strength to get up come dawnlight.

"Given Meera's track record, are you surprised she's willing to risk everything for a few end comforts?" Darmond remarked from under the cover of his hooded cloak. His blue eyes held hers as she looked up at his comment. Katula ignored him and kept her concentration on whatever was in front of her.

"What the *rot* is your problem?" Meera shot back, still raw from their previous exchange.

"Seems you do whatever you want, whenever you want, no matter who bears the consequences of your decisions," he replied, not backing down.

"*I'm* the one who bore the consequences!"

"I'm not talking about your wound, Red. I'm talking about *all* of Tersaith. It isn't just your life or our lives on the line. Lord Agnarr thinks you have information about the weapon, and if he gets a hold of it, entire *kingdoms* will suffer. The whole point of me taking out the two Grendolen guards was so they wouldn't know you *existed*! Have you forgotten this whole rotting mess revolves around you?"

His words cut deep, but she refused to admit it. "If I hadn't helped you, you would have been killed or captured, leaving Katula and I without a guide to navigate the mountains," she charged.

"Tea's ready," Katula interrupted, holding out two steaming mugs. Both Darmond and Meera paused in surprise.

"How'd you do that?" Darmond asked, looking perplexed but grateful.

"How many times must I explain it?" Katula sighed, falling back into her usual regal posture. "I am a Matuian s*agen*. I used the Elements."

"Gracious! This is actually really good," Meera admitted, taking a long sip. "Doesn't taste anything like the tea I drank back in Notabi. What's in it?"

Curious, Darmond took a sip of his, but didn't seem at all as impressed.

"It's one of my grandmother's special blends," Katula said, not making eye contact as she readied a small pan of food to cook. Meera watched with interest as the Matuian mixed several Elemental vials together in a bronzium bowl and then placed the pan of food over top. Within moments, the pan's contents began sizzling. The sound prompted Meera's stomach to grumble loudly.

"Sorry," she said shyly. "It's been a long while since I've had a hot meal."

Darmond slowly nodded. "Perhaps a hot meal could do us all some good," he admitted, the heat in his words dissipating.

"Like it or not, we're stuck with each other until we make it to Vardia," Katula reminded them, bringing back the sensitive subject. Meera looked up at her, but Katula's eyes stayed locked on the food she was tending to. "I've spent only a few weeks with the pair of you and I already know that we each are used to doing things on our own. But we can't afford to work that way anymore. From here on out, we have to work together, and that means we're going to have to start trusting one another."

Both Darmond and Meera mulled over Katula's words for a while before responding.

"I'm sorry," Meera finally mumbled, breaking the silence. Darmond looked up at her in surprise. "I'll... I'll be more careful in the future."

"I'm sorry, too. I know you were trying to help, even *if* your grand plan was to get yourself stabbed." An edge of laughter danced around Darmond's eyes. It seemed his jovial character was back again.

"I didn't get stabbed," she teased.

"Run through, then?" he suggested, chasing the tension out of the air. "Speaking of which, what on Tersaith did you do to their leader? Her face was… well she had *none* left. You almost had a clean cut-through, too. For a first-timer with the sword, it wasn't that bad of a job."

Meera realized she'd forgotten all about the white bird who had come to her aid during the fight. "Oh yes! I think it was some type of hawk. I'd spotted it several times during our journey out of Matui. It was white, with a light blue underbelly. I've never seen one like it in the forest before."

"A Moorland hawk did that?" Darmond exclaimed, looking impressed. "I've never seen one attack someone before."

"It was a *Moorland* hawk?" Meera gasped, considering the suggestion. How long had it been since she'd laid eyes on one? It felt like centuries ago. And yet, now that Darmond mentioned it, the connection was obvious. How could she have forgotten the very symbol that had been proudly displayed on the Moorland sigil? She'd not seen nor heard any sign of the bird since it had come to her aid, but now that she thought of it, she was unable to shake the feeling that it was somehow still close by.

"Dinner?" Katula called, breaking into their conversation.

A silence fell over the group as they hungrily ate their meal. It had been so long since they'd enjoyed freshly prepared food and each of them ate their fill. Once all the plates were empty, Katula told Meera and Darmond they could do the dishes since she had cooked, then left them to go burn Elements and pray for her people's safety.

Darmond's eyes flickered Meera's way and then back down at the terra.

"You go ahead and get some sleep," he said solemnly, motioning to Meera's bedroll. "I'll tend to the dishes and take first watch."

Meera considered fighting him on it, but she was suddenly hit with a wave of incredible drowsiness, so she accepted his offer without complaint. She was barely under the covers before a deep, unnatural sleep took over her.

Tiny hands felt their way across slick, mossy stone. Meera couldn't see the hands or the stones because it was pitch black every which way she looked, but she instinctively knew they were her own hands and that this was a memory from when she was young. Much younger. As she moved along in the darkness, her little heart pounded within her chest so hard it felt like it would break free. Fear pulsed through every vein, causing sweat to bead on her temples despite the dank chill in the air around her. Footsteps sounded from behind and accompanying them was a voice.

"Keep going!" the voice said. It belonged to another youngling. She couldn't see their face or form, but hearing that voice gave her comfort. She could trust *this voice.*

"How far do I go?" she asked. As the words passed her lips, the stone wall against her left hand disappeared. It was another tunnel, like the numerous ones she'd already come across.

"Not much longer," the voice assured her.

They forged their way forward together, the other youngling's steady footsteps a comforting presence behind her, until the dreaded moment when they came to a stop. Meera knew what that meant.

"Keep going straight," the youngling spoke, "until you come to another opening on the right. Take that tunnel. It'll lead you all the way out."

"You're leaving me?" her own voice croaked, already knowing the answer.

"I must go. I've got to find my family."

"Please don't leave!" she begged.

"I have *to. You can do this—just remember to take the right tunnel up ahead."*

"But where do I go *once I reach the end of the tunnel?"*

Her question was met with silence. The youngling was already gone.

A fresh wave of panic set in as Meera realized she was now all on her own. Hot tears streamed down her cheeks as she stood there, too terrified to keep going. Is this what Nihility was like? Where Yveth sent the souls of the damned? The dark so encompassing she questioned her own existence? Perhaps she had already died, and this was what awaited her on the other side.

All sense of time was lost to her in that dark pit of a place. Until, at long last, the pounding of her heart reminded her that she was real and very much alive. The realization propelled her to take a step forward, because she knew if she didn't, her end would surely come, and she didn't want it to happen in such a horrid place. She took another step forward. Then another. After what seemed like an eternity in the dark, her eyes caught a flicker of light ahead.

Drawn to it like a flowering bud to the sun, her footsteps quickened until she was running. Just as the youngling said, there was a tunnel to the right lit by a soft red-orange glow.

When she finally reached its end, Meera emerged at the base of a familiar cliff, the one Moorland castle and its imposing walls stood upon—walls that were ablaze and filled with screams of the dying.

Meera bolted upright from her bedroll, gasping for breath. It was still dark out and, close by, Darmond sat with his back against a tree keeping watch, and Katula still slept soundly in her bedroll. Meera never experienced a dream that vivid before. It seemed so... *real*! As she worked to steady her breathing, Meera recounted what had occurred in the dream's sequence and realized, with growing alarm, *why* it seemed so real. After cycles of burying the trauma, Meera had begun to remember what happened to her the night of the Moorland Massacre. The night her life changed forever.

CHAPTER SIX

Katula

"It's... spectacular," Katula stammered as she took in the awe-inspiring sight before her. To her right, Meera slowly nodded, also lost for words. After they had packed up camp, the trio and their mounts meandered their way through the rolling valleys along the foothills as the sun made its ascent into the sky. But it wasn't until they'd passed through the last dale and turned west again that they'd caught their first *true* sight of the Cassia Mountains and the imposing Ismoad Peak. Set majestically above the lands surrounding it, the snowcapped peaks were lit like an endless crown of beacons gleaming in the morning's golden light. It was truly the most captivating scene Katula had ever witnessed. She had studied facts regarding the range, of course, and had always been fascinated by the illustrations the texts provided. But nothing could have prepared her for seeing the real thing.

"They seem to stretch on forever," she remarked aloud.

"Looks that way, doesn't it?" Darmond nodded, less enthused. Having traveled the mountain passes several times, he'd grown used to the view, it seemed—one of the sole reasons her father had allowed him to act as their guide. Still, Katula couldn't imagine ever growing accustomed to such a grand view, no matter how many times she saw it.

"And Vardia is somewhere up there?" she asked, pointing slightly to the right side of the mountain walls.

"It's on Ismoad Peak but not set quite that high. Vardia is located about a quarter of the way up its base, on the other side of the mountain."

"It's so far away," Meera remarked, finally finding her words again.

"Yes, which is why we need to keep moving," Darmond noted. "There's a small cavern near the foot of the mountain I've used as a camp before, and now that we're traveling at a slower pace, even on horseback it'll take us a little over a week, at least, to reach it."

"You worry the Grendolens will spot us before we get there?" Katula inquired, reading his sense of urgency.

"They are the least of my concerns right now. As we climb higher, the temperatures are going to drop fast, and no mixture of Elements you can whip up will be able to keep us from freezing after duskfall, especially with those thin Matuian clothes you two have on or these light cloaks the chief provided. We may have hills and dales to hide in, but smoke from a fire would easily be spotted." Then he paused and looked both women in the eyes. "Prepare yourselves now. Until we reach the cavern and can light a fire, the weather is going to get rather uncomfortable."

"Let's not waste any more time then," Katula agreed, eager to get going.

They set out once more, and as the morning wore on, Darmond and Pignut fell back next to Katula and her tan mount, allowing Meera to wander ahead out of hearing range.

"So, what was in the tea, Prickly?" he asked her quietly.

Katula barely managed to hold back her shock. She'd guessed he'd wanted to ask her something but wasn't expecting *that*. Somehow, he'd figured out she'd spiked the tea she'd given Meera the night before.

"What makes you think it wasn't just tea?" she finally asked, keeping her composure.

"The tea you gave me didn't taste any different than plain old nettle tea. But Meera, on the other hand... If her reaction didn't give it away, her eyes surely did once whatever it was took effect." He paused and looked at her directly. "The question isn't whether you drugged her. I already *know* you did. The question is what you drugged her with and why?"

Katula kept her horse's pace while she mulled over how to reply. Darmond didn't seem the type that would easily let this sort of thing go. If she told him a lie, he most likely would figure it out and alert Meera to what she was doing. But if she told him the truth, could she trust him to keep it between just the two of them?

"It's a memory-enhancing Elemental mixture my grandmother gave me," Katula eventually admitted, opting to tell the truth and praying to Yveth that she wouldn't regret it. "She hoped it would help Meera recover the memories she's forgotten, ones of Moorland," she emphasized, "so that we might figure out what information Lord Agnarr is after, if Meera indeed knows anything at all."

Darmond pondered that for a moment before replying. "So why not be forthcoming to Meera about it?"

"My grandmother was concerned that if I told her, it could potentially affect the results. We need the memories to be remembered as naturally as they occurred when they happened. If I tamper with her knowledge, probe a little too much here or there on a particular path, I could end up inadvertently changing the way she remembers how a particular sequence of events occurred, thereby creating a false memory instead of revealing the truth of what really happened."

"And this mixture you're giving her... It's Elements, isn't it? Is it *safe*?"

"Yes, it is. And no, there will be no lasting physical side effects, if that's what you mean." A silence fell between them as Darmond considered his next response. It was a good while before he spoke, and when he did, he sounded more reserved than usual.

"If Meera's memories can be recovered, and this is the best way to do that, then I agree it should be done. But I'll be honest, I don't like keeping something like this from her."

"That's surprising to hear, coming from a professed spy."

"Oh, I don't mind being devious. What I have a problem with is giving Elements to someone I need information from. I don't want your concoctions to permanently damage—"

"You don't want to lose the possibility of learning about the weapon the Stone Key is connected to," Katula cut in bluntly.

"Exactly," Darmond noted without reserve. "Meera holds the only hope for the war against the Grendolens finally coming to an end."

Katula nodded. "I know what I'm doing with the Elements, Darmond. Meera won't be harmed."

"I still don't have to like them. And I certainly don't like giving them to someone without their knowledge. Let's just agree that as soon as it's safe to tell her, without tampering with her original memories, we do so."

"Agreed," Katula confirmed with a curt nod.

"Any idea of how long that may be?"

"I was given eight doses in total, to be given every four days. Last night I administered the first."

"So, seven more to go and then we can come clean?"

"My grandmother said that whatever Meera doesn't remember after the last dose is given will most likely have been permanently forgotten; meaning, even if she were captured by the Grendolens, they, too, wouldn't be able to recover any memories," Katula clarified. "If she shows no signs of remembering after that last dose, I don't think telling her about the Elemental mixture at that point would do any harm."

"Did last night's dose have an effect?"

"If it did, she hasn't said as much to me," Katula confessed. It was something to consider, though. She could hardly expect to suddenly become Meera's confidant. Why would the Moorlander want to share anything so personal with her? They'd never been close and certainly didn't count each other as bloodkin.

Quite the opposite, Katula thought, recalling the higher level of tension between them of late. Her solid black eyes glanced Darmond's way. He seemed to accept being their guide easily enough, but Katula knew better than to fully trust him. He had his own agenda that revolved around whatever the Resistance leaders assigned to him. If Darmond somehow managed to win over Meera's trust to the point where she told *him* what she remembered, Katula would bet her best arrow he wouldn't bother to disclose that information to her.

Yes, she had in her possession the Tercara Scroll, and, yes, Natta thought there may be a link between the key of stone reference and the weapon Darmond spoke of, but that didn't guarantee Darmond's loyalty to Katula's own interests. Her people's very existence was on the line. She couldn't risk the possibility of Darmond manipulating Meera into giving up their search for Pawtoton in order to follow him back to Midtier.

"The elixir wouldn't have acted instantly," Katula lied. "It will take a few doses before the effects kick in. We should know within the next few days if it's working."

If he suspected she'd weaved him a story, Darmond didn't let on. Instead, he gave her a nod and nudged Pignut to pick up his pace and put some distance between them before Meera grew suspicious.

Steadying herself with a deep breath, Katula focused her thoughts ahead toward the Tarmanon heir. With all the bad blood between them, it wasn't going to be easy to turn the tide and win over the woman's trust. Yet, Katula's impression of her adopted sister had already begun to change without her intending it to. If she was truly honest with herself, she had to admit she was even beginning to *respect* the other woman. Meera could have fled south with the rest of the evacuees, leaving the Grendolens far behind her. Or she could have stayed and died fighting them. But instead, the Moorlander *chose* to travel with Katula, even though they were not bloodkin and their true destination was unknown. In the few weeks Katula had spent traveling with her, she had begun to see the woman from an entirely different perspective. Yes, Meera was still just as impetuous as ever, but she was equally just as brave and willing to put her life on the line to protect Katula and a Midtierian spy she hardly knew. Perhaps it was time Katula swallowed her pride and worked toward making amends.

Darmond had been right about two things. The temperature *did* drop the closer to the mountains they climbed, and their thin clothes were woefully inadequate to combat it. It made reaching the cavern he'd spoken of and the firewood he'd stowed there all the more relieving once they arrived. Even the horses, which had greatly recovered since Katula had seen to administering them regularly with healing Elements, seemed to enjoy the cavern's enclosure. In total it took them five days of travel to reach the safety of the cavern. Katula hadn't been prepared for how grossly ill-equipped they were for the colder weather. It had become increasingly clear, the higher their path took them, how vastly different the mountains were compared to Matui. On average, the coldest it got back home was a few frosts, maybe a rare snow every couple of cycles, but even then, that would never be expected in the middle of Lyntensol. Yet, the mountains seemed indifferent to the rhythms of the Tersaithian calendar. Even though it was now the beginning of Regnamoad, the middle moad of Lyntensol, the mountain air felt brisker than any moad in Wyntersol Katula had experienced in Matui, and they were still *far* below the highcaps.

It had become apparent to her rather quickly why a location like Vardia was such a prominently visited market town. Without it, those traveling from the east headed west wouldn't last a day traversing the Cassias without the proper supplies and gear.

"You're confident we'll reach Vardia by tomorrow then?" Katula probed Darmond as she instinctively drew nearer to the fire he was building.

"So long as the weather holds," he remarked casually.

"What do you mean, holds?" she said, eyeing him. "Are you saying it could *snow*?"

"Possibly. The weather up here can be unpredictable. One moment it's sunny, the next you've got a full-blown blizzard on your hands." The way he said it made it sound like the notion amused him, but the thought of it snowing only made Katula more anxious.

"We can't afford to lose the lead we have over the Grendolens," Katula advised. "We've got to get to Vardia, trade the horses for supplies, and send a carrier pigeon to your Resistance about forming an alliance between my people before the enemy knows we were ever there."

"Beginning to see why I pushed you so hard to get here so quickly?" he mused.

Katula's response was to cock an eyebrow and scoot closer to the fire, which was finally generating a welcome amount of heat.

"At least now we can enjoy a hot meal without having to use up all your Elements," Meera noted to her. The woman had kept to herself the last five days, which was unusual since normally Katula couldn't get her to stop talking half the time.

"Any more of that tea left?" the Moorlander asked tentatively.

Katula avoided glancing Darmond's way before she answered. She had administered a second dose of elixir on the 3rd of Regnamoad, exactly one week after the first, but couldn't give Meera the third dose until two more days.

"We don't have much to spare. Let's have the usual and save the special blend for another time. In the meantime, why don't you two make dinner? I've got something I need to do." Katula didn't wait for their questions. She picked up one of her satchels and stalked past the resting horses and out of the cavern.

Bracing herself against the cold night, the Matuian wound her way around the rocks until she reached a secluded spot with a view eastward. There, she sat cross-legged and stared out into the darkness in the direction of her home. Leaving Matui to the likes of the Grendolens had been the hardest thing she had *ever* done. The others relied on her, though, to be the strong one. She couldn't let her fears affect the task she'd been given. Still, that last vision of her family paddling down the Tae River haunted her each day upon waking. Had the rest of her people managed to escape? What of the warriors sent to hold off the enemy? Katula sat there for a long time in prayer and in grief, until her limbs went numb from the cold and her empty stomach began complaining.

After they ate, Katula forced herself to stay up that night, intent on watching Meera for signs of dreaming. Her patience paid off. Sometime in the early morning, Meera began twitching in her sleep and mumbling incoherent words. While the woman said nothing Katula could make out, she at least knew the elixir *was* working. Now all she had to do was find out what Meera was dreaming about.

Easily spoken, yet formidable in execution.

Vardia was nothing like Katula had anticipated a market town to be. She had grown up hearing stories from Matuian traders about the busy streets and loud people that filled Vardia but had failed to envision just how diverse the population was. She had expected to see mainly Mountaineers, with their fur-lined clothing and shorter stature, just as depictions from Matuian traders described, and indeed, there were many among the overall populace. But in addition to them Katula caught sight of several groups of Lowooders, a good number of Midtierians, and, if she was not mistaken, even a few Kielese hailing from as far away as the western shores. Yet, seeing so many characters she'd envisioned from the historical texts come to life before her was dampened when Katula caught sight of a Matuian market trader.

The woman's calm demeanor told her the news of what had happened back home had not yet reached Vardia. Katula fought the urge to run over to the woman and tell her what had happened, to warn her the rotting Shadeblights may still be pursuing them. But she forced herself to keep quiet. In revealing her identity to the woman, Katula would be putting her in more danger. If the Grendolens followed them there, they would interrogate every living soul in or passing through Vardia. She was sure of it. Katula refused to risk another Matuian life. Cautiously, she pulled the hood of her newly acquired fur-lined overcoat lower over her head to keep from being identified. Katula's only solace was knowing that Darmond had been successful in sending several carrier pigeons to the Midtierian Resistance, just in case one or two went astray. Now all she could do was wait and pray Midtier would agree to a Matuian alliance, one that would mean taking back her forest.

It had been Darmond's idea for him to go on ahead of the women into Vardia and trade the horses in to acquire cold weather clothes so Meera and Katula could blend in better with the crowds. And it was a good one, Katula had to admit. Out of the three of them, Darmond was the only one who had any experience with market towns. Additionally, the women were more easily recognizable. Katula, because she was such a prominent figure to the Matuians. Every one of their market traders knew the chief's family and would recognize her instantly, even with the clay she'd used to cover up her facial tattoos. While no one outside of Matui would recognize Meera, her unusual eyes and bright red hair would certainly make her stand out and draw unwanted attention. If the Grendolens managed to follow them to Vardia and her description was given to them, the enemy would undoubtedly know she was a person of interest.

Even Darmond had been forced to give up the precious Grendolen armor he'd painstakingly carried with him across the plains. Watching him stash the bundle of armor within a crevice inside the cavern was nothing short of watching him part with a beloved family member. He may have even shed a tear or two, though the light was too dim without the fire going, so Katula couldn't be certain. Either way, she couldn't understand how someone could grow so attached to sheets of metal. Using a bow was the smarter way to go about striking an enemy down. They allowed one to reach the enemy long before they ever had a chance to reach you. Thankfully, Mountaineers often traveled with their bows to hunt game and traded regularly for Matuian arrows, so the full quiver Katula had slung over her shoulder added to the authenticity of her new attire. Indeed, she was glad of the extra warmth the fur generated, as the higher altitudes had proved too much for Matui's thinner, more breathable material.

Thinking of home, though, sent a ripple of pain through Katula. Passing the Matuian trader, she sent a prayer up to Yveth, pleading that the woman be spared if the Grendolens eventually arrived.

The buildings in Vardia were set directly on the terra, rather than among the trees, which baffled Katula until she felt firsthand the power of the high winds the town sometimes received. The older structures were built out of stone, the same brown stone that Katula had seen while ascending the mountain trails to reach the town. However, there were many new buildings as well, which were instead made of wood. But no matter what material was used in its making, every entrance, even back doors, had a covering over it. According to Darmond, it was due to the amount of precipitation the area received. Katula would have doubted the man, but within moments of walking the town's streets, it had gone from torrents of rain to sun and then switched over to a fine, blustery mist. Thankfully, her new Mountaineer clothes were not only fur-lined but also consisted of a thick hide on the exterior, which was freshly oiled, keeping her completely dry and warm on the inside.

Footsteps fell in place to Katula's right as Meera joined up with her. Each of them had their own list of items to procure before setting off, Meera's consisting of food. While the women had no experience trading outside of Matui, it would have been impossible for Darmond to gather all of their supplies quickly enough. Since time was of the essence, they opted to divvy up the coin the sale of the horses supplied, split up the supply list, and go separate ways, despite the obvious risks it posed. According to Darmond, the Mountaineers never dared traversing the higher altitudes without enough supplies to last at least one moad—a solid block of thirty-two days—in case they got stranded. However, once Katula heard about the unique snow huts Mountaineers used, which were able to withstand high winds and retain heat in freezing temperatures, she insisted they get more than one just in case the other broke. She was not about to be caught unawares by one of those blizzards she'd overheard the locals describing. Katula even went as far as taking it upon herself to be the one to barter for them. That, in itself, had been quite a challenge. It was harder than she thought to mimic the longer draw of the Mountaineer speech patterns, let alone learn to walk like them. They were stocky and adept at climbing, whereas her people were generally more slender and graceful in their movements.

"Are those the snow huts?" Meera whispered next to her in Matuian, taking a tentative look back at the elongated packs Katula was carrying. She, too, wore her hood up over her head to help cover her appearance.

"Yes. However, I was only able to get two," Katula confessed. "Apparently, they are in high demand at this time of cycle."

"They look like cloth-wrapped longbows, only larger," Meera remarked skeptically. "You sure they're the right ones?"

"Positive. I had the trader show me how to erect one before I completed the transaction."

"And it didn't make him suspicious for a Mountaineer to be asking how to set up a snow hut?"

"Not when you accuse him of trying to sell you defective ones," Katula countered triumphantly. "After that, he was quite eager to point out all the qualities his huts offered that the others didn't."

Meera nodded, impressed. "Not bad. I barely said a word myself, just pointed and grunted at the items I needed. It's been too long since I've spoken the common tongue regularly. It sounds off, even after all the practice I've had these past few weeks. I'll need to speak it more if we're to blend in with everyone else."

"As soon as we finish up here, we'll be heading deep into the Cassias looking for a place we aren't even sure exists with a Midtierian spy who speaks it fluently. You'll have *plenty* of time to practice," Katula noted dryly.

As if on cue, Darmond appeared up ahead.

"Ladies," he nodded from under his hood. "I can see from what you're carrying that you two fared well at the market." As he spoke, he directed them into an alleyway that led behind a row of buildings to a dead end at a small stable. There were larger ones situated all throughout the town; however, unlike these, the rest had been vacant save for a few horses and ponies. Curious, Katula went to inspect the stalls only to find it was not filled with horses at all.

"What in Nisri's name are *those*?" she cursed, momentarily forgetting to mask her accent or remembering that, as a Mountaineer, she would have known what the animal was. Darmond shot her a look of warning before answering.

"These gorgeous beauties will soon become our best friends," he said quietly, casting an eye about to make sure no one overheard. "Meet the ever hardy, yet mighty humble, Cassia Mountain goat, otherwise known as *tonga* in these parts."

Katula stared at the tall beast in disgust as a string of spittle slowly dropped from its mouth onto the stable floor. The thing had a pair of massive round horns that spiraled back from its head and curved around its sides. Its grayish hair, if you could call it that, was long and shaggy, and smelled like something had crawled up into it, got lost, and died. It was *hideous*.

"I'm *not* riding that thing," Katula vowed, this time remembering to keep her voice down.

"Aww, he's not that bad," Meera countered, stepping up to feed the animal a fist of hay from a nearby pile. Horrified, Katula watched as the tonga greedily took the offered food, covering Meera's hand in nauseatingly viscous slobber.

"His name is Signot, a 'steady friend,'" she announced matter-of-factly to the others, before suddenly blushing. "I mean... he looks like a Signot, so that's what I'll call him," she said awkwardly. "Can I ride him?"

"Call him whatever the rot you want," Darmond replied dismissively. "You and whatever provisions you managed to procure will have plenty of time to get acquainted topside."

Meera ignored Darmond's sarcasm in favor of petting the tonga's forehead, which the beast seemed to enjoy.

"I had no problem learning to ride a horse and I did it without complaint all the way here," Katula noted firmly. "But there's no way I am going to ride that thing further up into the mountains. Why can't we take the horses?"

"Horses aren't built for these peaks," he fought back sternly. "Tongas are. They have the hooves for the rocky terrain and thick hides for the colder weather. There's no way around it, so you'd best accept it. We're taking the tongas, so saddle up, Prickly."

"Fine," she sighed, crossing her arms.

"Which one do you want?" Darmond prodded, motioning to the two tongas left.

Katula glanced into the adjoining stalls. Each one had the same grayish-white shag as Meera's chosen mount, not to mention that horrid stench.

How in the depths of Nihility do the Mountaineers put up with it? Katula wondered to herself. *I can barely even breathe outside the stable.*

Comparing her two options did nothing to help her arrive at a choice, so she finally pointed to the one closest to her.

"That one," she said flatly.

Darmond nodded and left them to go finalize the sale. Within moments, he returned, along with a stable hand loaded down with heavy saddles. Both Katula and Meera grew quiet and backed off, allowing the stranger space to work alone without engaging in conversation, while he secured their saddles and Darmond tied down their supplies. The boy, however, had no wish to stay quiet.

"Norf, ye be 'eaded den?" he asked happily, in a thick Mountaineer accent. Katula cringed when she heard Meera give a grunt for an answer. She was going to have to say something before he grew suspicious.

"Dat we be," Katula replied gruffly, attempting to mimic the vocal sounds. The three had agreed to a false direction prior to arriving at Vardia just in case a situation like this one arose. The most logical direction was north, toward the area where the majority of Mountaineers resided. It was also the direction one would go if they were fleeing to Midtier. If the Grendolens came looking, hopefully that's where they'd assume the trio was headed.

"Dangerous te be travelin' dis time o' cycle," the boy warned. "Right blessed ye were we still had a few tongas left, eh? Most folk 'eaded 'ome a few moads ago. Dem dat stayed, won't be movin' on 'til Sumorsol."

Darmond had mentioned much of the same to Katula and Meera when they arrived at the market town. In the rising heat of Lyntensol, if *heat* is what you could call it, the temperatures on the peaks would sometimes rise above freezing causing melting to occur, posing a large threat for avalanches. Most Mountaineers chose to travel the routes in mid-Sumorsol, once the risk of dangerous melting was past and before the Harvestsol snows began. With it being Regnamoad 6th, the peak of Lyntensol, they would need to take extra precaution proceeding through what the locals referred to as the highcaps. Katula struggled to remember the excuse Darmond instructed her to give, but thankfully he picked up on her hesitation and jumped in.

"Right ye are, lad," Darmond readily agreed, easily falling into the local dialect. "But we be embarkin' on a pilgrimage, and de dead don't much like waitin' on de livin', do dey?" The explanation spoke volumes to the young Mountaineer boy, as it was customary for family members to pilgrimage back home to pay their respects upon receiving news of a loved one who'd passed from Tersaith into Yveth's realm. No matter where a Mountaineer roamed across the Cassias, if word had reached them of a loved one's death, they would drop everything and head back home. Darmond had said that to them, a pilgrimage was seen as a somber yet spiritual journey, a time for one to reflect on the life lived of the lost loved one.

"May their soul rest in Yveth's embrace," the boy replied, reciting a traditional message of condolence. Katula nodded, relieved that the conversation seemed to be over. The boy finished saddling the tongas in silence and once he was done, nodded to Darmond and left the three travelers in peace. Katula let out a soft sigh and let her tense muscles relax. Ever since entering Vardia, she felt exposed and had constantly been waiting for someone to realize she didn't belong. But despite her inner fears, she'd managed to keep her wits about her and even pull off a half-decent accent at the same time.

"All right," Darmond called, once he'd looked around to make sure they were alone. "Time to saddle up."

Meera, of course, climbed up her tonga with fluid ease. Katula, however, didn't move.

"Just pretend they are horses," he added coaxingly.

"How do you even mount one?" Katula asked, giving him a stare.

Darmond rubbed his dirty blond stubble before letting out a long sigh. "The next town we hit, you both owe me an ale. No, make that *two* ales, *each*." At that, he walked over to Katula's chosen tonga. The saddle provided a small rope ladder that was rolled up and stored when not in use. Darmond unrolled it and motioned for Katula to begin climbing. "Just place one hand over the other until you reach the top," he explained.

It took her several tries, along with Darmond's help, to finally get the hang of it before she was high enough to swing her leg over the saddle's seat. Thankfully, her tonga seemed impervious to her blunders and stood calmly munching on its cud. Once he was sure she was not going to fall off, Darmond turned his attention to Meera, who was deep into a one-way conversation with her tonga.

"You can converse with your new friend later. It's time to head out," Darmond pushed.

Meera nodded and had begun moving her tonga forward when suddenly she stopped and looked up at the sky.

"What is it? What's wrong?" he asked, thinking it was something to do with her saddle.

"I think I... I thought I heard..." she stuttered, looking sheepish. Darmond looked around.

"Heard what?"

"I... I think we need to hurry," she managed.

"I'm the one having to show you both how to mount and ride tongas, remember? If anyone needs to speed this up, it's you two."

"No, I mean, I think we need to leave. *Now*," she emphasized.

Katula caught a note of concern in the other woman's voice. "What's going on?" she asked Meera, suddenly alert.

"The Grendolens," Meera urged. "I think they're *here*."

"In Vardia?" Darmond asked, skeptically. "We put plenty of distance between them. They won't be rolling through these parts until at least another day."

But the look Katula saw on Meera's face said, somehow, she knew otherwise.

"How can you know—" Katula was cut off as a loud screech sounded from overhead. She looked up to see a large white hawk circling them from above. Meera saw it, too, and let out an audible gasp of surprise.

"I don't know *how* I know," Meera admitted. "I just *do*. Trust me, they're here!"

Confirming her words, sounds of commotion began to rise up from the eastern edge of the market town. Darmond cast a suspicious eye toward Meera before leaving her side to go mount his own tonga.

"Looks like it's time we put our backs to this town," Darmond advised. Once he was up and his ladder stored, he rode over to the women and tethered their lead lines together to form a single line, a precaution Katula was grateful for, as she did not want her ride to buck and run away with her while she was still on the back of it. Darmond led them out of the stable area and into the back streets of the town, careful to avoid the ever-growing sounds of panic behind them.

Even at a slow pace, Katula had a hard time staying on top of her tonga. Every step it took sent her stomach into knots as she tried to sway with its rhythm instead of against it. Infuriatingly, Meera rode along with hers as if she'd been *born* on the back of one.

That girl has an uncanny way with animals, Katula noted, looking back at the pair.

They were able to make it out of Vardia without being noticed, much to everyone's relief. The trail they took led to a crossroads, where you could head in three directions: north, south, or west, with east headed back into town. West was where they were headed, but when they reached the intersection, Darmond halted his ride and sat quietly, staring out ahead.

"What is it?" Katula asked nervously from the back of the line. But instead of responding, Darmond turned his tonga about and dismounted. Confused, she watched as he reconfigured the tethers so that Katula would be in the lead and his tonga was behind Meera's. "What are you doing?" Katula demanded more forcefully.

"I'm going back," he replied, breaking his silence.

"Why?" Meera asked, beating Katula to the question.

"If the Grendolens tracked us here, then I need to know how many of them there are, who's in command, and how much they know about *who* they're tracking. In other words"—he rubbed his hands together excitedly—"I need to do a little reconnaissance. Leaving that young stable hand behind bothers me, too."

"He didn't seem like a threat," Katula remarked. "Is this really about him or are you going back for that armor you're so attached to?"

"Threat, no. But he interacted with us, which means he's got information the Grendolens want," he explained.

"And what do we do if something happens to you?" Meera challenged angrily. "You're supposed to be our guide. We have no idea where to go! And why put Katula in the lead? She's obviously not comfortable with riding a tonga yet."

At that, Darmond's face grew serious. "Out of the two of you, I know *she* at least can be trusted. *You*, on the other hand, are known to fly off the cliff on your own anytime you feel like it. We already talked about this; *you're the target*," he emphasized, pointing at her. "That means *we* protect *you*." At that, he walked back to Katula, who'd stayed silent during the exchange.

"Take this road west until you reach the snowline. Make camp on the south side of the path; the cliffs there will provide better shelter from the winds. If all goes well, I'll meet up with you later this evening. If I'm not back by daybreak tomorrow, go on without me."

Katula kept her voice level, but inside everything felt far from fine. "Darmond, if you don't make it back, how do I locate Pawtoton, or *any* giants for that matter?" Those words were still hard for Katula to say after cycles of believing they were myths.

"Look for really, *really* tall people."

Katula gave him a glare. "You told my father you could guide us to Pawtoton," she countered, her anger growing close to boiling over.

"No, I said I could act as your guide in the mountains, which is precisely what I'm doing. However, if you insist on dragging us all over the frozen mountainside looking for mythical snow beasts and flying fire creatures, the only advice I am able to impart is to continue heading west."

"Why west?"

"No one goes west anymore. Too many passes are blocked by snow, even in Sumorsol. If you want to find a race of giants no one has ever seen, it stands to reason you should go where no one goes."

"Wait a moment," Katula stopped short. "If no one goes there, how do *you* know where to guide us?"

"Don't kid yourself, Prickly. It was either I agree to be your guide or die by a thousand Matuian arrows. So..."

Katula sat on top of her tonga, stunned.

"*You've never taken the western path?*" she stammered, her composure slipping.

"There's a first time for everything," he grinned. Before she could object, he stepped back and slapped Katula's tonga on its rump. Her ride lurched forward, sending her hands gripping tighter to the reins. By the time she recovered, Darmond was already walking back toward Vardia.

Katula had always been a capable individual. Growing up, she was the kind of youngling who never had to be coaxed into trying a new skill. Her mother had died when she was young, so Katula kept her father on his toes, running from one thing to another before he could catch up, and her intensity for conquering new challenges didn't slow down as she grew older. Only now, life seemed to be throwing her everything she wasn't prepared for. She was an apt warrior but couldn't use those skills to defend her people to the capacity that she wished. Here she was, high up in mountains she'd only read about, riding on top of a tonga no less. It was truly the first time she felt completely out of her depth. She didn't like it one bit. On top of all that, there was something else deeply unsettling her.

"Meera," she called behind her, daring to look back and risk falling off her mount. Katula watched with a mixture of awe and jealousy as the other woman expertly steered her tonga up alongside hers.

It must be a Moorlander thing.

"Yes?" Meera asked, oblivious to how natural she looked on top of the tonga.

"Darmond, going to Vardia..." Katula started, unsure how to bring the subject up.

"You think his leaving is suspicious and he's not to be trusted," she guessed aloud.

Katula's eyes widened in surprise. "Yes, actually. That's *exactly* what I was going to say."

"I agree." Meera nodded. "He may have agreed to be our guide, but I'm certain his loyalty lies with the Resistance and getting them what they want. Plus, I make it a point to never trust unusually good-looking men."

Katula cocked an eyebrow at that last bit but pushed on. "What the Resistance wants is you. Well, the information they think you have, and before Darmond found out about the key of stone reference in the Tercara Scroll, I wasn't so sure he would agree to being our guide. Now that he knows, I wonder if he will keep that information to himself. Perhaps his unexpected departure is more than just reconnaissance?"

"You think he's going to try and send another message to the Resistance to tell them about the scroll?"

"It's entirely possible. In which case our journey is already compromised. He could tell them everything, including where we're headed. Our only hope is that once we get far enough away from Vardia, we'll be too isolated for him to send any more messages."

"Rot," Meera cursed beside her. "You really think he'd tell them? I mean, he did save my life back in Matui."

"He helped because he had no other option and didn't want to risk losing you to the Grendolens," Katula reminded her.

Meera thought about that for a while before responding. "We could leave him in Vardia... take another path."

"Don't think I haven't considered it," Katula mused. Then, looking up at the massive white peaks towering around them, she added, "Truth is, I have no idea where to go or how to navigate this terrain. What if we get caught in one of those blizzards Darmond mentioned? Or our tongas bolt and run off?"

Beside her, Meera kept silent as their tongas plotted on.

"He'll come back for you at least, I'm sure of it. But from here on out, you and I need to trust each other. I know we've not always gotten along..."

"We *never* got along," Meera noted sarcastically with a slight smile.

"No, we never have," Katula admitted. "But now we're all each other has."

"So, just to get this straight, I'm headed to a land of myths, full of beasts that would love to eat me alive, with a Midtierian spy for a guide who'd kidnap me the first chance he gets, and the only person I can trust is the most, stubborn, hard-headed, humorless person I know?"

"That's correct," Katula said dryly.

"Rotting Nihility," Meera cursed with a smile.

The conversation seemed to be going well, so on a whim Katula changed the subject to something else that had been weighing on her.

"Back in Vardia... How did you know the Grendolens had arrived?" she asked, looking at the Moorlander.

"I overheard shouts coming from the town's center."

"From so far away?"

"I suppose so."

Katula let the conversation drop. She didn't want to pressure the woman too much, especially when she needed Meera to trust her enough to open up about the dreams she was having. Yet, Katula couldn't let what happened in Vardia simply pass.

I've got excellent *hearing, and I didn't hear any shouting until well after Meera first warned us of the Grendolens.* If something else tipped her off to their arrival, Meera wasn't telling her. At least, not yet.

CHAPTER SEVEN

Darmond

Sneaking back into Vardia proved trickier than sneaking out. Not that it posed a problem for Darmond and his superior sleuthing skills. By the time he made it back to town, the Grendolen soldiers had blocked off all roads leading in or out. But a few armed guards were hardly something to dissuade him. Realizing it had been quite a while since he'd played the part of old Faltiel, Darmond climbed a boulder just outside of the town's western road, hopped over the stone wall, and dropped soundlessly down into a small side yard belonging to one of the bordering homes. There, he was able to lift enough clothes from the drying line under the home's covered porch to take on the impersonation of Faltiel, an aged, crotchety old man with whom it was easy to fit in among crowds. Once he had assumed the role, it wasn't difficult to shuffle along the alleyways until he'd reached the outskirts of the main square.

"Move aside," his now gravelly voice called to those who ignored him. "No respect these days, I tell ye. Er'y one of ye's a rottin' plagueman, if I 'er saw one!" His curses caused a few spectators to turn around, and reluctantly, they gave him space. He stifled a chuckle. Sometimes it was just *too* easy. His enjoyment, however, was short-lived once he caught a glimpse of the main square.

From when he and the others had left the town until now, the Grendolens had not wasted any time setting up a spectacle for the locals. A makeshift platform with a wooden pole had been erected, which in Grendolen terms meant they'd built a miniature version of the Stands they had positioned throughout any territory the Emperor Lord Agnarr ruled. Examples would be set, and fear would be spread in order to gain control of the population. But the worst of it was who stood prominently on the platform ready to address the crowd.

It was just as he'd feared. They'd sent Faction Colonel Varcor Orna to command the force pursuing the Tarmanon heir. Not for the first time, Darmond cursed himself for failing to nab Meera before the Matuian soldiers caught him back in Wildwood. Out of all the officers he'd come into contact with while posing as a soldier in the Grendolen army, Orna was the one that had worried him the most. There was a *hollowness* to the man that didn't sit right with Darmond, and it had become obvious he wasn't the only one who felt that way within the Grendolen camp. On several occasions, he had witnessed the lack of restraint Orna had when it came to disciplining his soldiers, one such report going as far as leading to a soldier's death. Darmond had met with his fair share of bloodthirsty soldiers on the battlefield, but Varcor Orna was different. He lacked the restraint most people had, as if killing was as normal as sipping a cup of tea. It didn't faze him. It was *unnatural.*

Darmond shivered. He liked tea. It was a shame to associate it with the man.

More disturbing, though, was the fact that even after the death of one of his men, which had taken place in front of a whole assembly of soldiers, the faction colonel hadn't even been reprimanded for it. The Grendolens were led by a tyrant, and in Lord Agnarr's name they had massacred more than one kingdom, but part of the reason they had been able to conquer them was their army's strict code of conduct. Say what you will about them, the Grendolens were a disciplined bunch.

So why let things slide with Varcor? Why let the unruly pup out of its pen and reward him with a bone to chew on? Darmond asked himself. Especially when the bone Varcor was after was the heir Lord Agnarr had thought lost in the fires over a decade ago and only now resurfaced.

Then it dawned on him. Commandant General Doth would have *never* sanctioned this type of assault on Vardia. It was too unplanned, too rushed. If there was one thing Darmond knew about Finnik Doth, it was how impeccably by the book he played the rules. Seeing Varcor in the square told Darmond one thing: F.C. Orna had failed to capture Meera, and to get her back, he'd defied orders. Was Varcor Orna that desperate?

Another involuntary shiver shook Darmond. A desperate Varcor was dangerous. Any man openly defying a Grendolen commanding officer, not to mention the commandant general himself, not only risked their life but the lives of their family, even extended family, in payment for their misconduct. The Grendolens took controlling their people very seriously; leniency was not a term in their vocabulary. If Varcor was there of his own volition, it told Darmond he was confident in getting away with it. It was a unique kind of desperation. It meant the man was positioning himself to *take over* Finnik Doth's position.

Anger rose in Darmond as he looked out across the square at the Grendolens. It wasn't just the ruthless back-stabbing that made his blood boil, it was everything the Grendolens stood for. For the countless lives lost fighting to keep them at bay. For those who didn't die but were now enslaved under Lord Agnarr's rule.

For the difficult position they had put *him* in.

Darmond's thoughts were interrupted as a group of soldiers dragged one of the locals to the center of the town's square and tied them to the pole. His breath caught.

Sweet Yveth, no!

It was the young stable hand. Darmond cursed himself for failing to take precautions before he'd left to protect the lad. By the looks of it, the boy had already received a typical Grendolen greeting from several gauntlet-covered fists, which told Darmond the soldiers had successfully extracted the information they were looking for. The fact that the lad had been brought to face F.C. Orna, however, meant *he* was the example that would be made to any others in the town withholding details. Proving Darmond's guess, Varcor raised his arms to address the crowd.

"By order of his Imperial Highness, Lord Agnarr, ruler of the great and mighty Grendolen Empire, this town and all subjects within are now under his claim. All rights and privileges followed under the previous law are to be immediately revoked and are henceforth replaced with the Grendolen Creeds. A list of these creeds has been posted for your reference.

"To surrender to this change would be wise; to raise a weapon against it, grievous." Varcor recanted the words in a monotonous tone that one adapts after reciting something too often. He'd said it all before, many times, as each free town or village within the lands of Midtier had fallen under Grendolen rule.

"The citizen you see before you gave aid to three travelers that recently passed through this way, a man and two women, disguised as Mountaineers. They are wanted in connection with high crimes committed against our sovereign. Do not be so quick to forget that he is now *your* sovereign as well. You owe Lord Agnarr your allegiance in payment for showing mercy and allowing you to live. Many towns and kingdoms that came before you were not so fortunate."

Darmond glanced at the Vardians around him and wasn't surprised to see they weren't buying any of the rot pouring out of Varcor's mouth.

Good, he thought proudly. These weren't the same dejected faces he'd seen back in Midtier, the ones who had been fighting all their lives only to watch the battleline continue to push ever closer inward. The Vardians had plenty of fight in them, and from the look in the eyes around him, they were more than happy to prove it.

However, the more he dwelled on it, the more concerned he became. Even from as far away as he was, Darmond had a clear view of the faction colonel's face. He had a pale, almost sickly complexion, made even more so by the black oily hair kept cropped short around his face. Darmond expected that, having just dispossessed the townsfolk of their lands and freedom, the man might display a level of pensiveness about the possibility of revolt, yet there was nothing. On the contrary, it looked as if F.C. Orna was *bored* with the proceedings.

There's something not right with the man, Darmond thought. *He's not even concerned by the notion of a revolt. If anything, he looks as if he'd* welcome *the distraction.*

The soldiers accompanying the faction colonel also held dismissive expressions, which was even more unsettling. Darmond had hoped some of them would show a bit of regret for breaking their sworn oaths to Commandant General Finnik Doth, yet each of them seemed steady in their resolve to obey Orna. A coup such as this had never been done in the history of Grendolen so far as Darmond knew, and he knew a lot after a lifetime fighting against them on the borders of Midtier. To act so brazenly without fear of Lord Agnarr's retribution hinted at something that at first Darmond didn't want to believe but in the end was forced to consider seriously.

Varcor was operating under direct orders from Lord Agnarr. He *had* to be. It was the only thing that could explain why such a large number of soldiers would up and follow the man, and why the F.C. seemed so confident in ignoring Doth's orders. But that posed another question: Why did a man as powerful as Lord Agnarr go to the trouble of hiding his true intentions from his own commandant general in favor of trusting a lowly faction colonel, especially one so obviously void of self-control?

As he mulled over all this in his mind, four of Varcor's soldiers gathered around the stable boy, each adding their own pile of wood. Darmond's stomach turned sour.

I should have protected him, he thought angrily at himself. The boy's fate was sealed; his death would be slow and painful, an event meant to leave an impression on the crowd. Muttering under his breath, old Faltiel slinked away from the streets and back into an alleyway closed off from prying eyes. There, Darmond ditched his costume and quietly entered the back door of one of the buildings. As fortune had it, it was a tradesmen's shop. Without hesitating, he lifted a recurve bow, its string, and several arrows, then headed up the stairs, praying to Yveth the owner of the shop was one of those out in the crowds on the streets and not watching from his roof. Again, fortune was with him. He encountered no one on the building's second level or the roof, which ended up providing excellent cover. Keeping out of sight, Darmond strung the bow, readied an arrow, and sank into position. His weapon of choice had always been a blade. It made things more personal when it came to a fight, as both opponents knew the damage each swing could yield. One miscalculation, and you could lose an arm or your life, your soul sent to Yveth's realm or Nihility, whichever the Creator deemed appropriate. Bows were hunting weapons, or in this case, a weapon able to reach a target he couldn't risk approaching with a sword. Yes, he preferred a sword, but in a pinch, he wasn't bad with a bow. What he needed now was an opportune moment.

It came not long after Darmond took up his position on the roof, when Varcor went about selecting a short, curved blade from a box containing multiple instruments meant to inflict pain. It was one Darmond was very familiar with, specifically used for disemboweling someone while still alive. A new wave of anger rose over him. Because of his carelessness, this boy had been sentenced to a most excruciating death. Not only was he to endure the knife, he was to be burned alive too. Darmond watched from afar as a small puddle formed at the boy's legs upon seeing the blade. Losing himself to fear, the boy began screaming and fighting against his bonds. The crowd, too, began to stir. They didn't take kindly to the Grendolens' sudden arrival, and they certainly didn't condone what was taking place before them.

Come on, Vardians, Darmond thought. *Get angry! This is not* right*! I need you to fight back!*

To his relief, they did. It started with someone in the crowd cursing out loud at the Grendolens, then another telling them they weren't welcome and to leave their town alone. Before long, fury rippled through them all and they began to brandish weapons and push toward the Grendolen guards. Varcor Orna, however, seemed oblivious to it all, content to continue on with the curved blade in his hand.

Stepping toward the doomed boy, Varcor raised the blade. If Darmond waited any longer, it would be too late. Seeing his moment, Darmond took in a long steady breath, then held it as he took aim. He didn't release that breath until the arrow found its target. Upon impact, the boy's body jerked back, then slumped forward against the ropes with an arrow shaft protruding from his heart. Varcor Orna swiped his blade across the boy's abdomen anyway. The crowds went wild, and all Nihility broke loose on the square, but Darmond didn't wait around to watch.

Through his cycles working within the Resistance, Darmond had seen many towns fall to the Grendolens; some had put up a fight, others had simply given in. Those that did manage to overcome the enemy eventually fell once the Grendolen reinforcements arrived. Yet, he couldn't help but feel a sense of pride for the folks of Vardia. It took serious courage to take a stand against such a force, especially when the odds were so heavily stacked against them. Darmond's thoughts turned back to the boy, and with it came a heavy sense of guilt. Ever since learning the enemy was after the Moorland heir, getting her as far away from Lord Agnarr as possible had preoccupied all his thoughts. Had he stopped for a moment and thought about what would happen to the boy should the enemy find out he'd helped them, he would still be alive. Instead, the boy was dead, and by his own hand. A mercy killing, yes, but that meant little to Darmond, who would carry the weight of the mistake with him for the rest of his life.

There was *some* good to come out of going back to Vardia, though. Darmond had been able to confirm that Varcor hadn't figured out he was the one who helped Meera Tarmanon escape Matui. Eventually, they'd put it together and realize who he was. Eventually, his two new companions would too.

A bitter wind had begun blowing by the time Darmond made it to the point on the road where he'd instructed the women to turn south to make camp. This high up, snow lined the edges of the terra, giving a visual warning of how cold temperatures could drop at night.

They'd better have set up camp, otherwise, we're going to freeze our arses off. Much to his delight, his companions had not only set up both huts but from the smoke rising from the stove pipes, had also managed to get fires going as well. In the dim light of the evening the huts cast a warm glow in the area around them. While inviting, Darmond was glad they'd picked a spot surrounded by thick fir trees, as it not only provided shelter should a storm hit but also kept their presence hidden. And by the snowfall picking up speed around him, he guessed a storm was just what they were about to get.

The hut structures themselves were constructed out of five arched semicircles made from a light but sturdy wood found in the higher altitudes. When opened, the arched "ribs," as the locals refer to them, fan out to create a dome-shaped structure. A weather-tight, yet breathable, fabric woven out of tonga hair was then pulled over the frame and secured to the ribs. Each covering was outfitted with a reinforced flap near the back, opposite the door, which allowed for a stove pipe to fit through. The result was an incredibly strong structure, able to withstand blizzard gusts, while keeping the occupants dry and warm on the inside. Once erected, one hut could accommodate up to four people, and yet packed down to a semicircle that sat comfortably on the back end of a tonga. Thankfully for Darmond, Katula had insisted on getting more than one hut, which meant the women would share one and he'd get the other all to himself. It would be the first good night's sleep he'd had since he left the Grendolen barracks, and the sudden realization that he'd soon be tucked into warm furs brought on the exhaustion he'd been working so hard to hold back. Wearily, he checked on the tongas to make sure they had been fed. All three of the animals were circling in a tight formation, a telltale sign that snow was on the way. Deciding it was too late to wake the others and announce his arrival, Darmond opted to postpone their reunion until the morning.

Inside, his hut was every bit as warm and cozy as he'd imagined, and within a short time, he had a pot of water heating over the stovetop. He was in the middle of hanging his furs up to dry, when a neatly wrapped bundle sitting on his bedroll caught his eye. Curious, he opened it to find a bit of smoked meat, some cheese, a piece of bread, and an apple. His stomach growled. How on Tersaith had he gotten himself stuck traipsing through the Cassias with two of the most bull-headed women the world had ever produced? It was a question he pondered away at as he greedily ate the food they'd generously provided him. That, and Meera Tarmanon's unusual eyes. Not that the ones she had looked bad or anything. On the contrary.

Don't go there, Darmond, he warned himself. *You know better than anyone that's not something you need to go getting entangled with. Rot, you're far too involved* already! *If she ever figured out how, she'd bury one of those arrows she's so fond of right into your middle. Best stick to the plan.* With a resigned sigh, he tossed the now empty bundle of cloth aside and went about sullenly sipping on his tea as snowflakes softly fell overhead.

By morning, the storm had vanished, but it left behind a fresh blanket of snow, clear blue skies, and a bitter cold wind, all of which made for two miserable companions who were unaccustomed to such low temperatures. Darmond shifted on his tonga and looked back at the women trailing behind him. Both of them wore their fur-lined hoods secured so tightly around their heads, he could barely see their faces.

"Warm enough?" he mocked.

"It's too rotting cold up here," Katula cursed, attempting to pull her hood tighter.

Meera nodded in agreement, before giving Darmond a look.

"How in Nihility can you stand this wind without your hood on? It's cold enough to freeze a Jynyn's balls off!" He didn't know what the rot a Jynyn was, but the comment made Prickly *actually* crack a smile, something he didn't think she was capable of doing. Darmond ran his hands through his blond hair and gave his head a shake.

"Cold air gives you good locks. I can't let this gorgeous mane of mine be tucked into a hood all the time, now can I? It's got to *breathe*."

Both women gave him blank stares in response.

"Spend enough time up here and you'll grow used to the cold," he added more seriously.

"I highly doubt it," Katula remarked. Changing the subject, she added, "I didn't see you pack up your armor this morning when we broke camp."

Darmond's jovial countenance fell. After what took place in the square he'd had not wanted to ever go near that Grendolen armor again. Even if it was a work of art.

"You didn't go back for it, did you?" Katula pushed.

"No, I didn't."

"What did you find out?" she pressed.

Glad for a change in topic, Darmond filled them in.

"The man tracking us is Varcor Orna, and until recently, he was a faction colonel under the command of Finnik Doth, Lord Agnarr's commandant general. However, it seems that's not the case anymore."

"How so?" Meera asked from the back of the line.

"Varcor has taken control over the force sent with him and is now acting of his own accord, or, if my suspicions are correct, acting under the command of Lord Agnarr himself," Darmond explained.

"Why would Lord Agnarr betray his own commandant general?" Katula asked.

"A question I would greatly like to know the answer to myself," he agreed. "Yet the issue that should concern us now is the man Lord Agnarr has conspired with." Darmond brought his tonga to a stop and waited for the others to reach him before continuing. "The man is *cracked*. I've seen a lot of rotting maggots in my life, but believe you me, this man's actions prove he's given birth to them all.

"He's *dangerous*. Worse still, he's determined and desperate. A determined, dangerous, desperate man," Darmond emphasized. "He's the type that won't stop the hunt until his prey is caught. And even then, he'd probably go on."

Meera's red eyes flickered down, unable to meet his.

"How much time do we have before he catches up?" Katula demanded, always getting straight to the point.

"We took the last tongas Vardia had to offer, which means his only option would be to travel on the horses they rode to Vardia with," he explained.

"Aren't horses faster?" Meera said worryingly. Darmond nodded slowly.

"Yes, but using them up this high comes with incredible risk. They're not made for these cliffs or the cold. One storm and they'd be in serious trouble. Tongas are slower, but they're made for this terrain. And trust me, sooner or later, a storm will hit, and that will give us the advantage."

"We had a storm last night. It didn't seem too bad," Meera remarked.

"Last night's storm was like a gentle mist compared to what the weather up here is capable of."

"So we pray for bad weather," Katula noted sullenly.

"Exactly that," he confirmed.

Three weeks later, not one flake of snow had fallen. Within that time, it had also passed Regnamoad 14th, marking Darmond's birthday. They celebrated with a slightly larger dinner that night, and Darmond made the women promise to buy him a giant-sized pint, should ever they make it to Pawtoton and discover giants liked ale. Once a week, Katula had continued to bring out her "special" blend of tea and watch Meera readily consume it. It had become somewhat of a tradition. Ever since Darmond's conversation with the Matuian, he'd kept count. Meera had been given the Elements five times so far, with the sixth due that very evening. He knew Meera had begun to have dreams, and he was well aware Katula also knew and hadn't told him. It didn't bother Darmond. He would have done the same if he were in her shoes. But it did mean he'd have to try and gain Meera's trust in order for her to open up to him about whatever it was she was remembering.

Before duskfall that evening over the highcaps, however, they spotted the line of Varcor's men snaking around one of the peaks they'd traversed several days back. The hunter was closing in on its prey. Realizing they were losing their lead, Darmond ignored his own advice and pushed the tongas as fast as he dared around the icy cliffs, keeping their direction always headed west. The higher they climbed, the colder it grew, and before long even Darmond had pulled on his hood. Tucked behind the sparse evergreen trees, sheets of ice blanketed rocky ledges, a dangerous sign of recent thaws and refreezes. For three more days they serpentined their way around the icy, clear weathered cliffs; however, Darmond could tell the strain was starting to take its toll on his companions. He'd pushed them as much as he dared, but clear skies for them meant clear skies for those pursuing them. He'd begun checking behind them like he'd taken on a nervous tick, knowing that at some point he'd look to find Varcor staring right back at him.

Rot, why won't you send a storm, Darmond cried to the skies silently. He had never been a very religious person in the past, but recent events had caused him to call on Yveth a lot more frequently of late than he was used to. Looking back, he noted that both women looked exhausted, with dark circles under their eyes, the only part visible through the thick furs closed up around their faces. He had allowed them to make camp, but woke them early every morning, before the sun came up. Other than the brief sleep, the only time he allowed their caravan to halt was to relieve themselves or when the tongas needed to be fed and watered. Katula even dug into her precious reserve of Elements and mixed up concoctions for them to drink down that would fill their bellies. He'd refused, of course; you could never trust what was in those things. Yet, both women drank them without a thought, and it seemed to work, as it kept them more alert. However, the longer they took it and went without a proper meal, the more ragged they appeared. Katula said it had something to do with the mixture wearing off the more your body took in. It seemed to Darmond that if you could concoct a potion to keep you fed, why couldn't you concoct one that kept working? The Matuian sagen had actually *growled* at him when he'd mentioned this enlightening thought, though, so he'd decided to leave well enough alone.

Overall, both Katula and Meera hadn't complained one bit about how sore he knew they must be, especially since they weren't used to riding tongas. Even an experienced rider like himself had to dismount and rest at some point; the question was, where? Looking ahead confirmed there'd be no stopping point for a while yet, as they were reaching a dangerous section of trail. To the right was a sheer drop-off and to the left stood high cliffs where fresh snow had fallen on the mountain cap above.

Great, just what we need, he complained to fate. Wearily, he pulled his tonga to a stop.

"Water and feed your tongas," he called a bit more quietly than normal.

"What's wrong?" Katula asked, immediately picking up on the change in his tone.

"That," he said, pointing to the snow-covered cap above them, "is an avalanche waiting to happen." He let them take in the spectacle before continuing. "From here on out we move slowly and, let me *really* stress this part, *qui-et-ly*. The slightest sound can trigger a cascade. I don't want to even hear your tonga pass arse-air, got it?" The two women nodded solemnly and dismounted. As punctual as ever, Katula was the first to finish watering her tonga, but instead of mounting, she walked over to where Darmond stood, inspecting the trail ahead.

"One sound and the snow falls?" she repeated, giving him a skeptical look.

"There's no way of knowing exactly what will trigger it," he explained, "but if it *is* triggered it would be more like an unstoppable wave rather than a fall."

"But we were able to dig out our huts after the snow a few weeks back. How *much* snow falls in a wave?"

"It's much heavier than it looks because of the melting underneath," he tried to explain. "Dry air makes for lighter snow, whereas wet air means heavier snow. However, that rule means nothing if you're dealing with such a massive amount of the rotting stuff, such as what's up there." Darmond paused to look up at the snow-covered cliff, trying to find a way to explain the severity of the situation to someone who'd seen about two snowflakes in their whole life. "If we were to trigger an avalanche here, enough snow would fall to cover and hide this trail for *cycles* unless someone took the time to dig it out. But even then, it would take an army..." Darmond stopped mid-sentence and turned to Katula who, surprisingly, held a rare smile on her face, if only a slight one. "You're a clever one, Prickly, I'll give you that," he admitted, flashing a grin.

"We may not be able to stop the Grendolens completely, but if we were to trigger an avalanche after we passed to cover the trail, it would delay them, at least. Right?" she reasoned.

"It would definitely give us enough of an advantage to put a fair distance between us and the enemy," Darmond agreed, rubbing his thickening beard. "We'll have to time it right, though, and make sure we're well away from the area before triggering it."

"I'll let Meera know," Katula said readily. Darmond stood there for a little while longer, contemplating the plan and exactly how to best carry it out. Katula's rigid demeanor had been a thorn in his side ever since Matui, but he couldn't dismiss the fact that her plan was a good one. Truth be told, he was a bit annoyed he hadn't come up with it himself.

Noting both women had finished and mounted their tongas, he left his post and mounted his own. However, no sooner was he up than a strong gust of wind blew over the mountain cap from the south, down toward them like a solid wall, threatening to push them over the cliffs. Completely abandoning his orders to be quiet, he yelled back at his companions to hold on, hoping that they had the good sense to keep their tonga's reins tight and away from the ledge. As soon as the wind abated, he looked behind him and let out an audible sigh upon seeing both Katula and Meera were still there, although visibly shaken. The next gust of wind he heard before it hit. Looking up, he saw the telltale signs of a storm peaking over the tip of the snowcap, and from what he could see, this one was going to be serious.

"A storm's brewing," he warned, raising his voice dangerously high in competition with the wind. "We've got to get across this pass before it hits." His words were lost as a series of sharp gusts blew past. To make matters worse, he realized that in his haste to mount, he'd forgotten to secure the tonga tethers. If one of them strayed from the narrow pass, he wouldn't be able to pull them to safety. Hoping the women heard his words and followed him, he led his tonga out onto the pass's ledge. Halfway across, the stormfront crested over the mountain, unleashing the blizzard he'd spent the last few weeks praying for.

Even with his familiarity with tongas, he struggled to keep the beast as far away from the drop-off as possible—partly because the tonga's instinct was to huddle together with the others in order to protect themselves from the storm, and also because he couldn't actually see the rotting ledge anymore in the sudden whiteout. He gave up looking back to check on Katula and Meera. If he couldn't see his own hands in front of him, it was pointless to try to locate the others. All he could do was press on and hope he was headed in the right direction. In moments, the temperature plummeted, making what was already cold now dangerously bitter. He could feel the snow accumulating on the frost that had formed on his eyebrows, and even with the thick gloves he wore, his fingers were going numb around the reins. As he struggled forward—at least he hoped it was forward—a large crack sounded as lightning struck somewhere above him. A sense of dread filled Darmond as a roaring sound quickly grew over the loudness of the storm. Hoping his companions were close enough behind him to hear his warning, he cried, "AVALANCHE!"

CHAPTER EIGHT

Meera

According to the sparse Matuian records she'd researched about her homeland, Moorland received a good amount of moderate snowfalls in the three moads of Wyntersol. However, even without remembering most of her previous life there, Meera knew the coldest moad in her homeland was in no way as terrible as the incredibly bone-chilling cold the blizzard had thrown at them. She had been prepared for a myriad of challenges along the journey: hunger, injuries, illness, and even battle. But this was something else entirely. It was so cold, she could scarcely take in a breath without feeling like her lungs would freeze over, and that was with all the furs wrapped around her face. Desperately, Meera struggled to pull her hood tighter while trying to keep Signot on the path ahead. She'd lost sight of Darmond almost instantly when the storm broke, and couldn't see Katula anymore, so she had to rely on her instinct to get her across the pass. She knew the drop-off was somewhere to her right, so she kept Signot pushing ahead to the left as much as possible, just in case she was wrong. She'd rather the two of them run into the cliffside than suddenly find the terra gone out from underneath them. Meera could feel the beast she was riding tense up, and a mere moment afterward, a bolt of lightning struck above, accompanied by a massive clap of thunder. If a slight noise from a tonga could start an avalanche, then surely that abrupt sound would call the entire mountainside of snow down upon them. Not knowing how much longer she had until she reached the other side of the pass, she urged Signot into a run, her senses alerting her to a danger she could not see.

Hurry, Sig! We're out of time, she thought in her mind.

Sensing its own peril, the animal sprang to life and bolted forward, its thick muscles easily supporting Meera as they bounded through the quickly gathering snow. Even through the storm's fury, an unmistakable roar gathered above them. Heart racing, she leaned down against Signot and *willed* him to go as fast as he could. As if he understood, the tonga's speed increased. They were traveling so fast now that the snow stung Meera's eyelids. She was navigating blind and hoping with all her heart she knew where the rot she was going. Suddenly, the roaring sound was upon them, thundering like a herd of a thousand tongas on the run. It was in that moment, with the deafening loudness surrounding them, that Meera felt something within tell her to pull right.

Right is where the ledge is, though, she panicked, second-guessing her intuition. Yet, the urge to go right was so strong, there was no ignoring it. Against all reason, she pulled Signot's reins in the opposite direction just as the avalanche crashed down behind them. Meera opened her eyes as the tonga obeyed, half expecting to see their doom flash before them, but instead she was greeted with a thick grouping of fir trees on all sides. They'd reached the other side of the pass.

Her shock of surviving the ordeal was quickly put aside, however, when she nearly collided with Katula's unmanned tonga. Pulling back hard on the reins, Meera stopped Signot and quickly dismounted. Even within the confines of the trees, the snow had grown thick, with some banks already coming up to her knees. Walking was difficult. After struggling her way through the snow, she did a quick assessment and found no trace of the tonga's rider.

"Where is Katula?" Meera yelled to the animal, over the storm. The tonga only stamped and rolled its eyes, clearly shaken in the aftermath. Realizing her own panic would only stress the animal more, she forced herself to slow down and breathe in more calmly. Gently taking the reins and pulling the tonga's head to hers, she spoke aloud.

"I need to find her. Can you show me where she is?" Meera felt the animal relax against her but only after it let out several loud aggravated snorts and stamps. Rubbing its forehead, she pulled back slightly and looked into its eyes. She watched as the whites disappeared and calmness overtook them until all signs of stress were gone. She'd always had a way with animals. She'd grown up spending more time alone with them than with people. But the way the tonga's eyes connected with hers felt... *different* somehow. It was something deeper. Something that both amazed and frightened her at the same time. Until that moment, she hadn't thought about Vardia and how when the white hawk called out from the sky, she had known, beyond any doubt, the bird was warning her of the Grendolens' arrival.

Am I losing my mind? Am I really considering the possibility that this tonga understands me? Despite feeling foolish for even thinking it, she decided to try something.

"Show me where your rider is." She half hoped nothing would happen, even though she needed to find Katula. Pins and needles shot through Meera as the beast responded to her request and made its way past Signot, who'd thankfully stayed where she'd left him, and led her through the snow-covered evergreens until it came to a stop next to a thick snowdrift that had gathered against the tree trunks. The tonga let out a mournful cry that pierced through the storm's rage, making Meera jump. The instinct she'd felt during the storm hit again, only this time it told her Katula was under the snowdrift. Dropping down to her knees, Meera desperately began scooping out piles of snow, hoping her instinct would serve her well once more. After several moments of frantic digging, her gloved hands hit something soft. Working fast, she cleared Katula's crumpled frame off and dragged her out from the drift. Right away, she noticed dark bloodstains in the snow where Katula's head had been resting. Pulling back the woman's hood, she checked for signs of life and let out a relieved sigh when she confirmed she was still breathing. As gently as possible, she turned her over to get a better look at her injury, which proved difficult in the blizzard's fury. The base of her skull was matted with snow and frozen blood.

Katula must have hit her head against one of those trees when she fell. If Meera didn't get the Matuian warm soon, she was going to freeze to death before Meera could tend to her wound. She couldn't waste time questioning her newfound instinct with animals. Whipping around, Meera called out for Signot. Within moments his snow-matted head appeared through the storm.

"I need you to find Darmond and his mount. If you come across either of them, bring them back to me." The notion that Signot would understand even half of what she just said numbed her more than the cold, yet the tonga let out a call and began forging its way through the blizzard. As Meera watched him disappear into a world of white, she turned her attention back to Katula. Fresh blood christened the snow around the Matuian's head. Not knowing what else to do, Meera sent up a prayer to Yveth. As she did, a wave of exhaustion like she'd never felt before hit her. It took all the strength she had to pull Katula away from the trees and toward her tonga.

Thankfully, Katula's tonga had managed not to lose the supplies or the hut it carried during the ordeal. After a bit of a struggle on her own, Meera was able to erect the hut and even get the stove lit. Once she'd pulled Katula in out of the blizzard, she retrieved the rest of the supplies from the woman's tonga, which she knew included Katula's precious satchels of the Elements. While the stove's belly began to glow with warmth, she put a pot of water on to boil, then turned her attention onto Katula's wound.

"You know, it would have been a lot easier if I'd been the one to get hurt," she complained aloud to Katula as she rifled through the medical supplies. "I have no idea what the rot to do, let alone what Elements to use once I've cleaned the wound." Leaning down, Meera pushed the unconscious woman onto her side so that she could take a better look at the injury. The now-melted snow and blood had matted together with Katula's green hair, preventing Meera from seeing the full damage done. Annoyed, she got to work cleaning, but when she finally managed to get through the mess, there was no evidence of a wound at all. Confused, Meera began looking through the woman's hair for any sign of the wound's location, but again, everything looked normal. Panicking that she'd missed seeing a more serious wound elsewhere, she stripped Katula down to her undergarments to check. Yet, no injury was found. Completely perplexed, and still fighting the incredible exhaustion that had come over her, Meera covered the sagen up in fur blankets and sat down on her own bedroll. Where had all the blood come from if not Katula? A sound from outside the hut broke her thoughts.

Throwing on her thick coat once more, she opened the hut's flap to see Signot had returned. Behind him stood Darmond's tonga, and despite the snow still blowing, she caught sight of a rider on top.

"You found them!" she exclaimed, a wave of relief washing over her. Katula's tonga called to his companions, and the other two returned the greeting.

But as Darmond's tonga grew close, she realized the man was slumped over rather than sitting up. Not waiting for the tonga to make its way to her, Meera ran to meet it out in the storm.

The tonga greeted Meera with a tired bleat before setting itself down beside her so that she could reach its rider. Grateful, Meera nodded, letting out a bewildered "thank you" before pulling Darmond off his saddle. A quick assessment showed he had smacked his forehead against something and knocked himself unconscious, but there was no blood, nor did it look too serious.

He'll have a nasty headache when he wakes, and no doubt be more annoying than usual, but at least he's alive.

Looking back at his tonga, she put her hand on its head.

"Thank you, friend." Meera watched as the tonga stood and joined his two companions, which began circling together against the storm.

Back inside the hut, Meera scrambled through Katula's Elements until she found the vial labeled "Concussions" then poured a small amount into a cup, guessing at the dosage and hoping it would help rather than harm. Darmond let out a groan as she forced it down his throat but didn't fully come to. Satisfied he'd drunk enough, she set about stripping him of his wet clothing.

With both companions safely tucked into their beds, Meera stoked the stove once more before seeing to her own needs. It wasn't until she began to undress herself that the symptoms of shock fully set in. A cold numbness took over her mind as she struggled with shaking hands to undo her dressings. Once she finally made it under her covers, however, sleep would not come. It stood at a distance, taunting her, while she stared blankly at the hut's dome above. Outside, the wind continued to howl, and the snow continued to fall as she lay under her furs, vacant of thought. After what seemed like an eternity listening to the storm's rampage, sleep *finally* stepped closer and invited her weary soul into its restful folds.

Meera slept for two days. During that time, Darmond and Katula worked continuously to keep the snow hut clear from heavy snowdrifts, as the storm had not shown any signs of slowing down. They didn't bother setting up the secondary hut, as it had been damaged in the storm and meant wasting fuel for the stove. The huts could withstand strong storms, but too much weight on the dome's top could crush the frame, so Darmond set up shifts for Katula and himself to go out and clear the hut off. When Meera finally came to, it was the smell of freshly made panbread that pulled her back into the world of the living. For a moment, she thought herself back in her own hut in Notabi and wondered who had come to visit and brought fresh panbread with them. As Meera let out a slow stretch and lazy yawn, her other senses began to come around and her memory returned. Not ready to deal with all that had occurred quite yet, she forced herself to ignore it for the moment and focus on breakfast.

"Afternoon," Darmond greeted her. Sitting up, she found the Midtierian hunched over the stove, flipping several rounds of panbread, his hair perfectly framing his perfectly chiseled face. How annoying.

"Afternoon?" she asked, rubbing the sleep from her eyes and trying not to remember what he looked like without a tunic on. "How long have I been asleep?"

"It's the 24th of Regnamoad, Red. You've been asleep for two days straight." He sounded as if she'd accomplished some great feat. "Haven't missed much, though. The blizzard's still blizzarding out there, and until it stops, we're stuck here." Meera nodded, stretched again, and then gave her messy red mane a rake through with her fingers, hoping she didn't look as awful as she felt.

"Wonderful," she grumbled. "What have you two been doing while passing the time?"

Darmond pointed his utensil to the dome's door, indicating Katula was outside.

"I challenged her to a game of Bluff."

Meera laughed. "That was a mistake."

"Indeed."

"Matuians *invented* the game."

"So it would seem."

"Katula's face is practically made of stone."

"Like staring at a *rock*."

"It's impossible to tell if she's bluffing."

"I can confirm this."

"So how much do you owe her?"

"*Too* much." The two shared a smile before he resumed flipping pan bread. After a few moments of silence, Darmond looked up, his blue eyes looking more serious.

"I don't know how you found me out there, or Katula for that matter," he said. "The last thing I remembered was some tree branch deciding to get in my way of a perfectly executed dash away from an avalanche. Next thing I knew, I was waking up here. Katula and I know you were the one that found us. If you hadn't..."

He paused to scoop a round of panbread onto a waiting wooden bowl before continuing. "Well, what I'm trying to say is, *thank you*. I owe you my life. Katula and I both do."

Meera squirmed uncomfortably. What could she say in response? She could hardly expect either of her companions to believe the tongas had somehow *understood* her. She still wasn't sure that's what really happened. She'd been in shock and practically blinded by the snow. Reality would have seemed warped. Just thinking of trying to explain what she thought had happened made her head feel dizzy. They'd think she'd gone mad. *She* was certain she had.

"It wasn't me," Meera finally answered. "Your tonga brought you back to the others, as did Katula's. It was the animals' instinct, and I just happened to stumble upon them in the process." It was close enough to the truth that it was believable.

Darmond's eyes held hers for a moment longer as if he was weighing her words, but eventually he looked away.

"What's Katula doing out in the storm anyway?" Meera asked, switching the subject.

"It's her shift to clear the hut and check on the tongas," he replied. "She shouldn't be too much longer."

Meera nodded and went about getting dressed.

A little while later the flap to the hut opened, bringing in a whirl of cold and snow. Katula stood there, completely covered in white.

"You're up," the Matuian noted, seeing Meera as she pulled back her hood. "You saved our lives," she added, getting straight to the point in her usual curt way. "I don't remember what happened after I realized the avalanche had been triggered, but when I awoke, I found myself safe and warm. Thank you." Meera remembered she'd thrown the bandages used to clean Katula's head wound, or whatever it was that caused the bleeding, into the hut's stove to burn before she'd fallen asleep that night. Yet another thing she couldn't explain.

"Like I told Darmond, your tongas kept you safe. All I did was set up camp," Meera replied. Katula seemed content to drop the conversation there, and Meera was all too happy to oblige.

"Food's ready," Darmond called. "I think we can spare a few pieces of dried meat, too. We'll need to gather our strength before this storm ends." Meera's stomach let out a loud gurgle alerting the hut's occupants to how hungry she was.

"Sorry," she blushed. "I guess it's been a while since I've eaten anything."

"Dig in," Darmond replied, handing her a plate. As simple as the food was, Meera found it more than satisfying. She hadn't realized how famished she'd been. Thinking back before the avalanche, she realized they'd not eaten a full meal in days. While panbread was nothing to get excited about, the fact that it was warm and fresh made all the difference. There was freshly brewed tea too and

Meera didn't hesitate to down several steaming cups. She inquired about the special blend, but Katula insisted that they wait until after dinner later that night to enjoy some. There was just something comforting she found about holding a hot mug of tea in the confines of the cozy hut while the chaos of the storm billowed outside.

"Any idea where we are?" Katula asked Darmond once everyone had eaten their share. "I've been out to check on the tongas, but past that point, I can't see anything."

"I don't think we're far from where the avalanche occurred," Meera reasoned between sips of tea. "I didn't want to risk moving around too much in poor visibility, so I made camp in a small grove of trees the tongas had found."

"Do you think Varcor and his men will be able to cross the pass once the storm lets up?" Katula asked Darmond.

"If he or his men manage to survive this blizzard, it will take them a moad, if not two, to dig their way across," he smiled happily. "I doubt their horses fared well either. Trust me, they're not going anywhere fast."

"Then we have the advantage we needed," Katula noted. "As soon as the storm slows, we move out."

"Whoa, there," Darmond replied, holding up his hands. "We'll need to let the tongas rest first even after the storm subsides. They've been out there circling through this whole thing. And that's *after* we pushed them hard to reach the pass."

"Darmond's right," Meera said, inspecting the inside of her tea mug instead of meeting their eyes. "If we don't rest them, they won't get us any farther ahead." She could almost *feel* their exhaustion from inside the hut as soon as she said it. A sudden wave of her own exhaustion hit her at the same time. Was it wrong to go back to sleep as soon as you'd woken up? Fighting the urge, Meera asked for another refill of tea.

"Then the tongas rest. We don't want to push them and risk their health. Otherwise, our hard-won advantage over the Grendolens would be for nothing," Katula reasoned. "But the moment they *are* rested, we move out."

The other two nodded in agreement. After some time sitting in silence, Katula stretched and pulled out a pouch full of wooden dice from her pack.

"Anyone up for a game of Bluff?"

The following day, the storm's fury finally ended, leaving behind cloudy skies. The three travelers decided it was a good chance to investigate their surroundings and see where they'd ended up. The pass they had so narrowly escaped plummeting to their deaths from led to a rather large plateau, which backed up to the mountainside's cliffs. It was much larger than what they had anticipated, and despite the recent snowfall, underneath the drifts grew the lush, hardy grasses tongas thrive on. However, the real discovery was when they came across red flowers peeking out of the shallows where the higher snow drifts couldn't reach.

"Hey, aren't those the same flowers we saw glowing in Wildwood?" Darmond asked Meera curiously.

"They are," she replied, looking baffled. "How on Tersaith can the same flowers grow this high, in such a colder climate?"

Katula pulled out a small knife and cut one of the flowers off at the stem to inspect it. "You've seen these flowers before?" she asked, her voice full of concern.

"Yes, back in Noto Wey and again on the night we camped on the border. I didn't know western Matui had such unique flowers," Meera said.

"It doesn't," Katula noted. "Wait, you said they *glowed*?"

"Like little flames. It gave me chills," Darmond replied, exaggerating a shiver.

Seeing the concern on Katula's face, Meera stopped. "What's so odd about the flowers?"

"Follow me and I'll show you," Katula replied. She led them back into their hut and, once they'd hung up their furs, took out a leather tube and placed it into her lap. As soon as she was sure she had their full attention, Katula pulled off the top and carefully unraveled a long scroll of parchment.

"The Tercara Scroll," Meera realized, catching her breath. She had heard its text quoted many times by the sage but had never actually seen it with her own eyes.

"*This* is the scroll that references the key of stone?" Darmond asked excitedly. Katula nodded as she reverently surveyed the ancient text.

"See anything familiar?" the sagen asked them.

Meera gasped. “The flowers illustrated all along the sides” she exclaimed. “They’re the same!”

Katula nodded.

“What’s the significance?” Darmond asked, not catching on.

“The red flowers you see depicted here?” Katula noted, pointing to them. “The Tercara Scroll refers to as Wildfire flowers. They decorate the script because they are a symbol of the Ancients, Darmond. Yveth’s god-kin.”

“Wildfires,” Meera breathed. They sure looked like little fires when they glowed at night.

“I still fail to see how this is some type of discovery,” Darmond countered.

“These flowers haven’t been seen since the Ancients walked Tersaith,” Katula explained.

Darmond’s eyes went wide with understanding.

“You’re saying these things haven’t been seen in over three thousand cycles?”

Katula nodded in confirmation.

“Then what the rot are they doing suddenly making an appearance?”

“My question exactly,” Katula replied. “If we were to run into them once, it would be a grand thing, a miracle of Yveth. But to see them pop up everywhere we travel... We can’t ignore it. My word as a sagen, there’s a sign here, I’m just not sure what that sign is yet.”

The day after the discovery of the Wildfires, the sun reappeared again and the tongas were found no longer resting but grazing on the vegetation that they had churned up with their wide hooves. It was a sign that it was time to get moving again. They'd brought provisions for the tongas, knowing that the higher the altitude they were traversing, the less likely they were to come across food. However, their own supplies had been quickly dwindling. The location they'd stumbled across after the avalanche was a rare find and one they might not come across again. Staying up in the highcaps for too long meant they risked starving their tongas. With each of the travelers eager to locate a passable descent out of the sparse terrain, they broke camp on the 27th of Regnamoad and the caravan once again headed west.

Rather than leading as he'd done in the past, Darmond positioned himself in the back of the line so he could stay behind and cover their tracks just in case no other snow fell before Varcor's men cleared the pass, if indeed any survived. Instead, Meera led, having located the best way out from the plateau the day before. Much to her relief, the path she'd found took them away from the dizzying heights, down into the heart of the mountains. But, despite the change of scenery, it proved a tight fit for their tongas to pass through. With towering rocky walls jutting up on both sides of them, they were forced to go single file, and even then, it was a tight squeeze. By midday, they'd reached no end to the narrow passage, and Meera found herself actually missing the views from the cliffs, despite the danger they'd posed. A pensive silence had also settled over the travelers. It felt wrong to converse in such a space. Only that left Meera with her thoughts, and most of them had to do with the vivid dreams she kept having of late, ones that were painful to recall.

It was obvious no one had ventured down the trail in many cycles, and perhaps that was how the mountain preferred it. The farther they rode, the more closed-in Meera felt, as if the walls would shut in on them and trap them there forever. She also began to feel her first few hunger pains, which was odd, as she'd kept herself fed and they hadn't run out of food. Yet the feeling persisted until she could no longer ignore it. Annoyed at her stomach, Meera reached back to her saddlepack to grab something to eat again, when she heard Signot's own beastly stomach rumble.

I'm sorry, Sig. Hopefully we'll reach a good grazing spot soon, she thought in her head, giving his neck a rub as they rode. Signot seemed to enjoy the attention and lifted his head higher, giving a call out to the other tongas. To Meera's amazement, all three simultaneously picked up speed, and suddenly the hunger she'd felt was met with a rush of adrenaline. She'd still not faced what had happened the day the blizzard struck, naively hoping it would just go away. And yet, here she was again, experiencing something that couldn't be explained. Had the hunger she felt before come from *Signot*? The moment she'd thought those words to him, his demeanor changed, and she could swear to the Watchers she'd *felt* that change. Had the tonga just read her mind and she his?

What the rot *is happening with me? Either I'm losing it, or the lack of oxygen up here is getting to my head.* Was she really going to consider she'd communicated with the tonga? Try as she might, she couldn't deny the hunger she'd felt just moments ago, a deep hunger that Signot surely must have been feeling by now. First the dreams and now this. It was too much. All Meera wanted to do was forget any of it happened. The trail, however, was *so* boring and there was nothing to do. Curiosity finally won over. After shoving down a gulp of fear, Meera hesitantly leaned in on her saddle toward Signot's head.

Slow down, she thought in her mind. She tensely waited, but nothing happened. She tried again, only this time she willed Signot to slow down as she thought the words, and sure enough the tonga did. Meera's stomach soured.

No! That's impossible!

She tried again, willing the tonga to speed up. He complied.

Rot. Rot, rot, rot, rot! She *wasn't* going mad. What in *Nihility* was wrong with her? Realizing she wasn't making it up meant she had to face the truth. This type of thing had happened before. Ever since she'd run into that white hawk back in Matui, she had begun experiencing unexplainable things—feelings that were not her own but, rather, impressed upon her. No. More like *willed* upon her, just as she had willed her thoughts into Signot.

Somehow, she was communicating with them, and they, her. Terrified of what that meant, she kept silent the rest of that day.

CHAPTER NINE

Katula

"What do you mean, it's a dead end?" Katula demanded, awkwardly steering her tonga around the others to get a better look. Darmond made no reply, and she soon found there wasn't need for one once her eyes locked on to what the other two had been staring at. They'd spent the entire day meandering at a snail's pace through the mountain's confining crevice way, only to find it stopped at a dead end. The rock walls they had squeezed their way through suddenly divided to ring around a flat circle of land. But it wasn't just the dead end that had caught everyone's attention. Scattered throughout the plain stretching before them stood the remains of massive stone structures, long since abandoned.

"Maggots," Darmond cursed under his breath.

"Giants," Katula breathed in awe. The structures *had* to have been made by *giants*! One carved block of stone was twice her size. A sinking feeling hit her. Was this what was left of Pawtoton? Had they come all this way only to find what they were after had died out long ago? Katula knew the others were wondering the same thing.

"What do we do now?" Meera wondered aloud.

"Let's double-check and see if there's an exit," Darmond suggested. "There may be a hidden path somewhere." The three of them rode their tongas around the ruins, checking in every crevice for a way out until they came back to the narrow entrance they'd entered from. It was truly a dead end. That meant the only way out was back over the pass where the Grendolens were waiting for them. It was a serious blow to them all.

"Let's make camp," Katula ordered. "It is almost sundown and there's nothing else we can do tonight. Perhaps in the morning's dawnlight, we'll find something we missed."

"There's *got* to be a way out," Meera protested. It was more of a plea than said in confidence.

"Katula's right. Let's make camp before nightfall. Those clouds over there promise snow," Darmond said, nodding to the south rim. "Tomorrow I can double back and see if we missed any other passages along the way."

"What do we feed the tongas?" Meera questioned. "There's not a blade of grass to be seen in this desolate place."

"We still have a little of our reserve feed left," Darmond confirmed.

"That's not enough," Meera pushed. "They're *starving*."

"What is it you think I can do?" he shot back, growing angry. "I can't conjure up food out of thin air, can I? Ask the all-knowing sagen, maybe she can conjure up something with her Elements."

"The only reason we are here is because you said you *knew* these trails," Meera retorted.

"I had no choice in the matter, and you know it. If you had come with me to Midtier you would have been nice and safe by now and I could be off to the alehouse trying to drink away any memory of this whole *rotten* thing! But *no*, we *had* to go west. We had to look for beasts and giants because Prickly here has an old scroll that said so. And let's not forget, I've risked my life several times trying to get you two where you wanted to go. But go on," he taunted Meera, "blame me when the results are what I warned would happen."

"Do you expect me to feel sorry for you?" Meera countered. "Katula and I have suffered incredible loss at the hands of the Grendolens. It may seem absurd to be out here looking for myths, but it is our best shot at stopping the Grendolens."

"I've lost more than you know," he growled.

"Your precious suit of armor? How could I forget!"

"Meera!" Katula yelled, finally stepping in. "We've *all* suffered loss thanks to those rotting Shadeblights! We're tired, hungry, and almost out of daylight. The two of you need to get over yourselves and help me set up camp before it gets too dark." Darmond and Meera both wiped the surprised looks off their faces at her outburst before nodding and silently splitting ways. Glad for the silence, Katula went about completing her own chores. Meera took it upon herself to see to the tongas being fed, and it was then that Katula caught the Moorlander undergoing another deep conversation with the animals. Not sure of what to make of it, Katula eventually walked over to Darmond to help erect the hut.

"I'm worried about her," she said quietly, nodding in Meera's direction.

Darmond took a glance and then shook his head. "She's talking to the tongas again, isn't she?" he guessed.

Was that a slight grin she just saw flicker across his face?

Oh, rot. She had been so worried about finding Pawtoton and gaining Meera's trust, she'd missed what was right in front of her. The man was *smitten* with her sister. No wonder they kept arguing like an old couple. That's all she needed to add to her list of ever-growing concerns. How close had the two gotten? Had he talked with Meera about her nightmares? Did he know something more about the Stone Key even now? Trying not to panic, Katula kept her voice calm and pushed on with the conversation.

"Yes, she is. I find it... disturbing," she admitted.

Darmond shrugged. "The woman is a flaming pain in the arse."

"No argument there."

"But I don't think it's anything to worry about. Red's just... well, *Red*. Maybe it's some odd Moorlander custom. Besides," he added, "if we're stuck here for much longer, I might try talking to the tongas myself pretty soon, just so I don't have to talk to you two."

Normally, his humor would annoy Katula, but after the argument they'd had, she took it as a sign things were being smoothed over. Still...

"It's not normal," she pushed, "*even* for a Moorlander. She spends all her time talking with them and..."

"And not with us?" he interjected, guessing at what was truly frustrating her. Rotting Nihility, the man figured her out. Time to come clean.

"I've administered seven doses of Natta's elixir, and she's not said one thing to me about her dreams, even though I know she's been having them. Has she spoken to you?"

"No," he answered regretfully with a sigh. "And after how I spoke to her just now, I doubt she'll count me as one of her confidants. How much of it is left?"

"Only enough for one more dose."

"You plan on giving it to her tonight?"

"That's what I had in mind."

Darmond fell silent for a moment as he finished tethering one of the hut's straps. "I know you said you don't want to do anything to alter what she remembers, but what if we were to go about helping jog her memory in a different way?" he proposed.

Katula cocked an eyebrow in interest. "What do you have in mind?"

After it had grown dark and the snow Darmond had predicted would come set in, the three travelers huddled around the hut's stove as Katula handed out freshly made tea. The act had become a beloved ritual after so many days living in close quarters together. However, this time would be the last dose of elixir Meera would receive in her tea. Katula feared that if the woman didn't recall the past events in her younglinghood after this dose, any information they could use against Lord Agnarr would be lost forever.

"It's a shame we didn't procure any Moorbrew back in Vardia," Katula said casually as she handed Meera her spiked tea.

"Mm, this is the good blend," Meera noted after taking a sip.

"And sadly, the last of it," Katula replied, trying to sound casual.

"It's not Moorbrew, Prickly, it's Moor*dew*," Darmond corrected her, taking his own mug when offered and getting back on subject.

"It would have been nice to enjoy a sip or two to fight off this cold weather," Katula responded.

"I didn't peg you as the drinking type," he replied.

Meera took a long sip of her tea and let out a content sigh.

"There's a vast difference between being a drunkard versus being a *connoisseur* of good spirits," Katula retorted. "Besides, everyone knows the best grain spirits found on Tersaith came from Moorland."

"True enough," he nodded. "And none better than Moordew." Without warning, the Midtierian launched into song.

"From a land of moors and white fog,
Hails a drink high above your low grog.
Golden be that sweet liquid's hue,
Favored by the kings be Moordew."

Katula cocked her eyebrow.

"What in Nisri's name are you singing?"

"It's a drinking song!" he countered. "Don't tell me you don't have any of those in Wildwood."

"It's Matui. And no, we don't."

"That's a *rotting* shame. Next alehouse we hit, you two can buy those drinks you owe me, and we'll get a couple of rounds going. There's nothing better than a lively alehouse tune to sing your troubles away."

"Everyone sings it together?" Meera asked.

"Of course!" Darmond grinned. "Here, I'll sing another verse and then you two have to repeat the lines of the chorus after me."

"There is no other of its ilk,
Better than mother's own milk.
Distilled from Yveth's best brew,
Be the savory taste of Moordew."

He looked at the women and grinned. "The next lines you're meant to echo.

"Raise a glass!" he shouted.

"Raise a glass?" Meera timidly said.

Katula just crossed her arms and stayed silent.

"Lift a flask!"

"Lift a flask," Meera repeated a little louder.

"And drink one and all to Moordew!" he ended. "That last part you sing along with."

"And here I thought Moorlanders were odd." Katula sniffed.

Darmond ignored her. "There's a whole lot more to that one, and the chorus keeps getting bigger. The trick is to sing all the lines without messing them up, which, if you've knocked back a few Moordews, isn't easy. Prickly over there has no idea how much fun she's missing out on."

"Just because we don't make a spectacle of ourselves at alehouses doesn't mean we don't know how to have a good time," the Matuian shot back.

"Oh, so you *do* drink in that big forest of yours," he teased.

"As it happens, my father kept several bottles of Moordew in our family storeroom," Katula acknowledged.

"I didn't know Moorland was known for brews," Meera confessed softly.

"Moordew wasn't just any brew, mind you," Darmond said. "It was the drink of the reigning monarchs. Your parents would have toasted to celebrations with it." He paused for a moment and then gave Meera a look. "Wait, are you saying you've *never* tasted Moordew?"

"Darmond, I was a youngling when I left."

"Never stopped me," he remarked.

"Why does that not surprise me?"

"They didn't have any in your village back in Matui?" he pushed.

"Notabi was too small to have an alehouse of its own. Besides, even if I stopped by one in the other villages, there's no way I could have afforded it."

"Maggots," he cursed, shaking his head. "You've not lived unless you've had one too many Moordews and woken up face down in a tonga paddy the next morning."

"That sounds... anything *but* appealing," Meera replied, scrunching up her face in disgust.

"Don't listen to him," Katula interjected. "One glass or two won't do any harm, but I'm not sure we'll be able to find it anywhere. It's been out of production since... since the massacre." Katula hadn't meant to bring up the horrid event so openly. Shooting a look at Darmond, she pleaded silently for help.

"Oh, there's still some to be had," he said, quickly covering up her blunder.

"You think there are still bottles of it out there after all this time?" Meera asked curiously.

"It was a major export of Moorland for centuries," Darmond replied. "There's not a prominent alehouse I've come across that doesn't have a few bottles left in reserve. It just costs a whole lot more now. But, seeing as though you've never tried it and you happen to be Moorland's long-lost heir, I'd say that's a good enough reason to mark with a tasting." He smiled, before adding, "And I'm sure Katula would be *happy* to part with a few halfspritts to see you try a glass."

The Matuian let out a snort and pointed to the Midtierian. "*You're* the one who owes *me* after losing so poorly in Bluff," she countered smugly.

Darmond returned a flat stare before continuing. "What else haven't you tried?" he asked, directing the question to Meera.

"I did try some brown ale once while trading in Saby Wey," she recalled.

"Ale. *Once*." Darmond staggered, aghast. "What about saps?"

"Not tried any of those either."

"*None*?"

Meera shook her head.

"What about red saps?"

"Nope."

"Blue saps?"

"Never."

"What in the name of the Seven Sisters do they drink in Matui, then?" he cursed, genuinely shocked.

"We *have* spirits in Matui," Katula said defensively, raising her chin.

"Through trade, not craft," Darmond pointed out. "If you had brewcrafters, alemakers, or sapsmiths living among you, it would be more readily available and you wouldn't have to trade for it."

"Matuians craft *arrows*, not spirits," Katula retorted proudly.

"Was Moorland also known for its saps?" Meera asked them both, bringing the subject back to her homeland without either's aid.

"No, unfortunately. The weather on the moors wasn't good for growing sap vines. The best sap fruit hails from Tersaith's southern regions, where the sun is hot in Sumorsol and there are warm rains in Wyntersol."

"You seem to know a lot about Moorland," Katula commented dryly, still feeling a bit on the defensive side. "How did a Midtierian learn so much about the lands to the east?"

It was Darmond's turn to shoot Katula a look, but Meera also seemed eager to hear his answer, so he gave in. "You don't live in Midtier without coming into contact with travelers on a daily basis. Even after the massacre, it wasn't unusual to see a few Moorlanders stop in for supplies on their way through town. Put a few ales in a man and he'll talk. You can learn a lot from someone spilling out their troubles over a glass of spirits."

"Wait. Are you saying you've talked with Moorland *survivors*?" Meera gasped. This was news to Katula as well, who'd always heard there were none.

"A few, yes, but..."

"I'm not the only one," Meera breathed to herself, red eyes wide in wonder. "I always thought I was the only one left."

"Meera," Darmond said slowly. "It's no good thinking of them as Moorlanders anymore. Those that survived have embraced life elsewhere, with new identities so as not to be tied back to their homeland. It is better they keep it that way, at least while the Grendolens hold the advantage." There was a tenderness in his voice that Katula picked up on that hadn't been there before now.

"Still," Meera said a bit groggily, "it's good to know some of them survived." The redhead let out a yawn and placed her empty mug aside. "I'm sorry, but I think the exhaustion is finally catching up with me."

Katula and Darmond exchanged glances.

“I think we could all use a good night’s sleep,” he said.

“Same here,” Katula agreed. But once the others were asleep, and only the soft glow from the stove lit the tent, Katula lay there, tense with worry. Had she and Darmond pushed the subject of Moorland on Meera too strongly? If she did remember anything of her dreams, would those memories now be altered because of their forced conversation? The next time she offered tea to Meera she’d have to tell her the truth about the elixir and why they ran out of the “good blend.” How would the Moorlander react once she found out? Eventually, Katula found sleep, but it was a restless, agitated sleep, right up to the point where Meera’s blood-curdling screams ripped her from her slumber.

As soon as she came to, Katula saw Darmond had already woken up and gone to Meera’s side. Alarmed, Darmond attempted to shake Meera awake.

“Is this what the elixir is supposed to do?” he demanded of Katula, raising his voice over the screams.

“I... I don’t know,” Katula stammered, uncertainly. “Meera!” she called. “Meera, can you hear me?”

Seeing there was no response, Darmond tried again. “Meera! Wake up!” Suddenly, Meera stopped screaming and sat up so fast, she nearly smacked into Katula’s head.

“IT’S KILLING THEM!” she sobbed, her eyes wide with fear.

"Meera, you've been dreaming," Katula said, trying to reason with her. But the woman shook her head violently in protest.

"No! You don't understand. Something's out there attacking the tongas. Signot's hurt!"

"What? How do you know that?" Katula asked, confused. Even as she said the words, Meera sprang from her bedroll, pushed past Darmond, and headed for the hut's door.

"Meera, you can't go out there without your furs!" Darmond cried after her, realizing the Moorlander was barefoot and in her undergarments. But his words were lost as a burst of snow blew in the hut at Meera's leaving. Before Katula and Darmond could throw on their furs and go out after her, a deep resonating howl sounded outside, echoing around the ring of rock walls and sending Katula's hair standing on end.

"What the *rot* was that?" Darmond cursed, grabbing for his sword. Katula snatched her bow and quiver, wasting no time trying to answer what she didn't know. Outside, they found Meera had already made it over to where the tongas had grouped together around Signot, who lay bleeding in the snow. There was no sign of whatever had attacked the animal, but the low cloud covering and steady snowfall made it difficult to see much of anything past their camp. Readying an arrow, Katula blinked her Matuian black eyes over to their night vision and scanned the edges of the cliffs around them, pensively waiting for anything to reappear.

"What in Yveth's creation is big enough to attack a tonga?" Katula called nervously to Darmond.

The Midtierian shook his head as he kept his eyes on the perimeter and his sword at the ready. After a few moments of inspecting Signot, Meera stood up, her underclothes now covered in the animal's blood.

"How is he?" Katula called across the distance between them. The Moorlander shook her head.

"Not good," her voice trembled. "He's lost a lot of blood. Whatever did this, was big enough to—"

Her words were cut off as another ear-piercing howl sounded from behind her. Jumping in surprise, Meera turned around and began slowly backing up. Out of the darkness, a massive beast covered in white fur stood up on its hind legs and let out another resounding howl as if to challenge her.

"Rotting Nihility, it's *behind* her!" Katula yelled. Darmond bolted for Meera before Katula's words were out. Muttering a curse, Katula followed in pursuit, but already she could see there was far too much distance between Meera and themselves. The beast *towered* over the tongas, making Meera look like a tiny mouse in comparison. Katula sent two arrows straight at its hairy head as she ran, but just as they were to hit their mark, the beast dropped on all fours and charged for the Moorlander. Desperately, Katula sent two more arrows its way. This time they hit, one grazing its shoulder and one penetrating its massive thigh. It didn't even slow the thing down. Letting out a scream in desperation, she tried to quicken her pace.

Meera, however, did not run. She stood knee-deep in snow in her bloodied undergarments and stared down the beast with more courage than Katula had ever thought the woman capable of. As the beast closed in on her, it released another bone-chilling howl. It was *anticipating* its kill. Tears clouded Katula's eyes as the realization set in that neither she nor Darmond were going to make it there in time.

That's when it happened.

Meera began to *glow*.

Both Darmond and Katula came to a sudden halt at the sight. All along her pale skin, the Moorlander's veins turned red, as if they had caught fire from within. Just before the beast's massive frame collided with Meera's, she lifted her hands before her like a shield and let out a defiant scream. The white beast, with all its rage, fangs, and claws, suddenly slammed into an invisible barrier before the woman's glowing form. The collision was *so* violent, the beast's body was instantly torn asunder. Pieces of it flew, scattering in all directions, save where Meera stood. Around her a wide circle had formed, and all the snow within had vanished. Then as quickly as it had happened, it was over.

Trembling, Meera turned toward them, and for a brief moment, her glowing red eyes held theirs, then she let out a frosty breath and crumbled into a heap on the thawed terra.

Katula was the first to wake up the next day, followed by Darmond. Meera, however, slept as if in a trance, and would not wake no matter how hard they tried to rouse her. The glow they had seen during the night had faded almost as soon as Meera had collapsed. Unsure what else to do other than let their friend rest, Katula and Darmond dressed and went to check on the tongas, expecting Signot to have succumbed to his injuries during the night. But what they found only brought more questions. Within the circle that had melted where Meera had stood, waved thick, lush grass that all three tongas were feasting on. Outside the circle of grass among the giant ruins stood bright red flowers popping up through the snow. Darmond and Katula ran over to inspect Signot and found his wounds nearly healed.

"Darmond, what in Nihility is going on?" Katula exclaimed, her black eyes wide in disbelief. "Signot should be *dead*, but these wounds look like they've had a *moad* to heal."

"Where did the grass come from?" Darmond finally managed, in a daze.

Katula just shook her head. Around the circle of grass, she could see the remains of the beast. It *hadn't* been a dream. Visions of the beast's demise replayed through Katula's head over and over. She had begun to suspect Meera was somehow able to communicate with animals, more than just having a good instinct with them. She thought herself crazy for even thinking it, but Meera somehow *knew* Signot was being attacked. How else could she have known? And what about the beast? Something twice the size of a tonga instantly fragmented into a thousand pieces after impacting a wall of... of *water*? A wound that should have been fatal had miraculously healed overnight. Grasses that didn't grow at high altitudes had appeared where they weren't before. Wildfire flowers kept appearing wherever they went.

Katula's face clouded over.

"Darmond," she said in a low voice. "What if we've had it wrong the whole time?" The Midtierian stood silent, unable to look away from the scene before them, so she pushed on. "What if Meera doesn't have *information* about the weapon? What if—"

"—she's the weapon Lord Agnarr is after," he finished for her, the words catching in his throat.

Grimly, Katula nodded. "It would explain why he's so intent on hunting her down."

They needed answers, but to do that they needed Meera to come out of her coma-like state.

"I think it's time I used the Elements to wake her up," Katula suggested.

"If she really did all the things we think she did, she may *need* to rest," he warned.

She was about to comment when a flick of movement caught her eye. "We're not alone" she whispered, suddenly tensing. Darmond's head didn't move, but she knew his eyes were scanning their perimeter.

"There, to the left. Something just moved," he confirmed. Katula locked eyes on an area near the ringed wall, which was covered with a bank of snow after last night's weather. Worrying it was another one of those beasts come to have another go at their tongas, Katula turned to go retrieve her bow. Out of nowhere, a fist of bones met with her face, knocking her flat on the terra. She was vaguely aware of Darmond's body dropping down next to hers. A large tonga skull sauntered into her blurred vision just before she was hit again and slipped into unconsciousness.

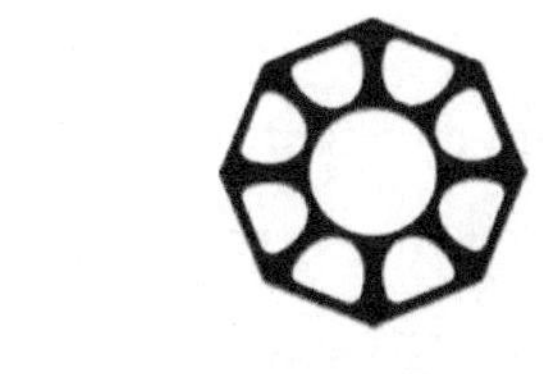

CHAPTER TEN

Finnik

Finnik stood like a stone, overlooking what remained of the once-thriving mountain town of Vardia. Many of the wooden buildings still smoldered from the fires Varcor and his men were responsible for kindling. Bodies of the fallen townsfolk scattered the streets, left unburied or tended to. Varcor had even burned the loft where the carrier pigeons had been kept. The Mountainmen had fought back, though. There were clear signs of a skirmish, and once Finnik came across the public execution Varcor had set up in the town square, it was obvious why they revolted.

Finnik shook his head in disbelief. Under the Grendolens' previous leader, this kind of savagery would have never happened. There was supposed to be an *order* to things. Vardia was a key trading center and could have been of great value to the empire, had it been spared. What lay before him now was the result of chaos. Varcor was *reckless*, and Lord Agnarr, for reasons Finnik could not deduce, kept allowing his behavior. Deep down, he knew that if Varcor and his men managed to capture the Tarmanon heir, his treasonous acts would be forgiven, and it would be Finnik's head that would burn—something he *didn't* relish happening. If he was going to survive this, Finnik needed to catch up with Varcor, deliver his due punishment, and capture the heir for himself.

To find out a spy had lived among them and gained their secrets was one thing, but to find out Varcor Orna was working against him was another. The man had boldly defied Finnik's orders by leaving Wildwood and making for Vardia, where he made sure anyone left around worth interrogating information from was eliminated. It was clear now to him that Varcor moved to strike Finnik from his position as commandant general and claim it for himself. It seemed the only logical reason behind his movements and betrayal. That kind of betrayal was just another reminder of how much the governing forces of Grendolen had changed since Lord Agnarr's rise to power. Never before would his people have even considered such an act.

Finnik's only consolation was that the Tarmanon heir had managed to once again slip through Varcor's grasp. Varcor's need to risk pushing his men into the unpredictable mountain terrain, on horseback no less, proved as much. It was no easy feat moving that many troops through such narrow and dangerous pathways. It would slow Varcor's progress down considerably.

It was up to Finnik to make sure he took advantage of that fact.

"Commandant General, sir?"

Finnik turned to find one of his soldiers standing to attention next to him.

"A rider arrived just now, sent here from our troops stationed in Wildwood. A message was sent by carrier pigeon, all the way from the Midtier lines."

This perked Finnik's attention. He'd been waiting for this.

"The letter," he demanded, holding out his hand.

"Here, sir," he obeyed.

Finnik took it, wasting no time breaking its small seal and decoding its contents.

Commandant General,

I found your question most intriguing, as no plans for the Resistance to infiltrate your command have been brought to my attention. I can assure you my position within the Resistance remains uncompromised, thus I am confident in my previous statement. However, the level of skill you described in the operative does indeed sound familiar. There is one among the Resistance whom they favor when carrying out extensive reconnaissance, but this is where I falter.

The spy of whom I refer to goes by the name of Darmond. I was not able to acquire a surname, unfortunately. Even so, you may find this next bit intriguing. According to my sources, the Resistance believes him to be dead, having never reported back after his previous mission several moads ago.

I will continue to investigate and send my findings forthwith.

Long live Lord Agnarr and the Grendolen Empire!

Your faithful servant,

KB

Finnik crumpled up the letter in his fist. It had left him with more questions than answers.

A ghost with no surname, he thought to himself, mulling over the new information. If his own informant in the Resistance had been compromised, he would have known by now, so he had to assume the Resistance truly believed their spy dead. But if he wasn't, and Darmond was the one who'd infiltrated Finnik's ranks and stole the Moorland heir out from underneath his grasp, under whose command was he taking orders?

Had the spy gone *rogue*? If so, what were his intentions with the heir?

Finnik furrowed his brow. He needed to capture the remaining Tarmanon and meet this spy face-to-face. But before he got to that, he'd need to deal with Varcor's treachery, and Varcor was already so *far* ahead of him. Time was not on his side. Finnik rubbed his temples, his aching bones temporarily distracting his attention. When had age crept up on him? It seemed like every day he woke to a sore back and complaining muscles. Perhaps that was why Varcor Orna felt he could use this time to strike against him. Finnik looked around at his soldiers. Did they *all* think he wasn't up to the task? It used to be that old age meant you were considered wise, not useless. Setting his jaw, Finnik pushed his thoughts from his mind. He wasn't about to sit down and let Varcor take what was his. He still had plenty of fight left in him.

Turning to the soldier, Finnik gave his reply. "I want Vardia's pigeon loft up and running again within the week. Bring our own from the coast if you have to. In the meantime, tell the rider to return to Wildwood and send a coded message in response. Our informants are to pursue information about the spy at all costs. *Any* details found, no matter how small, are to be sent to me *at once*." The soldier respectfully saluted before running off to obey. Finnik watched his departure as he contemplated his next steps.

At dawnlight the next day, after having respectfully buried the dead, Finnik Doth promptly departed Vardia, along with two units of his most trusted men. If Varcor Orna wanted to expend all his energy pursuing the Tarmanon heir, let him do all the hard work. But sure as the Grendolen Empire was strong, Finnik would be waiting to retake what was rightfully his once she was caught.

CHAPTER ELEVEN

Meera

It was the absence of cold, that bitter, bone-chilling cold of the highcaps she'd grown used to bracing herself against, that brought Meera out of her deep slumber. Instead of howling winds and endless snow drifts, she found herself peacefully encased in a soft warmth that felt *so* comforting, she briefly wondered if she'd died and passed over into Yveth's realm. Confused and feeling slightly dizzy, Meera slowly came to and opened her eyes to find herself lying in an oversized bed. Not a bedroll or cot, a *real* bed, with a luxuriously thick mattress, soft sheets, and the fluffiest pillows she'd ever rested her head on. Her eyes opened wide as she took in the bed's carved canopy and the room in which it sat. A *large* room, filled with very *large* things. Her feet hardly reached the middle of the bed, making it long enough to fit someone more than double her size.

A bed built for giants, she realized startlingly. Suddenly, she clutched for her hawk pendant at her chest, worried it had been stolen. When she felt it still hanging around her neck, she let out a sigh of relief and continued to look around the room. The craftsmanship that had gone into carving the furniture seemed far removed from the mental image of the drooling, bloodthirsty behemoths the Matuians had described in their stories of giants. Massive gold-framed paintings and tapestries lined the walls, and a pleasant floral fragrance hung in the air. Directly across from the bed stood a grand fireplace made of carved stone, yet no fire burned within its hearth.

Odd. It feels so warm.

To Meera's right were two large windows covered in thick green curtains blocking out the light. Curious to see where she was, Meera pushed aside the cloudiness in her head and climbed down from the bed. After steadying herself from a dizzy spell, she quietly padded over to one of the windows. She was surprised to find someone had dressed her in a clean nightshift. One made for someone slightly larger than herself. A giant youngling, perhaps?

If the room had come as a shock to her, it was nothing compared to what she saw *outside* as she peeked out through the curtains. Two, maybe three stories down from where she looked, ornate gardens decorated a generously large courtyard filled with flowing fountains and a wide array of colorful flowers.

Blommamoad flowers, Meera realized with a start. Wherever she was, it was somewhere that didn't receive the harsh bitter winds of the higher altitudes. Thinking of the snowy Cassias brought her a reminder of her companions, so she left the window, tiptoed over to the room's door, and slowly pulled it open. It led out into a sitting room area, dressed as elegantly as the interior of the room she woke up in but void of anyone in it. Another three doors lined its walls, one of which held a set of heavy double doors.

I bet my best arrow that's the way out.

But Meera wasn't ready to bolt for the exit just yet. Hoping her guess wasn't wrong, she snuck across the sizable sitting room to one of the smaller doors. Sending a quick prayer of thanks to Yveth for the doors not squeaking, Meera poked her head into the room. While hers had been decorated in rich greens, everything in this one was blue, save for the tuft of dark green hair sticking out of the sheets. It took longer than she expected to wake Katula, but at long last the Matuian began to stir.

"What's going on?" she demanded groggily.

"Shhh!" Meera replied, putting her hand over Katula's mouth. "I think we've been drugged, so you may feel a bit dizzy..."

Before she could finish, Katula sat up too quickly and clutched her stomach with a moan. "I don't feel so good," she mumbled. "Where am I?"

Meera spotted a pitcher of water by the bed and poured a glass for Katula. "You're not going to believe this..." She smiled excitedly. "I think we're in *Pawtoton*."

Katula's brow wrinkled as she took a drink. "What? How?" she whispered back in between sips.

"You tell me," Meera replied, "you're the one with the black eye. The last thing I remember was Darmond singing some song about Moordew, then I woke up here. What happened to you? How'd we get here?"

A shadow fell across the Matuian's face as she gingerly fingered her bruised eye.

"Do you remember anything?" Meera pushed.

"That and a *lot* more," Katula said hesitantly before switching the subject. "What about Darmond? Have you found him?"

"No, but your door was the first I tried and there's another out there." Meera helped Katula until she was steady enough on her feet to go explore. Sure enough, the third door led to a room decorated in yellows, where the Midtierian lay snoring in bed. It took them even longer to wake him, but once he came to, he bolted upright, fists in the air. Both women jumped back out of the way.

"Giants!" he growled with his eyes narrowed.

"Shhh!" both women hissed in unison.

Blinking away the fog of whatever they had been dosed with, Darmond slowly lowered his fists and looked around his room. "This doesn't look like a giant's den. Where the rot are we?" he demanded. Then he looked down. "And where in *Nihility* are my clothes!"

"Meera thinks we're in Pawtoton," Katula replied. "And judging by the size of the furniture and rooms, I'd say that's an accurate assumption."

"*Pawtoton*? You've got to be joking," Darmond sighed, while awkwardly tucking his covers around his waist.

"No," Meera chimed in, "no joke. And wherever we're at, it's a *grand* building, at least three stories high. I saw it from my room's windows. I haven't seen anything like it since I was a youngling. There's a massive courtyard with gardens and fountains below."

The man let out a low chuckle and rubbed the back of his neck. "Giants with a flair for ornamentation," he mused, shaking his head blankly. "Why not? Everything else on this trip has been just as... unexplainable." His blue eyes darted Meera's way and she didn't miss the wariness behind them. She remembered the argument between them when they had come across the dead end and wondered if he was still upset at her.

"I don't understand how we ended up here, though," Meera said, trying to move on. "How did you two get black eyes?" Darmond's face fell as he exchanged glances with Katula, and this time Meera couldn't ignore it. "*What*?" she said flatly. "Both of you have a look. What's going on? *What don't I know?*"

"You don't remember anything about the night we camped at the dead end?" Darmond pushed uneasily.

"I remember the argument," Meera admitted. "Oh, we had more of that good tea, now that I think about it. And Darmond sang a song, right? Yes, it's coming back to me now. The last thing I remember was finishing the tea and going to bed." No sooner were the words out of her mouth that a memory surfaced. Meera went quiet and sat down on the edge of Darmond's bed.

"Meera? Are you all right?" Katula probed.

"I remember dreaming," she whispered hesitantly as the memories of her younglinghood came flooding back. Painful memories. Memories of the night the massacre took place. But there was more stored in her mind than just her past. Visions of a frighteningly large beast in the snow began to return.

Signot had called out to her in her dreams. Meera had found him dying in the snow, his blood everywhere. She remembered *feeling* the presence of what had attacked him before she saw it, a hunter, dangerous and hungry, lurking in the shadows. Something within her instinctively knew the beast had attacked the tonga in order to lure *her* outside. Rage over discovering its devious plot ran through her. It had felt as if her blood were boiling on the inside.

But it wasn't just the anger that had run through her. It was something... *impossible*. Her veins had begun to *glow*. All sounds and happenings outside of herself had faded away as she had turned to face the beast that hunted her. It, too, knew she was aware of its intentions, but it refused to back down now that its prey was out in the open. As it had stepped out from the shadows, Meera remembered feeling her blood turn to liquid fire. The heat of it had been so intense, she had begun to shake under its pressure. When the beast charged for her, the energy within rose until she felt as if her body would explode like a sage's experiment gone wrong. She remembered realizing the snow around her had begun to melt, turning into droplets that gathered at her feet, as if the water had been *drawn* to her. And somehow in those brief moments, Meera had known, without any doubt, it was. The water had obeyed her will.

Just before the beast's massive jaws sunk into their target, Meera had lifted her hands and *propelled* the water outward. The impact between water and beast was so shockingly violent, it took her several moments to remember to breathe in the aftermath. But when Meera did finally remember and she gasped in fresh air, the energy flowing through her was almost too much to bear. She had felt so *alive*, buzzing with energy, yet numb to everything else, until her eyes fell on Signot. Just as surely as she knew the water had been hers to command, Meera knew she had somehow healed the tonga of its wounds. That was when she remembered her human companions and turned to see their faces staring back at her in terror. Not because of what the snow beast had done, but because of what *she* had done. After that, everything went black.

"Meera?" Darmond called softly, rousing her from her memories.

The concern in his voice pulled her back to the present, but she didn't want to look either of them in the eye. She didn't want to see their looks of terror ever again. "Signot," she whispered, already knowing the answer. "Did he survive?"

"His wounds were... They were completely *healed*, Meera," Katula replied, uncharacteristically unsteady. "It was as if they'd happened moads ago. *How?*" she breathed. "How did you do it? How did you do *any* of what you did?"

The fear and uncertainty reflected in her companion's words mirrored her own. She couldn't blame Katula for feeling that way, but it hurt, nonetheless. "I don't know," she admitted at last. "I don't know *how* I did it. I just... did. It felt almost instinctual. I can't explain it."

"It's happened before, though, hasn't it?" Katula pressed, crossing her arms. Begrudgingly, Meera nodded.

"I think so, with that white hawk, Tymmon."

"Tymmon?" Darmond repeated.

"I gave the Moorland hawk I kept seeing a proper Moorlander name. He was the one that alerted me to the Grendolens while we were in Vardia."

"I *knew* something else was going on when that happened," the Matuian narrowed her eyes.

"A bird told you they were coming," Darmond stated flatly.

"I know it sounds ridiculous. *Absurd*, even! I'm as confused as you both, trust me," Meera pleaded, before growing more serious. Her voice faded to a slight whisper. "And it didn't just happen in Vardia." She took in a long breath before continuing. "Tymmon came to my rescue back in Matui. Remember the Grendolen soldier with the mauled face? He fought her off long enough for me to grab her sword and use it against her."

"The bird fought with you?" he asked, looking bewildered.

"He somehow *knew* I was in serious trouble. I thought I was imagining it at first. I thought I was losing my mind. That was the first thing that happened that made me wonder. And your tonga," Meera said to Katula. "He was the one who helped me find you both after the avalanche. Without him, I'm sure I would never have been able to locate you in that whiteout." Meera thought about stopping, but she was on a roll, and *rot,* it felt good to get it all out. "There's more."

Katula raised an eyebrow but nodded for her to continue.

"You'd fallen off your mount during the avalanche and hit the back of your head against a tree," she explained to the Matuian. "There was so much blood, I thought you were dead. I... I didn't put it together until now, but when I went to clean your wounds, there were none."

"You *healed* me," Katula realized, aghast. Meera nodded hesitantly.

"I think so," she admitted.

"I had my suspicions after the avalanche. I remembered hitting my head but didn't have a wound. I thought perhaps I'd just hit my head too hard and dreamt it up. And you took so long to wake up afterwards."

"Your wound," Darmond suddenly remembered, "the one you got in Matui. You said it healed a lot faster than it should have."

"That's right," Katula agreed. "I knew the salve would help keep away infection, but when we looked at it again, it was almost healed. Now it makes sense. You healed yourself somehow."

"Well, it doesn't make sense to me," Meera retorted. "I don't know how I'm doing *any* of this. What's *wrong* with me?" Meera realized her hands were shaking, and she clasped them together to try and make them stop. Neither of them responded to her plea. How could they? None of them knew what was happening to her.

It was a long while before Darmond finally spoke up. "I think it's time we say what's on everyone's mind."

"You think *I'm* the weapon, the Stone Key that Lord Agnarr is after." A knot formed in Meera's stomach as Darmond nodded solemnly. Somewhere in the back of her mind, she realized she'd been wondering the same thing. What else could it mean?

"It's the only explanation that makes sense of all this," Katula noted gravely.

"What does it mean, though? How dangerous *am I*?" Meera pleaded, trying to hold back tears.

"I don't know," Katula admitted. "But let's not jump to any conclusions until we know more."

"What do you propose we do, then?" Darmond questioned.

"Against all odds, we now find ourselves in the exact place we were hoping to end up," the Matuian noted. "If my grandmother was right, and the giants possess large libraries, then perhaps those same libraries will hold the answers to some of the questions we have. Perhaps we can talk our way into touring them and getting a better look at their contents."

"By now the Pawtotons will have had plenty of time to go through our personal belongings, which means they've locked eyes on your people's scroll. I'm no expert, but even with one look at it, I could tell it was old—*really* old. They'll have questions of their own we don't want them getting answers to," Darmond warned.

"No doubt they've found the scroll and the Elements," Katula agreed. "I would even go so far as to say the reason they had us drugged was to give themselves more time to investigate our belongings. But that's why I made this journey, to request their help in keeping the Tercara Scroll safe."

"Our belongings aside, what about Signot and the other tongas?" Meera asked worriedly.

"I'm sure they're being taken care of," Darmond assured her.

"What do you think they'll do with *us*?" she wondered aloud.

"If they only wanted our possessions, they wouldn't have taken such great pains to bring us here and put us up in this grand place,"

Katula noted. "I think Darmond is right. Their curiosity has been piqued by what they found going through our things. They want answers just as much as we do, so we use that to our advantage."

"Agreed, but like you said, the want for answers will go both ways," Darmond cautioned. "If they were to find out what Meera did..."

It pained Meera to see the Midtierian unable to finish the sentence, but she knew he was right. What would the giants do if they found out?

"Don't worry, Meera," Katula said, seeing the concern on her sister's face. "That information stays strictly between the three of us."

Not long after they ended their discussion and turned their attention to investigating their rooms, a knock sounded on the sitting room's large double doors, ushering in their first glimpse of a Pawtoton giant. She was easily twice as tall and wide as Meera and came bustling in with a hurried expression on her unusually pale-skinned face.

"May I be the first to extend to you each warm salutations," she greeted them hastily, making a point to give them a quick grin. "My name is Reyna Osberry. You may refer to me as Matron Osberry. I am the manageress here at the Residence. You find yourselves the favored guests of our Esteemed Supreme Sovereign Matriarch Ayris Pagor Hilderman Fielder the Third, most blessed ruler of Pawtoton."

All three companions stood there for a moment, eyes wide. The giant wore what looked to be a uniform consisting of a bodice and long skirt dyed deep red and lined with rich embroidery and kept her snow-white hair twisted up in an immaculate chignon. She was the complete *opposite* of what any of the myths and stories described. She was also in quite the hurry.

"Have you no thanks to impart?" she demanded, taken aback by their stupor. "It really is *quite* an honor. No Lowlanders have ever set foot before in Pawtoton, least of all within the Residence's walls."

"Our apologies, Rey...," Katula began.

"Matron Osberry, if you please," the giant cut in curtly.

"Of course, Matron Osberry," Katula repeated flatly. Meera tried not to smirk, but it wasn't easy. "I am Katula, daughter of Matui's chief, granddaughter to our sage, and sagen to my people. These are my companions, Meera, also of Matui, and Darmond of Midtier." Without missing a beat, Katula had kept Meera's identity secret, and thankfully, neither she nor Darmond reacted to the change. "You will accept our deepest apologies for our reactions. Until this point, we were unaware your people even existed. It is a lot to take in."

Despite Katula's usual curtness, her words seemed to please Reyna, who nodded in understanding and waved her hand around the room.

"The grandeur of the Residence *is* enough to impress even the wealthiest of dignitaries among our kin, yet as being Lowlanders accustomed to more humble means, it must truly be a life-altering experience indeed."

Darmond let out a snort and Meera could practically hear Katula's blood curdling next to her.

"Life-altering, yes," Katula echoed coolly.

"Excuse me, Matron Osberry, but can you please tell me where our tongas have gone? Are they all right?" Meera asked.

"They are being seen to with the utmost care, I can assure you," the giant replied with an air of offense. A chime sounded in the room distracting them from the bizarre conversation.

"What is that?" Darmond asked, pointing to the round device with numbers on the room's fireplace mantel.

"That is a reminder that I am out of time to explain what a clock is and how it functions," the giant said hurriedly. "We have exactly one hour to get you ready for your appointment before the honorable sovereign and high council, and judging by the state the three of you are in, we're going to need every single minute to accomplish the task."

"We're going to see a... *queen*?" Meera stammered, still getting used to the idea that giants didn't wear loincloths and chew on the bones of younglings. Well, at least the loincloth seemed to be a myth. Eating bones was still up for debate.

"Esteemed matriarch," Reyna corrected. "And it was she who requested your presence, so you must not delay. My, my! Two honors that have never before been bestowed upon Lowlanders such as yourselves," she tsked aloud as she pulled on a long, braided cord by the wall. "It will be the talk of all Pawtoton for cycles to come." In moments, a group of servants dressed almost identically to Reyna and all with the same pale skin and white hair came bursting through the suite's doors.

"Before you governs the most esteemed and just ruler who presides over the Great Creator Yveth's chosen and ordained Preservers, that which reside in her gifted and protected land of Pawtoton, the honorable Sovereign Matriarch, her Supreme Majesty Ayris Pagor Hilderman Fielder, of the great and noble Fielder House."

Meera and her companions cast glances at one another as the long and drawn-out introductions were bellowed out before them. The words spoken reverberated loudly across the polished stone that neatly covered the walls, floors, and massive pillars lining what Reyna had referred to as the High Council Chambers. The high council members themselves stood silently in the shadows, staring at them from both sides of the room, but it was the sovereign, seated on a throne set on a platform directly before them, that had captured their attention. Ayris Pagor Hilderman Fielder held their gaze with an intensity Meera found difficult to ignore. She, too, had the same snow-white hair and pale skin, as did every giant in the room. Deep age lines creased around her icy gray eyes as the sovereign studied the "Lowlanders" from above with fierce scrutiny. Despite the matriarch's many cycles, it was obvious her mind was still sharp as a Matuian arrow tip. Meera took in the grand hall in silent wonder until her eyes paused on something familiar.

"Katula, look at that symbol," she whispered excitedly, nodding to the banners that hung on both sides of the sovereign's throne. Katula's black eyes went wide in recognition. The symbol displayed was none other than a Wildfire flower with its base connected to a tied scroll. The giants, it seemed, had knowledge of not only the Ancients, but of their symbol, a Wildfire flower.

"Looks like we've come to the right place," she quietly replied.

"My Supreme Sovereign," a well-dressed giant continued, "today, that which is the thirty-first day of Regnamoad, in the Tersaith Cycle of 3131, are approached by three persons of Lowlander descent who, through your immensely generous nature, were temporarily pardoned of our most just law of No Admittance, brought within our sacred boundaries, their wounds tended to and mended by our most highly trained healers, and provided stately accommodations within your very Residence, have humbly come before you to request your audience."

Meera could tell by the hard look in Katula's eyes that she wasn't the only one feeling belittled. The way the giant had worded it made it sound like they had requested they see the sovereign in order to thank her for drugging and abducting them. She also wasn't sure what the No Admittance law was and she certainly didn't like the sound of it being "temporarily pardoned" either.

On the throne, the elderly sovereign gave the man a slight nod, indicating she accepted the "request." The speaker then turned to them. "You have been given permission to speak with our most Esteemed Sovereign Monarch. When addressing her, you will preface your words with *Most Supreme Sovereign*. Please signal if this command is understood."

Knowing they had to play along in order to find the answers they needed, all three nodded. Seeing their response, he stepped back from them, bowed to the sovereign, and took up a standing position nearby. The Most Supreme Sovereign took her time looking her guests over before finally addressing them.

"Not for over a thousand cycles, have any of my predecessors allowed a Lowlander to pass into our sacred lands. I, however, being of a generous spirit, have allowed in *three*." An excited murmur rose up from the high council members. "As a courtesy for bestowing the privilege you have taken advantage of, I would have your names and the true reason for trespassing on our borders admitted before this high council."

Meera wasn't sure whether it was the way the sovereign worded her demands, the constricting bodice Reyna had dressed her in, or a combination of both that caused her to squirm in place. Whatever the reason, she was glad someone else other than herself spoke first.

"I am Sagen Katula of Matui, daughter of Chief Usoti, who rules the seven sacred villages of the Matui Tribe, and granddaughter of Matui's sage, master of the Elemental arts." Gone was any hint of unease or intimidation from Katula's face. With an air of the same pride, Katula stared down the sovereign as an equal, no doubt purposely omitting the giant's title in her address. Several audible gasps had arisen from those in the room at the mention of the Elements, but the sovereign herself did not respond, so Katula continued. "You charge us with trespassing on your borders, yet you took no pains to mark them, thus warning travelers of their existence. You praise yourself for giving us such honored accommodations and yet you drugged and abducted us against our will. You hold our belongings hostage, yet insist we owe you our deepest gratitude. After the insults you've thrown at us in the short time we've been cognizant, I'd say it is you and this high council of yours who owes *us* an apology, a thorough explanation of your misconduct, and the immediate return of our belongings."

A massive grin spread across Darmond's face as he gave Katula a nod of respect.

The high council, however, were anything but amused and thrown into a frenzy of anger until the sovereign motioned for them to calm down.

"It seems our intentions have been lost in translation," the sovereign replied coolly once the whisperers in the chamber dissipated. "Your reaction is not unexpected. As a point of fact, it was calculated you would assume as much, as you are of Lowlander descent and are therefore unaccustomed to the more civilized culture of the Pawtoton people."

Katula opened her mouth to fire back a heated reply, but the sovereign pushed on.

"When our guards came across your camp, they could only assume you had picked that location because you were unaware of its dangers. Death's Doorway, it was once called by the mountain men when they roamed our people's ancient ruins. It is home to the Night Hunters, great and fierce beasts who use the terrain's impasse to capture their prey. You must know this, as the remains of one were found scattered among the place. Although, how you managed to take down a beast of that size remains a mystery. Nevertheless, your company of three was already down one member, who, upon our inspection, was found to be unconscious, and the two of you remaining were weak, dehydrated, and near collapsing from exhaustion when we found you.

"We could have left you there, let the other Night Hunters who were eager to avenge their fallen kin finish you off. Instead, we showed mercy by taking you in and nursing you back to health. The medicines that kept you sedated were only to ensure your own safety, none of which was done under the lock and key of a cell. Your belongings *were* taken, but only because had we left them in the impasse, they would have been ransacked by the Night Hunters and destroyed. So, I will ask once more, what is your true reason for seeking us out?"

Maggots and rot, she's good! Meera had thought Katula's response would have left the sovereign speechless, but the giants' leader had effortlessly turned things back on them. Seeing the conversation would go nowhere if some truths weren't given, Katula relented. *Slightly*.

"On the 16th of Lyfmoad, an armada of Grendolen ships was spotted off our coast, bearing an army ten thousand strong. Knowing we could not hope to hold back such a force, my father gave the order for our people to evacuate. We three fled Matui and arrived in Vardia, a small trading town on Ismoad Peak, on the 6th of Regnamoad, where we were able to send word through carrier pigeon to Midtier, in hopes of seeking an alliance and gaining the numbers we need to push back the Grendolens once and for all."

"Am I to believe the sole purpose of your journey was to secure a Midtierian alliance?" the sovereign charged.

Katula faltered slightly, casting a glance at Meera. Knowing the Matuian was wondering just how much she should reveal, Meera shrugged indicating surrender. *Might as well tell her what we came here to say*, her look said.

Taking a deep breath, Katula launched into it.

"As I told you, I am sagen to my people. I come from a long line of Matuian sages, dating back over three thousand cycles. No doubt, after inspecting our belongings you have come across several things of great value to my people. One of them is what we refer to as the Tercara Scroll." At this, gasps from the high council members erupted from all sides but Katula ignored them. "It was the Ancients themselves, Yveth's god-kin, that bestowed the honor of safeguarding the scroll to my people, and in return, educated our sages in the Elemental arts."

More cries of alarm sounded, this time requiring the sovereign's servants to hush the crowd in order for Katula to continue.

"You will have found the Elements within my possessions, as proof of what I have said. As guardians of the Tercara Scroll, we could not allow it to fall into the enemy's hands. It was our sage, my grandmother, who gave me the task of seeking out Pawtoton, where she hoped you would extend the courtesy of safeguarding our most precious relic within the vast libraries you are rumored to hold." While Katula's admission seemed to shock the council members, the sovereign looked unshaken.

"There was another item found in your belongings you still have yet to account for," the ruler pushed. Katula cocked her head, confused, so the sovereign added, "A red flower." Meera watched as understanding flooded the Matuian's face. It was the Wildfire Katula had picked back on the plateau after they had survived the avalanche.

"We came across the flowers growing on a plateau, nearly buried by snow in the highcaps of the Cassia Mountains."

"Our guards witnessed them in bloom when they found you on Death's Doorstep." That was news to Meera, but it was clearly not to Darmond and Katula by the looks on their faces. "Do not pretend you are unaware of their significance, Sagen Katula, as I suspect you know very well they are Wildfires. Their discovery has been the forefront of discussion since your fellowship was rescued. There has not been a reported sighting of one for over three thousand cycles."

"Not since the Ancients left Tersaith," Katula cut in with a curt nod. "Three millennia, and then suddenly they appeared. It is a sign I did not think should be ignored, which is why I kept one, in hopes of studying the find further. That," concluded Katula, "is a faithful narrative of why we stand before you today."

The sovereign cocked a white eyebrow in disagreement and turned her attention onto Meera. "The Matuian named you as one of her own people. However, it is easy to see you are not of Matuian blood. Your name has roots in Moorland, does it not? And yet, there's not a soul in Pawtoton who does not know about what happened to that ill-fated kingdom."

All eyes turned to Meera.

Rot.

Unbidden, she remembered something Darmond had said during one of his long-winded spy stories along their journey. *If you sew in enough truth, they'll blindly accept the false threads weaved into the story.* She'd have to reveal her identity in order to overshadow what she didn't want the giants to find out.

"Meera Tarmanon is my rightful name. I am the only surviving heir of Hathmoor and Torma Tarmanon, the last reigning monarchs of the Kingdom of Moorland." Another round of gasps sounded throughout the large room. "I sought refuge with the Matuians, who took me in after the massacre of my people, and have lived among them ever since. When the Grendolen armada arrived, I gave Chief Usoti my promise to protect Katula during her journey to find Pawtoton and request the safekeeping of the Tercara Scroll." As soon as Meera mentioned the scroll, the council's anger rose again.

"As you see, the explanations you two have provided takes my own people by surprise, as what you say is quite impossible on two accounts," the giant's leader explained. "Firstly, within the vast libraries you correctly assumed we hold, sit multiple records of Moorland's Tarmanon line. You in no way resemble their lineage."

"Told you," Darmond whispered to Meera flatly.

"The Tarmanon line had green eyes and brown hair," the sovereign continued, "which you clearly did not inherit. Secondly, and most importantly, the entirety of Pawtoton's existence is due to a promise our *own* people made to the Ancients, back when they roamed this terra. We are the *Preservers* of its history, Sagen Katula, the guardians of all its knowledge, and as such, we have in *our* possession the only four Tercara Scrolls ever to be scribed by the Ancients themselves. It is *we* who were given them in exchange for the Ancient's knowledge of the Elemental arts. The scrolls and Elemental knowledge are *exclusive* to my people."

Meera turned wide eyes to Katula, who'd gone almost as pale as the giants. The Ancients gave them *four* Tercara Scrolls in exchange for knowledge of the Elements? It was the same exact legend the Matuians held about their own scroll.

"I *am* Meera Tarmanon," she eventually replied, "and I can prove it." Meera untucked the large pendant that she'd kept hidden against her chest and held it high for all to see. In the light reflected off the chamber's interior, the polished octagonal green crystal, wrapped protectively around a white Moorland hawk's wings, shone bright for all to see. "This belonged to my mother, Queen Torma Tarmanon," Meera stated, "and has been passed down to each of the Moorland rulers for countless generations. Upon my parents' deaths, it passed to me."

"She *is* the heir," Katula insisted. "I was there when Meera was found on our borders and brought before my father. I was a youngling, like her, but her appearance I'll never forget. Her clothes were scorched and bloodied, and she had breathed in so much smoke, our healers struggled to clear her lungs. But through all the healing rituals our sage and elders performed, Meera refused to part with that pendant. It could not be pried away from her. My people may not have seen eye to eye with Moorlanders, but we were versed in their customs. The pendant she wears is an heirloom of the Tarmanon line."

Darmond stepped forward and cleared his throat.

"Your honorable sovereign, you've heard from my companions here, but not as yet from me. I am Darmond of Midtier, and under orders from the Resistance, I, too, have confirmed she is Meer—"

"I am quite aware of the Resistance and of who you are," the sovereign cut in with a wave of her hand.

"Uh... you are?" Darmond stammered, taken aback. "I mean, I know stories of my great deeds have spread far and wide, but I didn't realize—"

"Must I repeat myself? We are the *Preservers* of Tersaith's history, Darmond of the Resistance. There is not one thing that occurs on this planet's terra that escapes our notice."

"Yet, you seem quite unaware the Ancients charged *my* people to guard the Tercara Scroll in exchange for knowledge of the Elements," Katula pointed out. "You say you made a similar promise to the god-kin to protect the scrolls in your possession. We have a similar past. It was the illustrations within the scroll I bore here that helped me identify the Wildfire flowers we found."

Protests over Katula's claim arose again from the high council until the sovereign had them quieted down.

"I warn you, what you say borders on *blasphemy*, Sagen Katula. The Ancients made it very clear it was only with our Preservers they struck the pact with. This they accounted for in the very scrolls *we* guard to this day. You must see now, why finding a similar scroll in your possessions, along with both the Elements and a clear knowledge of how to use them, is rather disconcerting to our high council." She let that hang in the air for a moment before continuing. "That, and up to this point you have only provided us with half-truths. Darmond, you may be connected with the Resistance, but seeing as though they think you dead, I doubt you are here acting under their orders." Both Meera and Katula wheeled on the Midtierian in surprise, but he refused to meet their eyes. The sovereign turned to the women. "He failed to mention that to you, did he? And while you two claim your journey to find us is tied to the scroll you wish us to guard, neither of you have yet to make mention of the large Grendolen force that has been tracking you since Vardia."

Rot! They know about that?

"We believe their force to have succumbed to an avalanche in the Cassian highcaps," Katula admitted.

"Curious..." the sovereign mused. "I should have thought admitting the Grendolens were after the heir would have strengthened your argument of Meera being who she says she is, yet you chose to withhold the connection."

Meera took in a slow breath trying to calm herself. The sovereign had known Meera had been telling the truth but had been pressuring them in order to gain more information from them. Meera inwardly chided herself for underestimating the woman. The Pawtotons seemed to know a whole lot more than they should. But *how*?

The sovereign fell quiet for quite some time as she contemplated their conversation, but at long last she spoke up.

"You were right in seeking us out," she said, her tone softening slightly. "The Grendolens' hold on Tersaith has been steadily growing for some time now—a concern, I believe, all in this room share. You may rest easy, however. Our borders cannot be found by anyone but our people, a safeguard set in place by the Ancients that has *never* faltered. I will grant you the asylum you seek. Your company of three and the scroll you bear are safe from the Grendolens while within Pawtoton territory. How long we *allow* you to stay, however, will be determined at my sole discretion.

"That being said, I believe it is of the utmost importance to ascertain whether or not the scroll you possess is in fact a fifth Tercara Scroll, and as such, will be made a top priority for our Preservers to determine. This, of course, will only be done with your permission, Sagen Katula, as you are its bearer and, despite your ill Lowlander misconceptions, we are not thieves. Although, I must point out that it would be advantageous for you to allow us to study it as a courtesy for using our sacred lands as your sanctuary. I also must insist that you meet with our Elementists so that we may further understand just how deep your sages' understanding and practice of the Elemental arts go."

Meera could tell the woman's pretentious nature was getting to Katula, but the Matuian hid it with a curt nod. "Agreed, so long as we three are present during the study of my people's scroll *and*, that we have your word that once research is concluded, *no matter the outcome*, you will relinquish it back into my care."

It was the sovereign's turn to agree, although she looked just as uncomfortable doing so.

"Now that we have at last settled on terms we can all agree on, I will assign to you one of our most highly decorated Preservers to oversee the scroll's research and who will also act as your guide during your stay in Pawtoton."

You mean your spy, Meera thought smugly. With a wave of her wrinkled hand, the sovereign motioned to a giant standing nearby to approach.

"Sagen Katula, Darmond of the Resistance, and Meera *Tarmanon* of Moorland," she emphasized, acknowledging publicly that she had accepted the Moorlander's identity, "I present to you our grand preserver and foremost historian of the Tercara Scrolls we possess, Everard Bookman."

CHAPTER TWELVE

Katula

Despite the giant's obvious role of keeping the sovereign informed of their movements and discoveries, Everard turned out to be much more pleasant to converse with than the manageress, or even the sovereign, for that matter. After their meeting with Pawtoton's leader came to an end, Everard escorted Katula and the others from the High Council Chambers and gave them a tour of the Residence. It was still so bizarre to see a person of Everard's size walking, making sure his pace was slow enough so that her smaller gait could keep up alongside him. Katula found herself staring in wonder at the giant more often than offering her own remarks on their grand surroundings. Not that it was easy to get a word in. The friendly giant, it seemed, was fond of words, and went to great lengths to use as many as he could when talking.

Instead of wearing a uniform like the Residence's servants, he was dressed in an impeccably tailored dark blue vest, matching waist jacket, and crisp brown trousers, all of which were embellished with the intricate embroidery Katula had seen on many of the sovereign's high council members. His white hair was shaved on both sides with a braid extending from the top of his head down to his back. Several bronzium beads decorated his beard, which was forked and braided together at the bottom. But his appearance and size were nothing compared to his incredible intellect and vast knowledge of Tersaith, which became apparent during their extensive tour of the place.

How do the Pawtotons know so much about everyone else on Tersaith when no one even knows they *exist*? Katula wondered. It was the question that had nagged her ever since her conversation with the sovereign, and one she meant to find out the answer to during their stay.

"Here we are at last," Everard announced, flashing a warm smile at the three of them. Before his outstretched arm stood the double doors leading to the suite they had woken up in. On each side stood a new pair of guards staring blankly out at nothing. "Inside, you will find a generous spread of food. After you have supped, Matron Osberry will come to collect you once again so that we can begin looking into the scrolls our people both possess together. Will an hour of time suffice your needs?"

Katula gave the giant a confused look. "We're not used to your... *clocks* yet. How long would that be?"

Everard blushed with embarrassment. "Goodness me! My deepest apologies, Sagen Katula. Of course you are not familiar with them. I will be sharper in the future, you have my word," the giant readily insisted. "Matron Osberry will come to collect you when the short hand reaches the number two and the long hand reaches twelve."

"Two it is then," she said.

As soon as they were in the room and the door closed, Darmond let out a long sigh and flopped down longways on one of the plush couches that decorated their sitting room.

"Anyone else notice the two guards posted outside our door?" he asked with an annoyed tone.

"How could we not? They're wearing armor made out of tonga bones," Meera replied, wandering over to take a look at the food left for them.

"You'd think they'd be hard to miss, wouldn't you?" Darmond said with a yawn. "At least now I know I wasn't imagining things when they knocked us out in the dead end before dragging us here."

"Looks like they've assigned us a spy, too," Meera added.

"Spy?" Darmond mumbled, on the verge of sleep.

"*Everard*," Katula emphasized, catching on to Meera's concern. "He's the giant that gave us the tour just now. We'll need to watch ourselves around him. He's a lot easier to talk to than the other giants we've met so far, and I'm betting that's not a coincidence. They're hoping we'll confess to him whatever it is we haven't told them yet."

A snore escaped from Darmond's direction, bringing Katula to a stop.

"Wake up," she called, throwing one of the many pillows at him.

"*Maggots*, Prickly!" Darmond cursed. "Can you not relax for one moment and let a man get some shut-eye?"

"In case you've forgotten, we've been asleep for the last three days," she reminded him. "We've only got so long to talk before Everard returns, and I for one would like to use that time to figure out what exactly we want to keep from him and what we want to let slip."

Darmond let out another long sigh but eventually sat up. "Fine," he said, rubbing his hand through his dirty blond hair. "But don't expect me to contribute anything cohesive to this conversation until I get some tea in me. That meeting with the sovereign and her high council was enough to do my head in."

"Speaking of which," Meera broke in. Both women crossed their arms and stared down at Darmond.

"What?" he asked, feigning ignorance.

"You're *dead*," Meera pointed out.

"*Thought* to be dead," Darmond corrected with a finger in the air.

"You said the Resistance *sent* you," Katula pushed. "Hard to do that if they think you're dead."

Darmond got up and went to pour some tea left brewing by their food. "My last mission didn't go so well," he said in between sips. The women didn't budge, so he begrudgingly continued. "I was leading a small reconnaissance team across enemy lines. The Grendolens had been pushing hard the last few moads and their tactics showed they were preparing to move deeper into Midtier, only we didn't know when. That was my company's task, sneak into the command tent and make a copy of their latest plans. Only, that didn't happen."

"What did?" Meera probed.

"We were ambushed not long after we crossed into their border. *Someone* alerted the enemy we'd be there."

"A *Grendolen* spy within the Resistance," Katula guessed.

Darmond took a long swig of tea and slowly nodded. "That's the conclusion I came to, yes," he said grimly.

"So what happened to you, to your men?" Meera pushed.

Darmond's blue eyes looked up at them hauntingly. "They died. Every single member of my company was killed in the attack."

"Except you," Katula noted.

"Except me," he echoed bitterly. "I managed to escape, steal a uniform, and pass off as a newly recruited Grendolen soldier. It was just for survival at first, until I could sneak my way back into Midtier. But then I realized the only way I could find out who the spy was that set us up would be to stay and gain some information." He took another swig and then looked at Meera.

"That of course, led me to find out about the plans they had for *you,* Red. I couldn't report back, though. Not with an enemy spy unaccounted for, and I couldn't very well allow Lord Agnarr to get ahold of the Moorland heir. Not with the whispers I was hearing about a weapon you might have knowledge of. So I did the only thing I could do. I went after you myself."

"Why didn't you just tell us this in the beginning?" Meera asked, sounding hurt.

"You already thought I was working with the Grendolens. If I'd told you the Resistance hadn't sent me, there was no way Katula's people would have let me walk out of Matui with you two. Besides," he added, flashing his familiar grin, "I've got a reputation to keep. I can't go blurting out my mishaps to everyone I meet."

"A bit of humbleness would do you good," Katula mused.

"Why, Prickly, was that a *joke*?"

She didn't answer, but the corners of her mouth hinted at a smile. Katula let Darmond assume she believed his words, but the truth was, she'd spent enough time around the man to know the information he had offered up was given too readily. It had the air of being rehearsed. He'd done exactly what he'd been schooling Meera and herself on during their frozen journey over the Cassias: feed someone a tapestry fat with truth and they'll overlook the lies you've weaved in.

Or information left out. Yes, he was still hiding something, that much Katula was certain of. She just wished she knew what it was.

After finishing their rather tasty meals, the three of them sat together in the softly padded sitting room seats, sipping what they all agreed was some of the best-tasting tea they had ever had. Even Meera proclaimed it nearly rivaled Katula's special blend. It was a reminder to Katula that she had yet to confess what she had spiked the tea with.

"I'm beginning to think Pawtoton and I got off on the wrong foot," Darmond said, happily downing the hot liquid. "If their ale is half as good as their tea, I may never want to leave."

"Focus, Darmond," Katula chided. "Accidentally stumbling across the giants' border is one thing; going about finding the answers we need is entirely another."

"Fair enough," Darmond murmured, losing his humor. "And if we're going to do that, we need a better understanding of the information we're after." At that, both Katula and Darmond turned to Meera expectantly.

"What?" she asked, confused.

"I think it's high time you shared what it is you remembered in your dreams," Darmond replied quietly, giving a glance toward the guarded doors.

"It may help us narrow down exactly which answers we are looking for," Katula, gently urged.

"How do you two know I've been having dreams," the Moorlander charged defensively. Katula quickly replied in case Darmond confessed about the tea and ruined everything before they could get the truth out of Meera.

"That night with the snow beast. You woke us up because of a nightmare you were having."

Darmond shot a glare at Katula but Meera was too preoccupied with her thoughts to notice.

"Honestly, I'm not sure if what I remembered will help anything at all," she admitted. "Truth is, ever since we left Matui I've been having dreams. Well, the same dream, really. It keeps reoccurring. But it comes in bits and pieces, and every time I try to put the pieces of the puzzle together, they don't seem to fit."

"Meera, even if it's in fragments, we may be able to help you piece it together," Katula reasoned. "Sometimes just talking through it helps." She had never doubted Natta's abilities as a sage; however, Katula had begun to wonder if too much time had passed in between Meera's last dream and the present. Three days was a long time to go without Meera orally recanting what she remembered. It could be that whatever she had remembered had faded by now. "Here," Katula said, pouring Meera another cup of tea. "My Natta always says a hot drink calms the nerves."

"Thank you." Meera nodded, picking up the cup and cradling it in her hands.

"Why don't you try describing the parts you remember, even if they don't make sense," Darmond suggested.

"At first, I didn't see anything. I just remembered voices... and *smells.*"

"Can you describe them?" Katula pushed. She watched as Meera's eyes unfocused and slipped from the present and back into another time.

"There were screams," she said softly. "Screams and the smell of... of *burning flesh.* Just the thought of that smell makes my stomach turn. I remember I was hiding. There was a large table; I was looking out from underneath it. I was looking for shoes."

"Shoes?" the Matuian asked.

"Yes," she whispered back. "Black boots. I was looking for them, praying he hadn't found me. But it was too late." Tears began running silently down Meera's cheeks as she finally faced the horror of that night out loud. "Mother gave me her hawk pendant and told me to hide, so I did. I never did see his boots when I looked out from under the table, though. I saw *her*. He had *killed* her. She was just lying there, her eyes still open. But she looked too pale and her blue dress had turned red. I disobeyed her orders and left my hiding place to crawl to her even though she had made me promise I would stay hidden. The smoke was so thick, and I remember stifling my coughing so he wouldn't hear me."

Katula watched as Meera subconsciously clutched for the hawk pendant kept safely by her chest. "Mother's throat had been slit. I knew she was dead, and I knew I should be quiet, but I cried. I cried *so hard*. I... I couldn't hold my tears back.

"It was hearing Father's voice that gave me pause. Father was fighting *him*, the one who killed Mother. They were shouting at each other within the smoke and flames. He was looking for something and Father refused to give it to him. Father knew I was supposed to be hiding but he saw me through the smoke and yelled for me to run. That was when I heard *him* shout my name," Meera whispered, her body shaking with pain. "Lord Agnarr. He had *betrayed* my family. *My people.*"

Meera's companions let her quiet sobs run their course without interruption. It had been too long since she had faced the truth, and they weren't about to hinder that.

"I never saw him kill Father," she finally continued. "The smoke was too thick. But I heard his final screams telling me to run. So, I did. Lord Agnarr followed. I could hear his footsteps behind me. I remember tripping over something and crawling. I knew I was somewhere near the back of the feast hall, so I was looking for the old servant's door. But..." She paused. "This is where my memory falters."

Abruptly, Darmond rested his hand on Meera's shoulder.

"I am so sorry," he said softly. "I'm sorry you had to remember that."

Katula shot him an annoyed glance for cutting Meera off but also moved closer to comfort her sister.

"I had forgotten what Mother looked like," the Moorlander mumbled, still surrounded by her memories. "She was so *beautiful*, so *kind*. And Father, he was a strong and noble king. I remember now. They both loved me, so very much." Meera cried openly, then, not caring whether her companions saw or thought her weak in doing so. "All this time I had forgotten what they were like, if they had cared for me, and now I remember. I remember how much I loved them and how much I loved Moorland."

"Those are the memories to hold fast to, Meera," Katula advised, patting her shoulder awkwardly. She had never been one to show physical displays of affection, but Meera's loss was a painful reminder to Katula that she had no way of knowing if her own people, along with her family, had managed to safely escape Matui. "Knowing what happened to your parents *needs* to be remembered, but the good memories are the ones you want to keep close to your heart. In time, they will overshadow the dark ones."

Without warning, Meera leaned over and hugged Katula in a tight embrace. Hugging was not a thing Katula, daughter of the chief and sagen to her people, did. After a few awkward pats on

Meera's back, the Moorlander pulled away and began wiping her eyes.

"Sorry," Meera said through a weak smile. "I'm an absolute mess, aren't I?"

"No need to apologize," Darmond replied, his face holding more concern than usual. "I doubt Katula or I would act any differently if we had to go through remembering what you just did."

A knock at the door interrupted them.

"Looks like our hour is up," Katula guessed.

"Watch yourself with this Everard," Darmond quickly whispered to them.

"Yes, he does seem much nicer than the sovereign," Meera noted.

"He's nice, nicer than any of the other Pawtotons we've met so far," he agreed. "Which is why we need to be on our guard more than ever. Nice people tend to get folks talking about things they shouldn't. We don't want the giants to get wind of what you... er, what you can do, Red. If they found out what really happened to that snow beast... Well, let's just make sure they don't."

The three companions nodded their heads in agreement.

A moment later, the doors to their suite opened and issued in Reyna, who looked just as hurried as ever.

"I trust the meal was to your satisfaction?" She didn't wait for an answer. "I am here to escort you to Grand Preserver Bookman, and we must leave promptly if we are to stay on time."

"Where are we to meet with him?" Katula asked.

"The *Red* Library," Reyna emphasized.

"I don't remember passing any libraries on our tour earlier."

"No, indeed. They are far too large to fit in this humble wing of the Residence. There are eight libraries in all, and each holds an extensive collection. The Red Library itself contains our oldest and most sacred texts. Never before have Lowlanders been given access to its contents."

"What a privilege," Katula mocked under her breath. She knew the truth of it. The only reason the sovereign was giving them access to historical records was because she suspected they were keeping things from her, and she wanted time to figure out what those things were.

They found Everard sitting at the large table in the Red Library surrounded by piles of books, scrolls, and manuscripts he had already gathered for them to review.

"Come in, come in!" his deep voice bellowed. "Matron Osberry, you have my deepest gratitude for escorting our honored guests here."

To Katula's surprise, she saw a blush form on Reyna's cheeks.

"But of course, Grand Preserver Bookman. I am only a ring away, should you need *anything* during your time here," the manageress gushed.

"Actually, now that you mention it, seeing as we'll most likely be at it for some time, some tea and pie might be nice for our guests to enjoy."

"I'll see to it right away," Reyna replied, giving a slight bow. As soon as she left Everard turned to the others and clapped his oversized hands together.

"Alone at last!" he said with a ready smile. "Reyna may seem a bit hurried at times, but I can assure you she's as genuine of a giant you will ever meet! Now, I am sure you all must have so many questions, and I'll be happy to answer them. But first, introductions! *Real* introductions, not the formal ones given to the sovereign. Then tea and pie!"

Katula was shocked to find herself actually smiling back at the man. She never smiled. His jovial mood was infectious. Darmond was right, this giant *was* dangerous.

"Meera Rammel Lavonna Tarmanon," Everard addressed, with a bow. "Let me be the first in Pawtoton to extend my condolences for the atrocities carried out on your homeland. What happened in Moorland remains one of the most difficult modern accounts I have studied and has always brought me grief, although I know it does not compare in any way to your own."

"Uh... thank you," Meera stuttered, taken aback by the unexpected exchange.

"Katula, daughter of the High One," Everard said, surprising her by addressing her formally in the Matuian language.

"*How*... How do you know..." Katula stammered.

"Your language?" Everard interjected with a smile. "I make it a point to know as much about the cultures I study as possible. Although, I admit, my people were vastly unaware your sages studied the Elemental arts. I shall never forget the look on the sovereign's face when she was presented with your satchel's contents," Everard chuckled lightly.

Katula was surprised by his casual comment, but the giant was all smiles.

"I must say, I am looking forward to taking a closer look at the scroll you bear. I had a brief glimpse when your possessions were brought to us; however, I did not wish to trespass and cause ill will between our two people before we were properly introduced, so my initial view was only in passing. We could view it now, in fact. Do you have it with you?"

Katula eyed the giant warily. "I did promise your sovereign you could view it; however, she also swore to allow us to see the ones you possess. Once I am satisfied we have had that chance, I will hold to my word."

"That is quite understandable, my dear." He nodded. Unfazed, he turned to Darmond.

"Darmond, the *spy* of Midtier!" Everard thundered with a grin. "Reading accounts of your interactions on the frontlines is more exciting than some of the best novels we've collected on the subject. And that's saying something, as I've read them all!"

"You've read *books* about me?" Darmond gasped, looking both surprised and pleased.

"Indeed, I have, sir," Everard readily replied. "Your work with the Resistance has been vital to the fight against the Grendolens. While the sovereign may not say it, you have our deepest respect for the sacrifices you have given in service, and I am very glad to see you are alive and in good health, contrary to the latest information coming out of Midtier."

Both Katula and Meera stared wide-eyed at Darmond, unsure what to make of the heroic deeds Everard mentioned, let alone that the giant knew about them.

"Forgive me, Everard, but I don't understand. How do you *know* so much about us? Where are you getting all this information from?" Katula asked incredulously.

Everard let out a carefree laugh. "So many questions, I know, I know! I promise I will answer them all over tea and pie," he said happily.

Katula let out an impatient sigh but took the time to look at her surroundings. Surveying the room, it was not hard to figure out why it was called the *Red* Library. From the soft fabric on the chairs they sat on, to the carpet and curtains, everything was lavishly decorated in a deep dark red.

Gracious, these giants like to coordinate their colors.

The rest of the library was constructed of dark stained wood and housed countless shelves filled with all kinds of histories. Katula found herself growing curious. She had always loved books, especially ones that contained historic tales of the past. When she was a youngling, she would spend ages imagining the lives of those who came before her and how they must have lived. What they wore, how they talked, what they believed in, their day-to-day lives—so many mysteries waiting for her to piece together and solve. The realization that the texts within the Red Library housed records of tribes and civilizations she did not yet know about almost took her breath away.

Seeing her interest, Everard noted, "This library houses the oldest texts we have in Pawtoton. Some manuscripts even date back to the time of the Ancient Ones themselves, although their age requires very careful handling. I have already compiled a few items that reference signs and omens in connection to Wildfires. I thought that would be a good place to begin our study, considering their sudden arrival." The door to the Red Library opened, letting in Reyna holding a large tray filled with food.

"Ah, here we are!" Everard announced with a satisfied grin. "My, my Reyna, you certainly have outdone yourself. This is a lovely spread."

The manageress beamed. "You just be sure to share some with our guests, Grand Pres— *Everard*," she corrected.

Four sets of cups, saucers, and plates with fresh pie were set out for each of them. After the full meal they'd just eaten, Katula wasn't sure she had room for any of it.

"Ring if you need me," Reyna said before taking her leave.

All eyes turned to Everard. "All right, all right!" he laughed, holding his massive arms up. "A promise is a promise." He took a sip of tea and a rather large bite of pie, then swallowed. "*Now*, I'm ready to answer your questions." He grinned.

"Where exactly are we located?" Meera asked right away. "When your guards found us, we were high in the Cassia Mountains, where it snows even in Sumorsol. We must have traveled a long distance to have reached such a warm climate."

"Very clever deductive reasoning, Meera," Everard praised. "However, you are no more than a two day's journey away from that spot and are still within the Cassias."

"But how can that be?" she replied in disbelief.

"Pawtoton is a unique place," Everard explained. "It rests within a protective ring located on the leeward side of the mountain and encircled by cliffs too dangerous for even a giant to climb. You came here by way of the only entrance that accesses the interior, a passage created by the Ancients themselves, that runs underneath the rock and stretches to the windward side. No man comes through it unless we allow it, and even then, those we bring through are blinded and drugged to protect its location."

Which means they're not going to let any of us walk out of here with that information, Katula warned herself. Would the sovereign really put them to the sword once she got the information she wanted? *No*, Katula thought. *She's the type of person who would get her Elementists to concoct an elixir to clear our memories and then drop us off somewhere within the mountains.*

"If you are so cut off from the outside, how is it that you know so much about us?" Meera asked, cutting into Katula's thoughts. "No one outside of Pawtoton even knows of your existence. Giants are a thing of myths, of *youngling's* stories!"

"And yet you sought us out," Everard countered thoughtfully.

"It was a risk we had to take," Katula explained, "and almost gave up on."

"Well, I for one, am glad you didn't." The giant smiled. "The answer to your question is a rather complex one." Several more bites of pie were consumed before he continued. "As the sovereign explained, we were appointed by the Ancient Ones over three thousand cycles ago to be the Preservers of Knowledge. For a millennium we did just that, traversing all of Tersaith, gathering what texts and histories we could find, as well as recording new accounts as time progressed. Most likely, this is where your tales of our people and vast libraries came from. We were known throughout the kingdoms back then. It was during that period, however, we began experimenting with the Elements beyond what the Ancients advised within the Tercara Scrolls left to us. You see, there was once a time we were not as you see us now, with this milky white skin and hair or larger stature. No, in fact, once we were of many shades, as broad a spectrum as those who wander the known parts of Tersaith even now, and of similar height."

"What happened to cause the change?" Darmond asked, happily helping himself to a slice of pie.

"Since our promise to the Ancient Ones there have always been two classes among our people, the Chroniclers, who retrieve and record historical accounts, and the Preservers, who safeguard and study them. As you can imagine, after one thousand cycles, the amount of information we had gathered had grown beyond our natural ability to retain."

"You mean to say you weren't just physically recording history, you were trying to *memorize* it all?" Darmond asked in disbelief.

Everard nodded enthusiastically as he finished his tea. "Exactly that," the giant replied. "Blinded by our passion to expand our cognitive abilities, our Elementists pushed past the limits set by the Ancient Ones. An elixir was created that enhanced our retention capacity far beyond what we ever imagined. For generations, every Preserver took it. Gradually, we began to notice side effects. Nothing serious at first, so we took no heed to the warnings. The elixir's positives outweighed its negatives, or so we thought. So we continued its use, even to the point of administering it to our infants." The giant stopped and shook his head sadly. "By the time we realized our error, it was too late. You see, it did not just expand the amount of knowledge our minds could retain. It began mutating within, more rapidly than our Elementists could control. Not only did it grow our minds, it grew our bodies to *accommodate* our larger minds. It wasn't until our physical forms began to change that we figured out what was happening. Misery's Milk, they called it, the elixir's given name within our records, on the account that its milky color also spread through our skin and hair. Here we are, thousands of cycles later, and its effects have never worn off. We are forever changed." Everard stopped and sat back, letting his guests take the information in.

"How does that explain the more recent knowledge you have about us?" Katula pushed, still confused.

"Only the Preservers took the elixir, the Chroniclers did not," he replied. "When it was determined the changes to the Preservers were permanent, it was decided our people would stay within Pawtoton, and only our Chroniclers, who were unchanged, were allowed to live among Lowlanders."

"Are you saying there are Chroniclers out there wandering Tersaith still making records?" Darmond asked incredulously.

"Precisely!" Everard smiled widely. "Without them, we could not hope to have gathered as much information as we have."

"Look, I've traveled to many places in my time, and not once have I heard of or seen a Chronicler," Darmond countered.

"And you wouldn't," the giant replied. "Outside Pawtoton, the term Chronicler is unknown. They keep to themselves and are very adept at blending into their surroundings. If you haven't noticed them, it is because they didn't want you to." Katula could see Darmond was having a hard time accepting this new bit of information.

He prides himself on his own ability to hide among crowds. It's probably a shock to realize that not only do these Chroniclers do the same, but they've done so right under his nose.

"Everard, if the Chroniclers know so much about Tersaithian history, why did the sovereign and high council know nothing about Matuian history?" Katula asked, remembering the Pawtotons hadn't known their sages studied the Elemental arts.

"Ah, yes." The giant nodded, rubbing his beard in concern. "If you do not mind me saying, Sagen, your people are quite good at keeping to themselves. While Chroniclers are excellent at blending in, none were able to pass off as Matuian traders and cross into your borders. Very little is known about the Matuians. I believe the... shall we say, frustration, you saw within today's appearance before the sovereign matriarch was a reflection of our own pride. It is not easy to admit we may not be the only ones who keep to ourselves at the behest of Yveth's god-kin. But come now!" He clapped, suddenly changing back into his cheerful self. "We've been gathered together to confer about a topic that I have always taken a keen interest in, the Ancient Ones, and there is *much* to discuss!"

Katula found herself smiling back at the giant again and was beginning to realize it was impossible for her not to. But inside, she wondered if the information Everard had revealed about the Chroniclers unable to pass off as Matuians was correct. *Someone* had found out Meera was alive and alerted Lord Agnarr to her whereabouts. Could it have been a Chronicler?

CHAPTER THIRTEEN

Darmond

After enduring an entire afternoon among dusty books and mundane chatter, Darmond was convinced he'd succumbed somewhere along their journey only to end up being tortured in Nihility. It was a far cry from the blaze of glory in battle he had always imagined his end to be. Reading had never been his strong suit. Too much sitting. Not enough *doing*. He was much more adept at dealing with *tangible* objects. Give him a tool, and he'd build a village. Put a weapon in his hand and he'd smite the enemy legions into the Netherealm, eternally lost to the dark void among the stars. Why write words on paper when you can be the one to inspire them? Which reminded him, he should ask Everard to see all those novels written about his adventures.

The meeting with Everard went on throughout the day. The elusive Tercara Scrolls, the ones held in Pawtoton and the one Katula kept, never made an appearance. Trust, it seemed, was hard to come by. At long last, they were forced to halt their research in order to prepare for yet another meal, this time dinner with the sovereign. However, within each of their rooms, a consolation prize awaited them. Seeing the round tub filled with steaming water and bubbles upon entering his private quarters was *almost* as good as spotting the glass of brew spirits sitting on the small table next to it.

Yveth, bless the giants!

He hadn't had a decent wash since he left the Grendolen camp in Midtier, and his own smell was starting to get to him. Wasting no time, he stripped and grabbed the glass. Moments later, Darmond lay back in the tub lazily sipping on a very finely crafted distilled brew while the grime and stress of the past sol floated away. For just a little while, he was content to let Tersaith's problems be put on hold.

From what he gathered during their painfully extended study session, the Ancients were as pretentious as they came back in the day. Why people back then felt they had to use ten times as many words as was needed to say something was beyond him. They were always speaking in riddles and never getting to the point. Thankfully, the giant, Everard, seemed to understand what the passages meant, but even his simpler explanations were sometimes difficult for Darmond to wrap his head around. In the end, they had been left with more questions than answers. Typical. He'd been hoping things would be a bit clearer. *Yes, the Wildfire flowers are a good omen; you've got great things coming your way!* Or, *Seeing a Wildfire means certain death; flee for your lives!* Instead, the manuscripts rambled on about how Wildfires are a sign of the Ancients, which Katula had already concluded. The only new bit of information they had gained was that the Wildfires had died out during something the manuscripts referred to as the Cleansing. But not even Everard knew what it meant, so it left them with another unanswered question to add to their ever-growing list.

Darmond finished his brew, heartbroken there wasn't more, and dunked under the soapy water as his mind switched its thoughts toward a certain redhead. When he embarked on his mission to find the weapon Lord Agnarr was after, Darmond had expected the usual life-threatening situations he always got himself into and was so good at getting out of. But Meera was an encounter Darmond had been completely unprepared for. She was stubborn, hardheaded, and a rotting pain in his arse when she wanted to be. So why in Nihility had he begun looking forward to their witty exchanges? He had even begun finding her constant chatter with wildlife, dare he admit it... *endearing*.

But all that had changed the night the snow beast had attacked. Even now, recalling the image of Meera's glowing figure facing down the beast and tearing it to bits sent chills down his spine despite the hot bath. A deep wariness had awakened in him that he could not shake. How did Meera possess such power? What *was* she?

Since that horrible night, he had been plagued by conflictions. Meera was innocent in all this, that much he knew. But the fact still remained, she possessed powers she didn't know how to control, at least not yet. Meera had gone into a coma-like state after facing the snow beast. What would happen to her if she was forced to use her power until it ran out? Could it? Lord Agnarr would use Meera to conquer the free lands of Tersaith if he got ahold of her.

Darmond wasn't going to fool himself, though. If the Resistance found out, they, too, would use her to fight back the Grendolens. He was also certain that if either side couldn't figure out how to harness Meera's power, her life would be forfeit. You don't let a dangerous weapon wander Tersaith for someone else to figure out how to use it against you.

Darmond had sworn oaths to the Resistance, and up until now, that had felt right. He had always intended to bring Meera back to Midtier and hand her over, hoping she knew something that could aid in their fight against the Grendolens. But things had changed. They changed the night Darmond realized Meera could be the weapon. If he turned her in now, they would use her power until she was all used up or kill her if they couldn't. He was *sure* of it.

All this thinking meant he was at a crossroads. Either he betray Meera and hand her in to the Resistance to be used against the Grendolens, or he betray the Resistance and risk the surrender of Tersaith's remaining free lands to the Grendolen Empire. While he pondered over his predicament, however, his mind wouldn't stop conjuring up images that had recently kept popping up when he least expected them to. Images of a redhead whose laughter put him at ease, whose curved frame caught his breath, and whose lips...

Rot, who was he kidding? He didn't know how it happened, but somewhere along their journey west, Darmond had fallen for Meera. He would *never* betray her to the enemy or the Resistance. She'd hooked him good. Probably used some of that glowing power of hers to do it too. Deep down, though, Darmond knew nothing would ever come of it. Pursuing any relationship was *completely* out of the question. Meera's inexplicable powers aside, she had remembered everything about the night her parents were killed. It was only a matter of time before the full account of what happened came out, and when it did, Meera would know the truth about him. It crushed him to acknowledge it. Darmond blew out the last of the air in his lungs and resurfaced, casting a sullen glance toward his empty brew glass, wishing it was full again.

Maggots and rot, man! Pull yourself together! Best remove yourself from her life as much as possible. Once she finds out the truth, and she eventually will, you'll be glad of the distance you put there. Angry he gave himself such good advice, he banished his thoughts and began scrubbing himself clean until his skin was raw.

A little while later, Darmond was clean and dressed in a new pair of clothes Reyna's crew had left for him. He suspected they were meant for a Pawtoton youngling but had been taken in and let out in certain areas to accommodate his size. It wasn't a perfect fit, nor was the traditional dress of the giants his particular style, but they were clean and not one hole could be found, which was more than he could say about the clothes he had on his back when the giants found him. With his shoulder length hair clean and brushed, and his thickening beard nicely groomed around the edges, he cleaned up well. After the internal conversation with himself earlier, he was more determined than ever to hunt down any details he could about the weapon so he could move on from the mess he'd gotten himself into.

Feeling confident about his mission and the next steps he needed to take, Darmond walked into the sitting room to wait for the others. Katula was the first to emerge, wearing a dark-green dress with light green and white embroidery. It, too, looked to have been a youngling's attire quickly tailored to accommodate a woman's form.

"I don't think the Pawtotons know what to do with my green hair," Katula remarked, her black eyes looking down at what she wore. "They keep dressing me only in green. I look like a walking mound of moss."

"At least you match," he joked. "I think they stuffed me in youngling's *play wear*. I look like a garden plot, all bright colors and flowers."

"Hopefully that tailor Reyna mentioned will be sent soon," Katula confided, cocking an eyebrow and giving Darmond a once over.

The door to Meera's room opened and the two of them turned to greet her, but she didn't emerge.

"Meera?" Katula called curiously.

"I'm here," the Moorlander said flatly, "but I don't want to come out."

"That bad?" Katula replied.

"You know those orange berries they have decorating the vases in the hallways?" Both Darmond and Katula grimaced as Meera slowly appeared at her doorway wearing an intensely orange colored dress that clashed with her red hair.

"I look like I belong hanging off a fruit tree," Meera complained. The sight was so comical, Katula *actually* laughed. Darmond just grinned. It was a *terrible* color on her, and yet there were those lips, looking as tempting as ever. It was the first time he'd seen her with her hair let loose and not tied up or braided. Red waves framed her face, cascading over her shoulders and down her back. He hadn't realized how thick it was. Had her eye lashes always been that dark and long? Ignoring her was going to be harder than he thought. Realizing he was staring, he dropped his grin and left the two women to go look out one of the suite's windows.

"I think we *all* look a little... out of place," Katula conceded, trying to comfort Meera. "I'm so used to blending in with my surroundings, wearing bright colors feels... uncomfortable."

"To say the least," Meera agreed.

A knock sounded on the suite's door, signaling Reyna had arrived to take them to dinner. As usual, she was in a hurried mood but made sure to tell them she thought they all looked wonderful in their attire before leading them down the grand staircases and into the belly of the sovereign's Residence.

Darmond's travels had taken him many places, and in that time, he had seen and visited some opulent establishments, even if he hadn't necessarily been invited to them. Within some of those lavish homes, he had feasted like a king over food and drink, but none of those experiences compared to the dining room that awaited him there. Hung from the ceiling were twelve massive chandeliers, all lit and sparkling. Running along both sides of the grand hall stood rows of tall windows, providing a generous view of the sun setting over the mountains. It was obvious the room could accommodate multiple tables, but only one was set. It was large enough to seat at least twenty giants on each side. On the far end of the table, five plate settings were laid out, two on each side of the table and one at the end. All the serving dishes were made of red crystal and sat on a bright white cloth that spanned the entire table length. Running down the table's center were four tall flower urns, also made of red crystal and filled with white flowers and stems full of the clustered orange berries the giants seemed so fond of.

Reyna left them at the door, where a server dressed in white was waiting to take them to their seats. To Darmond's dismay, he and Meera were seated next to each other, with Katula sat opposite. A few moments after they arrived, Everard was escorted in and led to the empty seat by Katula.

"Ah, I see they've provided you with some evening attire." Everard smiled, flashing his white teeth. He, too, wore something similar to what Darmond had been given, although not nearly as... flowery.

"Yes, very generous." Meera nodded, casting a look at Katula when Everard wasn't looking. Another server approached the table.

"Tonight, the sovereign has requested *red* be served with the meal. Would you like to partake or decline?" the server asked.

"Red?" Meera asked those at the table inquisitively.

"Sap, my dear," Everard explained happily. "Our Wanpa region makes excellent red and blue saps."

"Well then, if it is unique to this area, I should take the opportunity to try it, shouldn't I?" Meera grinned, glancing at Darmond. Had that dimple on her cheek always been there when she smiled at him? He gave a curt nod and tried his hardest not to seem too interested.

"Very good." The server bowed. "Any others that would like to partake?"

Darmond and the others nodded, so the server left to go fetch the sap. Unbidden, fragrant scents drifted his way, and he was enjoying them until he realized they were coming from Meera's direction. Yveth must be having a laugh.

Maggots, where's that sap?

A different set of doors opened, this time issuing in the sovereign, dressed in a bright yellow frock embroidered with green leaves and red, blue, and white flowers. She was led to the head of the table, where the server pulled out her chair and helped her take a seat. Ayris was up in age, but her eyes still held a fire behind their gray color. The moment she was in her chair, the server with the sap arrived and poured for everyone. Everard gave the three visitors a look that said to follow his lead, then stood and held out his glass. Darmond and the others quickly followed suit.

"To the Honorable Sovereign Matriarch," his voice boomed. "May Yveth bless her with a long and peaceful reign." Finishing his toast, Everard took a sip from his glass and sat back down.

Darmond downed the entire glass and looked to the servant for a refill.

"Thank you, Everard." The sovereign nodded, lifting her own glass to take a sip. Then, putting the glass down, she looked at the others. "Tell me, how much progress did you make today on your visit to the Red Library?"

"Not much, I'm afraid," Meera admitted. "The manuscripts we looked through spoke often of the Wildfire flowers and their link to the Ancients, but we found very little on what a sudden appearance of them would mean."

The sovereign looked to Everard for confirmation.

"Indeed." He nodded. "The passages are vague when it comes to interpreting any sign one may take away from it. However, there is one advancement we did make. It was only one reference, but it was not a term I have come across before. In one of the manuscripts it referred to the disappearance of the Wildfires as coinciding with something called the Cleansing."

The sovereign shook her head. "I've not heard of the term either," she admitted, her aged face wrinkling.

"According to the text, before the Cleansing, Wildfires were very common throughout Tersaith. It was only after it that they were no longer seen," Everard added.

"We were hoping to return tomorrow and continue our research with Everard. With your permission, of course," Katula remarked to the sovereign.

The old woman didn't respond right away. Instead, she took another drink of sap and eyed each of her visitors one by one before answering.

"You have it, of course," she said, before adding, "and beginning tomorrow afternoon, Katula, you are to meet with our Elementists, as you promised."

Katula nodded.

"Darmond, we have extensive martial facilities that I think would suit your interest while Katula is otherwise engaged."

Anything was better than sorting through piles of text and it would give him a chance to put some distance between Meera and himself.

"I would be honored to visit them, Sovereign," he replied readily.

"Am I to go with Katula?" Meera asked uncertainly.

"If you would like, you can remain with Everard in the Red Library. After hearing your report today, it seems the answers we are looking for may be harder to find than we had hoped, and Everard has expressed his admiration for your detailed research. Both sides would benefit from any additional time you can spare, don't you agree?"

Meera gave an enthusiastic nod.

It didn't go unnoticed by Darmond that the sovereign had so easily separated the three of them. *Don't let her age fool you. This one's old, but she's still as cunning as a fox.*

The meal was everything Darmond had hoped it would be, several courses filled with more food and drink than he could possibly stomach. It was a welcome change from the stale bread, moldy cheese, and diluted tea they had survived on. The conversation stayed light, switching over to Pawtoton and the towns within it, until at last the meal came to an end and the sovereign bid them good night.

"Well, then my friends," Everard bellowed. "I better be off home and let you all get a good night's rest."

"You don't live here?" Meera asked, surprised.

"No, no, my dear!" He smiled. "I have a home of my own, on the edge of Tawok, the name of the town the Residence is located in. Pawtoton is quite large and has several sizable towns. My area of Tawok, however, is known for its beautiful views of the countryside. Perhaps before all is said and done you three can come visit?"

"That would be lovely," Meera thanked him.

"Wonderful! Tomorrow we'll continue our research and plan the visit then." He nodded, rising from his chair. "Enjoy the rest of your evening, my friends!"

With Everard gone, Reyna reappeared and escorted them all back to their suite. With a full belly and a long day behind him, Darmond found himself rapidly crashing toward sleep.

"Ladies, I'm calling it a night before I collapse on one of those soft chairs," he announced with a yawn.

"That makes two of us," Katula agreed.

"Three," Meera added, also yawning. "See you all in the morning."

Glad to be back in his private room alone, Darmond barely managed to undress before slumber overtook him.

For once, Darmond finally got to sleep in. Breakfast had well passed when he finally managed to pry his eyes open. The first thing that caught his notice was a tray by his bed table with a pot of that delicious Tawoken tea waiting for him.

Unending tea and brew... I could get used to this.

A little while later he was dressed and sipping on his third cup when he finally stepped into the sitting room. He found both women standing by the windows looking out over the garden.

"Good morning," he greeted them cheerfully. His words went unnoticed. "If you're really into formal gardens, I should show you around Midtier. They're quite common in the northwest." Again, no answer. Growing concerned, he walked over and joined them to see what could have caught their undivided attention. Upon reaching the window and taking a look for himself, a world of red greeted him.

"Oh."

"They appeared overnight," Katula explained in a hushed voice. Sprouting up through the Residence's well-kept gardens, stood hundreds, maybe even thousands of blooming Wildfire flowers. The gardens were *blanketed* in red. Darmond pulled his eyes away from the spectacle to glimpse at Meera, who had kept silent. The broken cup on the floor didn't escape his notice either. The worry on her face said what her absent words didn't.

"I'm surprised they didn't wake us up for this," Darmond remarked, turning his attention back to the garden.

"They didn't wake us for breakfast either," Katula noted. "It's almost as if they wanted to keep this discovery to themselves for as long as possible."

"I bet the sovereign had her Elementists out there on their knees studying them since before dawnlight," Darmond remarked.

"It's what I would do if I were in charge," Katula admitted. "There's no reason for Ayris to trust us at this point. We are, after all, the ones the Grendolens tracked through the Cassias. If something like this happened in Matui while unexpected visitors were there, I'd be racing to figure out what was going on."

Again, Darmond noted Meera's silent stare. Something deeper was bothering her. Something more than just the unexpected appearance of the flowers. He was about to inquire if she was all right, when he remembered his promise to himself not to get involved any more than he already had. Pushing her from his thoughts, Darmond forced his attention back on the present.

"If the Pawtotons did find something out about the Wildfires, I bet my good looks the old fox tasked Everard to look into it," he mused.

"What, you mean she had him researching throughout the night?" Katula questioned.

"Exactly. And if he did find something, I guarantee Ayris wouldn't oblige us with what it is they found."

"Perhaps it's time for a heart-to-heart with our new friendly giant," Katula surmised.

Darmond grinned. "Lead the way, Prickly."

In keeping with the Residence's strict schedule, Reyna appeared at their suite precisely ten minutes to ten o'clock in order to lead them once again to the Red Library. Darmond was finding more and more that he was not fond of the time-keeping mechanism. Meals. *Meals* were how normal people should keep track of their day. Morning tea comes before breakfast, followed by a mid-meal enjoyed with an ale, afternoon tea, evening dinner, and a late-night brew before bed. It was a *perfect* system.

As he suspected, Everard was already in the Red Library working on texts that looked different from the ones they had reviewed the day before. *Those circles under his eyes say he's been here a long time already.* Darmond wasn't fond of the sovereign, and Reyna was one scream away from an avalanche. Other than those two, he hadn't really interacted with anyone else in Pawtoton, save Everard. If Everard was the exception, he was glad of it. The giant's jolly disposition had grown on Darmond, even in his short time knowing him. Although he suspected the giant was reporting about them behind their backs, he didn't get the feeling Everard was the type of person to do so unless pressured to.

"Everard!" Darmond called, greeting the giant with a pat on the shoulder, which, even sitting down, came to the same height as his own head. *Rot, I feel like a youngling again.* "You look *exhausted*, my friend. Should we call for tea?"

"Ah, welcome, welcome! No. Thank you, though. I've had several cups too many already," the giant replied with a tired smile. "But don't let that stop you from enjoying some."

"Seems like they've had you working overtime," Katula mentioned unreservedly, as she took a seat in one of the oversized chairs. "Did we not arrive on time?"

Darmond shot her a look warning her to back off. Going full force on someone like Everard was only going to make him clam up and keep his secrets to himself.

"No, no, you are quite on time," Everard replied. "However, there has been a development."

"Oh?" Katula said, trying to look surprised.

Maggots, she'd make a terrible spy. She should leave this sort of thing to the professionals. Darmond rubbed the back of his head and attempted to keep himself under control.

"Yes, indeed," Everard replied, growing serious. "The rest of you may want to take a seat. It looks like we'll be in for another long research session today."

"What happened?" Katula pressed.

"Another Wildfire appearance occurred overnight it seems; this time within the Residence's very own gardens in full sight of the staff," the giant explained.

"Which means word of it will have reached all three towns by now," Darmond noted.

"How come?" Katula asked, confused.

"Large houses like these run on the rumors. I should know, back in Midtier I started quite a few myself." Darmond grinned proudly.

"You are correct, I'm afraid." Everard nodded. "Knowledge of their sudden appearance has spread, and many have taken the sighting as an ill omen. People are starting to panic. As it says in the second Tercara Scroll, 'A seed of fear only sprouts disorder,'" the giant quoted. "The sovereign requested my presence soon after their discovery, and I have been here ever since, trying to locate any bit of information I can about why the flowers would suddenly be appearing."

"Have you found anything?" Meera asked, finally breaking her silence.

"Unfortunately, not." Everard frowned.

Darmond was so used to seeing the giant smile, the frown looked completely out of place.

"But, with you all here now, I'm sure we can make quick time of it." With a clap that echoed through the room, Everard began passing out books and manuscripts to each of them. The Pawtoton Tercara Scrolls were still absent, and he noticed Katula hadn't offered to share the Matuian scroll yet either. They had a scroll stand-off, it seemed. No one was willing to go first.

Darmond sat there blankly looking at the book he'd been given, his mind otherwise occupied. He'd been ready to work his sleuthing skills in order to gain information from Everard, but the giant had given it to them freely, without reserve. He seemed genuinely interested in working with them, despite his sovereign's suspicions. It meant one or two things. Either the giant was naive and trusting of everyone he met and had a natural inclination to spill all, or...

He already knows something, Darmond reasoned, growing alarmed. Enough to trust them with the information he so freely gave. With a start, Darmond realized the giant had employed his *own* advice. Sew in enough truth and they'll blindly accept the false threads weaved into the story. So what was it Everard already knew?

CHAPTER FOURTEEN

Meera

The dream Meera recalled of her younger self fleeing Moorland had continued to revisit her. Each time it replayed in her mind, she relived the horror of her parents' deaths and felt the terror of being pursued by their murderer. It always ended with her reaching the old servants' tunnel, a part of the dream she hadn't told her companions about yet, where another youngling had helped lead her to its secret exit. As much as it pained her to remember what happened, in a strange way, it was also comforting. The dream's reemergence helped awaken the fond memories she'd shared with her parents, something Meera never thought she'd recover. But those good memories came at a heavy price. The trauma of seeing her parents' deaths play out over and over again was beginning to take its toll. Sleep didn't come easy, and when it did, it was fitful and left her waking drenched in her own sweat.

The dream's sequence wasn't always exact either. Sometimes, it would allow her to find the tunnel's exit; other times the musty stone walls would crumble in around Meera and bury her alive, forever in the dark. The times when she did manage to make it out, she was forced to watch the once tall, proud walls of Moorland castle burn until it was reduced to charred ruins.

But on this particular night, the dream did neither. Clawing through the vines and old brush covering the tunnel's opening, little Meera emerged to find a small clearing, void of any fire or terrible screams of the dying. She instantly knew where she was, even though her younger self had never been there. It was the meadow she often visited back in Matui's forest. Through a sooty, tear-stained face, she gasped in awe, overcome with disbelief. Even in the dark of night, its beauty brought comfort to her. She was *safe* here. All fear momentarily forgotten, her little feet padded out into the tall grasses, drawn toward the meadow's center. It was bidding her to come, and she was happy to comply. Why had she been so worried before? The closer she got, the more at peace she felt. A giggle escaped Meera as she began to run, letting the grass tickle her outstretched arms. At last, she made it to the meadow's center and stopped there to look up in wonder at the Watchers, full and in their brightest phases. What had pulled her there?

She looked down at her feet and saw it. One solitary red flower, glowing bright as a candle flame. A Wildfire. Entranced by its beauty, her miniature hands couldn't help but reach down and pluck it from its stem.

The moment she touched it, a searing heat began to race through her veins. Instantly, Meera changed. She was no longer the small, frightened girl that had constantly revisited her dreams, but a woman, whose face shone with strength and determination. Gone was her charred and dirty dress. In its place, she wore a long tunic of undyed linen that splayed into four strips at her middle and billowed around her linen-wrapped legs. Tied about her waist was a dark red sash, the same color as the boots on her feet.

The heat coursing through Meera spread into every part of her until her eyes began to glow. Her skin looked like it was made of marbled liquid fire and felt just as hot. Yet, it caused no pain. All around her, the small meadow was bathed in an orange and red light. *Her* light. Then the meadow began to stir. Meera gasped as she became physically *aware* of every living thing within the clearing. She felt each blade of grass, tree, animal, insect, rock, and even the terra itself *wake up*. And they *rejoiced* at her presence. She could hear them singing of her return.

At the sound of their melody, something instinctual took over Meera. Bending down, she placed both hands on the terra and felt them waiting just below the surface. Thousands upon thousands of the Wildfire seeds were buried underneath. They had been lying dormant all this time, patiently waiting for this moment, and now at last, they could fulfill their purpose. Something deep within Meera's core began to emerge. It expanded until she felt like she would burst. With all the strength she could muster, she willed the power through her hands and into the terra. Then she called out to the Wildfire seeds.

Awaken!

And they obeyed her command.

Meera bolted upright from her sleep. Gasping for air, she looked around the room wildly, temporarily forgetting where she was.

Once her senses returned, she realized she'd soaked through yet another nightshift. Traces of her dream lingered on in the back of her mind. She'd heard sap could affect the senses. How much did she have to drink last night?

Too much, apparently.

Letting out a sigh, she climbed down from her giant bed and headed over to the small bowl and wash bin that had been provided. Peeling off her drenched clothing, she made quick work of washing up and then got herself dressed.

It was too early to ring for breakfast, so she helped herself to a cup of hot tea that had been placed in their suite's sitting room earlier that morning. Still feeling a bit groggy, Meera slowly walked about its large interior, sipping her tea and trying to clear her mind. She tapped at the clock's glass face, opened every drawer she could find, and inspected the craftsmanship that had gone into making the furniture until her cup was nearly empty. *Anything* she could do to take her mind off her dream. Breakfast time came and went but Reyna never showed, nor did Meera's companions rise. Meera's thoughts, however, kept her from noticing. Eventually, long after the sun had risen and copious amounts of tea had been consumed, she made her way over to one of the large windows and drew back its heavy curtains. Meera's cup fell from her hand and shattered on the floor as she let out a gasp. The Residence's garden had been taken over by Wildfires.

She wasn't sure how long she stood there staring. At some point, Katula emerged from her room and came over to inspect what it was that had captured Meera's attention. The Matuian must have read the worry on Meera's face and knew better than to inquire how she was feeling, so they stood there together in silence. Had her dream been more than just the result of drinking too much sap? Were the flowers covering the gardens below connected to those in her dream somehow? She would have laughed off the suggestion if it weren't for what she remembered happening to the Night Hunter only days prior. Just recalling the event made her skin grow clammy.

What if I'm *what the Wildfires are warning everyone about*, she suddenly wondered. Darmond eventually joined them and fell into silence once he realized neither woman wanted to make conversation. Images of the Night Hunter being ripped apart replayed in Meera's mind over and over again. If she was the weapon everyone was looking for, perhaps that was why the Ancients were sending the Wildfires. They were warning all Tersaith of the danger she posed.

Meera's stomach clenched. She felt sick. She didn't want to hurt anyone. Wouldn't a weapon crave to kill? Yet, she hadn't hesitated when staring down the beast who'd harmed Signot. And if she was truly honest with herself, she had *enjoyed* the feel of power coursing through her body when it happened. An involuntary shiver washed over her. She needed answers. No matter what she found out, she had to know once and for all what was happening to her.

Late into the day, well past lunch and nearly at the end of their session in the Red Library, progress was made, though it was not by Meera.

"Everard, listen to this," Katula called, sitting up in her chair.

The sudden sound of her voice woke Darmond with a start, who had fallen asleep with his head resting on an open book. "Mm?" he asked, dazed.

"It's a passage from a manuscript that references the Tercara Scrolls, specifically mentioning the Cleansing," Katula explained. The giants had yet to bring out the actual scrolls they claimed were written by the Ancients, so Katula had also kept hers safely guarded. "Only a small fragment is legible, the rest is too degraded to make out. It reads, '...in the hope that what we record on these pages will not be forgotten and fade out of memory, much like the Cleansing already has; surely the darkest period this world has ever known.'" Katula looked up at Everard. "What do you think it means?"

"I think it means we can now assume the Cleansing held a negative connotation," he replied, his thick eyebrows furrowed with thought. "Whatever happened during that time, was seen as something awful enough for the people of Tersaith to make sure it stayed buried."

Their conversation was interrupted by a knock at the door. Meera looked at the clock on the wall and saw the short arrow pointing to number four. *Right on time, Reyna.* Sure enough, the robust woman opened the door without waiting for a reply.

"I hope you three have saved some energy for the afternoon," she warned.

While Katula looked reluctant to go, Darmond's face lit up. Reyna quickly ushered Meera's friends away from the table and on to their afternoon activities, leaving Meera and Everard alone.

"Well, now." The giant clapped happily. "I hope that you don't mind spending a little extra time here without the others. I know I can be incredibly boring, but the truth of it is, I requested you stay."

His admission caught Meera's attention. Enough to tempt her out of silence. "Why me?" she asked curiously.

"Remember when I mentioned I had read the account of the Moorland Massacre?" he asked. Meera nodded. "My research on it led me to track down more information about your homeland."

"Did you find anything?" Meera questioned, her interest piqued.

"More than I thought I would," Everard said excitedly.

"But the fires... Wouldn't any records have been destroyed?"

"Sadly, many of them were. However, our Chroniclers were able to save a select few before they were burned. Being that they are considered modern records, they are held in the Blue Library. I would be happy to take you there, if you would like to go see them."

Meera's heart skipped a beat. Records from Moorland, *written* by Moorlanders! It was the closest she would ever get to learning about her own people.

"What about the sovereign's orders for me to research the Wildfires with you here?" she asked hesitantly. Everard ran a hand along his braided beard while he contemplated how to answer.

"The way I see it is, if the Wildfires are truly a sign from the Ancient Ones, then the sovereign will get her answers when she is meant to, and no sooner. In the meantime, I have dedicated my whole life to preserving the history of this world. What is the point of housing these records, if the people who are recorded in them can't benefit from their very existence?" The giant laid his oversized hand gently on Meera's shoulder. "I would be remiss to not allow you the opportunity to reconnect with your homeland. After all, as the heir to Moorland, they *technically* belong to you." Everard winked and gave her a pat. "Shall we?"

"Yes, please," she managed with a small smile.

The Blue Library was much different than the Red Library. It had more windows, allowing light to filter in, and it was considerably larger. Where the Red Library had one table, its blue counterpart had *seven* running down a wide central aisle, flanked on both sides by rows and rows of bookcases packed with books, scrolls, trinkets, and texts. Other giants, presumably historians like Everard, occupied the space, some hunched over tables researching, others slowly perusing the bookcases in search of whatever it was they were currently studying.

"Over here," Everard called to Meera in a whisper.

As quietly as possible, she followed behind him as he wove his way through the maze of knowledge. Halfway back on the left side of the room, he stopped by a bookcase where one of the shelves was only a fourth as full as all the others.

"Here we are," he announced quietly.

Meera watched anxiously as Everard gently pulled the shelf's contents out and handed some of them to her to carry.

"Let's find a table for you, shall we?"

Together, with arms full, they walked to the back of the room, picking the last table, the farthest away from the occupied ones. Meera sat down and began looking through the records that had once sat proudly on the shelves within Moorland castle. The maps in the collection were brilliantly illustrated, depicting territory borders, farmlands, and even the layout inside Moorland's stone fortifications. Others were so detailed, Meera could make out the names of streets that had once crossed through a myriad of homes, businesses, and buildings. Then she came across an illustration of the castle itself. It stood proud above the moors, with strong turrets watching protectively over those below. Meera seared the image into her mind, willing away the memory of it engulfed in flames the night she escaped. *This* was how she wanted to remember her home, as it once had been back when she ran through the castle's halls barefoot, playing hide and seek with faces that had faded away from her memory with time.

"Here, look at this one," Everard said, sliding over a volume he had been paging through.

Meera leaned over and took the large book from him. Inside held the recorded lines of succession for those that had ruled over Moorland. "It dates all the way back to the founding," Meera gasped. "Nearly seven hundred cycles ago! Every monarch that ruled is listed."

"All the way up to the Tarmanon line," Everard noted, turning the pages until he reached the right section.

"'Medomon Tarmanon,'" Meera read softly, "'crowned king in T.C. 2922.' What does T.C. stand for?" It was a term Matuians didn't use so she was unfamiliar with it.

"Tersaith Cycle," Everard explained. "We use the cycles to keep a record of time. The current cycle is 3131, which, if I am calculating correctly, means your particular line ruled over Moorland for nearly two hundred cycles."

"3131... over three thousand cycles," Meera mused. "Do the cycles date back to when the Ancients left Tersaith?"

"Ah, right you are, my dear. A very good guess," the giant acknowledged.

Meera turned back to the book and swept her finger over where her father's name was written. "'Hathmoor Tarmanon, crowned king in T.C. 3098.' It mentions mother here," Meera said, showing Everard, "but it doesn't list me. All the other rulers had each of their heirs listed. Why not me?"

The giant cocked his eyebrow, seeming also confused at the omission. "Mm, that does seem odd, now, doesn't it," he replied, taking the book back to give it a closer inspection. "Although, it could be that the heir was only listed in the book after they were crowned. This would have saved the recorder from having to cross any entrees out if they had succumbed to an illness or died before accepting their role." It sounded plausible, but there was something in Everard's voice that told Meera he didn't believe it to be true.

"Your people have been living here since the Ancients left Tersaith, correct?" Meera suddenly asked, changing the subject.

"Yes, we have. Over three thousand cycles," he replied.

"In the seven hundred cycles Moorland stood, it grew quite large. How is it that the Pawtotons have not? I would think by now your population would have far surpassed these protective walls and their boundaries," she noted.

Everard chuckled. "You're quite observant for a Lowlander," he jested. "Remember the account I told you about how we came to look as we do now? It affected us in more ways than just our appearance." A sadness fell on Everard's face, causing Meera to regret asking her question. "Birth rates also declined. To this day, it is rare for a couple to have more than one or two younglings. Many cannot conceive at all."

"Oh, Everard, I am so sorry," Meera replied, putting her hand on his arm. "I didn't mean to bring up such an unpleasant topic."

"Not at all, my dear," he said through a weak smile. "It is the loss of life we have experienced that has made us realize how precious the lives that we do have are."

Meera smiled back at the giant sitting beside her. Just like Darmond and Katula, somehow, in the short time they had known each other, he had managed to push through her self-reliance and become her friend.

"Seeing these," she said, turning her attention back to the Moorland records, "means more to me than you'll ever know. I can't thank you enough for bringing me here."

"It is a pleasure, and *true honor*, to share them with you," he replied genuinely.

For a time, the pair turned back to their reading. How incredible it was to step back into a time before Moorland fell! Meera became so engrossed in reliving the good parts of her past, she was unaware of how much time had passed until she felt a kind of tug within her mind. Lifting her head, she looked around and realized most of the other giants had left the library. She was about to ask if Everard was ready to go, when she felt another mental tug.

"What is it?" Everard asked, noticing her movement.

"You'll have to excuse me for a moment," she replied hesitantly, as she stood. It felt like something was calling to her. *Beckoning* her. Something she'd felt before. Looking around the room, the pull she felt loosened its grip until her eyes locked on one of the library's long windows. Whatever it was that wanted her was coming from outside. Slowly, she walked over to the window, curious to see what it was that was drawing her.

Also curious and a little worried, Everard quietly followed behind. Outside the library's window stood a grouping of trees that held clusters of the same orange berries Meera had seen throughout the Residence. As soon as she saw him, she understood why the pull had felt so familiar.

"Tymmon," she whispered with a smile upon seeing the white bird.

"Is someone out there?" inquired Everard.

"Not a person," Meera replied, grinning. "A hawk."

The giant leaned closer to the window and followed her gaze. "A *Moorland* hawk," he said aloud in surprise. "I've read about them, of course, but have never seen one in person. Nor have I heard of an account of their kind being seen in Pawtoton." Everard looked down at Meera with questioning gray eyes. "How did you know it was out there?"

Meera kept her eyes on Tymmon instead of facing the giant. She scolded herself internally for drawing attention to her feathered friend, not to mention the unexplainable connection she had with it. Once again, she used Darmond's advice and told a half truth.

"I heard it call out," she lied. "It's been following me ever since leaving Matui. I know my memory of my homeland is spotty, but I do remember it was believed Moorland hawks could sometimes form bonds with people. I think this one has bonded with me. He must have, to have followed me this far." In truth, Meera was shocked Tymmon had managed to find her. She hadn't seen him since he had warned her about the Grendolens in Vardia. Seeing him alive gave her more joy than she'd felt in a long time.

I don't know how you found me, Ty, but I'm sure glad you did.

The hawk let out a screech and hopped down onto a lower branch. She got the distinct feeling Tymmon wanted her to come outside.

"Everard," Meera called, turning to face him. "Would it be all right if I go see him? Just for a few moments? It may sound silly, but he's the only other Moorlander I know, and I feel a sort of kinship with him."

The giant smiled and nodded. "Of course, my dear! We have a spare few minutes. We should, however, get back to the Red Library soon, or we'll be missed," he warned. "I don't believe either of us wants to face the sovereign if she were to find out we had been remiss in our studies." With a wink, he led Meera over to the back of the room near their table and showed her a door that led outside.

Tymmon was busy preening himself when Meera walked up under the tree where he sat. The pulling sensation that had tugged at her insides dissipated once she drew close. During her journey that led her to Pawtoton, she had felt a similar connection with the tongas, but it hadn't been as strong as she felt with the hawk. On a whim, Meera decided to test out a theory. Looking at the bird, she tightened her jaw and tried to reconnect the invisible tether that she felt pull at her before.

Nothing happened. Narrowing her eyes, she willed the bird to call out. Again, nothing happened. Letting out a sigh, she sat on the terra and watched Tymmon continue to preen himself, seemingly oblivious to her presence.

Rot. I don't understand! Why can I connect with Ty at times and at other times, can't? Knowing she was running out of time, Meera gave up trying and fell into her old habit of talking to the bird out loud.

"So, where exactly have you been?" she asked, knowing she wouldn't get an answer. "While you've been flying about the mountains, enjoying the views, I've been slowly losing my mind over things I can't explain." Meera took a quick look around to make sure no one was within hearing distance. "Wildfires keep popping up everywhere I go, and I can't help but wonder if they are warning others of what I can do.

"I had a dream last night, Ty. One where I... I told the flowers to grow, and they did. *They did.* Yes, a certain unnamed amount of sap may have been consumed beforehand, but when I woke up, there they were, Wildfires covering the gardens! Was it a coincidence?" Even as she said it, she knew in her heart it wasn't. There *had* to be a connection. The dream had felt too real for them not to be. That burning surge of fire that had run through her in her dream... Meera froze and her eyes grew wide.

That's why the pulling sensation feels familiar! It was the same feeling that she'd felt in her dream when using her powers to grow the Wildfires.

Meera decided to give her test one more try, only this time, she didn't focus on Tymmon. Instead, she thought about the dream, recounting the liquid fire that had coursed through her veins. Instantly, her core ignited like dry tender. The familiar fire began pouring through her, making its way through her body. Staring at the hawk in wonder, she willed it to spread through her, just as it had done in the dream.

Tymmon stopped preening. As assuredly as she'd felt the presence of every living thing in the dream's meadow, she felt her connection to the hawk click into place. Except this time, instead of being pulled to the bird, Meera pulled back. Lifting her arm, she beckoned Tymmon to join her. The hawk let out a loud screech and flew down toward her, landing on her arm. She wore no bracers to protect herself, though, and his talons sank easily through her sleeves and into her skin. The pain was an afterthought. As soon as they touched, Meera knew, even though she couldn't explain how, that they were bonded to one another. Tymmon could sense her thoughts, and she could sense his. And when he spoke, his voice thundered inside her head.

"The big one watches! The big one knows!"

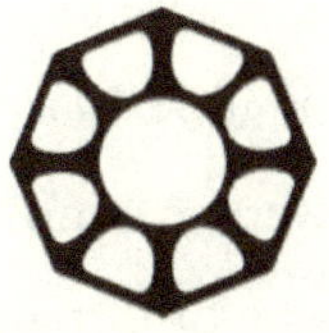

CHAPTER FIFTEEN

Finnik

Several weeks of enduring freezing winds and icy conditions left Finnik questioning whether traveling by sea might not seem as bad as he once thought. He'd taken the time to make sure they'd packed enough provisions before leaving Vardia, so his soldiers weren't without sustenance, but the ill-favored weather had relentlessly battered them raw since leaving. All around him, Finnik's men were showing signs of fatigue, their mounts looking even worse. He'd had no choice in bringing the horses; it was either that or walk, and already they were far behind Varcor Orna. But several had already succumbed to the conditions, and Finnik knew that before they caught up, more would join their fallen kin.

At long last, however, one of his scouts came back with the news he had been waiting for. Orna's camp had been spotted a day's ride from their current location. They were closing in.

"He, too, lost a great number of his horses. My men witnessed several piles of bodies that succumbed to the weather as well," F.C. Han Wesdo reported at the evening's camp.

"How many can we assume perished in the avalanche?" H.C. Baska Sarrel asked with an intense look on her face. She of course had pleaded with Finnik to allow her to come and deliver a swift end to Orna and his followers. All those in attendance had sworn to Finnik again after learning of Orna's betrayal. They knew, just as he did, that if Varcor brought the Moorland heir before Lord Agnarr, they all would share in the shame and punishment. It was their contempt for the man and determination to meet him in battle that had given them the endurance to continue through the Cassias in pursuit, despite the adverse conditions.

"I cannot say for sure. Most of the casualties were thrown over the cliffs, but recent snows made it hard to determine numbers. However," Wesdo added, "judging by the size of their camp, they're in no condition to put up much of a fight."

This was good news indeed. It seemed Varcor still hadn't managed to locate Meera Tarmanon and had crossed paths with a dangerous storm that had wiped out over half his soldiers and mounts, completely stalling his progress. Finnik had originally planned to allow the traitor to find the heir for him and then have him executed, but this information changed things entirely. Finnik had only to surround Varcor's camp, dispense his due consequence, and go after the heir himself once again. It would put him back on track.

"We push hard tomorrow," Finnik announced, having made up his mind. "Make for the pass and reach Varcor's camp before sundown. Let's show him what happens to those who betray the empire."

Around him, heads nodded and saluted, revenge burning in their eyes.

As fortune would have it, the sun shone brightly the next morning, giving good visibility. With an early start, they made good time and reached the pass where more than half of Varcor's soldiers had met their end. The sheer amount of snowfall Orna's men had cleared was staggering. Finnik was impressed. It was a massive feat to manage with such low numbers. Yet, a sizable path had been cleared all the way across the pass and over into a tree-lined plateau where, at last, they spotted Orna's camp. Just as F.C. Wesdo had reported, it was less than half the size of the soldiers Varcor had left Vardia with. In accordance with Finnik's plans, his own soldiers fanned around the front of the camp as they made it across the cleared pass and formed ranks. Finnik nudged his horse forward past his men until his eyes landed on Varcor.

Orna stood outside his command tent and casually watched Finnik's approach. Thick furs now covered his black Grendolen armor, his dark facial hair was matted with frost, and his pale skin pink with cold. All around him, his soldiers were appearing from their tents looking just as ragged and weather-beaten as Varcor. Finnik hoped his men didn't look as bad off themselves. They certainly hadn't lost as many to the cold, but it had hit them hard. His men were all primed for a fight, but now he wondered if it would even come to that. As soon as all his men were in place, Finnik dismounted and addressed Varcor so that all could hear.

"Varcor Orna, as a right bestowed upon my station, Commandant General of the Grendolen Military, by our emperor, Lord Agnarr, you have been hereby found guilty of treason and stripped of your title, Faction Colonel. Surrender now, and I will allow all personnel who accompanied you the opportunity to rejoin my ranks and thus gain back the honor they have lost."

"Mercy, is it?" Varcor mused.

"For your men," Finnik clarified.

"Ah, I see. And what of the Tarmanon heir?"

"She is no longer your concern."

"The problem with you, Finnik, is that you're *too* predictable. That's why a Resistance spy was able to infiltrate your ranks."

Up to that point, Finnik wanted nothing more than to wipe the smug look off Varcor's face.

He knows about the spy?

"It's why you failed to see my coup in the first place," Varcor continued, "and more importantly, it's why you believe you now hold the upper hand."

The hair on the back of Finnik's neck stood. Behind him, he heard his own soldiers dismounting and readying their weapons. A pit began to form in his stomach as he caught sight of movement from behind the plateau's tree line. In disbelief, Finnik watched as hundreds of additional soldiers emerged from the trees.

No! It's impossible*! F.C. Wesdo, had scouted the area, he*... Finnik caught his breath as Wesdo left his ranks and joined Varcor's. Beside him, H.C. Sarell cursed in anger.

"Traitor!" she spat, enraged. "You'll be the first my blade cuts down, Han!"

"Orna proposed a deal I couldn't pass up," Han Wesdo confessed casually.

Finnik just stood there, stunned. It made no *sense*! Finnik had seen with his own eyes the bodies of Varcor's men that hadn't survived the avalanche while crossing the pass. The number of soldiers surrounding the plateau were far more than what Varcor had left Vardia with.

"How?" Finnik breathed to himself out loud. It was then he realized many of those emerging from the trees weren't wearing Grendolen colors but were clad in hooded black cloaks. All this time, Finnik had thought Varcor was out to take over his position as commandant general, but now it looked as if the man had even *higher* ambitions. Had he made a pact with someone *outside* of the empire?

"Varcor, what have you *done*?"

"Done? I've only done what I was ordered to do."

"Who *are* these people? Who have you allied with?"

Varcor cocked his head in what Finnik guessed was a look of surprise. It was hard to tell in one so emotionless.

"You still don't get it, do you, Doth? I really don't know how you managed to hang on to your position so long. You think I've betrayed our emperor."

"What other conclusion is there?"

"What else indeed," Varcor mused. "Above all else, I serve Lord Agnarr. You *know* this, and it is why you never suspected what is truly going on. Or, perhaps you just refuse to acknowledge the truth."

"Say what you mean, man!" Finnik growled, tiring of Varcor's display.

"I am acting under orders from Lord Agnarr *himself*," Orna replied. Gasps from Finnik's men arose.

"*What*?" Finnik recoiled.

"I have orders to bring back the heir, and hereby relieve you of your duty," Varcor clarified. "What did you think would happen after failing to not only capture the heir but allowing so many Matuians to escape their punishment for harboring her?"

Visions of the last commandant general and his family being burned alive resurfaced in Finnik's memory. His whole life had been given in service to the empire. Countless generations of Doth's had served in the Grendolen military. Even as a youngling, Finnik's father had begun training him in the art of war. While other younglings of his station played, Finnik had spent his time learning complex battle strategies and training in martial arts. He knew no other life. He had believed in one thing, the might of the Grendolen Empire. Then Lord Agnarr came into rule and things began to change.

Varcor was right. Finnik *had* been denying the changes he'd seen taking place. He had held on to the hope that the empire would correct Lord Agnarr's shortcomings, that once the ruler was gone and another put in his place, things would be righted again. But here, faced with the reality of his current situation, that faith faltered for the first time. In overtaking Finnik's position as commandant general, Varcor Orna threatened the empire's stability. For how could a people succeed if their own leaders corrupted the foundations within? Before Lord Agnarr's rule, there would have been a process carried out to replace Finnik, should the public feel it was his time to retire. There would have been an order to things. But rather than order it was chaos that Lord Agnarr was fostering. As Varcor's mysterious allies poured out of the woods and surrounded Finnik's men, his anger over what was being done to the Grendolen he had sworn to serve increased. Who else would take a stand for the laws that Grendolen had been built on, if not for him? Finnik was not ready to hand over the reins to Varcor, no matter who gave the command or how outnumbered he was.

"You are a disgrace to the empire, Varcor." Finnik spat. "A man without honor."

"I am a man loyal to my emperor," Varcor countered.

"An emperor willing to sacrifice the laws of his own people is nothing more than a tyrant and is no emperor of mine."

Behind him, Finnik's soldiers stomped their feet in agreement. Varcor, however, looked unfazed.

"And now I have your open confession," he said, smugly. "Treason isn't going to look well on the Doth family, I fear."

Finnik's eyes widened as Varcor's threat sunk in. His whole family would pay the price for the words Finnik had just uttered. But thoughts of his loved ones were put to an end at Varcor's signal.

With the wave of Orna's arm, his soldiers and cloaked allies sprung forward in attack.

Finnik gave no command or signal for his own loyal soldiers to fight back. They were ready and willing to fight for the Grendolen they loved. In one breath they were standing at attention, watching the verbal exchange, and with the next, plunging into the fray, weapons drawn.

Finnik didn't blame them, and he was quick to join in. He knew they were outnumbered and would probably lose, but he'd always wanted to go out with a sword in his hand, and what better cause than for the good of the empire? He just wanted to make sure Varcor Orna went out with him.

Neither one of them had worn helms, but hidden underneath Finnik's furs he wore his light Grendolen chainmail, a habit he had never kicked and one he was grateful for in times like these. No doubt Varcor wore his too. Fighting with a two-handed longsword without head protection, however, was an easy way to get yourself killed, and Varcor took advantage of it by attacking with a bold swing from above, intended to split Finnik's skull in two. Battle cries from both sides rose as the soldiers took up arms and flooded the snow-covered cliffside, clashing together like two dark waves on white shores. Finnik's cycles of training kicked in instinctively, allowing him to parry Varcor's heavy blow from above by using the man's own momentum to block the blade. In a blink of an eye, Finnik pulled his hilt up, intending to bring his own blade down on his opponent's head, but Varcor managed to recover control by punching Finnik in the nose with his pommel. A blinding pain ran through Finnik as he heard his nose crunch, just as he brought down his blade against Varcor's rib cage. Both men staggered back a few steps, attempting to recover. All around them soldiers fought, churning up the snow and coating it crimson red.

"You can't win," Varcor said, through staggered breaths. Finnik could see the blow he had dealt must have cracked a rib or two, judging by the trouble the man was having. Varcor had always been a heavy hitter, someone who ignored technique in favor of inflicting pain on others. Finnik had lost count of the number of times others would report injuries during sparring due to Varcor's lack of restraint. It had taken the threat of losing his position within the army to finally invoke a change in behavior. But seeing him now, the betrayer he was, Finnik knew he hadn't changed at all. Varcor had just become really good at hiding his true intentions.

"Maybe not," Finnik admitted, pausing to spit out the blood pouring out of his nose and into his mouth. "But at least I fight with *honor* and for Grendolen. You fight for nothing but yourself!"

Varcor's eyes narrowed

"This isn't a fight, Finnik," he replied bitterly. "It is a victory! You just don't realize it yet." Varcor lashed out once again, but this time Finnik was ready. He knew how to beat the man; after all, he had sparred and fought with plenty of fighters like him. The trick to fighting a heavy hitter was not only knowing the techniques to take them down, it was knowing how to do them *faster*. Finnik knew that in order to best Varcor, he needed to wear him out until he slowed and let his guard down. With his adrenaline pumping,

Finnik flew into action, blocking Varcor's swing and swiping the tip of his blade across the man's cheek. Blood oozed from the wound, but Varcor seemed unfazed. The traitor struck Finnik with another blow, one he managed to avoid and counterattack, but just barely. A barrage of swings came at Finnik, and after each, he was able to strike back and nick his opponent. Through the crowds of battling soldiers, they fought, circling closer and closer toward the cliff's edge, till at last Varcor started to tire out. He began to swing wider, allowing his midsection to become vulnerable. In his mind, Finnik saw the killing move he could deliver, and in that instant, he took it.

Pulling his hilt up, he dropped his tip and thrust it into the opening, underneath Varcor's armpit. It was the one place Finnik knew there was an opening in Grendolen chainmail. But in his confidence, he had again misread Varcor Orna. The moment Finnik went for the opening, Varcor's exhausted demeanor vanished. He had, once again, deceived him, and like a fool, Finnik had fallen for it. As Finnik lunged with his thrust, Varcor hit the blade slightly with his own, knocking its trajectory off. Finnik's sword passed behind Varcor's back, bringing him within grappling range. Using his right fist, Varcor delivered an armored blow to Finnik's unprotected skull, knocking him down in the snow next to the cliff's edge. The impact caused Finnik to lose his grip and drop his sword, which went tumbling down into the ravine below. Before he could recover his breath, Varcor stood over him and pointed his sword tip to Finnik's throat. All around him, he could hear the cries of his soldiers, some who were still fighting even though it was clear they had lost the battle. Finnik faced the realization that he would join the dead within a few moments, but not before he left Varcor something to remember him by. Staring past the blade at his throat into Varcor's eyes, Finnik managed a partial smile. That was all he could do with a broken nose and possible cracked jaw.

"You think you've won," Finnik baited him, his right hand reaching slowly for his hidden dagger. "You may kill me today and report back to your tyrant, but heed my warning. Those who serve chaos only bring about their own destruction. Chaos breeds what you have become."

"And what *am* I?" Varcor asked, a rare smile gracing his lips.

"A traitor," Finnik shot back, as he hit Varcor's sword away with his dagger and kicked his feet out from under him. Varcor fell to his knees, giving Finnik just enough time to strike, bringing his dagger down on the same cheek he had sliced before. The cut crossed the other, making it look like a "t." Finnik knew he wasn't close enough to sink the blade in the man's throat, so he had delivered a lasting reminder to Varcor of what he truly was. Varcor's retribution was instantaneous. With one hand he knocked Finnik's dagger away and with the other, he delivered a blow to Finnik's head. This time when Finnik's body hit the snow, he knew he would not be able to get up again.

"You think a few scars will haunt me?" Varcor cried, the open wounds bleeding down his cheek. "You have no *idea* what I've had to endure to get here, Finnik." Varcor pulled his clothes away from his neck, revealing a network of old scars underneath.

Finnik stared at the old wounds. What on Tersaith had *happened* to the man? Seeing he wasn't going to get a response, Varcor straddled him and brought his fists down on his face. After each blow, Finnik grew more disoriented until at last he began to black out from the pain. Finnik was dying. The cycles he had spent serving Grendolen suddenly weighed on him and he let that weight and exhaustion flood in. How had he not felt it before this? He was so tired. It was time to let go and move on from this world. For the first time in his life, Finnik wondered what would await him on the other side, if there was one at all. In the last moments of consciousness, he found himself doing something he never thought he'd do. He called out to the god he had spent a lifetime professing didn't exist.

Yveth, take me as I am!

At that very moment, a loud rumbling sounded beneath him, shaking his limp body. Finnik thought it was Death himself, come to take him to Nihility, but as a weight lifted from his chest, he realized it was Varcor withdrawing. Try as he might, Finnik couldn't open his swollen eyes to see what was happening. Another rumble shook under him, this time followed by shouts from Varcor's men. Finnik laid there helplessly as another rumble caused a splitting sound at his feet. For a brief moment, there was nothing but silence, then suddenly the ledge he was on fell away from the cliff and tumbled down the mountainside, taking Finnik along with it.

CHAPTER SIXTEEN

Meera

Meera whirled around to see Everard's pale face just before it disappeared from the Blue Library's window. Her heart skipped a beat.

"The big one knows!" Ty's voice said again in Meera's mind. For a moment, she sat there frozen in motion, hawk sitting on her forearm, wondering just how much the giant saw. From an outsider's perspective, she hadn't done anything or said anything out loud to Ty that would have seemed suspicious. Letting out a sigh of relief, she turned back to Tymmon. That's when she caught sight of a slight glow radiating from her hands.

Rot.

Everard may not have heard anything out of the ordinary in her interaction with Tymmon, but he certainly would have questions if he saw her glow. Yet the giant hadn't run off screaming in fear and calling for the guards. On the contrary, he had calmly turned away and went back to his books. Almost as if he had *expected* it. It was then that Meera realized something. Out of the three of them, Everard had spent more time with her than Darmond or Katula.

Was that intentional? Had the other activities her companions were sent to been at Everard's request so he could get closer to her?

He's suspected something since we met, she concluded, heart racing. Was the sovereign in on it? Were they already plotting against her? There was only one way to find out.

"He has the answers I need," Meera spoke internally to Tymmon. "*I need to find out* exactly *what it is he knows.*"

"Watch the big one," Ty replied, cocking his head so that one of his black eyes looked at hers.

"Don't you worry. I'll be careful," Meera said with a grin. A thought struck her. "*Ty, do you know where Evera... where the Big One lives?*" The hawk fluffed its white feathers, shaking its head.

"I'll take that as a no," Meera guessed, a little unsure. "*I need you to follow him tonight and find out where he lives. Can you do that?*"

"Follow the Big One," Ty replied, stepping along her arm as lightly as he could so as not to inflict pain. Meera took that as a yes. It was going to take a little while to get used to speaking to a hawk.

"Follow him, then come back to me at nightfall. I think it's time the Big One and I had a heart-to-heart."

Ty bent down and flapped his wings in preparation for flight. Grimacing silently as his talons dug deeper into her skin, Meera swung her arm out and up to give the hawk enough of a push to get airborne. The burning within her veins slowly drained away as she lost sight of Ty in the distance. Meera knew the moment her glow waned, as she felt a small wave of exhaustion hit. It was nowhere near as much as when she'd killed the snow beast, but there was no mistaking it. Weary, she got up and walked back toward the door that led into the Blue Library. Inside she found Everard hunched over the manuscripts as if he had never left to watch her from the window.

"My dear, you're bleeding!" he whispered in alarm upon seeing her arm.

Meera looked down to find her sleeve dotted with blood. She hadn't realized Ty's talons had dug so deep, and if she were to try and heal herself now, the giant would certainly have questions.

"Here, let me help you back to your room," Everard said, closing the books and rolling up the scrolls. Meera let the giant escort her back to the suite, where he quickly requested that one of the guards fetch Reyna for some bandages. While waiting for her to arrive, Everard grabbed a cloth from Meera's private quarters, wetted it in the nightstand's basin, and pressed it to her arm to stop the bleeding.

"This is my fault, I'm afraid. I should have never let you go out there," he said, shaking his head in frustration. "Reyna will never let me forget my error, and she'll be right to do so. Please forgive me."

Meera looked into the giant's icy gray eyes, trying to read the thoughts behind them. He seemed genuinely distressed over her well-being. Maybe it had been too bright outside for him to see her glowing skin. She wanted to believe he was her friend, but catching him watching her with Tymmon made her wary. If he did harbor the answers she was after, she didn't want him suspecting she knew he had them until she confronted him on her own terms.

"It's not as bad as it looks," Meera replied with a tired smile. "Besides, it was my fault for going out there without my bracers. I'm just so used to having them on, I forgot they weren't. No harm done."

Everard nodded, although Meera could tell he still put the blame on himself. Then a sheepish look washed across his face.

"If it's not too much to ask, can you refrain from mentioning this occurred outside the Blue Library?" Everard asked. "If the sovereign found out our efforts in the Red Library had been postponed, even for a moment, it would not go well for either of us."

"Of course," Meera replied. Despite her reservations about what Everard's intentions were, she was grateful for the small amount of time she had looking over records from her homeland. "Seeing those manuscripts with my own eyes will be something I hold dear for the rest of my days, thanks to you."

"Not at all, not at all." The giant quickly shook his head. "If someone does ask you where the incident took place, know that the Red Library also has its own courtyard."

Meera nodded but was interrupted from saying anything more as Reyna entered. "What in Nirsi's name happened?" she exclaimed, looking frazzled by the news of Meera's injury.

"It's my fault," Meera quickly explained.

Ignoring her, Reyna looked at Everard. "Well, I hope you're happy," she stated, placing her hands on her hips. "The sovereign will have you for breakfast when she finds out, and you'll be on the menu!"

"Now, Reyna," Everard pleaded, putting his hands up in surrender. "It's not what you think."

"You're absolutely right. It's not what I think but what the sovereign will think that's the issue," she countered, dropping her hands to look at Meera's arm. A momentary panic hit her, though, as Reyna pulled back her sleeve to inspect the wound, worried that she'd somehow healed it without realizing it. Thankfully, she hadn't. How on Tersaith would she ever get used to doing whatever it is she could do or *when* she did it?

"Truly, Reyna, it's my fault," Meera pressed. "I saw the trees in the courtyard and couldn't resist a climb. It's been so long since I've left Matui, I didn't realize how much I've missed the forest."

"We have kept you cooped up for far too long in that stuffy library, haven't we?" Everard replied coolly.

"Mm, mm," Reyna replied to them both, cocking her eyebrow. She continued to clean out the wounds and bandaged them while Meera and Everard stayed silent. Something told Meera Reyna knew they had weaved her a story, but the fact that she didn't confront them about it indicated she would keep that truth to herself and not share it with the sovereign. When she finished tending Meera's arm, she looked both of them in the eyes.

"No more *tree climbing*. Is that understood?" she demanded, crossing her arms.

"Yes, ma'am," they agreed in unison.

"I think you're right about one thing, though," Reyna added. "You all have spent way too much time cooped up studying. I find that when I'm stuck on a puzzle I cannot figure out, leaving it for a while and coming back to it helps give me a fresh perspective I didn't see before."

"Thank you, Reyna, but I don't believe the sovereign is interested in us taking a break," Everard replied.

"And miss the opportunity to show our Lowlander guests just how superior Pawtoton is to the rest of Tersaith?" she mused. "Yes, a tour of our great lands to remind them of what an honor it is for them to see it may be just the thing. Especially if that tour was given by none other than our top historian."

It was Everard's turn to cock his eyebrow before his face split into a grin. "My dear, Reyna, I do believe you are right," he smiled, rubbing his beard.

The door opened again, this time issuing in Katula, Darmond, and a giant with whom Meera was not familiar.

"Ah, perfect timing," Reyna called. "This is Arvon, the head tailor in service to the sovereign. He will help fit you all for new clothes."

"Welcome to Pawtoton, travelers," the giant bowed before giving each of them a good look over. "I can see why I was called away from my work. It seems your smaller frames were much too different to fit properly in our own clothes. No matter! I'll have you all wearing decent attire in no time."

"I'm quite fond of the ones I had," Darmond said, turning to face Arvon.

"Darmond, those were falling apart and smelled like they'd up and died," Meera remarked, folding her arms.

"I'll admit they were... in need of some assistance. But there's no way in Nihility I'm stepping out of here in..." He looked down at the very colorful clothes he was in, a bit lost for words.

"What my friend is trying to say is we need items that are more suited to hunting and traveling. Preferably like the ones we had when we arrived," Katula explained. "We have chips and will compensate accordingly." Meera didn't miss the fact that Katula had used the term "friend" in a sentence. What a change since they'd first struck out on their journey! Meera hadn't had friends before. It was... comforting to think of Katula and Darmond as friends.

"Not at all, not at all," Arvon replied, waving the idea away. "These will be a gift from the sovereign herself. No chips are needed. And I am more than happy to accommodate you with the styles you are comfortable with."

"Well then." Darmond smiled, patting the large giant on the arm. "You can use these as a guide." Darmond grabbed a pile of clothes from his room and handed them to Arvon.

"*These* are your clothes?" the giant stammered, picking through them. He leaned in and gave it a sniff, then recoiled. "I thought these had been washed!"

"They *were*," Reyna said flatly. "*Thrice*."

Everything was run by time in Pawtoton. From the moment you woke, the meals you ate, and to the time you retired at night. It was for that reason Meera made sure to wait until the small and large arrows were pointing to the number one before risking sneaking out of her room. Darmond and Katula had withdrawn to their private quarters around eleven, and judging by the snoring coming from both their rooms, Meera was satisfied they were fast asleep. She hoped most of the staff would be also tucked in bed by now but guessed there was still a guard or two posted outside their door.

Time to put this newfound power to the test once again. Meera made her way over to one of the tall windows in the sitting room and pushed back the curtain slightly, but it was too dark to see anything. She had expected that. Breathing in deeply, Meera focused her attention within and searched for the flame that she had felt before. This time it ignited on cue. Meera gasped as the burning sensation lit up within her middle and spread outward until it ran through her entire being. Instead of looking out the window, she focused her thoughts, targeting them at Tymmon.

"*I'm here,*" she said within her mind. "*Where are you?*"

A screech sounded out from somewhere in the gardens, but Meera didn't need to see where Tymmon was to know his location. She felt it. A good start so far.

"*There are guards outside my door. Can you distract them?*" Meera asked.

"*Be ready,*" Ty answered back. Meera left the window and padded over to the suite doors to listen. A few moments later, something smacked into the window at the end of the hallway outside with a thud.

"*Not so loud!*" Meera warned.

Tymmon gave no reply, but Meera heard someone walk over to the window to inspect the noise. Holding her breath, she turned the doorknob as slowly as she could and cracked open one of the wide doors. Sure enough, the single guard on watch was over by the window, looking out.

Meera quickly closed the door as quietly as she could and was about to turn down the hallway stairs when the guard gave up his search with a shrug. Meera froze, unable to move, even though her mind was already racing through excuses to tell him why she was out of her room. However, another thud sounded at the window. This time, both she and the guard could see a hawk-shaped smudge appear through the glass. Forgetting momentarily that the guard could turn around and see her, she stared incredulously at Tymmon and shook her hands in annoyance.

"*What the rot are you doing?*" she demanded.

"*Distraction*," the hawk replied as if it was obvious.

"*I didn't mean for you to knock yourself out in the process*," she warned.

Realizing she needed to use the opportunity while she could, Meera turned out of sight from the guard and snuck down the staircase. Tymmon didn't bother with a reply.

A few moments later, Meera passed through the garden doors and out into the night. She could feel Tymmon waiting for her somewhere toward the back, so she made for that direction. Sure enough, he sat on the limb of a short fruit tree, puffed up like a snowball.

"*Comfortable?*" she asked. The hawk fluffed itself and stretched its wings.

"*Night. Sleep,*" Ty replied.

"*Sorry, friend. You can sleep once you lead me to Everard's house,*" Meera acknowledged.

The hawk didn't respond in Meera's mind, but he did hop on to the arm she extended, this time reinforced with several layers of cloth.

"*Pain,*" he told her, cocking his head down to look at her other arm.

"*Not your fault,*" Meera admitted with a smile. "*Besides, I think the two knocks to your head against that window was enough to make up for it.*"

Ty fluffed himself again as if to wave off her comment.

"*Here,*" she said, patting her shoulder. "*I've worn a thick shawl so you can sit up here.*" The hawk walked up her arm to the spot she indicated. "*Ready*?" Tymmon clicked his beak in reply, clinging on to her shawl as she stepped forward into the dark.

Everard's house was farther out in the Tawoken countryside than Meera had realized. It took Tymmon and her quite a while to make their way outside of the town. *Too* long. Meera began to worry about making it back to the Residence in time not to be missed. But she had come too far to turn back by the time she came to that realization, so she pressed onward. Meera stopped at a crossroads surrounded by crop fields and looked around.

"*Where to*?" she asked Tymmon.

"*Dawnlight*," he replied, looking to the east. A short while later down the winding dirt road, sat a quaint-looking building with a thatched roof.

"*Big One lives here*," he confirmed. Meera thought she caught a note of anticipation in his words.

"*Thanks for your help, Ty*." Meera smiled gratefully. "*You can go rest now. I know my way back*."

The bird fluffed and walked down her arm. With a swing, she cast him into the air and felt the fire within her smolder out.

Now the real fun begins.

Meera slunk down and made her way over to one of the home's windows. It was covered by a thick curtain, but from what she could tell, all was dark within. Wanting to be on the safe side, she circled the house and came to a stop when she spied a small gleam of light peeking through a different window's curtain.

Looks like I was right. Everard has *been researching after hours.*

Breaking in wasn't hard; the giant hadn't even bothered to lock his front door. Staying light on her feet, Meera crept through the main sitting room toward the room where the light was coming from. Placing her hand on the room's door, she gently pushed it open, expecting to see Everard sitting at the desk, but instead the room was empty.

"Looking for me?" a voice cheerily said from behind her. Meera wheeled around as Everard struck a match and lit the wick of a lamp.

"How did you—?" Meera gasped.

"—know you were coming?" Everard interjected with a smile. "That part wasn't hard to figure out. But I must say, I wish you could have made it a little earlier than two in the morning."

"But you... you don't seem upset," she remarked, still trying to overcome her shock.

"Not at all." The giant smiled. "After you saw me watching from the library window today, I knew it was only a matter of time before we had this conversation. Thankfully for me, I've grown accustomed to late nights recently.

"Was it that obvious?" Meera asked tentatively.

"No more so than the fact that you figured out I know more than I've told you and your friends," he countered. "Now, then." He clapped his hands together. "We've got quite a bit to discuss before the sun rises. Shall I put on some tea?"

A short time later, Meera found herself sitting opposite Everard in one of his high-backed leather armchairs cradling a steaming cuppa.

"How did you know?" she asked the giant, referring to her ability to communicate with Tymmon. She had worked hard to keep her secret during her stay in Pawtoton, so it came as a surprise when he had known to watch her from the library window.

"The truth is, I didn't," he admitted, taking a sip of tea from his own mug. "I suspected one of you but wasn't sure which. Not until I saw you with that hawk."

"Suspected us?" Meera asked, confused. "Suspected us of what?"

"That one of you was the cause of the Wildfires appearing," he explained. "My theory was further backed when I happened upon it—one solitary sentence buried within the text of content unrelated to anything I was looking for."

"What did it say?" Meera asked, her curiosity piqued.

"That Wildfires did not just disappear around the time of the Ancient Ones. Rather, they *disappeared* because they no longer walked Tersaith," Everard replied, his face wide with a smile.

Meera sat back, confused. "I don't understand," she admitted.

"Think about it," Everard challenged. "If the Wildfires stopped growing because there were no more Ancients around, the only reason they would appear again is..."

"...is because the Ancients have returned?" Meera finished, catching on.

"Exactly!" Everard exclaimed.

"But what does that have to do with us?" she countered.

"Well it's quite obvious," the giant replied, leaning back and rubbing his braided white beard. "I knew one of you had to be an Ancient."

"A *what*?" Meera choked on her tea. "Everard, that is... that's *preposterous*! Not to mention, blasphemous!"

"Is it?" Everard asked, calmly taking another sip of his tea.

"How can you even question whether it is? The Ancients were *god-kin* to Yveth," Meera stressed, suddenly under the impression she had wasted a good night's sleep to hear nonsense. "I can promise you, neither I, nor Katula, or Darmond come remotely close to divinity."

"Oh, I am well aware," Everard laughed, his low rumble echoing through the dimly lit sitting room. "However, that is the exact basis of my theory. I don't believe the Ancients were ever gods to begin with."

"Were never gods to... Everard, have you gone *mad*?" Meera laughed, unsure what to make of him. "If others were to hear you speak like this..."

"Trust me, I wondered if I had gone mad myself," he admitted. "That is, until I came across the line about Wildfires. It pushed me to go back to other manuscripts we historians have deemed outside the sphere of the Tercara Scrolls and research them once more. And my hard work paid off."

"You found more evidence to support your theory?"

"Indeed." Everard nodded excitedly. "I found references that spoke of unique powers the Ancients held. Everything pointed back to the scrolls, but on this I can find nothing within them. Nevertheless, armed with this new information, and knowing I didn't have enough to prove my theory in front of the sovereign, I began watching you and your friends for signs I was right. It wasn't until I saw you with that bird today, that I knew without a doubt, I was."

"You think *I'm* an Ancient?" Meera choked.

"Well, I'm certain they didn't call themselves that at the time," the giant teased.

"Everard, be serious!" Meera retorted.

"I am," he replied without a smile this time, to show his sincerity. "At first, I suspected it was you, after all, those red eyes, the very color of Wildfires, and in turn, the color of the Ancient's symbol. However, then I watched Katula use her knowledge of the Elements in a way my people thought impossible and wondered if it was her. When I learned both of you admitted to coming across the Wildfires after the avalanche you survived, I realized finding out which of you was responsible for the Wildfires appearing was going to be harder than I thought."

"What led you to believe it was me?" Meera asked.

"The look on your face in the Blue Library when you *knew* the hawk was in the courtyard, even though neither of us could see it from the table," he admitted. "When I witnessed the bird's ease with you. When I saw your skin glowing, bright as a fire..."

Meera let her tea grow cold as she sat stunned. This whole time she had been looking for answers to explain how she could do the things she did, and now that an explanation had been presented, every part of her wanted to deny it. She thought back to the night the snow beast attacked. She had been trying to suppress the memory since it had occurred, afraid of facing it. The look in the beast's crazed eyes as it charged. The feeling as the fire ignited and pumped through her veins. The sickening crunch as the beast's body impacted water that had melted from the snow at her feet. The smell of the beast's innards as they split apart. The incredible exhaustion that washed over her as the fire within died out. Whatever had happened, it was much more than she felt when communicating with Tymmon.

"But, Everard, this doesn't make sense," she said aloud, shaking her head. "The Ancients haven't been around for *three thousand* cycles. How on Tersaith would someone just *become* one? My parents certainly held no such... well, whatever it was the Ancients could do. What exactly *could* they do?"

Everard leaned back in his chair with an empathetic smile. "Ah, yes, your parents. I'm afraid I wasn't as honest with you earlier today when we were looking through the Moorland ledgers. The omission of your name under theirs is something of note, I think. One we should probably look further into. As to what powers the Ancients possessed... In all honesty, I am not sure," he answered truthfully. "We know of accounts that claim they could enter one's mind. Others say they healed the sick or injured. There are texts describing great fortifications they grew from the terra itself, and even some that say they could control water."

"Oh," Meera moaned, feeling faint and going pale. "Everard, I think we're going to need something stronger than tea to drink."

The clock's arrows were just past the number five when Meera slipped under the bed covers in her private quarters. It had been a lot trickier to sneak back into the sovereign's Residence than it had been getting out. With dawnlight fast approaching, many of the house's servants were already up and about, getting a start on their day. Thankfully, the guard posted outside the suite door was fast asleep, which allowed Meera to sneak into the room without being noticed or calling for Tymmon to help out.

She ended up telling Everard everything she had been holding in, her dreams about the Moorland Massacre and of the Wildfires, of the Stone Key and the weapon Lord Agnarr was after, and what really happened the night the snow beast struck. Once she began recounting what happened, it all tumbled out. There were so many reasons she could think of to keep quiet, yet somehow, she instinctively knew she could trust Everard with her secrets. After all, if anyone would be able to help her figure out why she had the abilities she did, it would be him.

She had finally convinced him to bring out the four Tercara Scrolls the Pawtotons had and share them in hopes that they'd find some answers if they combined all five together. By the time the second round of brew spirits were finished, Everard had vowed to help her find out all he could about the powers the Ancient Ones possessed and not to reveal anything to the sovereign until Meera knew more. She had been surprised he agreed to hold back what he knew about her from Pawtoton's leader, however, he had explained that, although his allegiance was to his sovereign, no one would fault him for adhering to the request of a living Ancient One. Which sounded just as wild for her to hear as it was for Everard to speak it.

Sleep came easy to Meera despite the startling revelation unveiled in the dark hours of the early morning. Too soon after her head hit the soft fluffy pillows on her giant bed, sounds rising from the sitting room called her out of slumber. After a yawn and stretch, the memory of what took place between Everard and herself returned and a sudden excitement awoke within her. She wasn't *alone* anymore. She had someone who had the resources to help her figure out what she was. A new day meant another opportunity for them both to dig deeper, this time, at last, into the Tercara Scrolls. Now more than ever, Meera was ready to get back to the Red Library.

Jumping out of bed, she threw on her oversized clothes while taking stops to quickly down the steaming tea set out on her nightstand. Armed with knowledge she didn't have before, Meera swung open her room's door and strolled into the sitting room. That's when she remembered they were scheduled to go on the Pawtoton tour that day, rather than visit the Red Library. Meera's heart sank at the thought of having to hold in all that she knew and wait an entire day before she could join Everard in his research. Let down, she walked over to the sitting room table and poured herself another cup of tea before sinking despondently into the long couch next to Katula.

"Rough night?" Katula asked, giving her a questionable look. "You look like you didn't get much sleep."

"You could say that," Meera replied with a moan. Darmond looked like he wanted to ask her if she was all right but turned away disinterestedly. What was with him lately? Every time she saw him, he seemed moody and withdrawn.

The door to the suite opened suddenly, ushering in Reyna, who seemed unusually disturbed.

"I must apologize," the giant said, ringing her hands. "As you know, we were to send you on a tour of the Pawtoton countryside today, however, that has since been postponed."

"What's happened?" Darmond asked, growing alarmed.

"It seems Everard has had a breakthrough, and you three have been called back to the Red Library right away," Reyna explained.

"Breakthrough?" Meera questioned.

"Something to do with the Ancient Ones," Reyna explained. "But you'll need to ask Everard for the specifics, dear. I'm not one for the histories of the gods."

Meera's heart nearly leaped out of her chest. Had she been wrong to confide in him?

Yveth, please don't tell me he's gone and told the sovereign what he thinks I am! Setting down her tea, Meera stood up. "Whatever it is, it must be important," she replied, coaxing the others to get up.

"But we haven't had breakfast," Darmond whined, not making eye contact with Meera. Was he ignoring her on purpose?

"I've already requested food be sent to the Red Library," the giant replied with a wave of her hand. "Breakfast will be waiting there for you by the time we arrive."

With the promise of food in his future, Darmond got up and headed for the door.

Meera found Everard in his usual position, hunched over a pile of old manuscripts and books with a look of deep concentration on his face. If he had told all to Pawtoton's leader, he showed no signs of remorse. It was all Meera could do not to run over to Everard and shake the truth out of him. But Katula and Darmond were there, and they didn't know what Meera had revealed to the giant, or he to her, so she had to keep silent until an opportunity presented itself and she was alone with him.

"Ah, my friends!" Everard called, his deep voice echoing against the wooden walls lined with books. "I am so sorry to have had to call you away from your day of rest."

"Oh, seed cake!" Darmond grinned, going straight to the food.

"Yes, we heard you had a breakthrough," Meera stated, pensively waiting to hear his explanation.

"I couldn't sleep last night, so in the wee hours of the morning, I came back here to continue my work," the giant explained.

"Apparently you weren't the only one to miss out on sleep," Katula replied, looking at Meera. Ignoring her, the Moorlander walked over to the teapot and attempted to pour herself a cup through unsteady hands.

"I found it, my friends," Everard told them. "The answer we have been looking for about the Cleansing."

"And?" Meera pushed, unable to contain the suspense.

"What I found was a record, buried in the middle of a manuscript's text that provided more detail on exactly what was occurring during that time in history. And I must say, it was much darker than I ever imagined." Unable to contain her curiosity, Meera abandoned her teacup and plopped herself down on one of the library's large chairs.

"At first, I thought it was a record counting Ancient Ones visiting specific locations occupied at the time," Everard continued. "However, I then realized the numbers associated with the record were being *crossed off*."

"I'm not sure I follow," Katula said, standing with a plate of untouched food in her hand.

"I don't believe they were recording visits to the Ancients. Rather, they were recording their deaths," Everard explained with a grim look on his face.

"Ancients dying? Gods don't die," Darmond pointed out.

"They weren't just dying, Darmond," Everard said through clouded eyes. "They were being *executed*."

"What?" Katula gasped, setting her plate down. "That can't be right. You can't *kill* a god. A god wouldn't *allow* themself to be killed."

Meera looked over at the Matuian. Hearing this was just as difficult for Katula as it was for Meera, and Katula didn't even know the half of it. How would she react when she found out Everard believed Meera *was* an Ancient? Dedicating their lives to the Ancients was the very foundation of Matui culture. It would crush Katula if Everard's theory were true.

"Let's say you *could* kill a god. Why would you?" Darmond countered, asking what everyone else was wondering.

"That's exactly what I intend to find out," Everard replied, shooting a worried look in Meera's direction. He was thinking the same thing she was. Perhaps the reason the Ancients had been hunted was because of how dangerous they were.

They broke their session later that day for their individual lessons, giving Meera the opportunity she needed to talk alone with Everard.

"My dear, I am so sorry to have caused you anxiety about the breakthrough Reyna mentioned. I promise you, I will not betray your trust and will keep what we spoke of last night to myself until you deem otherwise." The giant smiled fondly.

"I admit, I was taken aback when Reyna said what she did, but I am also glad you came across the new information, as it has given us some more time to talk," Meera replied. With what Everard had uncovered about the Cleansing, they were able to focus their research that day on finding similar records. The result of which led to a sickening number of executions that had grown higher with each record they tracked down. It pointed to one possible outcome: the Ancients didn't leave Tersaith to live among Yveth's realm. They were hunted to the point of extinction. Which left Meera wondering the biggest question of all.

"Everard, if the Ancients were forcibly wiped out, how could I possibly be one of them?"

"That question has been on the forefront of my mind ever since I figured out what the Cleansing actually was," the giant replied with a sigh.

"Let's just say, some survived," Meera thought out loud, abandoning her chair to pace circles around the study table. "Wouldn't Wildfires appear for them too? Three thousand cycles is a long time to go without any reports of signs."

"An astute observation," Everard admitted. "One that also has me befuddled. If the abilities the Ancient Ones possessed are passed on through blood, it would be far too long within the family line to suddenly appear in you."

"Meaning?" she pushed.

The giant sat back and eyed her for a moment before responding. "It means, my dear, your parents may not be your parents after all. Which leads me to consider *who* your birth parents really are. Once we ask that, we are led to wonder *where* they are from. The final conclusion being: are there perhaps more Ancient Ones still living on Tersaith?"

CHAPTER SEVENTEEN

Katula

As much as it surprised her to admit, Katula had grown used to having Darmond and Meera around. She never really had strong friendships back home. It was hard for others to befriend the chief's daughter. There was a certain status that came with the title, and it tended to keep folks away. That, and Katula had never been a very approachable person. This she was well aware of, and it was why she had shied away from becoming the next Matuian Chief and chose instead to swear her vows as a sagen. However, since meeting Everard, things between Katula and her companions had begun to dissipate. Meera had grown more distant and kept most of her thoughts to herself. Darmond was acting moody and hadn't said one sarcastic thing during the day's *entire* study session—a clear sign something was off.

Katula knew exactly where to put the blame, though. Ever since the sovereign had split them up, they had grown further apart and right when they had just begun to trust each other. Darmond was sent to train with the Pawtoton Guard, Meera to study with Everard, and she to prove herself among Pawtoton's Elementists. Yes, they were given the mornings to research together, but nothing substantial had been found other than Everard's discovery of the Cleansing. Unfortunately, that had nothing to do with the questions she and her fellowship needed the answers to. They needed to know why the Wildfires were appearing and what the Stone Key was, the answers to which she hoped could be found in the Tercara Scrolls of Pawtoton—if indeed they were what the giants claimed. These were questions they couldn't risk asking Everard. But as of yet, not one of their scrolls had been brought before them to view. Which was why Katula had refused to show them hers. The fact that they had viewed hers already, even if briefly, angered her to no end. But there was nothing she could do about that now other than hope that their interest in studying it further would push them to reveal their own at some point. The question was just how long the sovereign would hold out before giving Everard the go ahead. Katula could be stubborn, too, but at some point, someone had to give.

With every moment of every day scheduled with meetings and activities here in the Residence, Katula had little time to wonder how her family and people had fared. In quiet moments, though, when her guard was down, the worry would sneak up and return, clawing at Katula's heart. How she longed for word to come, or a sign given, that her people had survived the Grendolen forces. Had the messages Darmond sent proposing an alliance between Matui and Midtier reached the Resistance? Or had the spy Darmond feared infiltrated them somehow managed to intercept the messages before they could be read? Katula could ask the sovereign if word could be sent by one of the Chroniclers, but something held her back. She didn't trust them, not when it was possible they could have been the ones who alerted Lord Agnarr of Meera's presence in Matui.

In the short while since their journey began, Katula had been through a lot with Darmond and Meera and had put her trust in them even if it was difficult. It had grown easier, though, the more she did it. They had formed a bond, one Katula found she had come to rely on. One that *meant* something to her. And she wasn't about to let the sovereign come between them and take that away. It was time she confronted her companions and made sure they were on the same page.

As much as she had boasted about being a sagen in front of Pawtoton's sovereign, Katula had to admit, the Elementists she was sent to train with were much more knowledgeable. This was proven by watching a Tawoken apprentice only ten cycles in age blend her own concoction of Elements to create an elixir that could correct blurred vision. Granted, the Elementists here had the advantage of being able to learn from *four* Tercara Scrolls, whereas she only had the one. That, and she had only been accepted as the sagen before leaving home. Katula had managed well on their journey from Matui to Pawtoton, but mixing simple medicinal elixirs or heating food without a flame was novice-level at best compared to those working around her now. In the small time she had spent among them, Katula had worked very hard to make it sound and look like she knew what she was doing.

The vast number of mixtures, potions, and concoctions the Pawtotons had developed over time was astounding, and despite Katula's reservations regarding her own ability, she felt herself drawn in and hungry to learn more. Within the first day, she had mastered the hair-growing mixture, as well as one that completely healed scars if the wound wasn't too deep or too old. Most of what she knew from her sessions with Natta the giants already knew. However, occasionally, she would come across a few that they didn't know about, such as the elixir to enhance a person's short-range vision or greatly increase the chances of giving birth to a healthier youngling. With the difficulty Pawtotons had carrying younglings to full term, Katula's additions to their records were more than happily received. In turn, the Elementists began to let their guard down and share more of their own private remedies with her. Even though Katula had been annoyed at the decision at first, the sovereign's decree that she study under their top Elementists had turned out to be a good thing. Combining her knowledge with theirs, Katula was already working on a mixture that could combat mental loss, specifically for the elderly. It helped that the Pawtotons had a *wealth* of Elements stored within the training hall, and even their own courtyard garden that grew the essentials as well as exotics brought up from the far south. With so much to work with, the possibilities for new elixirs were endless.

"Apprentice Katula?" one of the servants called from the training hall's door.

"Sagen, if you please," Katula replied through the scarf wrapped around her mouth and nose. Some mixtures were harmful if inhaled so the lead Elementists were strict about safety procedures when working with them. "What is it?"

"Two of your companions have arrived. I've requested they wait in the front," the servant replied.

"Thank you. I'll go to them in a moment." Katula nodded. As reluctant as she was to end the day's session, Katula knew getting Darmond and Meera to open up again was a higher priority. The fact that they were waiting for her outside the training hall was a sign that the messages she'd sent them had grabbed their attention. Hanging up her scarf and apron, Katula quickly cleaned her station and went to meet them.

"I see you got my message," Katula said in a serious tone upon greeting them at the door. Both their faces held worried looks.

"What's the emergency?" Darmond whispered, looking alarmed. Apparently, he had come straight from sparing with the guards because he was still covered in sweat and dirt.

"I came as soon as I got your note." Meera nodded, checking the area for any unwanted listeners. Katula had sent them both messages requesting they meet with her immediately, hoping it would sound urgent enough to gather them together.

"Not here," Katula said in a hushed voice. "Follow me."

Not waiting for their response, Katula led them away from the Elementist training hall and down a separate corridor toward what she hoped was the Gold Library. She had never been there before but had overheard one of the apprentices mention its courtyard had a gate door that led out of the Residence's grounds. Sure enough, after a few turns, they came upon the Gold Library. It was much larger than the Red, which meant they were able to weave their way through the room and exit out the door to the courtyard without any notice from those studying within. Once outside, Katula wound her way around the paths and garden beds until they reached the back wall, which was covered top to bottom with vines filled with yellow blossoms.

"What are we doing here?" Meera whispered, looking confused.

"Trying to find a door along this wall," Katula replied, feeling through the vines. A look back toward the library windows confirmed no one was watching, at least not yet. If they didn't find the door soon, they could be spotted and reported.

"Here," Darmond called in a low voice, waving them over. Meera and Katula joined him and gave the hidden door a push. It opened without issue, giving credence to what the apprentice said about it being used often by Residence servants. Within moments, they were safely off the sovereign's grounds and out among the streets of Tawok village.

"Katula, what's going on?" Darmond demanded, pulling her arm and bringing her to a stop.

"Just a little bit further. *Trust me*," she replied, yanking her arm back.

Darmond let out a sigh, but both he and Meera complied. After several turns through the town's back alleys, Katula came to a stop in front of a large stone building.

"This is it," she confirmed, noting the hanging wooden sign.

"The Tipsy Tonga?" Meera read, confused.

"You brought us to an *alehouse*?" Darmond gasped.

"Yes," she admitted without hesitation.

"I don't understand," Meera said, looking a little annoyed. "I thought there was an emergency."

Katula ignored her question. "Do you want to go back?" she challenged.

"*Rot*, no!" Darmond replied with a grin. "I'm not complaining. I'm so overjoyed I might even cry real tears. I just didn't think you were the type that would break us out of our pen for some spirits."

A hint of a grin played at the corner of Katula's mouth. What was it that Darmond had said to them during one of his stories along the highcap trails?

Put enough ale into someone and they'll be spilling their thoughts to you in no time.

Katula started for the front door, but Darmond held her back.

"Hold up there, Prickly," he called. "Alehouses cost coin and I'm fresh out of halfspritts."

Katula crossed her arms. "That's because you lost so horribly to Bluff," she countered. Katula pulled out her coin purse and gave it a shake.

"I've got us covered this time. But you *owe* me. Turns out Elements from Matui are considered rare here. They paid a nice sum for some of our most readily available ones."

Darmond stood back looking a bit stunned, then gave her a respectful bow. "Nicely done," he commended.

Meera, however, smiled but was distracted by something off in the distance. Katula followed her line of sight and caught a flash of white in the sky just as it flew behind a distant tree line. It was that hawk that kept following her.

"Are you two going to stand out here all evening?" Katula pressed, making for the door once again. This time they both followed without question.

The Tipsy Tonga turned out to be a well-stocked alehouse according to Darmond, who considered himself the foremost expert of the group. Within a short time, he had ordered a variety of saps for Katula and Meera to try, which resulted in a myriad of goblets filled with colorful liquids appearing on their wooden table. The interior of the place was cozy, with wood-paneled walls and a cheerful fireplace that matched its warm and inviting atmosphere. Around them hung various maps of Pawtoton and colorful tapestries depicting countryside scenes. They earned more than a few stares at first when they walked in, but Darmond's advice about acting as if you're supposed to be somewhere you aren't had worked, and soon enough, conversations picked up again and the newcomers were left alone. Mostly due to the alehouse goers gossiping about the strangers quietly within their own circles.

"According to the locals, the red and blue saps you see before you are from Pawtoton's western town, Wanpa," Darmond explained excitedly.

"What about the orange?" Meera asked tentatively.

"You know those orange berries they have everywhere? Apparently, it's made from them. Less potent than the others, though," Darmond explained.

Already Katula's plan was working. At least the two of them were interacting again.

"Maybe I should start with that, then," Meera said, picking up a goblet and taking a sip. Darmond let out a laugh as Meera's face scrunched up. "Oh dear," she managed after swallowing. "I'm not sure about that one."

Darmond and Katula each tried theirs. A sickening sweet liquid coated Katula's mouth, making her own face cringe.

"I see what you mean," Katula replied, shaking her green head of hair in dislike at the flavor.

"Too sweet," Darmond agreed before downing the rest in one large gulp. "You going to finish those?" he asked the two women. He emptied both their drinks before turning his eye on the next option. "Next, you need to try blue," he said, sliding the goblets over to them. This time they all drank together. The flavor of the blue was much more palatable, less sweet but full of flavor. Back in Matui, Katula often enjoyed a small glass of blue before retiring for the night. This variety, however, far surpassed what she had tried before.

"This is actually quite nice," Katula announced in a satisfied voice.

"Indeed," Darmond agreed. "Those folks from Wanpa sure know their saps. Meera, what do you think?"

The smile on her face said it all. "Now *this*, I like," she laughed before taking another sip. Darmond returned a smile and handed out the reds.

"Reds usually cost the most because they are considered the best. Give it a try and see what you think," Darmond pushed.

The drier flavor that hit Katula's tongue this time was extraordinary, far beyond her expectations. "Delightful," Katula said, giving a rare smile.

"I second that!" Meera agreed, lifting her goblet to them. The three of them fell into small conversation about their days and what they had been training or studying. It was the first normal sit-down they'd really had together. A short while later, a round of Moordew Darmond had ordered arrived at their table.

"It's time, Red," he said, sliding her glass over to her. Meera took it, swirled it around, and gave it a sniff. Her eyes brightened excitedly.

"I think I remember this," she said with a smile. "The smell... It brings back fond memories of... of home."

"Then I think it's time we say a toast," he advised.

"I believe the locals toast to the saying 'the Bygones,'" Katula suggested, "as a homage to the histories they keep."

"To home," he began, holding up his glass, "and to the Bygones."

"To home and the Bygones," the women echoed. Meera downed her glass in one go this time.

"Well?" Darmond asked.

A smile spread across the Moorlander's face. "Let's order some more."

Before long, Darmond had the entire alehouse joining in a rousing round of the Moordew drinking song, and with all the drinks in their systems, Meera and Katula happily joined in.

Verse One (Bard)
From a land of moors and white fog
Hails a drink high above your low grog
Golden be that sweet liquid's hue
Favored by kings be Moordew

Chorus One
(Bard) Raise a glass! (**Audience Repeats**) **Raise a glass!**
Lift a flask! **Lift a flask!**
(***Everyone***) ***And drink one and all to Moordew!***

Verse Two (Bard)
There is no other of its ilk
Better than mother's own milk
Distilled from Yveth's best brew
Be the savory taste of Moordew

Chorus Two
Hoist a jug! **Hoist a jug!**
Hold a mug! **Hold a mug!**
Raise a glass! **Raise a glass!**

Lift a flask! **Lift a flask!**
And drink one and all to Moordew!

Verse Three (Bard)
For those who are on the roam
Due to troubles or trials at home
Why not try something new
With a wee dram or two of Moordew

Chorus Three
Heft a crock! **Heft a crock!**
Heave a stein! **Heave a stein!**
Hoist a jug! **Hoist a jug!**
Hold a mug! **Hold a mug!**
Raise a glass! **Raise a glass!**
Lift a flask! **Lift a flask!**
And drink one and all to Moordew!

Verse Four (Bard)
No other glass ages so neat
Than barley's gold grains so sweet
If all the souls on Tersaith knew
Peace would reign, all due to Moordew

Chorus Four
Grasp a cup! **Grasp a cup!**
Clasp a pint! **Clasp a pint!**

Heft a crock! **Heft a crock!**

Heave a stein! **Heave a stein!**

Hoist a jug! **Hoist a jug!**

Hold a mug! **Hold a mug!**

Raise a glass! **Raise a glass!**

Lift a flask! **Lift a flask!**

And drink one and all to Moordew!

Verse Five (Bard)

For the sick it will keep at bay

And the sad it will wash away

Should you require a healthier you

Take a big 'ol swig of Moordew

Chorus Five

Clutch a tankard! **Clutch a tankard!**

Grip a flagon! **Grip a flagon!**

Grasp a cup! **Grasp a cup!**

Clasp a pint! **Clasp a pint!**

Heft a crock! **Heft a crock!**

Heave a stein! **Heave a stein!**

Hoist a jug! **Hoist a jug!**

Hold a mug! **Hold a mug!**

Raise a glass! **Raise a glass!**

Lift a flask! **Lift a flask!**

And drink one and all to Moordew!

Verse Six (Bard)
So a toast to Moorland, we sing
Till the pub's own rafters we ring
Give thanks for the grains they grew
And drink one and all to Moordew

Chorus Six
Clutch a tankard! **Clutch a tankard!**
Grip a flagon! **Grip a flagon!**
Grasp a cup! **Grasp a cup!**
Clasp a pint! **Clasp a pint!**
Heft a crock! **Heft a crock!**
Heave a stein! **Heave a stein!**
Hoist a jug! **Hoist a jug!**
Hold a mug! **Hold a mug!**
Raise a glass! **Raise a glass!**
Lift a flask! **Lift a flask!**
And drink one and all to Moordew!

Several songs and glasses of Moordew later, Meera needed no coaxing to start talking after Katula asked about how her study sessions with Everard were going.

"He knows *so* much," she replied, her red eyes growing wide. "Things I didn't even know *existed!* He took me to the Blue Library, you know," Meera continued, unable to stop herself.

"The Blue Library?" Katula questioned.

"Yes," she replied, growing subdued. "Moorland's records are held there."

"What *kind* of records?" Darmond asked, dropping his smile and growing concerned.

"All kinds!" she replied, oblivious of his change. "Maps, old treaties, royal ledgers. Even lists noting the favorite meals and recipes of the monarchs."

"I'm sure seeing them brought you some comfort," Katula noted.

Meera nodded. "It was. It's just... all soomuch, youknow?" she slurred. "The *whole* thing. *All* of it. All of the things. *Too* much."

"Sure looks that way," Darmond said, giving Katula a knowing look.

"It *has* been a lot," Katula agreed, ignoring him. She'd managed to get the Moorlander talking, and she wasn't about to cut her off now. "That's why it's good to discuss these types of things with those you can trust."

"Exactly!" Meera replied, eyes suddenly intense. "Thatsswhy I told Everard everything."

"You did *what*?" Katula spat, taken aback.

"Gracious, youlook scary when you're angry. Doesntshe look angry, Darmond?"

"I'm not too happy about it myself, Red," he replied, crossing his arms.

"Meera, we talked about this. He's reporting directly back to..." Katula paused and leaned in to whisper. "... to the sovereign. We *can't* trust him. How much did you tell him?"

"Oh, I didn't trust him." Meera said. "Aaat least not at first. But Tymmon helped me break into Everard's house annn he told me I was an Ancient. So, we're *realllly* good friends now."

Katula and Darmond both froze in their chairs and stared incredulously at her.

"I think it's time we cut her off," Darmond recommended, once he found his voice again.

"My head feels fuzzzzy," Meera remarked, looking more pale than usual. "Why is the floor moving?"

"Agreed," Katula replied flatly, her anger at what Meera had revealed growing. When Katula paid up and the Midtierian's last shot came, she eyed Darmond as he grabbed it and downed it in one gulp before they took their leave.

Halfway back to the Sovereign's Residence, Katula took a sudden right down a deserted alleyway. By now both her companions were feeling the effects of the night's splurge. She would have, too, only, before she left for the alehouse, she'd downed an Elemental elixir she'd whipped up that suppressed alcohol's effects. With the other two in tow and not fully aware of their surroundings or the right way back, they followed her lead without complaint. The stone road soon became a dirt one and led into the Pawtoton countryside. With the sun having set a while ago, night had fallen, and both crescent moons were out lighting up the fields with a faint bluish-white glow. Once she was certain they were not being followed, Katula pulled them off the road and sat them down on a large stone at the edge of a small woodland.

"I don't feel sso good," Meera announced, rubbing her temples. "My head is *pounding*."

"It's just one of the *many* bags hitched to the saddle when it comes to drinking," Darmond replied, rubbing his own sore head.

"I don't think aaanything could feel worse than this headache." The Moorlander winced. Looking around she suddenly realized they weren't back at the Residence. "Where are we?"

"We need to talk," Katula pressed, "and here is the only place we can safely do that without others listening in."

"We're talking. I'm talking. We're alllll talking."

"Why did you break into Everard's house?" Katula demanded.

"He saw me. Through the window."

"What window?"

"The Bluelllibrary's window."

"What were you *doing* out there?"

"Ty was there," Meera said matter-of-factly before looking over at one of the trees in the woods and smiling. Somehow Katula knew that same hawk was sitting in one of them.

"Ty?" Darmond repeated, head clouded.

"The Moorland hawk," Katula reminded him. "The one who warned her about the Grendolens in Vardia."

Understanding finally hit the Midtierian, and he let out a slow nod.

"What does Tymmon have to do with Everard?" Katula continued.

"He knewIcould talk to him," Meera explained, growing serious.

"You *always* talk with animals," Darmond pointed out.

"No, I mean he *knew*," Meera emphasized. "Everard knew I could talk to them in my head. That's how he knew I was an Annncient."

"A what?" Darmond barked with a laugh.

"AnnAncient" Meera repeated, growing annoyed.

"Look, Red, you're a *lot* of things, but an Ancient ain't one of 'em."

"Amm *too*," she argued, standing up. "I didn't believe him at first either, but... I can *do* things, Darmond..." Her voice trailed off as she swayed.

"The only thing you're going to *do* right now is upchuck those drinks you downed," he remarked, unaware of how upset she was getting.

"Meera, we know you can do things," Katula jumped in. "We've seen it with our own eyes, remember? But saying you're an Ancient... that's more than just jumping to conclusions. *That's blasphemy.*"

"Itisn't if it's true!" Meera blasted back, her cheeks flushed. "If youuu don't believe me, I'll prove it!"

Before either of them could respond, the Moorlander's skin began to glow. As she grew brighter, Katula felt the air around them change. Like the heightened energy during a storm right before lightning hits. Bending down Meera placed both hands on the terra and spoke something Katula couldn't quite make out. Instantly, the terra began to rumble. Darmond and Katula both gasped and backed up as little green sprouts sprung up by their feet and continued to grow at a rapid rate until they matured, blossomed, and began to glow right before their eyes.

"*I'm* the one making the Wildfires appear," she said defiantly, turning her own glowing eyes on them. "After three millennia of waiting for the Ancients' return, they have finally awoken."

Katula was too stunned to reply and just stood there staring at the red flowers now carpeting the area like a thousand small flames. Darmond must have felt the same because he stayed quiet too. Endless questions streamed through Katula's mind. What had she just seen Meera do? How could the Moorlander command nature like that? For countless generations, her people had believed the Ancients were gods—beings that had once graced Tersaith with their presence before leaving this world to live among Yveth's realm. How could she even begin to accept Meera as one of those beings? Yet, Katula could not deny the fact that there had been signs since meeting the woman that day in the meadow—Wildfires appearing wherever she went, her easy ability with animals, surviving the avalanche, the snow beast, and now *this*. What *was* Meera? Was Everard right? Could she be an Ancient? Was the powerful weapon Lord Agnarr after the power of the *Ancients*?

Katula never got to ask any of her questions at that moment, however, because Meera stopped glowing and slumped over. It was then that her stomach decided to rid its contents and upchuck them just as Darmond had predicted.

Katula looked over at the Midtierian, who was sitting on the rock looking blankly in Meera's direction. With Darmond still recovering from the shock, Katula realized what happened next would be up to her. It seemed that the only person who had put everything together before they had was Everard. Somehow the giant had figured it out. That meant he had access to information he'd withheld from them.

It was time Katula played the one leverage card she had in hopes that tempting Everard with a view of her Tercara Scroll would entice him to give her a look at the others.

Show me yours and I'll show you mine.

Their disappearance did not go unnoticed. Upon their return to the Residence, the three companions were immediately apprehended and brought before the sovereign. Darmond and Meera cowled before the tongue-lashing, wincing with pounding heads at the giant's volume. In the end it was Everard, not clear-headed Katula, who eventually managed to persuade his sovereign to give leniency. After all, what could they expect of Lowlanders? They were used to roaming freely, and being shut in was against their nature. It was only natural that they wished to explore. With witnesses from the alehouse pulled in to testify that all they had done was buy a few drinks, the three were eventually allowed to return to their rooms on the promise they would let their guards know ahead of time if they ever felt the urge to "wander" again.

The sun could not rise fast enough for Katula the next day. Now that she knew the next step she wanted to take, she was anxious to get going. She was *determined* to get a look at the Pawtoton Scrolls and figure out once and for all what Meera was. Katula rose as soon as dawn's light touched the sky. Knowing her friends would have quite the hangover, she used the spare time to mix up an elixir to help clear their heads. When they finally arrived at the Red Library that morning, under the watchful eyes of double the guards, the three of them were wide awake, clear-headed, and ready to fight. But that fight never came. As soon as the doors to the room were closed, Everard turned to them.

"There will be guards stationed just outside the library," he noted in a hushed whisper, "so we must keep our conversation quiet." Before Katula had a chance to get in a word, Everard continued. "I wish the three of you had consulted me before sneaking out last night. Had I accompanied you into town, our session today wouldn't be so guarded. But be that as it may, I understand why you did it. If I were in your small shoes, I wouldn't trust me either." At this, he gave them one of his warm smiles. "I assume you discussed what I told Meera?"

"That she is an... an *Ancient*," Katula whispered back, eyeing the door with unease. It was still so hard for her to say it aloud, let alone think it.

"Told us, and decided to *show* us," Darmond chimed in, refusing to look in Meera's direction.

"How so?" Everard pushed, looking eagerly at the Moorlander. Meera, it seemed, had no reservations about the giant and gave him a full account of how she grew the Wildfires. This, according to the giant, was irrefutable proof his theory was correct. "As I explained to Meera, there are several powers that the Ancients were rumored to have," he told the others excitedly. "They could read the thoughts of others, move water, heal, and—" He paused, looking at Meera. "—control terra or anything grown from it."

"You think that's how she made the Wildfires appear?" Katula asked, shooting her own look at the redhead.

The giant nodded.

Darmond said nothing and instead went to pour himself a cup of tea.

"I knew they were there," Meera said, breaking into the conversation. "I don't know how, but I *felt* the Wildfire seeds waiting for me to wake them up. They'd been waiting for three thousand cycles. It's the same feeling I get when Ty comes around. I know what he's trying to say, and somehow, I can let him know my thoughts in return."

"Thousands of cycles are my point," Katula countered. "Why now? If Meera holds the powers of the Ancients, how can they just suddenly reappear? After what we've found out about the Cleansing, it sounded as if..." At that Katula put her fist to her mouth, pressing her thumb to her lips and then touched her forehead as a plea to Yveth to forgive her for what she was about to say. "As if they all had been *executed*. If they were truly wiped out, how then, can their powers return?"

"I have been contemplating that very thing as well," Everard replied, "and I think I've come to a conclusion. If what we now know about the Cleansing is true, then it changes all we know, or what we thought we knew, about the Tercara Scrolls our people possess."

"How so?" Katula asked.

"Both our people have passed down the tradition of the scrolls, or scroll in your case, being placed in our care to guard, and in return, we were gifted the knowledge of the Elements, yes?"

The Matuian nodded.

"But what happens if we change that view?" the giant challenged. "If you were an Ancient whose people and histories were about to be erased from Tersaith, what is the *one* thing you would do?"

For a moment, the only sound in the library was Darmond sipping his tea.

"You'd want to find a way to *preserve* them," Meera gasped, catching on.

"Exactly," Everard beamed.

"But our scroll holds no such records," Katula countered. "I've grown up listening to my grandmother, our sage, read from it. It is full of wisdom and parables, but nothing remotely close to accounting the Ancients' records."

"That is *precisely* why it is such a mystery," the giant said. "It's the absence of that vital information that I think gives us a place to start." Without warning, he sprang his large body out of his chair and walked over to one of the bookcases lining the room. After shuffling several volumes around, he piled his arms full and brought the contents back to the table.

With great reverence, Everard placed four scrolls down before them. Realizing what they were, Katula sat there for a moment, taken aback by the giant's displayed trust until at last, she took a deep breath and walked over to the leather tube she brought with her. Out of it, she pulled the scroll from Matui and placed it next to the others. Even Darmond came over, teacup in hand, to look curiously upon the Tercara Scrolls. For a long while, no one made a move, the library's occupants too enthralled to take their eyes away from the records before them. Eventually, their curiosity got the better of them, and Everard and Katula wordlessly began to open them up.

Side by side, there was no doubt in Katula's mind that the Tercara Scroll from Matui was connected to the four from Pawtoton. Each one began its text with an ornately painted letter, surrounded by decorative illustrations that included depictions of mountains, looped knot work, water drops curved into spirals, and Wildfires. The substance used for the parchment was unlike anything else she'd ever seen. She knew that whatever the Ancients had used to create them had allowed the scrolls to be so well preserved. It wasn't just the illustration and identical artform that all five scrolls shared, however, but the language and calligraphy as well. Katula had spent most of her time before becoming sagen working with the Matuian scroll, so she was familiar with the language. If she were ever to return home and continue her training, she vowed one day to be able to speak the language fluently, just as her grandmother and all the sages that came before her did. Everard, too, could read the ancient script and, using his expertise, weighed in. The giant's eyes were alight with wonder as he inspected the scrolls.

"It is a complete set, is it not?" he gushed in a hushed tone. "My, what a sight!" He grew so excited, he rose and came over to give Katula a giant-sized hug.

Unaccustomed to such an outward display of affection, Katula just sat there rigid as a tree until Everard finished and sat back down.

"You can confirm they are linked?" she asked, trying to recover her dignity.

"Yes, yes." He nodded. "The language they spoke three thousand cycles ago was quite different from our common tongue, or even that of Matui," he noted. "However, as Grand Preserver, I am fluent." Taking hold of the fifth scroll, with Katula's permission, Everard poured over the text. His eyes clouded a short while later as he reached the end. "It is as you say," he confided to Katula, looking perplexed. "It is fascinating to see the Wildfires depicted on your scroll, Sagen, I must say! In fact, each scroll seems to have a particular art form illustrated around its edges, do they not?"

"Indeed, they do," Katula agreed. Her own scroll held mostly red tones to coincide with the Wildfires. However, the scroll with mountains held mostly greens. There were two scrolls with intricate knotwork, one filled with black infinity loops, and the other with purple knots intersecting like a looped four-pointed compass. The remaining scroll was filled with blue, spiraling water droplets.

"Unfortunately, I do not see that your scroll holds any vital records that would answer some of our questions. I was *sure* there was something to that."

"Maybe they didn't want their secrets to be known," Darmond pointed out, breaking his silence. All eyes turned to him. "I mean, if I was all-powerful and knew I was going to get the ax for it, there's no way I would share what I knew with the ungrateful wretches."

"Well, thankfully they *weren't* you, and did," she retorted.

"That's my point, Prickly," he said, raising his tea to her, and looking at the others. "You all don't get it, do you? The fact that there are records, records that don't say what they should say, means that the records show what they want you to see."

"What?" Katula shot, giving him a blank stare.

"They've *hid-den-it-from-you*," he emphasized slowly.

Once that sank in, Katula gave the scrolls a side glance. Could he be right?

"Think about it," he continued. "If what you know and can do is threatening enough for folks to want to wipe out your entire race, why would you put all that in a nice little bundle and send it off to folks who have no powers of their own to keep them safe?"

"But that's exactly what they did," Meera argued. "They gave the scrolls to the Pawtotons and Matuians to guard." Darmond pointedly did not look at Meera and instead replied to the others.

"And get your people killed in the process and risk losing the records once and for all? I don't think so," he surmised. "No, these Ancients were *professionals*. Take it from someone who knows."

"They filled them with enough content to give us purpose, but kept us unaware of their real intent," Everard realized aloud, running his fingers over his beard and nodding.

"Exactly."

"Which begs the question, where within the scrolls are the *real* records?" Meera asked Darmond.

Yet again, he refused to look her in the eye. It wasn't hard for Katula to guess why. She had a hard time doing it herself. It wasn't easy to wrap her mind around the Moorlander being an Ancient. Meera, though, had had enough.

"What the *rot* is wrong with you?" she demanded, red eyes flashing at Darmond.

When he still refused to turn her way, she grabbed his arm and spun him around to face her. The jerky movement caught him off guard and sent his teacup, contents and all, flying through the air. All four of them gasped as they helplessly watched the cup crash down onto the Matuian scroll. The cup broke into pieces and scattered the liquid onto the text. Their horrified looks were cut short as the door to the Red Library opened, ushering in a guard.

"Everything under order here?" the guard demanded of Everard. The four turned around, crowding together to hide the scrolls from view.

"Yes, yes, my good man," Everard assured the other giant. "All is well. Just a spilt cup of tea is all." The guard's gray eyes weighed them for a moment before he nodded and ducked back out of the room. As soon as the door closed, the four of them turned around to assess the damage. To Katula's utter dismay, the tea had permeated the scroll's parchment. Everard quickly sprang into action, whipping out a handkerchief from his pocket and gently blotting the excess liquid off it. Angry tears welled up in the Matuian's black eyes as she covered her mouth and sat down in one of the large chairs.

"*What have you done*?" she cried, looking at Meera and Darmond. Both of them had gone pale with guilt.

"I'm so, *so sorry*, Katula," Meera begged, tears forming in her own eyes. "I didn't think..." She trailed off, unable to finish.

"Can it be mended?" Darmond asked the giant. Everard finished sopping up the tea and held up the scroll to get a closer look at the text. Without warning, Everard left them and walked over to one of the library's windows.

"How bad is it?" Katula asked, drying her tears and joining him.

A huge smile spread across his face. "Darmond, you are a *genius*." He held up the scroll to the light. Confused, both he and Meera came over. There, written right over the scrolls black text, had appeared more of the Ancient's unique calligraphy.

"*How*?" Katula gasped.

"Just what *kind* of tea were you drinking, Darmond?" Everard asked.

The giant made short time of repeating the spill on each of the other scrolls, only this time he took much more care, dipping his handkerchief into a freshly brewed cup of an Elemental herbal tea mixture and gently dabbing it onto the parchment. Sure enough, each of the Tercara Scrolls held concealed text. As soon as all five had received the treatment, he took them to the window and had one of the others hold them up while he translated the text into the common tongue onto separate pieces of parchment. Soon, the four of them were back at the table inspecting the hidden content. It was clear that each scroll had its own unique text, and yet all were connected. All *except* the scroll from Matui. It, too, held the same language, but its writings were much more vast, and the calligraphy appeared to have been penned by a different author than the other four.

"It's a riddle," Everard said, leaning in. He took the pieces of parchment he'd translated the text onto and moved them about, rearranging them like a puzzle until he sat back. Katula read the lines quietly aloud so the guards wouldn't hear them.

"What is pure, yet unclean?
What is round, yet uneven?
What is accessible, yet hidden?
What is magnificent, yet minute?
What is cherished, yet irritating?"

"What do you suppose it means?" Meera asked.

"If we can answer the riddle, it may give us more insight," the giant explained. "But I think we should concern ourselves with what's on the Matuian scroll first." Everard picked up the parchment and read the verses aloud.

"The Shifter's grasp goes unseen,
Reaching deep into one's thought.
The Mender's ways puts wrong to right,
Healing the broken, sick, and rot.
Terra and rock, valley, and mountain,
Dance to the Builder's behest.
Yet not a drop of dew or a griever's tear,
Can escape the Summoner's request.
To each of these, only one of pure blood,
Will awaken the Tercara's call.
But take heed of those bearing Yveth's mark,
For red warns us they possess them all."

The Moorlander sat back in silence, her red eyes wide with wonder.

"Well, my dear," the giant mused, looking at Meera, "it looks like you finally have your answer. Here I was, thinking the Tercara Scrolls were named after the place they were penned. It turns out, I couldn't have been farther from the truth. If we are to understand the text correctly, not all Ancients shared the same powers. As a matter of fact, I would go further and say, most of them only possessed one. Shifters, Menders, Builders, and Summoners," Everard recited, looking over the text and matching up the scrolls. "Only those 'bearing Yveth's mark' had the power to control all four. It seems at last we know what you are," he said, smiling at her. "You are able to Shift into the minds of animals, to Summon water and sleigh the Night Hunter, to Mend your friends after the avalanche, and I dare say, perhaps even Mend yourself of burns the night of the Moorland Massacre, and Built a meadow of Wildfires. Meera Tarmanon, you my dear, are not just an Ancient, you are a *Tercara*."

CHAPTER EIGHTEEN

Darmond

Darmond watched as Meera considered Everard's words, his own mind at war with itself.

"A Tercara," she repeated, letting the term sink in. A word, he realized, that the Ancients themselves warned about. What had the scroll said? Beware? It confirmed his greatest fears and what he had been wrestling with in his mind ever since Meera began showing her abilities. *She* was the weapon. She *had* to be. Katula must have been on the same page as he, because her next question hit that very mark.

"How dangerous were the Tercaras?" she asked the giant.

"It would seem they were enough of a threat to bring about their executions," he replied, giving a sorrowful glance at Meera.

"Everard, there's something else we've withheld from you," the Matuian announced.

"The Stone Key?" he presumed, surprising everyone except Meera. "Yes, I know about the Stone Key. Meera told me the night she broke into my house."

Darmond and Katula gave their companion a side glance.

"Did she tell you our sage found a reference within the Matuian Tercara Scroll?" Katula pushed.

"Indeed, she did. Shall I take a look now, since we have it out?"

Katula nodded and let the giant look over the scroll once again.

"Yet," he read, "if we cannot find it in ourselves to extend the grace bestowed on us to those in need of it, how then, can we face Yveth in the end? Therefore life, the greatest gift of the Creator, must be held sacred. For does not a key of stone hold only death?" The giant laid the scroll down, sat back in his chair, and rubbed his beard in thought.

"They think I'm the weapon," Meera said, looking at the giant. "And as much as it pains me, I'm not sure they're wrong. But I don't see how the Stone Key fits into all of this. Lord Agnarr is searching for me because he believes I have this 'Stone Key.' I'm *sure* of it, Everard. Because if he *knew* what I could do... Well, I don't think he would bother with capturing me alive." Meera's red eyes welled with tears. All of this terrified her.

"This must be a lot to take in, my dear," Everard said in his comforting voice. "Yet here with you sits three who will stand by you and help in whatever way we can. Isn't that right?" he asked Katula and Darmond.

Darmond nodded with the Matuian, but the guilt he felt for ignoring Meera recently hit him in the stomach like a lap-loving tonga. He had tried so hard to push Meera from his thoughts lately, yet seeing her laughing and so carefree at the alehouse the night before only made the feelings he had tried to hide grow stronger. Then she'd suddenly gone from that happy person to glowing and growing flowers like the Ancient Tercara they now knew she was. Yes, her abilities frightened him, but it was the fact that he knew how frightened she was and still had the courage to tell them that put him to shame. Shame, because he didn't have the same courage to be as truthful to her.

Meera had nearly found out, too. When Darmond heard there were Moorland records within the Blue Library, he had considered breaking in and stealing them. But seeing the look on her face when she recalled her fond memories of home broke down his nerves. How could he take away that small joy she'd found after enduring a lifetime of sorrow? He couldn't bring himself to do it, even if it meant risking his own secret becoming compromised.

"Everard," Meera said, breaking Darmond's thoughts. "If Lord Agnarr finds Pawtoton, there's no telling what he'll do to your people."

A troubled look moved across the giant's face. "Yes, I have considered this. The sovereign is certain it can never happen, but that is based on the fact that it never has. Look within any historical record, and you'll learn quickly that a thing that is never is only a never until it isn't. Now that we know what is at stake, I wonder if we are not underestimating just how much Lord Agnarr is determined to find you."

"Then you're on board?" the Moorlander asked.

"On board?" Katula echoed, confused.

Darmond, however, was able to read their looks. "They want to test her abilities so she can use them against the Grendolens," he surmised grimly.

“We can hardly let Meera light up and grow flowers within the Residence’s confines,” Katula advised.

“Quite right, quite right,” Everard agreed. “Which is why I think it’s high time we followed through with the guided tour of Pawtoton, don’t you?”

“I do feel a bit of that Lowlander wandering coming on.” Meera grinned.

Everard delivered just as he promised, and the very next day, on the 5th of Blommamoad, the four of them were provided with packed lunches and a tonga-drawn cart to tour the villages of Pawtoton at their leisure. They set out after a hearty breakfast, with the sun still low and only just gracing the western cliffs with its beams. Several turns out of Tawok, and they were back on the same dirt road where Meera had Summoned the Wildfires, and they were still in bloom when they passed. The outlying fields of the village were full of crops, growing plump in the warmer climate. Every now and again, they would pass a farmer or two out among their fields tending their land, and they'd wave cheerfully as they drove by.

Darmond leaned his back against the cart’s wooden side as they rode along and breathed in deeply, smelling the fresh country air. After being trapped in the Sovereign’s Residence for what seemed like an entire moad by this point, Darmond was overjoyed to escape its clutches. He was used to life on the go, always moving between places, never staying too long. Maybe the sovereign wasn't too far off with Lowlanders and their wanderings.

Darmond had to hand it to the giants, they sure knew how to pick a spot. Rolling hills filled with valleys of small forests and quaint hamlets dotted the landscape. Everything within the cliffs was green and lush. It was like a hidden gem, a *living* emerald.

The waterfall could be heard before it could be seen. Darmond cocked his head when he realized what the sound was.

"Do you all hear that?" he asked excitedly.

"Indeed, I do! Give it just a few more moments..." Everard replied as he steered the cart around the bend. Clearing the trees, the grand waterfall came into view, and all three of Everard's guests gasped. Just like everything in the land of giants, the waterfall's size was *enormous*. Here, the cliffs bordering Pawtoton curved into a vast crescent carved out of the rock by the fast-flowing water. The basin below was wide enough that the entire village of Tawok could fit within and became the mouth of the two rivers that flowed through the area.

"Welcome to Pawtoton Falls!" Everard announced with a proud smile.

"It's stunning!" Meera breathed, eyes wide in awe.

"Its waters are considered sacred among my people," the giant explained. "Some say it is Yveth's own blood that flows for us, bringing life to us and our land."

"I can see why," Katula agreed, taking it in.

"Are you sure there won't be anyone around?" Darmond asked, worried about unwanted spectators.

"We'll be quite out of the way where we're going," Everard assured him.

They made their way around the right side of the waterfall, following a small trail that ran parallel to the basin's edge. Upon reaching the end of the trail, Everard pulled the cart off to the side and secured the tonga. After everyone grabbed their belongings, Everard instructed his guests to follow closely behind him.

"Ahead, the rocks may be slippery, so have a care with where you step," he advised. As they climbed higher, the sound of the falls grew louder, making it impossible for Darmond to hear what Everard was chattering on about. No doubt, some long-winded piece about the waterfall's history and whatnot. Giving up on trying to make out the giant's words, Darmond glanced behind them and nearly lost his footing. Stretching through the mist and rays of the morning sun lay Pawtoton, green and fertile. If the waterfall had caught his breath, this view hit him even harder. He had not seen a more happily situated landscape since he was a youngling, before the Grendolens had invaded. Would that he could be transported back to that time.

By the time they reached the edge of the falls, a heavy mist hung in the air and coated their clothes and hair, soaking them through.

The giant said something Darmond couldn't hear and pointed to the water, then ducked behind a rock and disappeared. Katula and Meera did the same, so he followed suit. Behind the large rock was a dark tunnel with slick-coated walls due to the constant moisture. Just when Darmond began wishing he had brought a torch, a light appeared in the distance. Following it led him out of the tunnel and into a hidden cavern hollowed out directly behind the waterfall.

"Here we are," Everard boomed, his oversized hands waving around.

"Impressive!" Darmond beamed, looking around with an approving nod.

"We needed cover, so I thought this would be the best place," the giant confirmed. The afternoon sun was still hitting the water's cascade, lighting up the hidden cavern behind.

"This is a good place to have Meera try out her Summoning, but what about the other things she can do?" Katula yelled, trying to be heard over the noise.

"Not to worry," the giant responded, digging into the sling bag around his shoulder and pulling out a glass jar.

"What's that?" Meera asked curiously.

"Terra," Everard said with a smile. "I figured it would be better for you to practice on this rather than pulling down the cliffs on top of us."

Darmond knew the giant was teasing, but the look of terror on Meera's face said she half believed him.

"Don't worry, you'll do fine," Darmond tried to assure her, placing his hand on her shoulder before he thought better of it.

When he realized what he had done, he gave her a few awkward pats before taking it off and trying to act normal.

Katula found a spot away from the water's mist and sat down, indicating the others to do the same. Once they were all sitting, she unraveled the Matuian Tercara Scroll.

"Let's start with what the Ancients called *Building*," the Matuian said.

Everard opened the jar and poured the terra into a pile before Meera.

"What do you want me to do with that?" Meera asked.

"You're the Tercara, you figure it out." Katula shrugged. "Try to move it or something."

Darmond watched as a moment later, Meera's skin began to glow.

"There, that's it!" Everard encouraged. "Do you *sense* the terra?"

Meera's glowing eyes turned upward. "I sense it *all*," she breathed. "Every rock, spec of terra, small seed, and... and *life*." At this, she looked at each of them, tears in her eyes. "I can *feel* life. In the water, in the terra, in the air. I can sense them *all*. It's... it's overwhelming."

"Then use that sense now and direct it into the pile of terra. Let all the others fade away. Concentrate only on it, Meera," Everard pushed.

Meera looked down in front of her at the pile. Sure enough, the individual grains began to stir. As Meera's concentration intensified on the pile, the grains gathered and formed until they took on the shape of a hawk. Moments after the terra formed into

Tymmon, the shape dissolved and fell back into a pile. Without warning, Meera slumped toward Darmond, suddenly taken over by exhaustion.

"Are you all right?" Darmond asked, catching her before she hit the terra.

"I... I think so," Meera mumbled, rubbing her temples. "I seem to grow very tired afterwards." Once she could sit up again on her own, Darmond and the others backed off and allowed Meera some room to recover.

"I don't like how this is affecting you," Darmond warned.

"I suspect the exhaustion comes from inexperience," the giant surmised. "You are overreaching, my dear. The more you acclimate to using your abilities, the easier it will be for you to direct your concentration into one thing, rather than all of them at once."

"It's all right," Meera said, looking a bit more recovered. "I just had to give myself a moment. I'm ready for the next one."

"How about Mending," Katula suggested. "This time try what Everard advised and concentrate only on what you need to Mend."

"What should I Mend?" the Moorlander asked. No sooner had she spoken the words than Katula took her belt knife and drew it across her palm. Fresh blood oozed from the cut and ran down her arm.

"Katula!" Meera gasped. "I'm not ready!

"Life never gives you time to prepare," the Matuian retorted in her usual curt manner. "Now, hurry up before I bleed out!"

This time, Meera's glow lit up the cave a little quicker than before. Cupping Katula's hand between her own, Meera fell quiet while she concentrated. A moment later, she let go. Everard and Darmond were ready this time and helped prop her up.

"Meera, I think this may be too much too soon," the Midtierian warned, worry etched in his voice.

The newly proclaimed Tercara ignored him and looked at Katula.

"Well?" she asked. "How did I do?"

The Matuian held her palm up. "It's as if it never happened," Katula replied, eyes wide.

Despite Darmond's warnings, Meera pushed ahead and attempted to Shift into Everard's mind. She had never tried Shifting into someone else's mind, only animals; however, Meera managed it with ease and relayed to the others what the giant was thinking. The blush on Everard's face when she noted his interest in Reyna, though, also alarmed Darmond.

Maggots!

Could she drop in on *his* thoughts any old time she wanted? There were things rattling around in there he didn't want anyone else, *especially* Meera, to know about. Everard suspected Shifting had been easiest for her because, out of all her abilities, it was the one she had practiced with most.

"The last is Summoning," Katula announced, giving the waterfall a look.

Meera nodded and slowly rose on unsteady feet. She walked as close to the rushing water as she dared before lifting her hands to it.

Her glow ignited and reflected off the water and onto Darmond and the others. As if the water were tethered to her hands, it parted in two as she spread out her arms. A ray of sun gleamed through the opening into the cave, momentarily lighting up the cavern. For a good while, Meera stood there, looking out through the water at the valley below. However, the over-extension of trying each ability finally took its toll when she dropped her arms. Immediately, the water rushed to fill the gap, cutting out the sunlight.

Everard caught Meera this time. When she didn't stir right away, Darmond chided the others for going too far and insisted he carry her back down to the cart while they grabbed their belongings. Once there, he laid her down, sat on the back of the cart, and waited.

"Ouch," she said, finally waking and rubbing her head.

"How are you feeling, Red?" he asked, turning around.

"Absolutely fine."

"Liar." He smiled.

She smiled back but then moaned with regret as her head pounded.

"You're pushing yourself too hard."

"I know," she admitted. "I just... I worry..."

"That the Grendolens will find you?"

"Yes. If they do, what will happen to all of you? To all of Pawtoton?" Reaching for his hand, Meera slowly pulled herself up and sat next to him.

"Meera," Darmond said, turning to look at her. "There's something I've been meaning to tell you."

Meera looked up at him and suddenly he lost all the words he had been prepared to say.

"You see, I… uh, well, *originally*, when I was… That is to say, back in my…" He turned away, ashamed he couldn't get the words out, but Meera smiled and cupped her hand under his chin. Turning his face to meet hers, she cut off his awkward attempt at telling her the truth. He sat there silently captivated in every way by the woman before him, intent on memorizing how she looked at that moment. So that when she did hear the truth and hated him for it, he could remember her as she was then. But Meera was not content to just sit in silence. Instead, she smiled that mischievous grin, which sent his heart pumping, and pulled his face closer to hers until their lips met.

Her kiss was warm and eager, and Darmond found himself unable to resist his better judgment. Pulling her body against his, he readily returned the kiss, savoring her taste and the feel of her soft lips against his.

All too soon, he heard footsteps returning down the path and had to withdraw. It was the hardest thing he had ever done.

The smile spreading across Meera's flushed face fell, however, when she saw Darmond's reserve.

"Oh," she breathed, quickly growing self-conscious. "I… I'm sorry. I thought you wanted…"

"No, no," Darmond quickly replied, realizing she had misread his expression. "That was… I mean, it was," he stumbled awkwardly, cursing his own stupidity.

Everard and Katula came around the bend, signaling Darmond to jump off the cart and put some space between Meera and himself.

"Ah, you're up and it looks like the color in your face has returned. How are you fairing?" Everard called to Meera as they made their way over.

"Much better, thanks," she replied, shooting an unsure glance Darmond's way.

"Wonderful!" The giant smiled. "I say we stop for some lunch and then continue the tour. I hear there are several tongas in the next town over who would be very happy to see you again. What say you?"

Meera flashed a huge smile and nodded. "Yes, please! It's been ages since I've seen Signot and the others!"

Glad for the distraction, Darmond busied himself with setting out the food. *Anything* to take his mind off those lips and the feel of her warm body wrapped in his arms.

It was duskfall by the time they found themselves closing in on Tawok's town borders once again. Darmond had never been so relieved to see buildings and crowded streets in his entire life. It signaled the end of a very long and uncomfortable trip in which he spent most of his time avoiding contact with a pair of red eyes. As soon as they passed through the gates leading into the Sovereign's Residence, he jumped off the cart.

"Where are you off to?" Katula demanded, giving him a suspicious look.

"Missed sparing today, but if I hurry, I can catch the tail end," Darmond replied hastily. "Be sure to tell Reyna so she doesn't think I tried to escape again," he added before dashing off. Making his way around the left side of the large building, he reached the militia's training grounds in record time. Just as he'd hoped, there were still a few guards practicing out in the yard, now dimly lit with evening lanterns. Grabbing a longspear and the youngling's leather armor the Tawokens had lent him, he ran out to meet the stragglers and joined in.

Darmond had always found solace in combat training. This time was no exception, as it felt good to move and stretch his muscles after sitting in the cart for an extended time. That and it allowed him to focus his mind on other things besides the awkwardness that he'd put between Meera and himself. Forcing those thoughts from his mind, Darmond pushed his body to the limits. Considering he was up against giants twice his size, it wasn't hard to do. Being smaller and quicker meant he had to keep moving to avoid his opponent's attacks and be fast enough to strike when he saw an opening. His spear wasn't as long as the ones the giants practiced with either.

On the first day out on the sparing field, after he was barely able to lift the one given to him in time to block hits to the ribs and chest, it had become unpleasantly obvious that he would need a weapon more tailored to his height and size. He still had bruises from that bout. Fortunately, Pawtoton guards start their training at a young age, so Darmond was able to switch out the larger spear for one their younglings used.

While the giants preferred to defend themselves with spears, Darmond had always felt more at ease with a longsword in his hands. However, you couldn't use one against such long spears, not when the giants wielding them were so well trained. Still, he enjoyed the challenge of learning to master new skills with other weapons, the spear, being one of them. It was one of the most basic weapons, and yet very difficult to perfect. It took great strength to maneuver it in such a way that both pointed at the enemy and blocked the user's body. Allowing the enemy to get too close meant the possibility of hand-to-hand combat, rendering the weapon useless—not that Darmond didn't enjoy sinking his fist into the opponent's face. But, when that face is a giant's, he was out fisted *and* out faced. Keeping that precious distance with the spear was vital to winning a sparring match.

Long after the guards withdrew from the field, Darmond stayed and ran through the new spear drills the giants had taught him. His borrowed clothes were drenched in sweat, and his muscles ached for him to stop, yet he forced himself to continue. Both expanding crescent moons were high in the night sky when Darmond finally put away the spear. Weary from his extended workout, he took his time winding his way through the Residence. He had just reached the massive staircase that led to their suite when a muffled noise coming from the direction of the Red Library caught his attention.

With it being so late, the hallway was void of servants or any other occupants, so Darmond decided to investigate. Despite being the only one up, he made sure to keep his approach as quiet as possible so as not to alert whoever was in the room—his spy habits kicking in without even realizing it.

Upon reaching the library's large double doors, he found them unguarded and one of them slightly ajar. Putting his back against the other door, he leaned over to peek in. At first, he thought he had interrupted a romantic interlude between Everard and Reyna, because he knew they were smitten, even if they didn't admit it. Darmond's breath caught, however, when he got a better look. Everard sat bound to a chair and was in the middle of being gagged by a figure in a black cloak. A figure *Darmond's* size. Three other black-cloaked assailants were looking through manuscripts sitting open on the library's table.

Maggots, they're after the scrolls!

Armed with only a side dagger he'd lifted from an alehouse-goer at the Tipsy Tonga, Darmond threw the blade at the figure next to Everard, hitting him directly in the throat and sending him writhing onto the floor as he bled out. A barrage of throwing knives flew at Darmond in retaliation from the other assailants, but they hit the solid door as he ducked back behind it. The moment he heard footsteps nearing, Darmond took hold of the door handle and swung it into the face of one of the intruders, breaking his nose and sending him thrashing on the floor. Not wasting any time, he pulled himself into the room, grabbed two of the knives stuck in the door, and faced the two men left standing. Out of the corner of his eye, he saw Everard working to break his bonds, but before he could get to him, the others attacked.

They were quick, quicker than him, even on a day he hadn't overworked himself. Within a breath, Darmond had been sliced in five separate places, thankfully, none that were vital. At least, not that he could tell. Darmond fought back, pulling out every move he had ever learned to keep from being overcome. As one of the men came down with his knife from above, the other went for Darmond's kidney. Sweeping his left arm up and around the front attacker, he managed to deliver his own cut as he pulled his blade around the man's upper arm. Simultaneously, he used his right arm to block the second attack from behind but took another cut to his forearm in the process. Ignoring the fresh pain from the wound, Darmond pulled his blade back in and up under the man's arm, sending his knife into the man's chest cavity. Before his attacker hit the floor, the other was already thrashing wildly at Darmond, attempting to nick a vital artery and bring a quick end to the fight. Darmond ducked and weaved in time to miss his advances, however, he could feel his already exhausted body losing the momentum from the adrenaline it had been running on.

An unexpected kick to an open wound on Darmond's thigh sent him to his knees, gasping for air. The cloaked man leaned over Darmond, grabbed his hair, and was pulling his arm back, ready to slice open his throat, when an oversized chair with a giant still attached to it smacked into the man's side. The impact threw Darmond sprawling onto the floor. Pushing aside the searing pain running through each of his limbs, Darmond staggered over to where Everard and his chair landed.

"Oh dear," the giant said in a shockingly calm voice as he lay on top of the man, still bound to the now broken chair. "I do believe my weight may have crushed him." Darmond looked at Everard for a long moment before laughing, despite the dangerous situation they had just survived.

"Here, let me untie you," Darmond said, reaching for the giant's bonds.

Once Everard was able to stand, the two of them returned to the assailant who had been knocked unconscious.

"I thought you said no one could find Pawtoton! Who *are* these people, Everard?" Darmond asked after they secured the unconscious intruder to a different chair.

"Chroniclers," the giant replied, his voice deep with sorrow.

"I take it from the look on your face, this was more than just a robbery gone wrong?"

"Indeed," Everard replied grimly. "They copied down something from our four scrolls and were demanding I give up the location of the fifth. Thank Yveth, you came when you did and that Katula had enough sense not to keep the Matuian scroll here."

"Did you see what they wrote?" Darmond asked.

"No, but that one over there put the note in his pocket," Everard replied, indicating to the Chronicler that Darmond had struck first.

Walking over to the robed man with the knife still embedded in his jugular, Darmond searched his pockets and pulled out a crumpled note with four phrases hastily scribbled on it.

"It's the hidden riddle" Darmond realized, handing the note to the giant.

"What is pure, yet unclean? Round, yet uneven? Accessible, yet hidden? Magnificent, yet minute?" the giant read aloud. "Yes, you're right, these verses are from the riddle."

"I thought the Chroniclers were basically, well, *your* people, Everard. Why would they need to sneak into Pawtoton and steal records?"

"A question I intend to get an answer to," the giant promised. "Right now, I can only assume it was because they did not want us to *know* they were after the Tercara Scrolls' information. But to assault me in the manner they did..." The giant staggered before adding, "not to mention they nearly killed you! These Chroniclers have broken their vows to the most *heinous* degree!"

"Why do you think they were after the information?"

"The better question to ask, I'm afraid, is who sent them after the information."

"I thought the only way in or out of this place was through some secret tunnel. How did they know about it?" Darmond asked, nodding at the bound figure.

"Secret to all those save Preservers and Chroniclers. How else would we have the records we do if they did not provide them for us?" the giant pointed out.

"I suppose this means the sovereign will be involved now," Darmond mumbled.

Everard winced. "I am afraid this is far larger than just a botched robbery, my friend. The betrayal of the Chroniclers means we can no longer trust *any* of the records they have provided us or were intending to provide. They have stripped us of our ability to carry out the promise we made the Ancient Ones all those cycles ago," the giant realized. "What we do from this point on will change the very grains of our culture."

"I'm sorry, Everard. Truly," Darmond replied, placing his hand on the giant's arm. The motion caused him to wince.

"You need to see a healer," Everard realized, taking in the amount of blood that soaked his clothes.

"I've had worse." Darmond winked with a grin.

The surviving Chronicler began to stir, drawing their attention.

"Looks like you're the only one left breathing," Darmond noted to the Chronicler through gritted teeth. "Which means *you're* the fortunate one who gets to answer the questions. Let's start by you telling us who you are and what in Nisri's name you're doing here."

There was nothing notable about the man's appearance, other than the matching black cloak he and his companions wore. Underneath, he was dressed in the same generic clothes as any Midtierian farmer would wear, and kept his beard and hair trimmed like one too. But then, Darmond remembered that Everard said the Chroniclers were trained to blend in with those around them.

Maggots and rot, they're almost as good at disguising themselves as I am!

Their captive didn't bother to respond, so Everard took a step closer.

"Why were you after the scrolls?" he demanded, looking into the man's hazel eyes. "Why steal what you could have asked to view without the need of secrecy?"

The man spat blood that was still flowing from his broken nose into Everard's face before spreading a defiant smile up at him.

"How can you *be* like this?" the giant exclaimed, losing his usual reserve. "Do you know what you have *done*? What will this do to Pawtoton?"

The man began laughing, and before Darmond could stop him, Everard backhanded the prisoner across the face. "You've violated every code we live by! You've broken the vow which our people made to the Terca... to the Ancient Ones."

Darmond shot Everard a warning glance, but it was too late. A sudden gleam broke out in the man's eyes.

"So you *do* have the fifth scroll, then," he wheezed through his bruised and bloodied face. "It is only a matter of time before the others find it."

"Others? *What* others?" Darmond demanded, growing worried.

"What do you need the scroll for?" Everard pushed, ignoring Darmond's question. "Who sent you?"

Suddenly, the man's body jerked and contorted within its constraints then froze.

"Is he dead?" Everard asked, unsure whether to approach him or not. Before Darmond could respond, the man's head rose, revealing cloudy *white* eyes.

Both he and the giant jumped back in surprise.

"Rot!" Darmond cursed, caught unprepared. "What in Nihility just happened?" Their prisoner moved his white eyes slowly around the room as if taking it all in for the first time, before settling back on Darmond and Everard.

"*You...*" the man growled through the same voice but with a different accent. "You have caused more trouble than I expected."

Darmond and Everard looked at each other, unsure which one the man was referring to.

"You have the fifth scroll," the man stated with a cock of his head, as if just finding out. Then a pleased smile broke across his face. "*She* is here as well. The scroll *and* the key. I could not have planned it better myself."

Before either Darmond or Everard could question the man, his head went limp again, and when he came to, his eyes were hazel once more.

"What the *rot* was that?" Darmond demanded, looking at the giant. "It was like he was... possessed or something."

Everard's face grew sickly pale. "Not possessed, *Shifted*," he whispered, his eyes turning to face Darmond.

"What, like Meera can do?" Darmond asked, incredulously. The realization of what the giant was implying hit Darmond in the gut like a kick from an angry war horse.

"You mean to say Meera isn't the *only* Ancient out there?" he demanded, running his hand through his hair nervously.

The giant nodded slowly. "And whoever that was now knows she's here and has the fifth scroll," Everard replied, piecing it together.

Darmond's head shot up. "The others," he breathed, remembering what their prisoner had said.

"What?" Everard asked, confused.

"Right before the second... *voice* appeared, he said there were others," Darmond explained, pointing to the cloaked man.

Everard's eyes grew wide. "Then that means..."

"Meera and Katula are in *grave* danger," Darmond interjected, before turning on his heels and running for the door.

CHAPTER NINETEEN

Finnik

The pain surging through his body told Finnik he hadn't died. *Yet.* It was so great, he wished he would. Twice before, he had come to, only to vomit before passing out again in agony. His head felt like it had been crushed under the cliff he'd fallen down on, his eyes were too swollen to open, and his ears still rang from the beating Varcor had delivered. He was certain he had a concussion and almost just as certain he'd taken permanent damage to one of his eyes. But he was alive, and it seemed his body refused to let him embrace death.

He hadn't moved since the cliffs had given away and dropped him down into the deep snowy banks below. Had a fresh snowbank not been there, or had it not been so deep, the fall alone would have killed him. Finnik lost track of time as he lay there, cocooned in the hole his body had made upon landing. The cold probably would have taken him, too, if he didn't have his furs on. The upside to the frigid temperatures, however, was how good it felt against his swollen extremities. Every once in a while, Finnik would grab some snow and shovel it into his mouth. His swollen jaw protested, but his need for water overcame the pain.

At long last, on day… whatever it was, Finnik was able to pry open one of his eyes. At first, the blinding light hurt nearly as much as moving his eyelid did, but after a while, he adjusted and was able to make out the cliffs above. That was when he spotted the boulders sitting directly to his left. They had been part of the cliffs he had stood on fighting Varcor. He had been fortunate not to have ended up under one of them when the terra gave way. Fortune, though, or fate? His memory of the fight came flooding back, and along with it, his last thoughts. Had he really cried out to Yveth in the end?

He tried opening his other eye, but it was still too swollen. It also felt *different* than his other, which made him wonder if he would ever be able to see out of it again. Giving up on it at the moment, Finnik worked on checking his limbs. Most of Varcor's blows had been to his upper body, mainly his face and skull, so the only bruising he felt elsewhere was from the fall. There again, fortune, or dare he say it, god, smiled upon him. So far as he could tell, his ribs only had minor bruising. Maybe a fracture or two, but no clean breaks. Sitting up made him want to retch again, but all that came were only dry heaves. His stomach was empty. *Too* empty. The thought of hot bone broth and how he didn't have any to sip on at that moment made him endure the difficulties of trying to stand. His head pounded like an eager blacksmith hammering out metal on an anvil and caused spots to clog the vision in his one working eye. Once his body accepted the fact that he was standing, he attempted to take a few steps.

And so it went on like that, one step at a time, until Finnik found he had walked to the newly formed rocky slope caused by the cliff giving way. Had it not been there, there would have been no way for him to climb back up to Varcor's camp at the top of the cliff. Yet another miraculous find for Finnik to ponder over. The climb itself was slow, just as all his movements had been, but eventually he made it to the top.

The campsite was mostly deserted, save for the bodies and a few tents left in a hasty retreat. Baska Sorrel was among the fallen. She had been loyal to the last, so Finnik took the time to see she was laid to rest properly before continuing. He was surprised to find a few supplies left within the abandoned tents. The supplies, along with the unburied dead and abandoned tents, told Finnik that Varcor had been in quite the hurry to pull out. It wasn't because the traitor had lost and ordered a retreat; he had clearly won. Which told him Varcor had either received word of where the Tarmanon heir was or had received new orders altogether.

What was it Varcor had said? That Finnik was too predictable? Was that why he hadn't realized Varcor was under orders from Lord Agnarr? Time and time again, Finnik had underestimated the man. Yet here he was, still very much alive despite Varcor's efforts. There was no way he could return to Grendolen, not after suffering such a humiliating defeat and certainly not after his treasonous words. He'd be put to flame the instant he entered the city. Once word of his treason reached Lord Agnarr, Finnik's family would be made to suffer, too, but he had no way of sending them a warning. His passion and pride for the empire and its people, however, were still burning strong, and he wasn't about to give up on them just yet.

He had no other option but one. It was time the tables were turned and Varcor underestimated Finnik. Hoping fortune was still with him, Finnik ransacked the rest of the abandoned tents. He was munching on some dried venison jerky when he came across what he was looking for. Varcor had said Finnik didn't know all that was in play, but the crumpled message in his hand now changed those odds. It was a message straight from Lord Agnarr himself to Varcor Orna. A message that revealed Lord Agnarr had sent Chroniclers to aid Varcor's army and that the heir had sought refuge in a place called Pawtoton. But that wasn't the biggest revelation. What took Finnik by surprise was who the message was addressed to. It was addressed to Lord Agnarr's *son*.

For the first time, Finnik was finally able to put the pieces together. Varcor's actions and ability to get away with all he'd done made sense at last. He wasn't just favored by the emperor, he was his flesh and blood. Finnik knew the emperor had younglings, *many* younglings. At age nineteen, Lord Agnarr had risen to power, the youngest ruler in the Grendolens' history. By twenty-two he'd conquered Moorland. Now, at thirty-eight cycles of age, he had expanded his family like he had the empire, keeping over fifteen wives and well over twice as many younglings. But none of them had been named heir to the empire as of yet. Varcor's desperation now spoke volumes. If he were the one to capture

Meera Tarmanon, Lord Agnarr would name him heir to the empire. Finnik would *never* have succeeded with his orders. Lord Agnarr, the emperor he had pledged his life and loyalty to, had struck Finnik off without a second thought. That realization sent ripples of anger sweeping through Finnik until it built up enough for him to make a decision—one he never thought he would make. With a renewed sense of purpose, he pocketed the message and finished combing through the tent.

Finnik was picking through the battlefield remains, searching for weapons, when he came across one of Varcor's mystery soldiers he'd allied with who, by some miracle, had survived. Seeing an opportunity, he checked over the man's wounds and found they wouldn't be fatal if tended to. So, Finnik got a fire going and set the man up within one of the abandoned tents. There, he cauterized the wound to stop the bleeding and waited.

It wasn't until the next day that the man finally awoke. Upon seeing Finnik, the man's hand went to his side, grasping for a cutlass that wasn't there.

"You didn't think I'd let you keep that, did you?" Finnik's ebony face frowned. The man winced at his sudden movement and grabbed his side.

"What did you *do* to me?" he asked through gritted teeth.

"I saved your life."

"*Why*?"

"Because you have what I want," Finnik said.

"And what's that?"

"Answers."

CHAPTER TWENTY

Meera

For the first time in a long time, Meera did not dream about the horrors of her past or her memories of escaping the fires. Instead, she dreamt of waterfalls and kisses, which, even in her sleep, brought a blush to her cheeks. That was why, when she felt someone rousing her from slumber, she had to fight the urge not to blacken their eyes with her fist.

"What in the *rot* could possibly be important enough to wake me in the middle of the night?" she complained, sitting up to face whoever dared disturb her.

In the darkness, a shadowed figure approached her bedside, causing her to sit back in alarm.

"Shhh! It's me, you dolt!" Katula whispered, covering Meera's mouth with her hand.

"What's wrong?" Meera whispered back once Katula took her hand away.

"Noises, in the hallway," Katula replied, nodding outside her private room. "Something about it just doesn't feel right."

Meera knew by now to trust the woman's intuition, so she climbed down from the large bed and pulled on the robe the giants had provided during her stay. Following Katula's lead, the two women tiptoed to the wall by her room's door and waited silently in the dark. Sure enough, Meera picked up the sounds of feet shuffling through their suite's sitting room, feet that weren't giant-sized. Whoever was out there was making their way through each of the private rooms looking for something. Or someone. Meera's heartbeat quickened as the intruders closed in on her own room.

"I don't have any weapons on me," Katula warned Meera bitterly. "Remind me to take that up with the sovereign when next we meet."

"Neither do I," the Moorlander complained.

"That's not *entirely* true," Katula pointed out.

"I am *not* ready for that!" Meera shot back, remembering how weak using her powers made her. Desperate for any weapon, Meera left her place behind the door and went to grab the pitcher sitting on her nightstand. In a pinch, she could break it and use the shards as a weapon. Passing the dresser, she spotted the heavy silver handheld mirror the giants had placed there for her use. Grabbing it, Meera made it back to Katula's side just as her private room door slowly swung open. Meera handed Katula the mirror, giving the woman a shrug when she looked offended by the offer. Despite her reservations, Katula took it.

Armed with a looking glass and pitcher, the two women watched as three cloaked figures approached the bed where Meera had been dreaming only moments ago. As soon as the intruders realized no one occupied it, they began rummaging through the dresser drawers looking for something.

"It's not here," one of them whispered.

"Neither is she," another replied.

She? An uncomfortable feeling washed over Meera as she realized they were referring to her. The Grendolens, it seemed, had once again caught up to them. Anger rose within Meera, and before she thought better of it, she kicked her door shut, locking the bolt, and faced the hooded figures.

"Good evening, gentlemen," she growled. The slam startled the men, but they quickly recovered. In the dim light, Meera watched as they unsheathed matching curved cutlasses.

"I'm not liking these odds," Katula whispered to Meera.

"Where is the scroll?" one of the cloaked intruders demanded, pointing his sword tip at the women.

"Scroll?" Meera feigned. "We're in Pawtoton, gentleman. They have libraries *filled* with scrolls, none of which are held in bedchambers."

The man ignored her and took a step forward to get a better look at the women in the darkness.

"One's a Matuian, which means the other must be the heir," he confirmed to his companions, growing excited.

The other two stepped up and also eyed Meera. "Hand over the Stone Key, Tarmanon bitch," the one on the right spat, pointing his blade at her throat.

"First they want scrolls, now they want keys," Katula mocked. "Seems they can't make up their minds."

The men ignored the Matuian and all three took a step closer to Meera.

"Any closer, and this jug will find its way down your jugular," Meera warned, tightening her grip on the handle.

"Give us the key and scroll, and your life will be spared," the middle one coaxed.

"I *have* no key," Meera replied. "But let's be honest with one another. Even if I had what you were looking for, you wouldn't spare our lives."

The man in the middle lifted his eyebrow and nodded. He was about to say something when his body began convulsing. Both Katula and Meera jumped back against the wall. The other two men flanking their shaking leader also took a step back but did not seem alarmed. As soon as the convulsions stopped, the man lifted his head and stared at Meera through cloudy white eyes.

"Meera Rammel Lavonna Tarmanon, heir to the Moorland throne. At last, we meet." He spoke calmly through a different voice.

"Who *are* you?" Meera demanded, taken aback by the unexplainable change.

"You don't look anything like them," the voice replied.

"Like whom?"

"We almost met, once, you and I, many cycles ago," confided the voice projecting through the man. "Your parents, however, got in the way."

Meera blinked in dismay. She was talking to the man who had murdered her parents. Who had burned her kingdom to the terra.

"Lord Agnarr," she guessed, through gritted teeth.

"I think about that night often, don't you?" he mused. "I was young then, and naively thought King Tarmanon would bow, without a fight, to my empire. But as you already know, he refused. For three cycles my armies fought Moorland, yet their defenses proved impenetrable. It took feigning an alliance and signing a peace treaty to finally gain entrance. I made sure to tell your parents before I killed them that there would be nothing left of their kingdom. Had I managed to find you among the flames, I would already have the Stone Key and you would never have had to go on the run. Yet, here we find ourselves." There was so much Meera wanted to say, wanted to *do,* to the man who had taken everything from her, but she found herself laughing instead.

"How pathetic is it to spend all this energy hunting me only to find out I don't have the very thing you want?" she snarled. "I have *no* key!"

"Do not *lie* to me, Meera," Lord Agnarr hissed, losing patience. "I *know* you possess it. Your mother wore it daily, but it wasn't there when I slit her throat."

Involuntarily, Meera's hand clutched the hawk pendant hidden under her nightshift. The moment she did, the white eyes of the man Lord Agnarr was talking through widened.

"So you *do* have it." He smiled greedily. "I don't *need* you, Meera Tarmanon. You can go live your life as you see fit and never be on the run again. Give me the Stone Key and the Matuian Tercara Scroll, and I will let you go."

Meera paused. Not because she believed the man, but because of what he had revealed. The Stone Key was her hawk pendant! That, coupled with the fact that Lord Agnarr hadn't mentioned her abilities, meant one thing.

I'm not the weapon, she realized, relief flooding through her despite her current predicament. Even though she was facing the man she'd spent cycles hating, Meera felt the heavy burden she had been carrying finally lift off her shoulders. She wasn't some ancient weapon built to harm those around her. Odd, that it was the person she hated most who delivered such good news. Still, if she wasn't the weapon, what then did the Stone Key, her pendant, unlock?

"Meera, the pitcher," Katula whispered next to her, nodding at it.

"So?" she replied, confused.

"It's full of *water,*" the Matuian stressed. Just as Meera caught her friend's meaning, the man Lord Agnarr was talking through stepped closer and suddenly froze.

"*Red* eyes," he gasped, face alight with utter shock. "You *can't* be..." he breathed. Not waiting for him to make the first move, Meera withdrew into herself and took hold of the flame, which was beginning to feel more familiar each time she used it. Instantly, her veins lit up, sending the fire racing through her. Soon the dark room held a warm glow, lighting up the three intruders. The two men flanking the one Lord Agnarr spoke through reacted first, stepping in front of Meera to protect their leader. But Katula was faster, and in a blink of an eye, she threw the heavy mirror she held at the head of the one closest to her. With his focus on Meera, the man didn't block the attack in time and received an unexpected blow to his temple. The force of the contact caused him to drop his sword, giving Katula the opportunity she needed to lunge for it herself.

At the same time Katula had charged at that man, Meera Summoned the water within the pitcher, pulling it out and containing it in a circular sphere-shape in the air beside her. With the pitcher emptied, she hit it hard against the wall, shattering it. The other cloaked man did not hesitate in his movements as he lunged at Meera with his curved cutlass. As she ducked to the side, narrowly missing his blade, Lord Agnarr, broke out of his stupor.

"*Do not harm her*!" he yelled at the man with the curved cutlass.

He knows *what I am,* Meera realized with a start. But Lord Agnarr's words came too late—Meera's assailant recovered his miss with incredible speed and would have landed a thrust to her torso had she not slammed a broken pottery piece into his thigh. The move wasn't enough to bring him down but only seemed to make him angrier. Her water sphere faltered, nearly falling to the floor as she lost concentration. Recovering, Meera quickly Summoned the water forward, aiming directly for the man's face until it enveloped his entire head. Panicking, he stopped his attack and began trying to push away the water. Meera held her hands out, commanding the water to stay where she willed it. Wildly, the man thrashed about in vain, unable to escape his fate.

Meera shot a quick look Katula's way and saw the man she had hit was back up and facing her with a knife he'd pulled. Katula had the man's sword, but she wasn't proficient with using one. Meera desperately wanted to help, but she didn't know if she could keep Summoning at the same time. It took all her concentration to keep the water from dissipating. Thankfully, she didn't have to wait long. After a few excruciating moments, the man trapped in water stopped struggling and fell lifelessly to the floor. With a gasp, Meera let the water drop, splashing over the man's body. Fighting the exhaustion that hit, Meera turned and found Katula had managed to nick her assailant's artery, sending him writhing on the floor and covered in blood. With Lord Agnarr's guards down, both women turned to face him.

"Now I understand why your parents hid you from me." His white eyes smiled, unfazed by his guards' deaths. "No wonder they refused a political marriage between our kingdoms. Had I known—"

At that moment, the bedroom door was kicked in, ushering in Everard and Darmond.

"Are you all right?" Darmond asked both the women, catching his breath.

"*You* again," Lord Agnarr hissed, white eyes narrowing. "I should have killed you when I had the chance."

"You've met before?" Meera asked Darmond, distrusting Agnarr's words.

"I've never met this man in my life," Darmond retorted defensively. "But we did just kill several of his companions downstairs and Everard's got another who had white eyes tied up and under guard."

"Not the man, the voice," Meera explained. "It's *Lord Agnarr.*"

Darmond's face grew dark as he looked the man over. "No, it's not," he replied, shaking his head.

"He knew about my parents," Meera stressed, annoyed Darmond didn't believe her.

"It's true," Katula confirmed, coming to stand by them.

"Look, I've seen Lord Agnarr before, and trust me, this man isn't him," Darmond countered.

"You've seen him?" Meera asked, rounding on Darmond. "When?"

Darmond's face suddenly fell and Lord Agnarr let out a satisfied laugh.

"Did he not *tell* you?" the emperor asked, looking at Meera. "It was thanks to him we knew you had survived the massacre! He told Varcor you were alive and *exactly* where to look."

Meera stood back aghast and stopped glowing.

"No," she whispered, turning pleading eyes to Darmond. But the guilt reflected within his own confirmed Lord Agnarr spoke the truth.

"I... I tried to tell you," he began.

"I *trusted* you," she breathed through gritted teeth.

"That is how it has always been with him, Meera," Lord Agnarr said, with a twisted note of tenderness to it. "Always looking out for himself, to the detriment of those around him. Just ask him what became of the men under his command when my own captured them. Out of them all, he is the only one left standing."

Meera stood there, too stunned to move. She wanted to believe it was all a lie; after all, it was Lord Agnarr telling her these things. But the look on Darmond's face told her it was the truth.

The hurt and betrayal she felt then turned to anger—a deep, seething rage that was all too easy to give into. Her glow returned and her exhaustion vanished, fueled with anger and flame burning *so* hot, she wasn't sure she could contain it. Shaking under the pressure, Meera turned back to the man Lord Agnarr was speaking through. That was when she hit a moment of clarity.

"You're *Shifting*," she realized aloud, her glowing red eyes looking directly at him.

The surprised expression that hit his face confirmed she was right. But it was more than Shifting. Lord Agnarr had looked into her eyes and realized what she was.

"You're a *Tercara*," she challenged, eyes narrowing.

A smile broke across the man's face. "Indeed, I am. Give me the Stone Key, Meera," Lord Agnarr demanded.

"You can't hurt me," she surmised. "Not when you're Shifting through someone who isn't a Tercara."

"*The key!*" he yelled, starting to lose control.

"You are in no position to barter."

The body Lord Agnarr had Shifted through was beginning to heave large breaths, as if it was suffering. It seemed he could only Shift for so long before it took a toll on the body he was using.

"That body is fading," Meera remarked, letting Lord Agnarr know she understood the full extent of what was occurring.

"There are a *thousand* more like him," Lord Agnarr noted, unfazed.

"Maybe," Meera replied, "but by the time you Shift into another, the Stone Key and I will be long gone." As soon as she said it, Meera Summoned the water on the floor and *willed* it into the man's orifices. Streams of water rose and gathered together then shot forward and found their way into his nostrils, ears, and mouth. As the body shook against the attack and Shifting, the white eyes began to fade.

"This isn't over, Meera," Lord Agnarr choked as his human vessel's lungs filled with water. "I know what you are now and that you have the Stone Key. My... army... will be there soon..." The moment the body of the man Lord Agnarr was Shifting through failed, the connection was broken and the cloaked man slumped dead into a heap on the floor.

Meera passed out moments later.

When she came to, Meera found herself back in her bed. The door to the room was left ajar, thanks to the kicking-in it took earlier that broke its hardware. The dim light streaming in the cracked opening revealed to Meera that she had slept through the night. Forgotten on the floor were the remains of a broken pitcher and splattered blood. The fact that they hadn't been cleaned up instantly told Meera something wasn't right. Out of habit, Meera clutched her pendant, the Stone Key.

There was no need to try and recall what had happened, it was all *too* fresh in her mind. Agnarr was a Tercara. He could Shift just like she could, only it was clear his skill at the ability far outweighed her own. He had actually Shifted into the mind of another person and completely taken over control of their body. The reality of it sent a wave of fear down Meera's spine. But there was more than just fear she was feeling. There was anger. Darmond had confessed to being the one who betrayed her to the enemy! It was his actions that had sent the Grendolen forces to invade Matui and force Katula's people to evacuate. Now, Lord Agnarr not only knew she was in Pawtoton but knew she had the Stone Key as well.

And he said his army would be here soon, she reminded herself with growing alarm.

Ready to unleash her fury on Darmond and figure out what to do about Lord Agnarr, Meera rose and stormed out of the room, forgetting she was still in her nightshift. Only it wasn't Darmond she encountered in the suite but Reyna and an entire group of guards, dressed in full suits of tonga bone armor. Meera's sudden appearance sent all eyes on her, causing her anger to falter. With an awkward nod, she looked over at the manageress for help.

"Matron Osberry?" she asked, unsure as to what was going on.

"My dear, I'm glad to see you're up." the giant replied. "I'm afraid I have terrible news. The Grendolens have breached the tunnel," Reyna confessed. "Led by Chroniclers, they have crossed under the cliffs and are marching toward Towak as I speak. They will be here by nightfall. You are no longer safe, I fear, within Pawtoton. The sovereign has tasked me with seeing you safely out of the village. But we must hurry. We don't have much time."

Meera stood there for a moment, trying to process what the giant said. It sounded all too familiar. Hadn't she just fled Matui because of the same thing, and even before that, Moorland? The Matuians had lost their ancestral homeland, and now the Pawtoton giants were about to have the same thing happen to them. Meera knew that if she fled once again, Lord Agnarr would only continue hunting her now that he knew she had the Stone Key. How many more kingdoms would fall in pursuit of it?

"No," she replied firmly.

"No?" the manageress repeated.

"I'm not going anywhere. I'm *done* running, Matron."

"But the sovereign..."

"The sovereign is going to need all the help she can get to fight off the Grendolens," Meera interjected. "I'm the one Lord Agnarr wants."

"You?" Reyna asked, looking as perplexed as ever.

Meera sighed. She didn't have time for this. "Reyna, where are my companions?"

"They, along with our high council, are currently meeting with the sovereign matriarch."

"Take me to them," she demanded.

The entire residence had been thrown into an uproar. As Reyna and the group of guards escorted Meera hurriedly through its halls, cherished items were being stowed and barricades were being assembled. Guards with their tonga helms ran past them from all directions, on their way to wherever it was they had been ordered to go. Meera thought they were headed toward the Residence's High Council Chambers, however, Reyna took a different turn and delivered her to a smaller room filled with anxious council members all vying for the sovereign's attention. Congregated around the old giant, stood what Meera assumed were her closest advisers. A familiar greenhead stood among them, but there was no sign of Darmond.

"Meera," the Matuian greeted her in surprise. "What are you doing here?"

"Don't you start," Meera warned quietly. "Where is everyone? Darmond? Everard?"

"No one has seen Darmond since last night," Katula acknowledged, "and after Everard gave a full account of what happened, he was sent to oversee securing the Red Library's contents."

"Everard gave a *full* account? How much does the sovereign know?"

Katula looked her in the eyes. "Everything," Katula confirmed. "But so far she's not revealed what Lord Agnarr is after, or what you are."

At least in that, Meera was comforted.

"Meera Tarmanon," the sovereign bellowed upon seeing her in the crowded room. "You should be halfway into the Cassias by now. Why are you *here*?"

"I'm not leaving," Meera stated, setting her jaw. "I intend to stay and fight."

"Very well," the old ruler agreed, waving her hands in surrender.

"That's it? You're not going to dissuade me?"

"Why? If you want to risk your life, that is your right. We could use all the help we can get. I only ask that you both report in to my military commander so he can position you properly." The sovereign turned to one of her guards. "See that their weapons are returned to them immediately."

The guard nodded and ran off.

"Any word of our prisoner?" she asked another guard.

"He has yet to talk, Supreme Sovereign." He bowed.

"Prisoner?" Meera asked.

"A man claiming to be the commandant general of the Grendolen army," the sovereign replied. "We are working to ascertain whether he is who he says he is. But that is secondary to coordinating our defenses, of which, as you can see, I am in the middle of," the sovereign stressed, losing her patience.

"You're busy here. Why not let Katula and I handle him?" Meera suggested.

The sovereign looked as if she was going to deny the Moorlander's request but instead waved another guard over. "Take them to the prisoner."

CHAPTER TWENTY-ONE

Finnik

Finnik raised his head as the giant guards opened the door to the room he was being kept in. *Giants*. Just another thing his aged mind hadn't seen coming. It had taken every ounce of strength he had to beat Varcor to Pawtoton. Had the Chronicler he'd interrogated not given up the location of the smaller tunnel entrance that passed under the Pawtoton cliffs, Finnik would have once again found himself beaten by the traitor. But Varcor had an army now and that large of a fighting force meant he had to move them through the larger tunnel at a slower pace.

The leader of the giants, the Supreme Sovereign, had, however, not taken kindly to Finnik's unexpected appearance when he was captured just within the boundary of Tawok village. It hadn't been his intention to get caught, of course. His plan had been to sneak into the town, locate the Tarmanon heir, and use her as leverage to negotiate his family's safety with Lord Agnarr. The way things had been going since his fall, with the cliff giving way before Varcor stabbed him through, the boulders just missing his head, the rockslide creating an exit out of the ravine, the message he'd found in the camp, and even the Chronicler who knew where the location of the tunnel, Finnik had begun to wonder if fortune was on his side. That, or his prayer really *worked*. Yet, now he sat, a prisoner of the giants, and most likely would be sitting there once Varcor's forces came rushing in. How he hated the idea of Varcor coming in to find him tied up like a stuffed pig ready for the feast. That was how he thought it would play out, until he looked up to find two women being ushered into the room.

"Leave us," the redhead said to the guards.

The guards themselves didn't seem so sure about doing so, but once the women produced the sovereign's signed permission to view the prisoner, they eventually complied. Alone with Finnik, the women came over and stood before him.

"Do you have a name, Shadeblight?"

With solid black eyes and dark-green hair, it was obvious she was Matuian, but the white tattoos around her eyes gave away her station among the woodland tribe.

"You're one of the chief's family," he stated, certain he was right. "Which means you must be the Tarmanon heir." He used his one good eye to get his first look at Meera. Finnik let out a long bitter laugh. "You don't know how many moads I spent under orders searching for you. And here you are, standing right before me."

"So, you *are* the commandant general," Meera surmised.

"Finnik Doth," he confirmed with a nod. Then, cocking his head, he noted the heir's appearance. "You have the same red eyes."

"Same eyes as who?" Meera asked.

"Lord Agnarr."

"Meera, he led the attack on Matui. Let's end him and be done with it," the Matuian growled, growing tired of the chatter and readying her bow.

"Yes, I am the one who led the attack on Wildwood," he confessed calmly. "But killing me now would be a mistake."

The Matuian hissed at his reference to Wildwood, but the heir jumped in before she could respond. "Why is that?"

"I have information you need."

The Matuian pulled back her arrow.

"Katula, wait," Meera advised. "Let's hear him out." Katula lowered her bow but kept the arrow nocked.

"Varcor Orna," the heir said, pulling Finnik's attention back to her. "That's who is leading the Grendolens. Am I correct?" He could tell she was testing him to see if he would tell the truth.

"Yes." Finnik nodded.

"He usurped you, didn't he?" she continued, making Finnik's weathered face wince. It was still hard to admit it, let alone hear it from the heir's lips. "If you're no longer in charge, why try sneaking into Pawtoton? Did you think you could capture me yourself?"

Finnik chose to stay quiet. If he could break free of his cell, there was still a chance of him making the statement a reality.

"If he won't answer then there's no need to keep him around," Katula noted.

The heir nodded and then thought of something. "I think we should try a different tactic," Meera suggested.

To Finnik's utter dismay, the heir began *glowing*. Before he could even start to comprehend what was happening, he *felt* her reach into his mind. His *own* mind! He sat there unable to move as he felt Meera unlocking the secrets he desperately needed to keep hidden. And before he knew it, she withdrew and once again, he had control of his own body.

"What in Nihility *are* you, woman?" he gasped, eyes wide with awe.

The heir ignored him. "Varcor is Agnarr's son!" she exclaimed to Katula.

The Matuian helped steady the heir as she struggled to stay standing.

"His *son*? That's all we need." Katula winced. "If Varcor has the same abilities..."

Meera shook her head. "I don't think he does, otherwise he would have found me ages ago. But Finnik's memories do caution me. Varcor was able to clear the passage of the avalanche far quicker than he should. He's been trained with the Elements too. I suspect his ability and knowledge of the Elements have aided him this whole time. It would explain how they cleared the pass so quickly. Finnik also intended to try and capture me and use me as leverage. But—" Meera paused, looking into Finnik's remaining brown eye. "I think he may have just changed his mind after what he saw me do."

Out of nowhere a feeling of shame washed over the old commander, and it wasn't one the heir was making him feel.

"Varcor is a Summoner," Katula realized.

Meera nodded then looked back at Finnik, who was still in a daze over what had taken place.

"Yveth heard you," the heir told him.

"What?" he staggered, even though he had heard her clearly.

"In your memories," she pushed. "You called out to Yveth and Yveth saved you. That is no small thing, Finnik Doth."

"*What are you?*" he asked again, unable to think of anything else to say.

"A Tercara." He didn't follow, so she added, "An Ancient."

Understanding hit him then. She was what Lord Agnarr was, that man who had used Finnik to put to flame and death so many in his name. The man who threatened the downfall of the Grendolen Empire. Finnik had seen what Lord Agnarr could do, what *abilities* he possessed. Facing that, who could stand against him? Yet here before him now, stood one who had those same abilities. Was the Tarmanon heir right? Did Yveth really hear his prayer? Had everything that had happened to him happen for a reason? Perhaps, just maybe, Meera Tarmanon could help him save the Grendolen Empire from Lord Agnarr, even if it meant it would require him to do the unthinkable. For the first time in a long time, Finnik felt a ray of hope.

"You're the only one who can stop him," Finnik announced with determination as he stood as tall as his restraints would allow.

"You *know* what Lord Agnarr is?" Meera asked.

"I know he has the same powers as you, and I know you'll need me if you wish to survive the force Varcor Orna has brought with him." He then found himself doing something he never would have thought possible within his lifetime. Finnik Doth, former commandant general of the Grendolen Empire, fell to one knee and pledged his life in service to the woman he had spent cycles hunting.

CHAPTER TWENTY-TWO

Katula

Katula stared down at the man before her with a mixture of shock and disbelief. He didn't seriously think Meera would buy his newfound loyalty to her. Proving her wrong, however, Meera nodded and called for the guards.

"Meera, what are you *doing*?"

"I'm going to free him," she said, looking back down on the scarred man.

"*We can't trust him*! He's the one who attacked my people. Rot, he probably led the attack on Moorland too!"

The guards entered the room and Meera requested they unlock his chains before she turned back to Katula.

"I *know* he was the one who burned Moorland to the terra. I saw him do it with my own eyes. I Shifted into his mind, remember? When I did, I saw everything. *Everything*, Katula," she emphasized, her red eyes wide. "His loyalty lies with his people, not Lord Agnarr. He'll do anything to keep Grendolen from falling prey to its leader's ill intentions. I don't know how else to explain it to you, Katula, but I know, beyond any doubt, that he will follow me, even to his death, if it means I can overcome Lord Agnarr and put to rights the Grendolen Empire. There are other things I saw, but we don't have time to stand here and chat about them. You'll just have to trust me on this one."

Katula stood there motionless as what her sister said sank in and she watched the guards release their prisoner. Out of his chains, Finnik again took to one knee and bowed before Meera, waiting for orders. If there wasn't an army on Pawtoton's doorstep ready to destroy them all, she might have allowed herself to laugh. Here was the Grendolens' famous general bowing before the Moorland heir. The irony was not lost on her.

"I think you'll be needing that eye back if we're to win this thing," Meera noted, placing her hand on his shoulder. The old ex-general stayed completely still as Meera used her abilities to try and Mend his wounded eye. Once finished, she took a step back, steadied herself from the exhaustion, and waited. Katula noted Meera grew less tired the more she used her abilities. She didn't even need her help standing up this time. Finnik, visibly shaken by what just took place, carefully unwrapped the bandage around his head that concealed the eye. Underneath, his wound had been put back to rights, mostly.

"I'm sorry Finnik," Meera apologized. "It had been a while since the damage was done and I could only do so much. How does it feel?"

Finnik slowly opened his Mended eye and blinked as it focused on the two women and guards in the room. Scars had formed around the socket, but the wounds were healed. The iris, however, was no longer brown but the color of ice, a light blue-gray.

"I can see," he breathed, trying to take it in. "Thank you, Lady Tarmanon." He bowed. "I am in your debt."

"You certainly are," Katula jumped in at last. "And don't you go forgetting it. Meera may be willing to trust you, but I certainly *do not*. One wrong move and my best arrow will be finding its way into your skull. Got it?"

Meera gave her a side glance, but Finnik nodded and lowered his head in respect and recognition. "I'd expect nothing else," he replied solemnly, looking at her with his different-colored eyes. "Your people," Finnik added, looking up at Katula. "By the time my troops reached the river down south, most of the Matuians were gone."

"*Most*?" Katula growled.

"Some did not fare well on the rapids. Those we caught were taken into custody. I do not know their current fate." A hurried knock on the room's door, however, broke the moment. A group of guards were waiting to escort the women to their respective places during battle but when Finnik attempted to follow them, he was stopped.

"I am sorry, but it was on the sovereign's orders that he stay here," one of the guards warned.

Meera turned to Katula. "You go on ahead. I need to go talk to the sovereign and sort this out." Katula teetered on whether to go with her but decided her time would be better spent getting ready.

"All right, you go talk to the sovereign. I'm going to go top side and check out the view," she replied, referring to the many archer's walks above the Residence. "I'll catch up with you in a little while. Meera," Katula called as she watched the red head leave, "be careful."

Katula's heart raced as she ran up the stairs to the archer's walks. She didn't have time to contemplate the unexpected exchange with the Grendolen, Finnik—the man who had attacked Matui, her precious woodland home. It was because of him that her people were now scattered about the Drylands. He was the reason she went to bed every night worrying about her family and whether her father and grandmother had made it somewhere safe. She would *never* trust that man, no matter how much he groveled. But Meera was her own person, and for some reason she believed Finnik's pledge.

Upon reaching one of the many walkways, she found a sizable group of fellow archers preparing their bows, checking their fletching, and filling braziers with oiled wood. All were giants, of course. All had larger bows and arrows. All of them were armed with Elements. Thankfully, Katula brought with her several quivers of Matuian-made arrows the sovereign herself had supplied her with, along with the satchel of weaponized Elements Natta had given her back in Matui. Joining the others, she began preparing for war.

Below, sprawled Tawok. Katula's vantage point provided a generous view of the town and its outlying farms. Large, neat lines of Pawtoton guards hurriedly ran through the streets in a practiced, orderly fashion, eager to get to their positions before the enemy arrived. Dodging out of their way were the very citizens the guards were laying their lives on the line for. Younglings, mothers, and the elderly alike ran to take cover and barricade themselves in the town's stronger stone buildings before the blockades being assembled prevented them from reaching their destinations. Tawok was no longer the sleepy village that only a short time ago Katula and her friends toured by tonga cart. It had been transformed throughout that day into a town readying for siege.

All too soon, the sun set and Katula and her archer companions caught their first sight of Varcor's forces. Black cloaks and armor intermingled with the red and yellow of the Grendolen colors bearing torches to light their way. The giants around her began howling and hitting their fisted bows against their bone armor, sending even Katula's hair standing on end. This was personal for them. The Chroniclers had betrayed their own people. Panicking, Katula realized Meera had never appeared.

Hurry up, Meera! They're almost here!

Briefly, Katula wondered where Darmond had gone off to. No one had seen him since the night before. She knew he had been hiding something but never guessed what it could be. If what Lord Agnarr said about the Midtierian was true, she assumed he had left Pawtoton in shame before dawnlight that morning. That both angered and relieved her. It angered Katula because of the hurt his actions caused so many. It relieved her because it meant she could temporarily forget about his treacherous ways and concentrate on the battle at hand.

The giants around her stopped their war cries, bringing Katula's thoughts back to the present. Sure enough, shouts and the sound of swords clashing had broken out at the edge of the town as the giants of Pawtoton and the forces of the Grendolen Empire crashed into one another.

The Battle of Pawtoton had begun.

CHAPTER TWENTY-THREE

Darmond

Darmond's worst fear had come to pass. Meera now knew he was the one responsible for telling Lord Agnarr to look for her in Matui. It was *his* weakness that had brought about the evacuation of Katula's people from their homeland. After decades keeping himself detached from forming any close relationships, he'd gone and mucked things up with the two friends who had been willing to give him a chance. In bitter shame, he had fled their suite after the bodies and damage had been removed from the skirmish and an unconscious Meera had been put to bed, anxious to put as much distance between them as possible.

What the *rot* was he doing in Pawtoton anyway? He should have left ages ago and reported back to the Resistance headquarters in Midtier where he could have spent his time hunting down the Grendolen spy hidden within their ranks. He had sent pigeons to them from Vardia warning of the spy, but the spy could have intercepted them. But as he stalked through the Residence toward the training hall to retrieve some type of weapon other than the knife he'd lifted, Darmond's footsteps slowed. Deep down he *knew* the reason he hadn't reported back. If the Resistance found out he was alive they'd want answers. Where was the Tarmanon heir? Did she have the Stone Key? What did it unlock and had it been destroyed? And if he reported to them that Lord Agnarr was a Tercara, that would only encourage questions about what Tercaras were and how he knew that information. If he returned to Midtier, Darmond was certain it would mean exposing Meera as a Tercara, further endangering her life. The last time folks knew what Tercaras could do, they tried to eliminate their race. Darmond may have been responsible for giving up Meera's location, but he wasn't about to deliver her to the wolves.

Realizing he couldn't go back to Midtier and knowing neither Meera nor Katula would want him to stick around, Darmond was at a loss of what to do. The Chroniclers had betrayed the Pawtoton Preservers by giving up their location to Varcor. They had come after Meera once, and now that Lord Agnarr knew she was here, there was no doubt in Darmond's mind the Grendolens would soon be arriving in full force. It wasn't just Meera that was in trouble, but Katula, Everard, and all of Pawtoton. Yes, he felt bitterly ashamed of himself, but he wasn't about to let that come between him and helping his friends. Even if those friends hated his rotting guts.

If he was going to help, though, training weapons twice his size wouldn't cut it. It was time he stole back what was rightfully his. Turning about, Darmond slipped into his spy habits and went to find where the sovereign was keeping his longsword.

By the time he tracked down where it was being held, duskfall could be seen through the Residence's windows. Since the breach and betrayal by the Chroniclers, the sovereign had tripled security within the property, making navigating the halls and rooms extremely challenging. But at long last, Darmond closed in on the storeroom he'd been looking for. As fortune would have it, only one guard stood by the door, the others posted in various places around the Residence no doubt. Without a weapon, there was no way Darmond was going to best the giant guard, but he'd come prepared. Reaching into one of his side pouches, Darmond gingerly pulled out a bundle of cloth. As steadily as he could, Darmond unwrapped the cloth to reveal a small vial filled with a bright red liquid. A shudder ran through his body. Ever since Varcor had forced him to drink Elements, Darmond *hated* being near them. But necessity dictates, as they say, and despite his wariness around the Elements Katula had brought with her, Darmond couldn't help but lift a vial or two once he heard what the more volatile ones were capable of. Happy to be rid of the thing, he quickly threw it around the corner toward the guard. At the sound of the glass breaking, a small burst of light flashed, and the contents began spewing smoke. No sooner had the guard looked down in confusion, than he breathed in the smoke and collapsed unconscious. Once the air cleared, it was no time before Darmond had the lock picked and he'd located not only his sword but also his daggers, throwing knives, and a well-crafted ax too beautiful to leave lying around unused. He was just about to lift a one-handed sword that had also caught his eye when he heard noises from the hallway outside the room. Fearing his location had been compromised, Darmond ran to the door and peeked out. He caught the tail end of a group of men clad in black cloaks headed in the opposite direction from the wing that held the suite where he and his companions had stayed. Which meant they could only be headed to one place, the sovereign's private quarters. Alarm bells sounded in Darmond's head. That many Chroniclers within the Residence meant the enemy had already sent enough numbers to push past the extra guards. This wasn't a small reconnaissance mission, it was an all-out *attack*! The battle Darmond knew would come was already here. The giant's matriarch was about to be assassinated! All previous plans were thrown out of his mind at that moment. If the Chroniclers were willing to try and take out Ayris Pagor Hilderman Fielder, that meant they were confident they'd win the war, and if they won, Lord Agnarr would undoubtedly capture Meera and get his hands on the Stone Key. Bolting out of the storeroom now armed with a proper number of weapons, Darmond ran after the Chroniclers.

The wing holding the sovereign's private rooms was vast, but locating the matriarch within its network of gilded halls wasn't difficult. Lining the corridors like a guided map were the bodies of the fallen, along with strange scorch marks left on the marbled floors and on the walls. Giants, with their tonga helms, made up most of the casualties, but even more disturbing were their wounds, which seemed to coincide with the scorch marks. Large burns still smoldered on their skin, the flames of whatever they'd succumbed to *so* hot, any metal within their armor had melted in place. Yet Darmond could see no evidence of a fire large enough to cause the damage. Bending down to examine the strange burns, he caught sight of a shard of glass. It was eerily similar to the vial he himself had thrown at a guard just a little while ago. With a hiss, he recoiled. The Chroniclers had access to the Elements, and they weren't playing nice. Realizing time was short, Darmond threw caution aside and began running in the direction the dead led him.

As he neared what he assumed was the sovereign's private rooms, the sounds of fighting grew louder. At least in that, he took hope. Fighting meant the Chroniclers hadn't succeeded in their mission. That meant Darmond had time. Slowing down, he readied the ax and one-handed sword he'd lifted from the storeroom. Coming to a junction in the hall, he stopped at its corner and risked peeking around. At the end of the corridor stood two enormous doors, ornately carved and gilded in gold, and thankfully still closed. In front of them fought a handful of giant guards against a mass of shorter black cloaks. Scorch marks lined the walls here, too, and a sulfur smell hung heavy in the air, yet as Darmond observed, he noted none of the Chroniclers were using their explosive Elements.

They've run out, he realized with a sly grin. While the Pawtotons had access to Elements themselves, the assassination attempt had caught them unawares, and none of the guards Darmond saw fought back with any Elements of their own. Darmond was just about to round the corner and join in the fun, however, when his ears picked up footsteps coming from the hall behind him. Instantly, his instincts kicked in and he ducked into one of the doors lining the wall. Leaving it cracked slightly, Darmond was able to make out three Chroniclers racing to join the fight. Each wore satchels that looked suspiciously bulky. It seemed the enemy had sent reinforcements. If the newcomers carried with them more explosive Elements like Darmond suspected they did, the last of the Pawtoton guards wouldn't stand a chance.

There was no time to think. Pulling open the door to the room he'd hid in, Darmond threw his beautiful, newly lifted ax straight at the back of the Chronicler last in line. There was a satisfying thud as it hit on target, but the victim let out an agonizing scream that alerted his two companions. In the same instant that the other two Chroniclers turned to see what had happened, the man with the ax embedded in his nervous system fell to his knees. Darmond readied himself for a fight, but the other two turned and high-tailed it toward the sovereign's rooms.

Craven maggots, Darmond sneered as they rounded the corner. It was then that the fear he saw on their faces registered. Looking down at the Chronicler on his knees, he realized why. *Rotting Nihility!* As the body fell toward the marble floor, Darmond swung around and threw himself into the room he'd just come out of. As he hit the floor, a massive explosion blew through the Residence, shaking its foundations. The reaction was so powerful, the door to the room blew off, flew over Darmond, and crashed against the room's opposite wall. Glass, wood, and gold ripped through the air in all directions.

Once the dust started to settle, Darmond uncurled himself and attempted to get up. His ears rung from the blast, making it difficult to gather in his surroundings. Touching his forehead, he realized he was bleeding. Several shards of glass had been lodged in his skin. As he pulled them free Darmond took stock of the damage. Debris coated everything. Glass crunched under his boots as he turned to the room's doorway, now void of a door. A giant hole stood where the door once did and smoke poured through the opening, its sulfuric smell making Darmond gag. As it cleared, he could see the hall where the center of the explosion occurred had fared worse. The Elements had taken out not only the walls lining the hallway but the floor as well. Leaning over, Darmond could see down into the hallway below. As his hearing began to clear, the sounds of fighting could still be heard around the corner. If one satchel of Elements could do that much damage, Yveth only knew how devastating *two* satchels full of the rotting stuff would be.

Using the remains of the hallway floor, Darmond scooted along the ledge and reached the corner of the corridor once again. With the ax irrecoverable and his one-handed sword lost in the explosion, he unsheathed his longsword and wasted no time as he rounded the next hall.

"Those two have more Elements," he warned the Pawtoton guards, pointing at the additional Chroniclers. "If they drop those satchels, your sovereign's as good as dead!" As he yelled over the fray, Darmond ran straight for the men holding the explosives.

Not surprisingly, a pack of black cloaks broke from the others to protect the two assassins. With a determined grin, Darmond raised his sword and charged.

Fighting Chroniclers was vastly different from fighting Grendolens. Under their black cloaks they had been given the same armor the Grendolens used; however, they fought with cutlasses, which were shorter than his longsword. No doubt they carried them because they were easier to conceal under their long cloaks. Their shorter swords gave Darmond the advantage, though, so long as he didn't allow the fight to get too close. He easily cleaved down two Chroniclers and was going for his third when one of the Elementist assassins decided to risk the loss of one of his vials in order to clear the doors to the sovereign's rooms. As Darmond swung with an overhead cut, the blast hit the terra beside them, throwing everyone in its radius to the floor. The Chronicler Darmond had been going for flew straight into him, knocking out his air as they hit and causing him to lose his grip on his longsword. He recovered quickly, but so did the Chronicler now lying on top of him. In a panic, Darmond grabbed desperately for the hilt of his sword but before he could find it, the man realized what he was looking for and placed a knee on Darmond's arm. Wordlessly, the Chronicler positioned his cutlass against Darmond's throat and was about to write a sad end to his epic tales, but in that moment, a spear shot through the opening under the enemy's arm with such force, it came out the other side. Darmond's eyes went wide as a bloodied tonga skull came into his view. Within the hollow eye sockets were two familiar gray eyes.

"*Everard?*" Darmond gasped.

"Greetings." The giant smiled, despite the chaos around them.

"How in Nihility...?" Darmond didn't even know how to finish the sentence. The only time he'd ever seen Everard use any kind of violence was when he'd *accidentally* tipped his chair on to a Chronicler and crushed him to death. The giant was always so, so... *peaceful*!

"It seems only fitting I save your life after you saved mine, wouldn't you agree?" Everard beamed. As he spoke a Chronicler wielding his cutlass came within striking range of the giant. Without any hesitation, Everard punched the man so hard, he went down without even a grunt and then turned back to Darmond to continue the conversation. "I heard you before, about the Elements. We'll need to find a way to reach those satchels and take out their bearers without giving them a chance to drop them." Still wheeling from the sight of Everard bloodied and dressed in armor, Darmond nodded and grabbed his sword.

"I'm open to ideas," he replied at last, standing. Everard nodded and went to pull his giant-sized spear out of the man he'd just impaled.

"Our guards seem to be holding but they don't need an army to get through those doors," Everard warned. "Just one of those satchels would be enough should they make it through."

"Then let's make sure that doesn't happen," Darmond agreed. Together, they turned and began fighting their way toward the two Chroniclers who held the Elements.

CHAPTER TWENTY-FOUR

Meera

It was no small thing to convince the sovereign to allow Finnik out of his cell. When the matriarch finally agreed, it was under the provision that he be placed directly under Meera's care. Basically, that meant if he did anything wrong, it would be Meera's head that would roll. But that didn't stop her. She knew the man who made up Finnik Doth now. She'd seen his entire life play out in the span of mere moments. She had seen his *soul*. He would protect her with his life. She doubted he would leave her side even if she commanded it. As soon as the agreement was met, the sovereign was whisked away to her private chambers, leaving Meera and her newfound bodyguard to arm themselves and catch up with Katula before Varcor's army arrived.

It was just after Meera and Finnik had been outfitted in armor and weapons that a massive explosion rumbled through the Residence.

"What the rot was that?" Meera exclaimed, grabbing hold of the wall to balance herself.

A grim look came over Finnik's face. "The only thing I know of that could cause that kind of damage would be the Elements."

Meera's eyes went wide. "Then they're in the Residence already," she guessed.

Finnik nodded. No sooner had she done so than the bells of Towak began ringing in alarm. Varcor and his army had arrived.

"We've got to hurry if we're going to catch up with Katula."

Finnik grabbed her arm before she could start running away. "I am sorry, Lady Tarmanon, but we don't have time," he warned. "If we're going to go after Varcor we need to go now before the roads are completely impassable." Meera cursed under her breath. Finnik wanted to take down Varcor just as much as she did, and doing so could stem the tide of war. Slowly, she nodded in agreement. Sending a prayer up to Yveth for Katula's safety, Meera and Finnik wound their way through the Residence's halls and out onto Towak's streets.

For a while they were able to travel unhindered, but all too soon, the roads grew thick with fighting, and they were forced to engage in battle. Time was forgotten. It wasn't until Meera caught a glance of the Watchers in the night sky that she realized how long they had been fighting. Every now and then they would catch a lull, giving them a few blissful moments to catch their breath before things picked up again. The Pawtotons had initially pushed back the tide, but eventually, the Grendolens gained more terra. Just as she predicted, Finnik had not left her side. Slowly but surely, the two of them fought their way through the streets of Tawok toward the heart of the Grendolen forces. With her bow returned, Meera let Finnik clear a path ahead with his Grendolen longsword, while she took out any others who tried to get in his way. Surprisingly, they made a good team despite never having fought alongside one another before. As the sun began to rise, they finally reached the outlying fields. Here, with open terra, the fighting grew dense.

"On your left!" Meera shouted at Finnik, warning him before she could get a shot off. The old ex-commandant skillfully stepped sideways, missing a swing from a Chronicler's curved cutlass. Finnik's own sword parried the cut, knocking the cutlass away before delivering a thrust to the man's torso. No sooner had the Chronicler fallen than Meera spotted another heading for Finnik. One of her own arrows took him out.

"It's getting a bit crowded," Finnik warned, closing the distance between them.

"Agreed," she said, sending another shot flying. "And I'm running out of arrows."

A familiar screech sounded above as Tymmon called down to Meera. He, too, had joined the fight despite her protests. Swooping in, his black claws and sharp beak sunk into a Chronicler's face. The man screamed as his skin was shredded and his eyes plucked out. Meanwhile, Finnik blocked another attack, but his opponent rushed into a grapple. His sword no longer useful, Finnik switched hands and drew his dagger. Meera tried aiming at the soldier to take him down, but he and Finnik were too close to risk a shot. Thankfully, Finnik was able to pin the man's arm using a grappling technique. With a quick motion, he snapped the soldier's arm in two. Crying out, the soldier let go of his own dagger, giving Finnik an opening to sink his into the man's throat. Breathing heavily from the exchange, Finnik quickly sheathed his dagger and turned to Meera.

"You know, you could always use your—"

"*Not yet*," Meera interjected, knowing he implied using her abilities. "I need to save my strength for Varcor."

He nodded, but she knew he wanted to take the man out himself. She had read his mind, after all. They were about to skirt around the thickest part of the fighting when a group of giants were simultaneously hit through the chest with a lance made of *water*. All five dropped dead instantly.

Meera turned to Finnik. "He's here," she announced grimly.

Without waiting, Finnik bolted forward, ready to deliver the blow that would bring an end to Varcor. Cursing, Meera nocked an arrow and went after him. None of the soldiers out in the field fought with Elements. Meera suspected all the Elemental supplies they had traveled with were being saved to use against the barricades at the Residence, where she and Finnik had witnessed their use more than once as they fought through Towak.

Varcor stood on the very same rock Meera and Darmond had sat on not too long ago after their alehouse excursion. All traces of the Wildfires were gone, having been trampled on by so many feet. Surrounding Agnarr's son fought a group of soldiers she assumed was his personal guard. On his cheek were two cuts in the shape of a "t" that Finnik had left—a permanent reminder of the traitor Varcor was. Lord Agnarr's son didn't see Finnik or Meera right away, however. All his concentration was on Summoning.

As Finnik fought to break through the guards, Meera saw the opportunity and took it. Aiming right at Varcor's head, she let an arrow fly. Its target was on point, but as soon as it neared, a shard of water flew to meet it, knocking it off course and rendering the shot useless.

"At last," Varcor called. "I was wondering if you were ever going to show." He looked down and saw Finnik. A rare look of surprise hit him. "You *survived*? I am actually quite impressed."

"We never finished our fight, *traitor*," Finnik taunted. "Come down and face me!"

"The last time we fought I was under orders not to Summon and reveal myself. But I am no longer under those restrictions. I'm afraid you are quite outmatched this time. And *you*," Varcor said, turning back to Meera. "A *Tercara,* so I hear. Tell me, just how much practice have you managed?" As he spoke, Meera saw water droplets forming at his feet. Realizing he was about to attack, she reached for the fire within. Gasps from both sides of the battle sounded as they caught sight of her glowing, causing a momentary pause in the fighting around them. Varcor's watershard flew straight for her head. Instinctively, Meera threw her hands up and tried to *will* the water away, but she couldn't. Varcor's will already had control over it and no matter how hard she concentrated, she couldn't break through. He was *much* more advanced in Summoning than she. Panicking, Meera changed the focus of her will and directed toward the terra. In an instant, the terra before her shot straight up into the air, creating a shield of rock, successfully blocking the water shard.

"You have no idea what you are doing, do you?" Varcor guessed. "I've had my whole life to master it. It's not something you can just pick up."

As he prattled on, Meera hid behind her rock shield and attempted to Shift into his mind, but again, his will proved too strong.

"It's an art one must practice at," Varcor mused, gathering more water to him. Hoping her shield would hold, she stayed ducked behind it. But Varcor sent more than one watershard this time, and they hit with so much force, it caused her shield to explode. Meera hit the terra and covered her head from the impact of flying debris. No sooner had she recovered, however, than she turned to see Varcor was already Summoning more. Again, she threw up a rock shield, and again it was shattered by the impact.

While Meera fought to keep herself from being impaled, Finnik continued to try and break through Varcor's guards. He was evenly matched, though. These were Grendolen soldiers, ones Finnik himself had made sure were trained well. They knew all his moves and they were not as weathered as he. As Meera ducked and weaved and threw up more rock shields, she could see Finnik beginning to falter. She tried closing in on his location, but Varcor realized what she was doing and strengthened his attack any time she got near. Too much of her concentration was being used as defense while attempting to focus on using two abilities at once and helping him. The guards also read the signs of Finnik's fatigue, and like vultures, began circling in. In despair, Meera realized she was never going to make it to Finnik's side quickly enough. But just as the guards cornered Finnik and he realized he had no way out, another sword came crashing into the fray.

Without hesitation, Darmond brought his longsword down on one of the guards so hard, it split the man's helm in two. Breaking through the guards' lines, he joined Finnik's side, and together they broke through and advanced on Varcor.

"What in Nihility are you *doing* here?" Meera yelled at the Midtierian as she ducked behind one of her rock shields.

"Trying to save your life," he yelled back, over the battle's shouting and clashes.

"By getting yourself killed?" she retaliated.

"I can't let you take all the glory, Red. I've got a *reputation* to uphold," he retorted with a grin. Varcor paused his attack on Meera and took note of the duo's advance. Realizing he was about to Summon watershards at them, she let her rock shield fall back into the terra and threw one up in front of her friends. But that was *exactly* what Varcor had been expecting. With a satisfied smile, he threw his hands at Meera and willed his watershards straight for her. Meera realized her mistake too late. As the shards were about to hit her, however, something large slammed into her right side, pushing her down onto the terra. The impact knocked her breath away, and she struggled for a moment to recover. As soon as she did, she sat up to find Everard lying next to her in his bone armor.

"Everard!" she exclaimed, shocked to see him on the battlefield. A warm smile slowly spread under the tonga skull.

"We couldn't very well let you fight him alone, my dear. Now, could we?" the giant asked.

"We?" she echoed. At that moment, an arrow whizzed by her head, taking out a Grendolen soldier just behind them. Looking back, Meera saw Katula standing proud and defiant, black eyes flashing with the adrenaline that comes with the heat of battle. Meera's smile fell, however, when she heard Tymmon's call. Too late, she saw her feathered friend dive toward Varcor. The Summoner shot one of his watershards straight through the hawk's chest. Tymmon screeched in pain and fell out of the sky onto the terra.

"No!" Meera cried, running to Tymmon's side. Without thinking, she placed her hand on the wound. Down through the torn skin and tissue her will traveled until it knew what was wrong and how to Mend it. Closing her eyes, Meera concentrated. What was torn apart began to reconnect and grow back together. She had almost finished when something impacted her right shoulder, sending her sprawling backward. Opening her eyes in surprise, she looked down to find a watershard-shaped hole in her *own* body. Pain overtook Meera, causing her to gasp as she clutched at the gaping wound. With wild eyes, she looked up at Varcor, whose face held a victorious smile.

"I could have ended you just then, Tarmanon *bitch*," he gloated, "but that would deprive me of watching you witness your companions' deaths."

Overcome by the exhaustion from Mending Tymmon and with pain, Meera struggled to get up. Ignoring her protests, Katula and Everard rushed in to help.

"How bad is it?" Meera asked the Matuian.

Katula took a moment to look over the wound. She was losing a lot of blood.

"Nothing a little bit of your Mending couldn't handle," she lied with a slight smile. Everard checked on Tymmon.

"You've stopped his bleeding, Meera," he encouraged. "You saved him."

Movement from where Varcor stood caught both their eyes. The man's body had begun to convulse. All too soon, Varcor's body settled, and he opened his eyes. They were cloudy white. Lord Agnarr was Shifting through his son. Seeing what had happened, Darmond and Finnik pushed even harder to reach the enemy, but the more soldiers and Chroniclers they took out, the more others filled their place.

"You don't look so well," Agnarr spoke to Meera over the fighting. The redhead gritted her teeth against the pain. "Varcor is talented at what he does. He's spent his life studying how to Summon and it was only fair of me to let him have his moment with you." A sickening grin ran across Varcor's face. "But he knew I would be the one to see things through to the end. After all, Meera, you and I share something no one else does. We are alike. *Kin*. It's only right that this conversation be between you and me."

"I am *nothing* like you," Meera spat.

"No, I suppose you are not," Agnarr conceded. "Here you are, gifted with the powers of the Tercaras, and you haven't the slightest idea of how to use them. A shame, really. Imagine what you could have become had you known! Together, we could have expanded the empire far beyond the reaches of Midtier. We could have unlocked the Stone Key and its secrets together."

"You don't strike me as one who would share," she shot back, sickened by the thought. Varcor's mouth let out Agnarr's laugh.

"Perhaps that's because I never met my equal," he sighed with a smile. "No matter. I'm here to give you one last chance, Meera. I want that Stone Key and this time I'm not leaving until I have it."

Against all odds, Darmond and Finnik had gained terra and had nearly reached the stone Varcor stood on. However, Meera wasn't the only one who noticed. "It's been quite entertaining watching your little fellowship band together, you know," Agnarr said to Meera, looking down from Varcor's perch at the two men. "No abilities whatsoever, and yet they still push on."

Meera watched helplessly as Agnarr used Varcor's Summoning abilities to gather water. Pulled out of the terra and air, the droplets came together forming large water spheres. They looked just like the one Meera had Summoned to kill the Chronicler who Agnarr had Shifted through the night before. Agnarr was going to make Meera watch her friends suffer in the same way. Katula rose from Meera's side and shot an arrow at Varcor. But Agnarr was Summoning through the man, and he was even more experienced than his son. He easily sent a watershard to intercept the shot while Summoning the water spheres over to Darmond and Finnik. The two swordsmen tried to duck and swing at the water, but nothing stopped their progress. In horror, Meera watched as both spheres covered their heads. The men fought with everything they had to escape, but the water followed their every move. As the men ran out of air, Agnarr turned back toward Meera and sent two more water spheres flying in Katula and Everard's direction.

"Stop!" Meera cried, unable to find the strength to help her friends.

Everard tried unsuccessfully to use his size to pound the water away, but Katula's stone-cold face never wavered. Even as she fell to her knees, her black Matuian eyes refused to look away from Agnarr in fear. Meera knelt there on the terra at a loss for what to do. All around her were the screams and cries of the dying. Fallen giants, Grendolens, and Chroniclers scattered the field, now a churned mess of dirt and blood. Her friends had come to fight alongside her and now they would pay with their lives because of it. They had believed in her. Believed she was an Ancient, a *Tercara*. It was her fault. *All* of it! Agnarr was right. She had *no clue* how to use her abilities. As she watched her friends begin to stop struggling and tire, Meera did the only thing she could think of. She sent up a prayer to Yveth.

Yveth's response was instantaneous.

Time itself *froze*.

One moment the chaos of war raged, and in another, not even a wisp of wind stirred. Meera gasped in a breath of air as the pain in her shoulder suddenly stopped. Shocked, she looked down to find her wound completely healed.

"What's happening?" she wondered aloud to a silent world. Meera's eyes widened when a voice in her mind answered back.

"You must not be extinguished, Creation," the voice said.

The sound echoed through Meera's body as if god were standing there before her.

"Yveth?" Meera guessed in awe.

"That is the name Creation has given me," the god confirmed. *"You must not be extinguished,"* Yveth repeated.

"I'm too weak," Meera admitted through tears. "I can't fight him."

"You have been given everything you need, Creation."

"I've tried! But they're dying, and there's *nothing* I can do to stop it!" Tears flowed down Meera's cheeks as she looked out over the frozen world to her friends, whose deaths had been momentarily captured in time.

"You are made of this world, Creation. It is a part of you. Call out to it and it will respond."

"How?"

"Ask it."

As quickly as time had stopped, it was thrown into motion again. All at once, the pain from Meera's wound returned and the sounds of battle filled her ears. Gasping on her knees, she caught herself with her hands. The moment she felt the terra, she remembered Yveth's words. *Ask it.*

So, she did.

Blocking out everything going on around her, Meera closed her glowing eyes and concentrated. Instead of forcing her will upon the terra, however, she opened up her own will to it. The terra's will immediately came flooding in as if it had been waiting to do so all this time. As the terra's will filled her thoughts, it, too, opened up in a way she had never experienced. It wasn't a forced thing, but something that, once it occurred, felt as natural as breathing. Their wills connected in a symbiotic way and the terra shared its will *with* her. The terra was dry. *Too* dry. The water it relied on to grow things had been used up by Varcor and Agnarr's Summoning. The terra was angry, and it wanted its water back. Meera decided to deliver it.

Lifting her head, the Tercara turned her glowing red eyes to Agnarr and his son. Agnarr saw her movement and looked over at her.

"What do you think you're going to do, Meera?" He smiled with an amused look on Varcor's face.

Her connection with the terra coursed through her body like nothing she had felt before. She could feel her wound closing as the energy built up within, renewing her strength. Her mind began to clear and a peaceful clarity blanketed her. Agnarr may have had a lifetime of learning his abilities, but he only ever forced his will on others, never considering the possibilities of allowing his own will to be used.

"Here you are, gifted with the powers of the Tercaras and you haven't the slightest idea on how to use them. A shame, really," Meera repeated, using his own words against him.

Varcor's head cocked sideways, showing Agnarr's confusion.

"You should have learned how to share." With that, Meera sent the energy that had been building up in her down through the terra and it responded in kind. All around them, the bloody fields began shaking. Varcor's wide, white eyes looked around in surprise as people from either side of the battle stopped fighting to try and catch their balance.

"*What are you doing?*" Agnarr demanded angrily.

"You were right about one thing, Agnarr," she said, looking up in defiance. "There *are* two of us now. The difference is, I have Yveth on my side." At that, a loud crack resounded through the field as the terra below Varcor ripped open. The newly formed chasm swallowed Varcor and the rock he had been standing on. Almost as soon as it happened, the terra closed back up on itself. The force of the event cascaded through the fields of Pawtoton. Trees were toppled, and both giant and man alike were thrown sprawling onto the terra.

With the last dregs of energy still flowing through her, Meera stood and ran to her friends. The water spheres that had nearly drowned them had burst, fallen, and had been readily absorbed back into the terra. Her friends were unconscious but alive. Darmond's heartbeat, however, was dangerously faint. Despite his betrayal, Meera couldn't let him die; not after what they'd been through and how hard he fought against Varcor and Lord Agnarr. In a last push of energy, Meera laid her hands on the man's chest and willed it to Mend. As she felt Darmond's heartbeat return, Meera's last remaining energy waned. Just before she slipped into unconsciousness, she caught sight of something unexpected in the early dawnlight: silver-armored Midtierians were rushing onto the battlefield and pushing back the remaining Grendolen forces.

CHAPTER TWENTY-FIVE

Meera

Three days after the Battle of Pawtoton ended, Meera awoke. She quickly realized the world had changed while she had slept. An alliance had been struck between Midtier and Matui once Katula's family connected safely with their southern tribal kin and had access to their messenger pigeons. Thanks to Darmond's messages of warning, the Grendolen spy within the Resistance, Kane Barnor, had been found, caught, and interrogated, allowing them to find out about Varcor's plans to assassinate Pawtoton's sovereign and his alliance with the Chroniclers. Within that day, the Midtierians sent reinforcements to aid the giants, turning the tide of the battle, and sending the Grendolens and the Chroniclers who sided with them into full retreat. It turned out that not all the Chroniclers had been aware of the betrayal, and those who had stayed loyal had begun to return to Pawtoton and help with repairs.

Among the messages the Midtierians brought with them were ones from Chief Usoti and the sage to Katula, letting her know they were safe. Upon hearing of the ex-commandant's heroic efforts against Lord Agnarr and his son, the Supreme Sovereign Ayris Pagor Hilderman Fielder granted Finnik Doth an official amnesty, however, despite his newfound freedom, he refused to leave Meera's side. The sovereign had also awarded Darmond and Everard the Pawtoton Medal of Valor after they thwarted a large-scale assassination attempt and were instrumental in saving the matriarch's life.

Upon reflection, Meera wasn't surprised to find that she, too, had changed. Had she really *talked* to Yveth? It all seemed like a dream now. In killing Lord Agnarr's son, she had revealed herself as a Tercara to the world. And the world wasn't quite sure what to make of it. As Finnik led her to the victory banquet the Supreme Sovereign was throwing in Meera's honor, some she passed along the way nodded in respect while others shied away in fear.

"Give it time, Lady Tarmanon" Finnik whispered, seeing Meera's concern. "They'll come around eventually."

The Tercara nodded but didn't feel as certain as her self-appointed guard. A rousing applause broke out once the doors to the feasting hall opened and ushered Meera in. As awkward as it was to have all the attention on her, Meera politely nodded and bowed before she walked up to join the sovereign at her table. Her hesitancy abated, however, when she caught sight of her friends seated at the large banquet table. Darmond was among them, and as fortune, or a lack thereof, would have it, the only vacant seat was between the sovereign and the Midtierian. After Meera was begrudgingly seated, their cups were filled with Pawtoton's last reserves of Moordew and a toast was given. A toast to the fallen, to the living, and to the return of the Tercaras. Once the signal was given for the feasting to begin and conversations arose from the many tables within the hall, Darmond turned to Meera.

"I'm sorry," he began.

Meera held up her hand, motioning that she didn't want to hear it, but the stubborn man continued. "I know you're upset, Meera, and you should be. I betrayed your trust—"

"You did more than that," she charged, turning hurt eyes on him.

"You're right, and I know that apologizing doesn't change what I've done, but it needs to be said. And I *am* sorry. But there's something else you need to know. Something I've tried over and over again to tell you." Darmond took her hands and for a moment she thought the conversation was going to get more awkward than it already was. "Meera," he said, swallowing his fear, "it was me."

"I *know* it was you," she shot back, confused.

"No, I mean, *I* was the boy who led you out of the castle tunnels the night of the Moorland Massacre."

Meera's eyes grew wide as understanding hit her. "*You*?" she breathed.

Darmond nodded. "My mother worked in the castle kitchens. I knew those tunnels inside and out. I came across you in the smoke and led you through a secret door the servants used."

"You're a... a *Moorlander*?" she asked, unable to process the news.

He nodded. "Darmond Ontrustor Reedmont, Cook Reedmont's second son," he reintroduced himself. "After the massacre,

I made my way over to Midtier and did my best to blend in. Varcor found out I was a Moorlander, though, when my men and I were captured. One by one, he had them killed, in hopes I would give up the information I had on you. I refused for as long as I could. *Truly*."

Meera's hands tightened around his as what Darmond said sank in.

"I withheld it to the end, you know," he added, looking up into her eyes defiantly. "But Varcor used the Elements. I fought against them," he promised her, blue eyes earnest. "I fought as hard as I could. But in the end..."

It was then Meera at last saw what had been right in front of her the whole time. Sticking out of Darmond's scabbard was the hilt of his longsword. The grip around the tang was bound in dark-green leather and its long crossguard curved upward into points facing the enemy. But it was the round disk-like pommel, with its golden inlay, that caught Meera's attention. The pattern was that of an octagon with eight indentations around a central ninth, the very same pattern that could be found on the bottom of the Stone Key's crystal, and one she remembered her father had been fond of. Darmond wore her father's sword.

"You *saved* it," she breathed, looking at his side where the sword rested. "Worrosarn, my father's sword!"

Darmond followed her gaze, then looked back in amazement. "Truth Defender," he breathed out loud, translating the name from Moorlander into the common tongue. "I found it lying on the floor before I found you that night. Couldn't bear leaving such a work of art behind for the flames to consume. I had no idea it was King Tarmanon's!" Darmond instantly started undoing the buckles of the belt that held the dark-green sheath, intending to give it to Meera.

"Don't," Meera said, stopping him, shaking her head. "I'm *glad* it was saved. All these cycles I thought it lost along with everything else. My father would have been proud to see Worrosarn wielded by a *true* Moorlander."

The two were quiet for some time before Meera finally spoke again. "Thank you," she said, still holding his hands. "Thank you for telling me the truth."

They held each other's gaze for a while. It wasn't a romantic look; Meera wasn't even sure the feelings they had shared before would ever be rekindled after all that had happened. What passed between them then was much deeper than a slight infatuation. It was a true understanding of who the other really was, and she found great comfort in it.

Breaking into the moment, however, the sovereign turned to address Meera.

"Do not think I have forgotten how much you and your companions withheld from me," the sovereign noted quietly, shooting a look Everard's way. "He tells me you possess the Stone Key Lord Agnarr is after."

Meera gave Everard her own glance before responding. The giant seemed uninterested in the food on his plate and kept aimlessly pushing it around.

"Yes, I do." she answered honestly.

"Then you know it *cannot* stay here." It was a statement, not a question.

"No," Meera conceded, "It cannot."

The sovereign considered her response for a moment. "If you find the weapon the Stone Key unlocks, you know that it must be destroyed." Instinctively, Meera felt for her hawk pendant. The Stone Key. She had carried it with her all this time with no idea just how important it was.

"Yes."

"Then I will supply you with whatever you need for the journey, providing you grant me one request."

At that, the old sovereign turned her gray eyes back to Meera. "What's that?" she asked.

"That you bring *him* with you," she said, referring to Everard. "Books and libraries no longer suffice his appetite. Battle has changed him. He needs answers, ones we all hope you find on your journey."

"I'd be more than happy to have him come with me." Meera beamed.

Everard picked up his head and looked over at the two. Upon seeing Meera's smile, he knew she had agreed to the sovereign's request. A large, familiar grin spread across his face.

"Where do you plan to start on your journey?" the sovereign inquired.

"We start by answering the scrolls' riddle," Meera replied, looking to Everard. The giant turned to the ruler and quoted.

"What is pure, yet unclean?
What is round, yet uneven?
What is accessible, yet hidden?
What is magnificent, yet minute?
What is cherished, yet irritating?"

The sovereign grew quiet, taking the words in before suddenly answering.

"A pearl," the giant's ruler proclaimed in her usual confident air. Everard's eyes went wide for a moment, then he smacked his head.

"Of course!" the giant cried excitedly. "How could I have *missed* that?"

"What does it *mean*, though?" Meera asked.

"It means we finally have our heading," Everard beamed. "We travel to Yveth's Pearl!"

EPILOGUE

Agnarr

Agnarr's body was thrown across the room, landing him against the wall and onto the marble floor of his bedchambers. Never before had he been so violently forced out of a body he had Shifted into. Picking himself up, Agnarr let out a growl loud enough to usher in two of his guards.

"Lord Agnarr," they addressed together, bowing in reverence. Red eyes still glowing and his anger still boiling, he lifted his hand at the unwelcome intrusion and willed the heart of one of the guards to burst within his body using his Mending ability. No sooner had the man dropped dead than Agnarr turned his attention to the other and snapped his neck with a mere flick of his hand. As the second guard fell, Agnarr ran his fingers through his red hair, casually stepped over their bodies, and headed down the corridor.

Varcor was *dead*. He had spent *cycles* experimenting on his many younglings with the Elements in hopes of breeding a Tercara army to secure his empire. But the only one who had shown any promise had been Varcor. And just like that, Meera Tarmanon had *killed* him. *She*, a Tercara *herself*! One with the Stone Key! Agnarr's steps quickened their pace. If the others of his kind knew what he had been up to, they could ruin everything. He had to get the Stone Key back before Meera found their bloodkin and figured out what it unlocked.

It was time he went after Meera Tarmanon *himself*.

APPENDIX

The Tersaithian Calendar

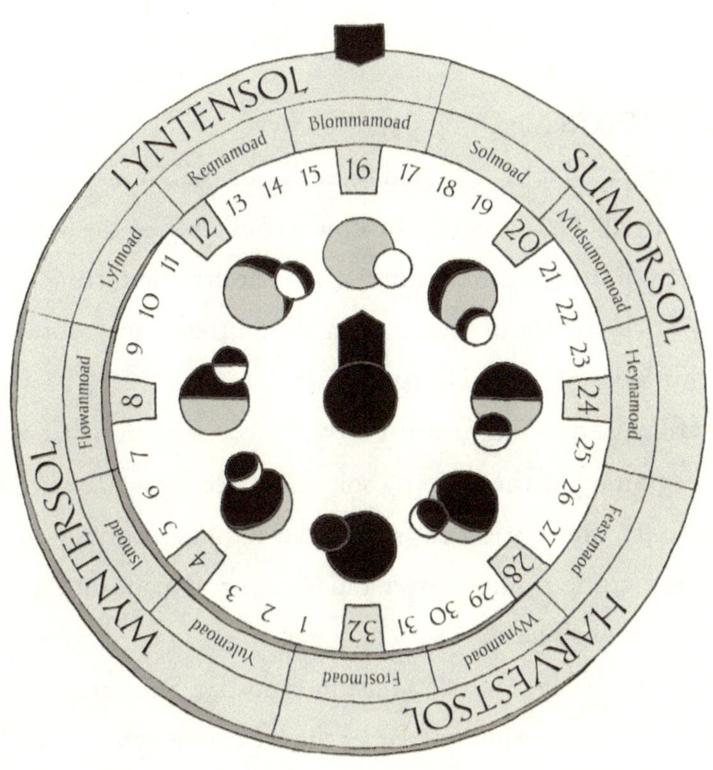

PASSAGE OF TIME

Cycle: Denotes the time it takes for the planet Tersaith to make one revolution around its sun/ equivalent to 384 Tersaithian days, twelve moads, or four sols

Sol: Denotes a length of time consisting of three moads broken into quarters to follow the cycle's weather patterns

Moad: Denotes a length of time consisting of thirty-two Tersaithian days

Week: Denotes a length of time consisting of four Tersaithian days

HOLIDAYS

Dawnday: 1st of Lyfmoad, first day of the New Cycle, celebrated by all Tersaithians with a meal consisting of the last saved items from storage and toasting to good health and fortune in the New Cycle. In Matui, they hang a Sasson tree branch above the tree hut's door for good fortune.

Lyfday: 16th of Regnamoad, a Lyntensol celebration that marks the beginning of the growing sol, celebrated by all Tersaithians with songs, brews, and ales, as well as an abundance of flowers and greenery strung around homes and villages and made into crowns to wear on one's head.

Midsumorday: 16th of Midsumormoad, a Sumorsol celebration that marks the longest day of the cycle, celebrated by all Tersaithians at duskfall with music, fires, and dancing throughout the night. Traditionally, males will weave a crown of ivy and present it to their female interest to wear as a token of their love.

Feastingday: 16th of Wynamoad, a Harvestsol celebration that marks the end of the growing sol, celebrated by all Tersaithians with a large feast, usually held outdoors, where every participant brings a dish to share. Music and dancing are not uncommon.

Frostlight: 1st of Frostmoad, celebrated by Matuians who walk among the forest at night with lanterns and sing the trees to sleep for Wyntersol.

Yuleday: 32nd of Yulemoad, a Wyntersol celebration, celebrated by all Tersaithians by decorating the interior of one's home or hut with evergreens, sharing baked goods with family or friends, and participating in a large bonfire with hot drinks and stories of the bygones.

Midwynterday: 20th of Ismoad, a Wyntersol celebration marks the shortest day of the cycle, celebrated by all Tersaithians by giving to those in need during the coldest moad of the cycle, whether it be through providing food, shelter, or any item one in need is without.

Lyflight: 1st of Flowanmoad, celebrated by Matuians who awaken the forest with their singing at dawn, in preparation for the coming Dawnday and Lyntensol.

MOONS AND CYCLES

Orynis: The name given to the largest of Tersaith's two moons (the Watchers) whose appearance is a hazy bright blue and is always seen directly behind Oryna at its left side.

Oryna: The name given to the smallest of Tersaith's two moons (the Watchers) whose appearance is chalky white, has several notable craters, and is always seen in front of Orynis at its right side.

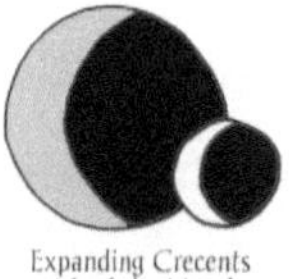
Expanding Crecents
4th of the Moad

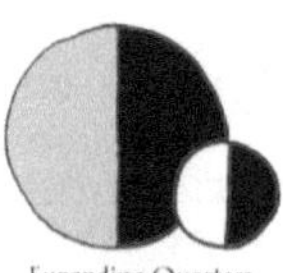
Expanding Quarters
8th of the Moad

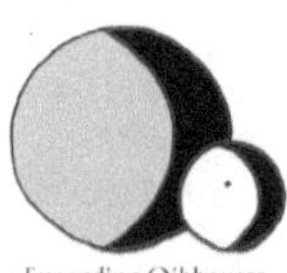
Expanding Qibbouses
12th of the Moad

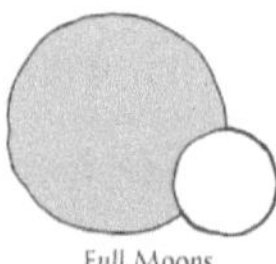
Full Moons
16th of the Moad

Withering Gibbouses
20th of the Moad

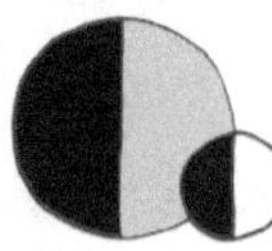
Withering Quarters
24th of the Moad

Withering Crecents
28th of the Moad

Dawn Moons
32nd of the Moad

Grendolen Military Ranks

Commandant Admiral: Oversees the entire Grendolen Navy

Commandant General: Oversees the entire Grendolen Army/ ten Hosts = 100,000 soldiers

Host Commander: Oversees five Faction Colonels within the Grendolen Army/ one Host = 10,000 soldiers

Faction Colonel: Oversees two Assembly Captains within the Grendolen Army/ one Faction = 5,000 soldiers

Assembly Captain: Oversees five Troop Officers within the Grendolen Army/ one Assembly = 1,000 soldiers

Troop Officer: Oversees two Unit Captains within the Grendolen Army/ one Troop = 500 soldiers

Unit Captain: Oversees five Soldier Officers within the Grendolen Army/ one Unit = 100 soldiers

Soldier Officer: Oversees twenty Soldiers within the Grendolen Army/ one Pod = 20 soldiers

Soldier: Base rank of military

Tersaithian Coinage

Chip: Tersaithian money/ 1 stamped Tin Coin

Tenner: Tersaithian money/ 1 Tenner equals 10 Chips / Copper Coin

Halfspritt: Tersaithian money/ 1 Halfspritt equals 50 Chips / Bronzium Coin

Spritt: Tersaithian money/ 1 Spritt equals 100 Chips / Cerulon Coin

Hightenner: Tersaithian money/ 1 Hightenner equals 10 Spritts or 1,000 Chips/ Silver Coin

Highspritt: Tersaithian money/ 1 Highspritt equals 100 Spritts or 10,000 Chips/ Gold Coin

Glossary

Afterealm: Heaven, to those on Tersaith who believe that when they die, their soul departs from their body and rises to meet Yveth

Ale: a beer or stout

Alemaker: A person who specializes in the making of fine ales

Ale-tent: A common term for a pop-up pub within a Grendolen army encampment

Ancients: The term Tersaithians gave to Yveth's god-kin, powerful beings that were said to hold god-like abilities that left the planet over three thousand cycles ago

Avron: Tawok's Head Tailor in service to the sovereign

Ayris Pagor Hilderman Fielder: The Pawtoton ruler, otherwise known as the Sovereign, Supreme Sovereign, or Sovereign Matriarch

Bae: The alias Darmond used while posing as a soldier in the Grendolen Army while spying for the Resistance

Baska Sarell: Host commander under General Doth's command in Lord Agnarr's Army

Bitun: Matuian warrior and personal guard to Chief Usoti's family

Blue Library: One of eight Pawtoton libraries on the Residence's property, this one specifically containing modern records of Tersaith

Bluff: A well-known game of dice that involves gambling

Bora Tree: A rare tree that only grows within Matui Forest known for its medicinal properties

Border Branch: A river originating in the southern Lornadian Range Mountains that splits into two smaller rivers, the Outer Branch and Border Branch/ Referred to as the Taw and Tae in Matui

Botana: Second largest town within Pawtoton—located to the southeast/ known for their cheese

Brew Spirits: Similar to bourbon, alcohol distilled from malted grain

Brewcrafter: Person who specializes in the crafting of fine brew spirits

Brown Library: One of eight Pawtoton libraries on the Residence's property

Cassia Mountains: A vast mountain range dominating Tersaith's middle and western regions, stretching from the Rivi Ocean to the eastern foothills

Cerulon: Blue metal mined widely on Tersaith/ used to make Spritt coins

Chroniclers: Pawtotons who seek out and record Tersaith's Histories

Copper Library: One of eight Pawtoton libraries on the Residence's property

Darmond: Spy for the Resistance/ grew up in Midtier/ born Regnamoad 14, 3102 T.C.

Dawnlight: First light of a new day

Death's Doorway: A dead end to the western path leading out from Vardia within the Cassia Mountains/ a favorite hunting ground for predators

Deltapoint: Location of the Grendolens' newest port town located within the Fertine Delta where their armada sets off from toward Matui

Donotabi: Roughly translates from Matuian into English as, "*trail that leads to Notabi*"—referring to the northern path leading out of Matui Village toward Notabi Village

Dorthrin River: Northern river flowing from Grendolen down into the Flats, it has two branches that split off: to the west it becomes the Cassia Rapids which ends at the Cassia Falls, and to the south a small branch becomes Clearwater Creek

Duskfall: Last light of the day

Eastland Ocean: A large ocean bordering the Tersaithian lands to the east

Elementist: The term given to those who study the Elements

Elements: Naturally occurring organic materials found on Tersaith, used to create elixirs or potions that can heal or harm

Emidd: Soldier officer in the Grendolen army and in command of the pod Darmond, under his alias Bae, infiltrated

Everard Bookman: Pawtoton's Grand Preserver and Foremost Historian of the Tercara Scrolls

Faltiel: One of Darmond's old man aliases that he uses while in Vardia

Fertine Delta: A delta located in the north where the Fertine River empties out into the Eastland Sea

Fertine River: A river whose origin is within the forested Lornadian Range Mountains and empties into the Eastland sea at the Fertine Delta

Finnik Doth: Commandant General of the Grendolen Army

Gentlefolks: A common term used when addressing a mingled crowd

Gerdiun: Soldier who left Finnik's command in favor of Varcor Orna, almost captured Meera in Matui

Gold Library: One of eight Pawtoton libraries on the Residence's property

Green Library: One of eight Pawtoton libraries on the Residence's property

Grendolen: Name of the empire Lord Agnarr rules, located to the far north alongside the Assiel Chain

Grizzling: A large bear-like creature with two sharp tusks protruding down from its top jaw, usually found in the northern foothills of the Cassia Mountains

Han Wesdo: Faction Colonel in the Grendolen Army

Hathmoor Tarmanon: Father of Meera Tarmanon, Fifth Tarmanon to rule over Moorland, his reign lasted seventeen cycles between 3098 T.C. to 3115 T.C.

High One: A formal way to address the chief of the Matuian Tribe

Highcaps: The higher mountain elevations

Ismoad Peak: The outermost mountain to the east of the Cassia Mountain Range, home to the town of Vardia

Jay: Naval Officer aboard the Grendolen Brig, the *Seventh Sister*

Jerrna Wess: Commandant Admiral of the Grendolen Navy

Jynyn: A very territorial monkey-like creature that dwells in Matui Forest, the males are particularly known for their large, blue-colored testicles

Katula Min: Daughter of Matui's Chief and Granddaughter of Matui's Sage/ becomes sagen, an apprentice to the sage, a lifelong commitment/ born Ismoad 22, 3104 T.C.

Kinblood: A term used to describe a blood relative or relation

Linklo: An alias Darmond uses while posing as a sailor aboard the Grendolen Brig, the *Seventh Sister*

Lord Agnarr: Self-proclaimed Emperor of the Grendolen Empire/ Born Solmoad 30, 3093 T.C.

Lowlanders: A Pawtoton term for anyone residing outside their borders

Marty: One of Darmond's drunken aliases he uses while in an ale-tent at Deltapoint

Matui: The name Matuians call their large, forested domain, stretching from the Eastland Ocean to the plains, and the name of their central, largest village / referred to by non-natives as Wildwood

Matuians: A seclusive people who broke off from their southern nomadic tribes and settled in a vast eastern forest/ Guardians of the Tercara Scroll

Meera Rammel Lavonna Tarmanon: Daughter of King Hathmoor and Queen Torma Tarmanon, last surviving heir to the Moorland throne/ Born Blommamoad 16, 3108 T.C.

Midtier: An area of land to the north of the Cassia Mountain Range containing many prominent towns and peoples/ Headquarters of the Resistance

Midtierians: The peoples native to a section of land north of the Cassia Mountain Range

Moordew: Moorland Brew Spirits, a major export of the kingdom before its destruction

Moorland: An area of land stretching across the northeastern moors that was once controlled by the Tarmanon line but lay in ruins since the Moorland Massacre

Moorlanders: The people that used to reside in the Kingdom of Moorland

Natta: A familiar name Katula uses to address her grandmother, the Matuian Sage

Netherealm: The Tersaithian term for outer space

Night Hunter: A large, white beast of prey found in the Cassia highcaps

Nihility: A void filled with unending torment that Tersaithians believe Yveth will send the damned at the time of their passing

Nisri: The Mother of Yveth, her name is sometimes used in vain as a curse word

Noiramite: Rare black metal mined in the Assiel Chain and used by the Grendolens for their armor

Notabi: The northernmost and smallest village of Matui, one of the seven prominent villages of Matui

Noto Eto: The northeastern village of Matui, one of the seven prominent villages of Matui

Noto Wey: The northwestern village of Matui, one of the seven prominent villages of Matui

Oryna: The name given to the smallest of Tersaith's two moons (the Watchers) whose appearance is chalky white, has several notable craters, and is always seen in front of Orynis at its right side

Orynis: The name given to the largest of Tersaith's two moons (the Watchers) whose appearance is a hazy bright blue and is always seen directly behind Oryna at its left side

Outer Branch: The western branch of the Border River/ Referred to as the Taw River in Matui

Panbread: A common type of flatbread that can be cooked in a pan

Pawtoton: Home of the Preservers of Tersaith's histories/ Located within the Cassia Mountains

Pignut: The name Darmond gives to his Grendolen warhorse, a chestnut brown gelding

Piwakey: Matuian word for a narrow wooden boat propelled by paddles

Plum Library: One of eight Pawtoton libraries on the Residence's property

Preservers: Pawtotons who guard Tersaith's histories in vast libraries

Red Library: One of eight Pawtoton libraries on the Residence's property, this one specifically containing the oldest records of Tersaith

Reyna Osberry: Pawtoton giant who is the Manageress of the Residence and prefers to be addressed by the title of "Matron Osberry"

Rivi Ocean: A vast ocean bordering the western lands of Tersaith

Runner: Matui term for a person who runs important messages between villages

Saby Eto: The southeastern village of Matui, one of the seven prominent villages of Matui

Saby Wey: The southwestern village of Matui, one of the seven prominent villages of Matui

Sabyto: The southernmost village of Matui, one of the seven prominent villages of Matui

Sage: Matuian wise woman and Elementist, a lifelong commitment

Sagen: An apprentice to the sage/ becoming sagen requires swearing a lifelong oath

Sap: Fine wines/ Tersaithian varieties including red, blue, and orange

Sapsmith: A person who specializes in the smithing of fine saps

Sasson Tree: A common tree found in Matui usually containing bioluminescent blue moss/ Its wood is used to construct Matuian bows and arrows

Shadeblight: Derogatory name Matuians use to refer to Grendolen Soldiers

Signot: The name Meera gives to the tonga she rode out of Vardia

Silver Library: One of eight Pawtoton libraries on the Residence's property

Span: A Tersaithian term defining a unit of linear measurement, similar to a mile or kilometer

Tae River: The name the Matuians gave to the eastern river flowing through their forest domain, originating from Border Branch, a large river in the north

Tannison: A vapor made of Elements that a Matuian Sage can make to ensure one is telling the truth once inhaled

Taw River: The name the Matuians gave to the western river flowing through their forest domain, originating from Outer Branch, a large river in the north

Tawok: The largest town within Pawtoton and home to the Sovereign's Residence

Tercara Scroll: An Ancient scroll given by Yveth's god-kin, the Ancients, to the Matuians to safeguard in exchange for knowledge of the Elements

Terra: A term referring to rock, dirt, or soil on Tersaith

Tersaith: The planet on which the story takes place

Tersaithians: All peoples residing on the planet Tersaith

The Cleansing: A term referring to a dark period of time that occurred around three thousand cycles ago when the Ancients walked Tersaith

The Residence: The official home of Pawtoton's Sovereign Monarch and location of Pawtoton's eight libraries

The Seventh Sister: A prominent constellation in the Tersaithian sky used by sailors to navigate/ The name of a two-masted Brig, pride of the Grendolen Navy

The Stand: The worst form of punishment in Grendolen or anywhere the emperor rules, where the offender is bound to a large spike and burned alive

The Tipsy Tonga: A festive pub located within Tawok, Pawtoton

The Watchers: The name given to both of Tersaith's moons, Orynis and Oryna

Tineu: A Matuian term for a meeting held by the chief

Tonga: A large beast resembling a cross between a mountain goat and a mammoth that resides within the Cassia Mountains

Torin: The name of the sailor Commandant Admiral Jerrna Wess yells at when Linklo incorrectly handles one of the topsail lines aboard the *Seventh Sister*

Torma Tarmanon: Mother of Meera Tarmanon, wife of King Hathmoor Tarmanon and Queen of Moorland

Tymmon: A white Moorland hawk Meera befriends, also known as Ty

Usoti Min: Chieftain of the Matuian tribe, son of the sage, and father of Katula Min

Varcor Orna: Faction Colonel in the Grendolen Army

Vardia: Market town on Ismoad Peak located within the Cassia Mountains

Varwonen: The name sailors gave to the brightest star in the Seven Sisters constellation, which helps them navigate

Wanpa: Smallest town within Pawtoton, located to the west, below the waterfalls/known for their saps

Youngling: A term used to describe children

Yveth: Name the Tersaithians gave to their god, the Great Creator

Missing Tersaith already? Scan the code to sing a round or two of "Moordew." No halfspritts required!

ABOUT THE AUTHOR

Arwen McCain is an author, artist, and musician. She lives with her family in the Raleigh, North Carolina area. When she is not writing epic fantasy novels, you'll most likely find her mentoring aspiring teen writers or tending her ever-expanding gardens. She also enjoys longsword fencing, archery, traveling, and reading SFF novels.

www.ingramcontent.com/pod-product-compliance
Lightning Source LLC
LaVergne TN
LVHW100501110826
845146LV00002B/474

* 9 7 9 8 9 9 9 4 6 6 4 1 9 *